The Owner's Temptation

The Black Ledger Billionaires

Rebekah Sinclair

This novel contains **mature themes, explicit content, and dark romance elements** that may be **disturbing or triggering** for some readers.

This book is **intended for adult audiences** and **reader discretion is strongly advised.** If any of these topics are sensitive for you, please proceed with caution.

- Sex Work / Escorting
- Toxic relationships & power imbalances
- Explicit sexual content & masturbation
- Sexual power dynamics & BDSM elements:
    - Binding and Sensory Deprivation
    - Consensual Sexual Punishment
    - Dubious Consent / Non-consensual Sexual Punishment
    - Non-consensual Scenarios (CNC Fantasy)
    - Primal Play & Chase/Capture Dynamics

- Explicit language & derogatory / degrading terms
- Physical violence & aggression
- Emotional trauma & disassociation
- Abduction & captivity
- Torture & mutilation (graphic)
- Gun violence, organized crime, and murder
- Stalking & Surveillance

The Black Ledger

Welcome to The Black Ledger

An elite, highly exclusive escort service where billionaires strike discreet deals, and escorts set their own terms.

~ No complications.
~ No attachments.
~ Just business.

But desire is never that simple.

Here, control turns into obsession, rules are meant to be broken, and the one risk no one dares take—falling in love—may be the most dangerous deal of all.

Because at The Black Ledger,
contracts are final...

But hearts were never meant
to be part of the deal.

Each book is a **standalone** with interconnected characters. ***No cheating***, ***no cliffhangers***—just powerful men, the women who bring them to their knees, and spice that will leave you breathless.

Thank you for choosing The Black Ledger and we hope you enjoy your contract.

Lucian Vale

*—**To my filthy little rabbit**—*

Look at you holding your smutty book.
Mouth parted. Thighs clenched.
Ready to soak up every filthy word like a good little whore.

Turn these pages just the way I like it—
Desperate. Obedient. Starving for more.

You were mine the second you cracked the cover, angel. And now?
I'm never letting you go.

See you on the last page, sweetheart.
I'll be waiting—
Hard, hungry, and ready to make you scream.

—The Devil—

The night is warm, the kind of perfect late-summer evening that makes everything feel a little more alive, a little more electric. The Masquerade glows against the city skyline, its sleek black exterior accented by golden lighting that spills into the night like a beacon for the elite.

It's exclusive, whispered about, wrapped in the kind of mystery that breeds rumors.

I'm not here for the mystery. I'm here for the free drinks.

Everline Consulting apparently always throws one hell of an Employee Appreciation Party and this year it's on the rooftop terrace of one of New York's most exclusive night clubs.

The Masquerade.

The buffet of food is delicious. The bar is... open and the music is feeding my soul.

"God, remind me why we don't go out more?" Harper leans in, her breath warm against my ear as we sway together on the dance floor. "We are *hot*. We should be out getting worshipped every weekend."

I laugh, tossing back the last of my cocktail before setting the empty glass on a passing waiter's tray. "Because we're broke."

She scoffs. "Empty bank accounts are temporary. Bad bitches are forever."

She twirls, her black dress clinging to her toned frame, while I follow, the hem of my form-fitting red mini dress riding up slightly as I move. I don't bother tugging it down.

Tonight, I want to feel *good*. Relaxed. And have fun.

It's not a private party so as the night wears on, more and more patrons find their way up here.

Our gold wristband gives us access to the rooftop VIP area where the drink and food are plentiful, but we've not left the dance floor in half an hour.

If I know Harper, she is one hundred percent looking for someone to take home for the night.

But me?

I sigh to myself, ridiculing my own ridiculous inner monologue.

I don't even know.

Harper smirks as we dance. "So. Word on the street is... this place has a sex club inside."

"You really shouldn't believe everything you hear from your hookups." I roll my eyes, lips quirking in amusement. "They're just trying to get in your pants."

"They're already in my pants," she shouts over the music. "And *they* say it's some *Eyes Wide Shut* type shit—like, a full-blown secret society."

"That's ridiculous."

"It's true!" She scoffs back. "They wear different color masks for different kinks." She explains. Her eyes alive with excitement. "That's why this place is called, The Masquerade."

Now that I think about it, there is absolutely nothing about masks with this place.

The ground level is an indoor dance club called Limbo. This rooftop is just an extension of it.

This is like—a ten-story building.

Now my mind is racing at the possibility this could be true and I feel my face heating up as I consider the possibilities. What people would be... doing in there.

What it would be like to walk through and watch. To be watched.

I shake my head is only to clear the thoughts I'm spiraling down. "You'd sell your soul for a masked orgy, wouldn't you?"

"Not my *soul*, just my vagina and my time," she teases, taking another sip of her drink. Then she levels me with a look. "Speaking of time, when are you gonna get back out there and find a piece of ass to satisfy you?

"Look, I was tired of faking orgasms for Ben." My voice carries a little too much over the music. I think my second cocktail is starting to kick in. "I don't feel like faking it for a stranger too."

"Oh honey," Harper looks at me like I have shit all over my face. "Are you saying Ben–Boring Ben—the *prestigious, accomplished, white-collar wonder boy*—was bad in bed?"

She puts her hand over her chest dramatically. "Pretends to be shocked."

"Hey, we were high school sweethearts." I defend myself of my naivety for the millionth time. "He was my first love. I didn't know better."

Just in time a server returns with a fresh drink for me.

"Girl, you still don't know better."

"God, tell me about it." Ben's idea of foreplay was turning over and asking me if I showered.

Then spicing it up meant going from missionary to doggy style.

But Ben was my childhood friend turned teenage boyfriend. I gave him my virginity, and we kept up our relationship long-distance through college.

We moved to New York together and I was certain we'd be getting married while Ben worked on his career.

Until I caught him fucking one of his coworkers.

Dickhead.

Not only did he leave me unsatisfied in the bedroom, but he also left me with an expensive lease for an apartment I didn't even want. Now I'm racking up credit card debt and blowing through my small savings to keep the rent paid.

I swear to God, I hate him.

But I'm glad I woke up when I did.

That life—the one where I gave up everything for the man in my life—it's not me.

It's not what I want.

"We're not leaving here until we find you some good dick." Harper takes it upon herself to begin scouring the crowd of faces. "This is my mission now. It's my purpose. You *will* get laid before I leave for my vacation."

"I'll be fine."

"Trust me, my dick-dar is always on point." She ignores me, sipping on her drink through the tiny black straw as her eyes move from person to person. "One look and I can tell if they can eat pussy like a pro or if they lick it like a fucking kitten drinking milk."

I choke on my cocktail, coughing as Harper pats my back like she *didn't just say that.*

"Jesus, Harper," I wheeze between laughs. "What the hell?"

She shrugs, completely unfazed. "I'm just saying, some guys lap it up like they've been training for the Olympics, and some?" She clicks her tongue, shaking her head in disappointment. "They treat it like a goddamn *sippy cup.*"

I'm *dying.* Tears prick my eyes from laughing so hard. "Oh my God, I hate you."

"You love me," she corrects, tossing back the last of her drink. "I need a refill."

She sways her hips, hands lifted over her head with her empty glass as she cuts a path through the crowd toward the VIP area.

One man turns to her, his hand on her hip as he dances with her while she passes.

I swear, I don't understand how she does that.

Just walks through a crowd and draws eyes to her.

I mean she's beautiful. Long brunette hair and olive skin but I'm beautiful too dammit.

We're complete opposites, my long auburn hair and

bright blue eyes probably makes me look like an innocent little bunny rabbit compared to the vixen stare she is giving this guys.

Harper keeps on walking, looking back at me with a smile and wagging her eyebrows.

The bouncer waves us through the roped entry to the VIP lounge and we stroll up to the bar.

"So, did that guy,–"

"Not even fucking close." She cuts me off, giving a nod to the bartender and holding up her empty glass. "That man is a two-pump chump. Guarantee it."

I shake my head, looking back in the crowd and trying to find him again.

Poor guy.

Harper is like a Venus Flytrap. Ready to sink her jaws into any man, chew him up and spit him out.

She claps her hands, turning around and leaning her back against the bar. "Okay, what are we in the mood for tonight, Sienna? Some chow-time in the bathroom?"

"Good lord." I look around seeing if anyone is listening.

"Someone to finger you in the rideshare on the way home?" She lists the option off like she's picking toppings for her sub-sandwich. "I'm personally looking for a cute face to ride."

"Harper!"

"What?" She shrugs as the bartender puts her new drink down, sliding it to her with a wink. "You know, a strong jaw, some stubble for a little extra–umph." She keeps her eyes on the bartender and nudges me with her elbow. "Please tell me Boring Ben at lease let you ride his tongue once or twice."

I wince, taking my tiny straw between my teeth.

Harper wears a look of utter disbelief. "I'm terrified for you actually."

"Can I be honest with you?" I look around again, making sure we're alone. She leans in toward me.

"Oh girl spill it. The tea is piping hot, I can tell."

I'm already blushing. I can feel my face getting hotter.

Just as I'm about to open my mouth, the words get stuck. Suddenly, I wish I hadn't said anything.

"Oh, no you don't. You can't back out now. Give it to me." She takes a long pull from her new cocktail. Her eyes focused on me like I'm about to tell her the secret to world peace.

"Ben never actually..." I'm not sure how to finish it but Harper seems to have caught on.

"Oh, you sweet summer child." She gives me a slow, pitiful shake of her head. "We are officially on booty-call duty for you. A man to stick his tongue as deep in your snatch as possible."

"Oh, my God." I give myself an actual facepalm, running my hand down slowly.

"And for the record, I want to stab Boring-Ben in his mediocre little dick."

I laugh, turning around with Harper to watch the dance floor too.

She starts calling out prospects, then immediately telling me why they do not make the cut.

I don't hear her, though, because I'm focusing every

ounce of my attention on the man walking into the VIP lounge.

Tall. Dark. Dangerous.

A tailored navy suit clings to his powerful frame, broad shoulders commanding the space like he owns the air itself. His sharp, steel-gray eyes scan the room with cool disinterest—until they land on me.

And then, for a *single* breathless second, the world *stops*.

I forget my name. I forget how to function as a human being. My skin feels too tight, my heart hammers in my ribs like it's trying to break out.

Holy *fuck*.

"See?" Harper is still talking, completely unaware that my soul just left my body. "That guy right there? *That's* the kind of jaw I'm talking about. Just the right amount of stubble to grind against—probably *phenomenal* at eating pussy."

I whip my head toward her, panic crashing into me like a freight train.

Because she's *pointing*.

At him.

Her eyes trail over him approvingly, dragging down the length of his broad frame, taking in the way his crisp navy button-down stretches across thick, powerful shoulders.

And *he's watching*.

His gaze locks onto mine—sharp, assessing, *dangerous*.

A flicker of amusement dances across his face as he takes slow, measured steps toward the bar.

Harper leans in, whispering conspiratorially, "We should ask him to *prove it*."

I swear to God, I'm going to *die*.

I shoot her a look of pure betrayal, but she only grins as the mystery man passes us, completely unbothered by our existence.

Instead, he stops at the far end of the bar, shrugging off his suit jacket in one smooth motion.

And *oh my God*.

Underneath, the black fabric of his button-down clings to the kind of body that shouldn't be legal. He's tall—easily over six feet—lean but *built*, the movement of corded muscle evident even beneath the expensive fabric.

Then, as if he knows *exactly* what he's doing, he rolls up the sleeves, revealing *tattooed forearms*.

I don't even know what the tattoos *are*—all I know is that my brain has officially short-circuited and I want to run my tongue up those tattoos.

Harper, of course, notices.

"Jesus, Sienna, you're *drooling*," she mutters under her breath, shoving her fresh cocktail into my hands. "Guard this. I have to pee, and when I get back..." She starts backing toward the bathrooms, pointing at me. "You're talking to him."

I will die first.

She disappears into the crowd before I can protest, leaving me standing there, gripping her drink like a lifeline.

It's not that I don't like sex. I do.

I love sex. At least, I like the idea of sex.

My partner was a piece of shit. Selfish in the way he never tried to make me orgasm.

Degrading in the way he made me feel down on myself for wanting more–other *things*.

Once, I wanted to blow him in a dark movie theatre. There was hardly anyone there and certainly no one around us.

You would have thought I asked him to let me castrate him, grill his dick on a bar-be-que and serve it to our fellow movie-watchers.

I exhale sharply, shaking off the weird flutter in my chest, and turn toward the bar—only to feel the mood *instantly* sour.

Because *fucking* Steve, my *dickhead* of a manager, in all his corporate mediocrity, waltzes into the VIP lounge with a damn *Bud Light* in his hand.

All this top-shelf liquor, and he goes with a basic-ass beer. Figures.

He spots me almost immediately and beelines straight for me, his smarmy grin making my stomach turn.

The closer he gets, the more my stomach clenches. I *already* know where this is going.

"Enjoying the party?" he asks, sliding up beside me like he belongs here. His tone is easy, conversational—too casual.

He's trying to make this look natural.

It's not.

I take a deliberate step back, but he mirrors it immediately, maintaining the space like he owns it.

I school my face into polite indifference, nodding. "Yeah, it's nice."

He hums, taking a sip of his beer, eyes scanning the VIP

lounge like he's just another *guy hanging out*—like he *isn't* actively *hemming me in* with his presence.

"You know," he muses, his voice taking on that fake *we're-both-in-on-the-joke* tone, "I've been meaning to talk to you outside the office. Things at Everline are... shifting. Some positions are opening up."

His eyes flick back to mine, just for a second. Calculating.

"I think you'd be a great fit for something *more*," he adds, voice dipping suggestively, his eyes doing the same.

I know exactly what he's doing.

The bait is to make it sound like an opportunity.

The hook, however, implies there's a favor attached.

The unspoken? *If you play along, maybe I can make things easier for you.*

I can't *prove* he's outright suggesting anything sleazy, but the *implication* is heavy enough to make my skin crawl.

I keep my expression neutral, giving the world's most *noncommittal* nod. "I'm sure a lot of people would be interested but Everline is not exactly where my career ambitions live."

Steve chuckles, shaking his head like I just said something *adorable*.

And then—he steps closer.

Too close.

I *feel* his body heat and on imstinct slide down the bar, trying to keep that distance between us.

The scent of cheap aftershave and beer wafts over me, as his fingers trail down my bare arm—slow, deliberate, testing. "I can see us–"

Oh *hell* no.

A chill races down my spine, and every muscle in my body locks up.

"Don't touch me."

I jerk my arm away so fast that the drink in my hand sloshes over my fingers—splashing against the front of his tan dress pants.

A dark stain spreads across his crotch.

"What the fuck, Sienna?!"

The outrage in his voice would be hilarious if I weren't *so pissed*.

I roll my eyes and look across the dance floor, searching for the bathrooms so I can just go find Harper.

Steve exhales sharply, running a hand down his wet pants, trying to *casually* wipe at the stain. He lets out a forced chuckle, but it's tight, clipped. Like he's tolerating me.

"Relax, would you?" he says, voice edged with frustration now. "It's a party. You should *enjoy* yourself."

He takes another step toward me, setting his bottle on the bar top.

I step back again, but this time—a barstool is behind me, blocking my retreat.

Steve notices.

His lips curl slightly, that *pathetic little smirk* reappearing like he's decided I'm only playing hard-to-get.

"Better yet..." he leans in, voice lowering like we're sharing some private secret. "*Maybe* we should enjoy ourselves—privately."

His eyes drag over my mouth.

"You know, I look at that *smart mouth* of yours every damn day, and I've *wondered* what it would feel like on my co—"

I don't let him finish.

Taking a step back, the stool slides out of my path and I throw the rest of Harper's cocktail in his *fucking face.*

"Don't you dare talk to me like that," I snap, my voice steady even though my blood is boiling.

Steve freezes, drenched in whiskey and humiliation.

A few nearby patrons glance over as Steve stands there, face red, jaw ticking as he calculates his next move. From the side of my vision, the bartender stands up straight. I can tell he's watching us and expect a bouncer at any second to kick me out.

I can see it in Steve's eyes—the fury, the *loss of control,* the way he's struggling to mask it.

He steps forward and I flinch in instinct.

"Consider yourself fired, bitch."

Then out of nowhere, a large, *tan* hand clamping around the back of Steve's neck.

Everything happens fast.

One second, Steve is standing there, gloating.

The next—h*is face meets the fucking bar.*

A sickening crunch echoes through night air as his nose breaks.

I *jump* back, eyes widening as Steve crumples to the floor, completely unconscious.

My mouth falls open.

My best friend, ten feet away, is frozen mid-step as she finally returns from the bathroom.

Tall, Dark, and Tattooed stands there like nothing *just happened*, adjusting the cuffs of his rolled-up sleeves, exuding pure dominance.

Patrons glance over, but no one reacts.

Like this isn't *unusual* here.

Like he *owns* this place.

"I–" I have no fucking idea what to say.

He reaches into his pocket, pulling out a sleek, metal cardholder. Smoothly, he slides out a single black card, then extends it between two fingers.

His voice is even. Controlled. Dangerous.

"Orientation is Monday."

I blink.

"Excuse me?"

He runs his grey eyes to Steve–still passed out on the ground–as if that should answer my question.

"You need a job," he says simply, then flicks his gaze down my body.

"And you're already wearing the right color."

And just like that—

He's *gone*.

he Black Ledger.

I flip the card over between my fingers, the weight of it strangely heavy. All black, sleek, expensive. The gold foil letters catch the morning sunlight streaming through my window. The front is stark—just those words.

The Black Ledger. No title. No job description. Just the name.

The back is even more cryptic.

An address. Nothing else.

I stare at it for another long moment before tossing it onto my nightstand, exhaling a groan as I flop back against my pillows.

It's nearly noon, and I'm still in bed.

Last night should have ended in disaster.

But somehow, it didn't.

Steve was carried out.

Literally.

Harper and I stayed.

We danced. We drank. We soaked up every second of the VIP treatment we didn't pay for.

Men surrounded us, offering drinks, offering their hands, offering to take us home. But none of them held my attention for longer than a passing glance.

Because no matter how hard I tried, I couldn't stop thinking about *him*.

Mr. Tall, Dark, and Tattooed.

The storm in his eyes.

The rough edge to his jaw, a shadow of stubble sharpening the cut of his cheekbones.

The way his dark hair showed the beginning signs of gray throughout.

An older man.

That realization alone makes something tighten in my stomach.

Fuck. He only looked sexier because of it.

I bite my lip, heat curling through me as my mind drifts *exactly* where it shouldn't.

His hands—big, warm, rough—gripping my hips.

His body pressing mine into the bar.

His mouth claiming mine—hot, hard, devouring—

I want to keep going with this fantasy but the buzz of my apartment intercom, shatters it like glass.

"Perfect timing, Harp."

I run a hand over my face, pulling myself together, and shuffle out of bed toward the call button.

A loud, pained groan crackles through the speaker.

"It's *me*," Harper moans. "Open the damn door. I'm

dying."

I smirk, pressing the button to let her in.

A minute later, she stumbles inside, sunglasses on, a bag of food in one hand and two obnoxiously large, iced coffees in the other.

"Well good morning." I fold my arms. "How are you feeling, sunshine?"

Harper flops onto my couch, groaning dramatically. "Like my soul left my body and I barely convinced it to come back. But I brought sustenance, so I expect zero judgment."

She waves the bag of food like an offering.

I snatch it immediately. "None given."

I unwrap my sandwich and take a massive bite, barely suppressing a groan as the greasy, carb-loaded goodness hits my tongue.

"So," I say through a mouthful, eyeing Harper over my coffee cup, "how was the bartender?"

Harper pushes herself up, tossing her sunglasses onto the table with a satisfied smirk. "Oh, babe, *phenomenal*."

I raise an eyebrow.

She stretches her arms over her head like a cat waking from a long nap. "Three orgasms. *Three*—and that was just round one."

I nearly choke on my coffee. "Jesus Christ."

"Oh, don't act so scandalized. It was art. Pure, unfiltered, *Michelangelo-sculpted-that-shit* level of perfection. And he's Italian. The tongue work? *Superb*. The stamina? *Elite*. And best of all..." She sighs dramatically. "He made me waffles afterward."

I chuckle, taking another long pull of cold coffee. "So, love at first fuck?"

She scoffs. "Please. *Love* is for people who don't have better things to do. I'm just saying, if I ever get a commemorative plaque for outstanding life achievements, *last night* is going on there."

Harper finally takes a bite of her own sandwich. "And, lucky for you," she pauses for a drink, "he has a friend."

"As most people do,"

Harper grins. "Are *most* people members of the nine-story sex club where they work?"

Reaching into her purse, pulling out two silver coins, she tosses them onto my glass coffee table with a soft clink.

Slowly, my gaze lifts to hers as I pick up one of the large coins.

They're thick, weighty-looking, and identical—both stamped with a bold, raised number *two* on either side.

She waggles her eyebrows, smug as hell. "Yeah, babe. *It's real.*"

"Whoa."

"And we're going."

"I'm not."

"Oh, but you are." Harper focuses on her sandwich like it's restoring her lifeforce.

It probably is.

I shake my head, setting the coin back on the table. "Harper, I *really* don't have the funds to go gallivanting through a sex club. Hi, your jobless friend. Remember?"

Harper waves a dismissive hand, unbothered. "I don't mean *tonight.*" She leans back against the couch, stretching her legs out. "My vagina is currently in recovery mode. Last night was a fuck-a-thon of Olympic proportions, and frankly, I need a *nap* before I can even consider stepping foot inside a place where people are actively getting railed."

I snort, shaking my head. "I repeat. I'm not going to a sex club."

"You *are* going to a sex club," she says, pointing at me with the last bite of her food. "I leave for vacation tomorrow, and when I get back? You better have a job and be ready for a night filled with *sin*."

I open my mouth to protest again, but she levels me with a look.

"Babe, The Masquerade is just the front. The *real* club is inside." Harper waggles her brows picking up a coin and tossing it back into my lap. "Nine levels of Hell, straight up to The Devils Playground. And these? These are level access coins. Number two means I got us into the 'soft exploration' floor. *Vanilla kinks, voyeurism, a little light bondage.*"

I blink. "You got *us* in?"

"Mhm." She takes another smug bite of her sandwich. "Well, my new situationship can get us in."

I set the coin down. "Yeah, *not happening.*"

There are more things to worry about. Like the fact I'm already drowning financially and now I have no job.

I groan, rubbing my hands over my face. The events of last night replay in my mind—getting fired, Steve getting his face *rearranged*, and then... *him.*

Mr. Tall, Dark, and Tattooed.

The raw power in his movements. The way his steel-gray

eyes locked onto mine, like he saw right through me. Like he *knew* me.

I bite my lip, hating the way my stomach clenches at the memory.

Nope. Nope, nope, *nope.*

Harper hums, eyeing me over her coffee cup. "You're thinking about him, aren't you?"

"Whaaat?" I draw the word out. My high-pitch tone giving away the lie.

She grins. "Ohhh, you *so* are."

I glare, reaching for my own coffee. "We're changing the subject."

"Fine. Let's talk about your new *mystery job* then." Harper nods toward the sleek black card sitting on my nightstand. "Did you look it up?"

I sigh. "Yeah. There's *nothing*. And it's not my new job."

She frowns. "Nothing?"

"Not a single mention of *The Black Ledger* anywhere. No website, no job listings, no sketchy forum rumors. Just..." I grab my phone and pull up the only thing I *did* find, turning the screen toward her. "...this."

A tall, sleek skyscraper. Black glass. The name *The Black Ledger* displayed in massive gold letters across the front.

Harper whistles. "Damn. That's... intimidating as hell."

"Right?" I murmur, staring at the screen. "It's like it doesn't exist."

But it does.

And I can't stop thinking about it.

Harper eyes me over her coffee cup. "So... are you going on Monday?"

I snort. "Or, hear me out... I could just sell feet pics."

She groans. "Oh, Jesus."

"No, I'm serious," I say, setting my phone down. "There's this woman on the internet who bakes cakes, and then—*steps on them*—barefoot." I gesture dramatically. "That's it. Millions of views. Thousands of subscribers. People are *paying* to watch her obliterate buttercream with her toes."

Harper stares at me, unimpressed. "So, your backup plan is to become a cake-stomping sensation?"

I nod. "I can step on cake. I have feet. I'm qualified."

She scoffs. "I don't think we're at feet-pic desperation levels yet."

"Yet," I mutter, sipping my coffee.

Harper stretches...again, groaning. "Look, all I'm saying is, you should go. What's the worst case that could happen? You walk in, it's sketchy as hell, you walk right back out."

I chew my lip and pull my auburn hair to the side, splitting it into three sections and braiding it.

It's a ridiculous idea. But is it really worse than where I'm at right now?

I have no job. No other immediate options.

Rent is bleeding me dry.

My credit card debt is stacking up.

The job market is garbage.

I'm going to spend the next few days sending out applications anyway. What else would I be doing on Monday?

At *best*, this is some high-paying job that I miraculously qualify for and has immediate openings.

At *worst*...

Well.

"I could get murdered in a skyscraper." I deadpan. "That would kind of suck."

"Agreed." Harper tips her coffee at me. "But I don't think killers walk around giving out business cards."

"You never know. It's working." I stuff the wrappers from our sandwiches back into the paper back.

"So, you're going."

"I'm thinking about it."

"You're going."

Yeah. I'm going.

Chapter 3
Sienna

I used to have a plan.

A *real* plan.

I was supposed to be someone. Someone important. Someone powerful.

The kind of woman who walked into a room and made people nervous.

The kind of woman who handled chaos like it was her job—because, once upon a time, that *was* the plan.

Law, PR, crisis management. High-profile reputation fixing. Something where I could control the narrative, smooth out disasters, make impossible problems disappear.

That was who I was *supposed* to be. A problem solver.

Instead, I spent years running damage control for *Ben.*

I let him convince me to put my dreams on hold—*our* future came first, he'd said. And somehow, along the way, I became *his* fixer. *His* crisis manager. *His* personal fucking PR rep, handling his life instead of my own.

Until he cheated.

And left.

And suddenly, I wasn't just *Ben's girlfriend* anymore.

I was nobody.

It's funny how you don't notice losing yourself in the moment. It happens so slowly, piece by piece, until one day you wake up and realize you have nothing that's truly *yours*.

For years, we did what *he* wanted to do. Hung out with *his* friends. Moved to *his* city. My life was built around *our* relationship, and when he was gone, I had no idea what was left of *me*.

I'm glad to be free of him, but I *hate* our fucking apartment.

Everywhere I look, I still see *him*.

Us.

The couple we used to be.

The barstools at the kitchen counter—we picked them out together. The rug in the living room when he spilled wine on it and blamed me. The spot on the couch where we sat, tangled up, pretending like forever was real? It's still there, like a ghost of something I can't shake.

I'm already working on erasing the past, one paycheck at a time.

The ugly framed photos, replaced.

The hideous curtains *he* liked? Burned in a metaphorical funeral of bad taste.

By the time my lease is up, this place will be nothing but a shell—nothing left of *him*, nothing left of *us*. Just an empty apartment for the next idiot in love.

And when I walk into my next home, it will be *mine*.

Not *ours*.

Not *his.*

Just *mine.*

With a sharp breath, I add a few more pictures to my Pinterest page of my dream living room and then slide my phone back in my purse.

Because today, I have other things to worry about.

Like the fact that I'm walking into a *literal mystery job interview* at a company that doesn't exist online.

I exit the subway, looking up at the tall buildings and sunny day as I fish my phone back out of my purse. My nerves suddenly spiking now that I'm here.

Looking at the time, I know Harper will be in the airport terminal waiting to fly out to Miami for two weeks. I tap my screen, sending my location to Harper along with a text:

> SIENNA: If I get murdered, this was my last known location.

A second later, my phone buzzes with her response.

> HARPER: You're so dramatic. 🙄 But also… good luck, bitch. 🏃‍♀️🔥💰 Manifesting hot men, a six-figure salary, and maybe some light choking. 😏

I snort, shaking my head as I slip my phone back into my purse.

God, I hope she's at least right about the six figures.

I take a final look up at the towering black skyscraper before me, its sleek glass exterior reflecting the bright midday sun. The massive gold lettering near the entrance is crisp, polished, intimidating.

THE BLACK LEDGER.

That's all that exists of this place.

Just this building.

A mystery wrapped in black and gold, somehow drawing me in like a moth to a flame.

I exhale, adjusting the collar of my blouse.

Red, of course.

It had stuck in my mind all weekend, looping in my head like a warning. Or maybe a sign.

"And you're already wearing the right color."

So, red it is.

A deep crimson blouse, tucked neatly into a sleek black pencil skirt. Black pumps. Gold jewelry. Power dressing at its finest.

It's a good look.

A lucky look.

At least, that's what I tell myself.

With one last deep breath, I step toward the revolving doors, pushing through as they glide open silently.

"Well..." I murmur under my breath. "Here goes nothing."

The moment I step inside, the space swallows me whole.

It's sleek. Modern. Expensive.

White marble floors stretch across the vast lobby, veins of gold running through them like lightning frozen in stone. The walls are a striking contrast—deep black with subtle gold accents, giving the entire space an air of quiet power.

The Black Ledger aesthetic is clear.

Black. Gold.

The same color theme from Friday night.

And red. The color of my dress that night.

Even the receptionist is wearing a stunning red dress that hugs her like it was made for her body. Paired with crimson lipstick, she looks like she belongs on the cover of Vogue, not sitting behind a sleek black desk, typing effortlessly on a glass keyboard.

Straightening my posture, I pull the black card from my purse and step forward, clearing my throat.

"Hi," I say, placing the card on the desk. "I was given this on Friday night. I was told to show up today?"

The woman looks at the card, then up at me. And smiles.

Not a generic customer-service smile, but one with amusement—like she already knows something I don't.

"Ah," she hums, looking at the card before giving it back to me. "Lucian hoped you would show up."

Lucian.

The name hits me like a shock to the spine.

So that's his name.

Mr. Tall, Dark, and Tattooed.

I blink, carefully keeping my expression neutral. "I think so? I, uh... didn't catch his name."

The receptionist gives me a knowing look, then gestures toward the far wall.

I follow her hand—

And my stomach drops.

There, just across the way, hangs an obnoxiously large, gilded frame.

A painting.

Of him.

Lucian.

Not a photo. A goddamn painting.

His powerful frame is captured in stunning detail—broad shoulders beneath a deep blue shirt, black slacks tailored to perfection, sleeves rolled up his forearms, revealing the tattoos I already know he's proud of.

But it's the eyes that get me.

Piercing. Sharp. Like they see everything.

Like they're looking straight at me, even now.

A shiver races down my spine.

Lucian Vale.

The receptionist stands, moving with the kind of effortless grace I'll never possess, and pulls a black folder from beneath the desk.

Ah.

A black ledger.

Of course.

She slides it toward me, along with a gold pen and a single sheet of paper.

"Sign this NDA first," she says smoothly. "You'll find out everything else in orientation."

I take the paper carefully, my fingers grazing the sleek surface. My eyes scan the document.

Standard legal jargon.

Nothing covered in orientation can be shared. No photos. No recordings. No discussions outside these walls.

A strict non-disclosure agreement, but nothing wildly different from corporate NDAs I've seen before.

Still, something about it unsettles me and something about this moment feels profound.

Like this is a turning point.

I could fold up the paper, hand it back, and walk out of here. I could forget about Lucian, the mystery, the goddamn painting that won't stop looking at me.

Or.

I could sign my name and go find out whatever the hell this is.

The revolving doors spin behind me, the soft hush of movement pulling my attention.

A woman with long brown hair steps inside, pausing as a small group of three other women pass her. She waits, then follows at a measured pace, her red dress standing out like a beacon.

She smiles warmly when our eyes meet.

Something about it feels... *reassuring*.

Like maybe I'm not completely crazy for being here.

My gaze drifts back to the painting.

Lucian. Watching. Waiting.

He's almost challenging me. Saying, *"I bet you won't."* With his sexy eyes and sharp jaw.

Well, watch me.

I exhale sharply, sign my name, and hand the NDA back to the receptionist.

She takes it without a word, then slides the black folder into my hands.

"You can go ahead and follow Elena," she says, nodding toward the woman in red. "She'll be leading orientation today."

I tighten my grip on the folder and turn toward her.

My heels click against the sleek marble floor as I follow Elena across the vast, echoing lobby. The gold veining in the stone catches the light, leading my eyes upward to the impossibly high ceilings. This whole place exudes power and wealth, like it was designed to remind you exactly where you stand in the hierarchy of the world.

Elena presses the elevator button, and the gold-trimmed doors slide open in near silence.

As we step inside, I glance at her from the corner of my eye. She's stunning—elegant yet approachable, the kind of woman who commands attention without demanding it. There's a quiet confidence to her, something warm but knowing.

And when she smiles, it's like she knows the joke everyone else does—except me.

The doors glide shut, and the elevator begins its smooth ascent.

"So," she says, casually, as if she's just making small talk. "You're the girl Lucian picked himself."

I stiffen slightly.

The way she says it—like it's a thing.

"Well, I'm not exactly sure what I'm getting into here," I admit, shifting the black folder in my arms. "So, I'm not sure why that's significant."

Elena studies me for a beat before her lips curve again. That smile.

"Lucian is very busy. He hasn't gotten into the selection process in several years, is all. It's just... a rare event."

Rare event.

I swallow, unsure what the hell to do with that information.

"So... when was the last time he 'picked' someone?" I

ask, my voice careful, because I have no idea how to phrase this.

Elena's eyes flick to the doors, watching as the numbers above tick higher. Then she glances back at me, something amused and unreadable in her expression.

"When he hired me."

Oh.

She says it like it's nothing, but her presence is still warm, steady—not threatening, not like this is some kind of competition.

And I appreciate that. It relaxes me, if only a bit.

The elevator chimes, the doors gliding open to reveal a sprawling room beyond.

Rows of sleek black chairs fill the space—about forty or fifty women, all of them stunning in their own unique way. Some are chatting, others scanning the room with sharp, calculating gazes.

I try not to panic-assess my place here.

Elena leads me forward, and before I can process anything else, a bombshell brunette steps into our path, grinning like she's got juicy gossip to share.

"My bestie, Eve," Elena introduces, warmth evident in her tone.

Eve's sharp brown eyes sweep over me in one quick, efficient glance.

"Is this her?" Eve asks and Elena confirms with a sharp nod, smirking, her voice honeyed and confident. "Gorgeous."

"You do know I can hear you?"

Eve's smirk only grows. "And feisty. I like her already."

And suddenly, my brain decides that maybe this is a modeling agency, and my first thought is...

I'm too short.

At 5'3, I'm basically hobbit-sized compared to some of these women. My heels give me a few extra inches, but still —not glamazon levels.

Elena gestures toward a long refreshment table against the far wall.

"We'll be starting soon. Feel free to grab something before we begin."

I'm actually thankful, because my nerves had kept me from eating earlier.

I move toward the table, grabbing a flaky croissant stuffed with ham and cheese, some fresh fruit, and a bottle of water that somehow looks expensive.

Even the damn bottled water is posh.

By the time I take my seat, Elena and Eve stand at the front of the room, their poised confidence silencing the low murmur of conversation.

The air shifts.

This is it.

The lights dim slightly, and a projector drops down behind them, sleek and precise.

Elena lifts a microphone, her easy smile never faltering.

"Welcome, ladies," she begins, her voice smooth and polished.

I brace myself, waiting for some kind of explanation— something that makes any of this make sense.

And then the screen behind her lights up.

A bold, striking logo appears.

The Black Ledger.

Black and gold. Sleek. Polished. Powerful.

And then, as if the room needed another dramatic moment, Elena delivers the final bomb.

"Welcome to The Black Ledger—the world's most elite and exclusive escort agency."

My brain short-circuits.

Excuse me?

Chapter 4
Sienna

My pulse pounds in my ears as Elena's words settle over the room like a thick, undeniable truth.

Escort agency.

The world's most elite and exclusive escort agency.

I stare at the bold gold logo on the screen, my mind struggling to reconcile what I'm hearing with the opulent professionalism of the building, the women, the meticulous secrecy of it all.

This is not what I expected.

A flicker of movement catches my attention—a woman stands abruptly, grabbing her bag and practically marching toward the door.

She's not the only one.

Two others follow, their heels pound sharply against the polished floor as they make their exit.

The tension in the air shifts, uncertainty swirling in the space they leave behind.

I can't blame them.

I should probably be doing the exact same thing.

But I don't move.

Instead, I sit perfectly still, my fingers tightening around the water bottle in my lap.

At the front of the room, Elena remains composed, completely unbothered by the few who leave. If anything, she expected it.

She simply waits until the doors ease shut again before continuing, her voice just as calm, just as poised.

"This is a choice," she says smoothly, her gaze sweeping across the remaining women. "A lucrative, life-altering choice—but a choice nonetheless."

A new slide appears on the screen behind her.

Elegant black and gold text lays out the rules of The Black Ledger.

You set your own terms.

You choose your contracts.

You decide if intimacy is involved.

I blink, rereading the words.

You choose. You decide.

I expected this to be black-and-white—either you're in, or you're out. Either you sell your body, or you don't.

But this?

This is power.

Control.

Eve steps forward, her sleek brunette waves catching in the light as she takes over.

"The Black Ledger isn't just an escort service," she says, her voice carrying a natural authority. "It's a world of power, influence, and exclusivity. Our clients are some of the most powerful men in the world—CEOs, politicians, royalty, elite athletes, and billionaires who need more than just sex."

She paces slightly, letting that sink in.

"They need discretion. Intelligence. Poise. Companionship that extends beyond the physical."

She gestures toward the screen as a new image appears —a list of high-end services their companions offer.

Attending galas and public events. Accompanying clients on luxury vacations.

Posing as a business associate or personal partner. Providing emotional companionship—whether intimate or not.

Elena steps in, effortlessly commanding the room with a quiet kind of confidence, and I suddenly understand why she's the one leading orientation.

She's not just experienced—she's elite.

One of The Black Ledger's highest-paid, most sought-after companions.

And yet... she doesn't sell intimacy.

Not once. Not ever.

Her contracts are strictly companionship-based, built on presence, influence, and the kind of poise that makes men crave her attention without ever laying a hand on her.

She's proof that this isn't just about sex.

It's about power.

But even with that realization, my thoughts spiral. Would I really do this? Could I?

Then another slide appears, and my lingering doubts begin to falter.

"Companions in training receive a salary of $10,000 weekly, as well as full access to The Ledgers exclusive spa." Eve clicks a button, and the next screen makes my mouth drop open.

"Once your sponsorship is complete and you are approved to begin accepting contracts, you'll be compensated well for your companionship."

She steps back. She and Elena watch the room as we take in what we see on the screen.

The Compensation

• $25,000 per week – Base rate for standard companionship

• $50,000+ per event – High-profile engagements

• $100,000+ per month – Exclusive contracts

• Negotiable bonuses for intimacy, discretion, and additional services

Holy. Fucking. Shit.

That's not just money.

That's life-changing money.

Money that could wipe out my credit card debt in a matter of weeks. Money that could pay off my lease and get me the hell out of that apartment. Money that could give me a fresh start.

My fingers press against the cool surface of the black folder in my lap.

I glance around the room.

Some women look intrigued, some excited, and others are clearly just doing the mental math like I am.

A few, though, sit rigid, discomfort clear on their faces.

One more woman quietly stands and leaves.

And yet—I still don't move.

Elena clasps her hands together. "We understand this isn't for everyone. That's why training comes first—so you can make an informed decision. No pressure. No obligation."

$10,000 a week just to be trained. It's unbelievable.

A contract flashes onto the screen.

"This," she says, "is your introduction contract. Signing it doesn't make you a Companion. It simply means you're open to learning."

My fingers tighten around the pen, my pulse hammering in my ears as I stare down at the contract.

I can walk away later.

Nothing is permanent. Nothing is binding me to this.

I can send out job applications. Do this for a little while —just until I'm back on my feet.

I can set my own terms.

I swallow hard, my gaze tracing over the elegant black ink of the agreement. The words feel heavier now, settling over me with an intensity I wasn't expecting.

Companionship. Discretion. Power.

It sounds... simple. And yet, my stomach twists.

I think about Elena—untouchable, desired, in control. But then I think about myself.

I'm not her. I don't have her confidence, her experience.

Hell, I don't have much experience at all.

A dull heat creeps up my neck. My only real partner was Ben, who barely put in any effort and never even—

I shake the thought away, suddenly hyper-aware of how little I know about pleasure—real pleasure. The kind that makes a person weak. The kind that makes them pay for it.

Am I even capable of this?

The question echoes in my mind, sharp and taunting.

I think of Elena and Eve, standing at the front of the room—poised, confident, completely in control. They are the kind of women who command attention, not just receive it. Who hold power over the men in their lives, rather than being at their mercy.

I want that.

I want to walk into a room and own my space, not shrink into it.

I want to know what it feels like to be desired—truly desired—not as an afterthought, not as something to be tolerated or overlooked.

I want to be the one with the power.

For once.

My fingers tighten around the pen, my pulse drumming against my ribs.

A voice in my head sneers, *You weren't even enough for your ex.*

I shove the thought down, refusing to let it sink its claws into me.

This isn't about him. It's about me.

I scan the contract again, my mind grasping at every rationalization.

It's not a commitment. Just training. A few weeks of learning, of discovering—of figuring out what I even want.

If I hate it, I'll walk away.

If nothing else, I'll walk away debt-free.

Ten thousand dollars a week.

The number alone makes my stomach tighten.

I could pay off my credit cards, wipe the slate clean. Get out of this apartment—out of the place that still smells like him.

I could start over. Really start over.

My eyes flick to Elena again.

She built a life on her terms. She carved out space in a world that would have gladly overlooked her.

I want that, too.

I want to know what it's like to choose—not just settle for what's given to me.

I take a breath, steadying myself.

Then, slowly, deliberately, I pick up the pen.

And I sign.

The rest of the day is a whirlwind.

Orientation, as it turns out, isn't just sitting through an initial presentation. It's paperwork. So much paperwork.

Non-disclosures, tax forms, health disclosures. Contracts covering conduct, compensation, client selection, personal boundaries. It's an avalanche of fine print, and with every page I sign, the weight of what I'm stepping into settles heavier on my shoulders.

Then come the measurements.

A team of well-dressed women—somewhere between stylists and tailors—take my height, weight, bust, waist, and hip measurements with the kind of precision that makes me feel like a mannequin.

"For wardrobe," one of them says briskly, jotting down numbers. "Everything you'll need will be provided."

That includes access to the Ledger spa.

A private tour takes us through a sleek, high-end space designed to cater to everything—hair, nails, tanning, massages, waxing, facials. It's indulgence on another level, all pristine marble and warm lighting, the air scented with something rich and expensive.

"And it's all included," Elena tells us with an easy smile. "You represent the Ledger. The Ledger invests in you."

I watch as one of the other women—someone who sat two rows ahead of me earlier—books herself a full-body massage and a hair glossing treatment like she was born for this. I, on the other hand, still feel like a fraud, like at any second someone is going to point at me and demand to know what the hell I'm doing here.

By the time we're finally released, only twenty of us remain.

I wonder how many of them will still be here when training is over.

I wonder if *I* will still be here when training is over.

And yet, despite the uncertainty pressing at the edges of my mind, one thought stays at the forefront all day.

I wonder if Lucian is here.

If he knows I showed up.

If he even remembers me from Friday night.

Probably not.

And it shouldn't matter.

But the fact that it does? That I catch myself hoping for a

glimpse of him as I move through the building? That's a problem.

When I finally step outside, my purse is heavier than when I arrived—not just with the weight of everything I learned today, but with $1,500 in cash.

For a single day.

For signing my name.

I barely breathe as I call Harper, pressing my phone to my ear as I walk toward the subway.

The second she answers, her voice is expectant, giddy.

"Soooooo?"

I exhale, shaking my head.

"You're never going to believe this."

Chapter 5

Sienna

I've spent an two entire weeks training to be a high-end escort.

If I had told myself a month ago that this would be my life, I would have laughed—loudly, obnoxiously, probably while choking on my coffee. But here I am, standing in front of my mirror, dressed in a silk robe after another long day at The Black Ledger, assessing myself with a sharp, critical eye.

Because this isn't what I expected.

Not even close.

When I first walked through those gilded doors, I assumed the job would be one thing—gorgeous women on the arms of wealthy men, playing the role of an adoring date. I thought maybe there would be etiquette lessons, some coaching on conversation and charm. Maybe even a little training on how to fake interest in old-money assholes who talk about their hedge funds too much.

And yes, those things do exist. But what I didn't expect?

The depth of control these women have.

Because being a Ledger Companion isn't just about being wanted—it's about commanding attention.

The first few days were a crash course in poise.

How to walk into a room and own it. How to control body language in a way that draws eyes without even trying. How to sit, stand, cross my legs, tilt my chin—each movement deliberately designed to radiate confidence.

By week two, it had become something more intense.

How to read a man's desires before he even speaks.

How to redirect power back to myself in every interaction.

How to command a room, not just be present in it.

Eve has been leading most of our training since Elena took on a contract the same day I walked through those doors.

She's sharp, no-nonsense, and effortlessly elegant—a woman who moves like she already owns whatever space she's in.

"You're not here to be a pretty accessory," she told us in one of our first sessions. "You're here to be a luxury—an experience men pay for because they can't have it anywhere else."

She makes it look so easy.

The other women? Some are already thriving. Some, like me, are still finding their footing.

Because this?

This is so much more than I ever imagined.

I also didn't realize just how impossible it is to gain access to The Black Ledger.

It's not just elite—it's untouchable.

You can't buy your way in. You can't apply. The men who hold Ledger contracts are hand-selected, their membership approved only after months of scrutiny.

No leaks. No scandals. No accidental exposure.

And that's exactly why they pay millions.

Two new recruits leveled up to Companions already. It seems they had *previous experience.* Three others left so there are fifteen of us now.

I'm fine remaining in the learning phase, applying for jobs and getting my $10,000 a week.

I glance at my phone, pulling up my bank app. My second paycheck hit today, and the first thing I did was pay off one of my credit cards.

One down. Two more to go.

I paid my rent and added to my savings without even batting an eye and there is still plenty of money left for the week ahead.

I take a deep breath, staring at the numbers. The relief is undeniable.

If I just stick this out a few more weeks, I could have everything wiped clean.

Harper is back from vacation, looking ridiculously tan and far too pleased with herself when she plops down on my couch.

"So..." I lean back in my chair, crossing my arms. "Did you miss me, or were you too busy sexting your Italian-situationship, Adriano?"

Harper rolls her eyes, but the smile she tries to fight is telling.

"Oh, please." She waves me off, pretending she's

completely unbothered—but I see the way she fidgets. "We were just talking. You know, casual. A little light conversation."

I narrow my eyes. "Uh-huh. Light conversation."

She sighs dramatically, then finally admits the truth.

"Fine. Maybe Adriano texted me the entire time I was gone. And I might have replied... frequently."

I grin. "Mmm-hmm. You like him."

"He's hot." She takes a dramatic sip of her coffee. "He's temporary fun. I'm not looking for a boyfriend anyhow. You know this."

I raise a brow. "Suuure. And does your temporary fun know that? Because it kind of sounds like he wants to see you again."

Harper glares, but she can't hide the truth.

She's smiling.

Not her usual predatory, man-eating smirk—a real, soft, I-might-actually-like-this-guy smile.

And I love it.

I lean forward, teasing. "It's okay to admit you have a heart in there, Harper. I promise, I won't tell anyone."

She snorts, flipping me off before shoving her sunglasses back onto her face.

"Shut up and let's talk about getting to the second item on your to-do list."

I laugh, shaking my head.

She puts her hand up like a fake notepad and mimes holding a pen with the other.

"You were to have a job. Check."

"That's a partial check. For now, only."

"Sure, sure. We'll be sure to make a note of that." She pretends to push up some nonexistent glasses before getting back to her pretend list. "So looks like all we have now is... ah, sex club time."

I grin, but my cheeks warm instantly. "So, about that..."

Harper arches an accusing brow at me. "If you went without me already, Sienna, so help me—"

I burst out laughing, shaking my head. "No! No, I swear."

She huffs, clearly skeptical. "Good. Because if my best friend experiences her sexual awakening in a nine-story sex club without me there, I will never forgive you."

I roll my eyes. "Well, lucky for you, one of my trainers is taking a group of the new girls to *The Masquerade* tonight."

Harper perks up immediately. "Oh? Now that sounds like an event I need to be a part of."

I snort. "I don't think plus-ones are allowed."

Harper smirks, reaching into her purse and pulling out two silver coins, rubbing them together between her fingers. "Oh, babe, don't forget I've got my own access."

I shake my head, trying to focus. "Okay, well, the thing is... *Ledger* girls get *full* access. To all nine levels of Hell."

Harper's jaw drops for a single dramatic second before she lets out a gleeful squeal. "You better get in there and go *fuck the Devil himself.*" She clasps her hands together, eyes wide with mock reverence. "I hear he plays exclusively on the top floor."

I snort. "Who do you *hear* these things from?"

She shrugs, completely unbothered. "Adriano, of course."

Before I can protest, she's already grabbing her phone, fingers flying over the screen. A second later, she gasps, lighting up like a damn Christmas tree.

"He's free tonight!" she practically sings, bouncing in place. "He'll meet me at the club. Level Two."

I stare at her, barely processing how quickly she locked in her plans. "You just summoned him like a damn demon."

"Damn right," she grins, wiggling her phone. "And now, we get ready."

The Masquerade looms ahead, its sleek black exterior gleaming under the golden glow of its entrance, a quiet promise of indulgence and secrecy. The low thrum of music pulses beneath my feet, a heartbeat of something unknown waiting inside.

I'm dressed exactly as Eve instructed—all black. My dress is sleek, hugging my body in all the right places without being too revealing, paired with sky-high heels that make my legs look miles long.

Harper, in contrast, is a vision in white; the *Level Two: Lust* color code. A barely-there mini dress, her signature confidence accompanies her.

An incredibly tall, muscular and tan man is looking at us like we're walking steaks until I realize it's Adriano. I hadn't seen him since that night on the rooftop party but I notice my friends smile grows.

She looks like temptation wrapped in a bow, and she knows it.

She smirks at me as we near the entrance. "Ready, babe?"

"Go have fun." I tease and she flips her hair over her shoulder, looking back as me.

"Go do all the things I would do."

When she reaches Adriano he wraps an arm low around her back and pulls her in for a toe-curling kiss.

Yeah, *situationship*, my ass.

Just beyond them, I spot Eve and two other trainees.

I swallow, glancing up at the looming club doors. *Ready* is a strong word.

Tonight, is about applying what we've learned in training—holding ourselves with confidence, commanding attention without demanding it.

Eve said our wristbands would be *look, don't touch* for the night, a safety net for us to observe, to absorb, to ease into this world. But she said we shouldn't worry about anyone approaching us anyhow.

No one will interfere with a *black mask*.

A guest can only wear a black mask by invitation from the Devil himself.

That's what Eve told us during training. And yet, no one explained who *he* actually is. A figurehead? A myth? Or a man?

I guess I'll find out soon.

Eve strides ahead with effortless confidence, leading us past the long line of eager guests waiting outside. The doorman clocks her immediately, nodding in recognition before pulling open the heavy doors without hesitation.

No words are exchanged.

No questions asked.

Just silent acknowledgment as we step inside.

Behind us, the line groans with collective frustration, but no one protests. The Masquerade has its own rules, its own hierarchy, and we're apparently above the waitlist.

Inside, the first entrance is deceivingly normal—a dimly lit lounge with moody lighting and a slow, pulsing bass humming beneath the chatter of the evening guests. But we don't stop there.

Eve leads us past a set of velvet ropes, where another level of security waits. Here, the shift in atmosphere is palpable. The air is charged, thick with exclusivity.

Two men stand beside the entrance to what I assume is the real club, both dressed in all black. One wears a sleek tailored suit, the other... a simple pair of slacks and a black leather collar that sits snug against his throat.

My gaze barely flicks toward him before I look away, my cheeks warming.

"Pick your poison," the suited man purrs, sweeping his hand across a red felt board lined with a selection of black masks.

Each one is different. Some simple and elegant, others more elaborate with intricate designs or embellishments. A few are animalistic—sharp, pointed fox masks, curved feline styles.

I reach for one with sleek black bunny ears.

Eve hums, a slow, knowing sound as she watches me fix it over my eyes, adjusting the elastic band beneath my hair.

"Oh, going for prey tonight, Sienna?" She fastens a delicate lace mask over her own face, eyes twinkling with mischief. "I *do* love being chased myself."

I swallow, pulse kicking up.

Prey.

The word settles over me in a way that makes my skin prickle, but I square my shoulders, determined to play along.

"Maybe I just like the aesthetic," I say, forcing a smirk as I meet her gaze.

Eve laughs, looping her arm through mine as she leads us toward the next set of doors. "Oh, sweetheart," she murmurs. "Aesthetic or not... the wolves in here will see you for exactly what you are."

As doors open, and the Masquerade swallows us whole, I wonder for myself, what exactly that could be.

Chapter 6

The moment we step onto the second floor, the atmosphere shifts.

It's warmer here, heavier, infused with something I can't quite name. The lighting is low and decadent, casting everything in a golden glow. Wall sconces flicker against dark velvet drapes, the soft hum of music weaving through the murmur of voices.

Lust.

The second floor of The Masquerade. Where all desires begin.

I lift my glass of champagne, taking a slow sip as my gaze sweeps the room. The bubbles fizz against my tongue, but the light taste does nothing to soothe the anticipation curling low in my stomach.

Harper is already inside somewhere with Adriano, leaving me with the group of Ledger girls, each of us marked by our black masks and red wristbands. *Look, don't touch.* That was the rule for tonight. A safety net. But as I take in my surroundings, I wonder if watching is all we're supposed to be doing.

The first area we enter looks almost normal—like any high-end cocktail lounge in the city. Plush booths curve around intimate tables, expensive liquor gleaming in delicate glasses.

A woman reclines against a velvet chaise, her silk dress slipping down her shoulder, exposing a sliver of lace. A man beside her trails his fingertip up her bare thigh, his expression unreadable. She doesn't flinch. She doesn't stop him. If anything, she leans in.

I swallow hard, fingers tightening around my glass.

Further in, the setting becomes more deliberate. *Designed.*

Rooms framed by sheer curtains, alcoves lined with plush seating. The air hums with something electric, something slow and indulgent.

A blindfolded woman sits in a silk-draped chair, her posture relaxed as a man lifts her hand to his lips. He kisses the inside of her palm, then the tip of each finger, his movements slow, reverent. She shivers.

A velvet massage table sits a few steps away, a woman sprawled across it, her mask tilted slightly as strong hands work warm oil into her back. She exhales, tension melting beneath each firm press of his fingers.

My skin prickles.

This is what Lust is about. Not just sex, but sensation. The slow unraveling of control.

I take another sip of champagne, forcing my gaze forward.

Deeper in, the boundaries between spectator and participant blur. A couple sprawls across a chaise lounge, half-dressed, moving together in a slow, intoxicating rhythm. Another woman kneels between a man's legs, her lips parting in a whisper I can't hear.

My stomach tightens.

I expected this. I *knew* what kind of club The Masquerade was. But knowing and witnessing are two different things.

And the realization that unsettles me the most?

I *like* it.

The warmth pooling low in my stomach. The slow, insidious pulse between my legs.

Arousal. Curiosity. An aching kind of awareness I can't ignore.

I exhale sharply, glancing at the other Ledger girls. Some of them are wide-eyed, others are scanning the room like they're calculating possibilities.

The blonde beside me murmurs, "If this is just the second floor..." She trails off, taking a sip of her drink.

I nod absently.

Because if this is just *Lust*—

What happens when we go deeper into Hell?

By the time I step off the elevator onto the fifth floor, *Wrath,* I am practically panting.

Not from exertion.

From something deeper.

From the slow, building heat that has been coiling inside me with every floor we've ascended.

Gluttony was indulgence. Decadence. The kind of pleasure meant to be consumed in excess.

Greed was power. Control. A floor where submission was currency and dominance was the only acceptable form of wealth.

Somewhere between the champagne, the lingering touches of bodies brushing past me, and the raw, unrestrained nature of *Greed,* I lost my group.

They were taking a tour of each floor so if I just keep going up, I'll find them eventually.

The shift is immediate. The moment I step into the dim, red-lit expanse of *Wrath,* the space is not just darker. The very atmosphere is–*heavier.*

The walls are lined with black leather panels, the scent of it mixing with the sharp tang of something electric. Anticipation. Submission. *Pain.*

I hear it before I *see* it.

The unmistakable crack of impact.

The quiet, shuddering inhale of someone *taking it.*

Then another *slap.*

I round the first corner, heels clicking slowly against the polished floors, as I walk straight into *something primal.*

A large open area stretches before me, a raised platform in the center where a man and woman play out something rough and raw.

She's bent over a padded bench, her wrists bound to the legs with deep red rope. A man stands behind her, shirtless, powerful, a leather paddle gripped in one firm hand.

He drags it down the curve of her back, his other hand smoothing over her flushed skin.

Then—

Crack.

The paddle meets her ass, a delicious moan spilling from her lips.

My stomach clenches. My thighs *press together.*

The room is filled with *watchers.*

Not just here.

Everywhere.

Some standing near the stage, some lounging in the dark corners, some sitting in chairs that line the perimeter of the floor. Their eyes track the movements of the participants.

And now...

Their eyes track *me.*

A slow chill rolls over my skin—not fear, *not even close.*

Awareness.

One by one, the patrons of *Wrath* turn their attention toward me, their gazes sliding over my body, assessing, lingering.

Not judgmental.

Desirous.

I don't even realize how my posture has shifted, how my body has adjusted. *Like my training.*

Back straight. Shoulders rolled. Chin lifted.

My mask hides me, but it also *marks me.*

Black mask. Elite. Untouchable.

But the rabbit: Prey

I swallow, but I don't lower my eyes.

Instead, I *let them look.*

I just became the ultimate forbidden fruit, and they all want to take a bite but none of them can.

My nipples tighten against the soft fabric of my dress. Heat pools low in my stomach, spreading between my thighs, soaking through the lace of my panties.

They *want* me.

And *God help me,* I *love* it.

Something is emboldened within me, and I turn my back to them. My head is the last thing that turns as I slowly look away, heading back to the elevator. The predators here want to give chase and catch their prize but it's against the rules.

Because the black masks belong to the Devil.

And it's that thought that runs through my mind, some kind of possession taking me over that makes me push the button for the topmost floor. My wristband, the key that makes the floor light up as the elevator rises.

The doors glide open with a soft chime, and I step into *The Devil's Playground.*

Heat wraps around me immediately, thick and cloying, laced with the scent of expensive cologne, leather, and sweat mingled with the unmistakable perfume of *sin.*

The room is massive, dimly lit, and thrumming with pleasure. Velvet seating. Mirrored walls reflecting bodies locked together in hypnotic, indulgent rhythms. The air hums with moans and whispered filth, a sensual symphony of surrender.

But none of it holds my attention.

Not when *he's* right in front of me.

A woman is stretched out, arms pinned above her head,

legs spread wide and bound with sleek black cuffs. She's laying on a contraption, suspending her in a work of wicked engineering, floating midair, held up by chains that disappear into the darkness above.

She's helpless. Powerless.

And at the mercy of the man between her legs.

The Devil himself.

His face is hidden, buried between her thighs as he devours her.

The *only* thing I can see is the mask resting on top of his head.

Sculpted black. Curling horns.

It's *him.*

Not just a title. Not just a whispered legend. *The Devil is real.*

A shiver rolls down my spine as his hands flex, fingers digging into her thighs as he holds her open. I watch, rooted to the spot as his head moves, the slick sound of his tongue stroking into her making my own thighs clench.

Her moans rise, a breathless, broken wail as she *shatters* around his mouth.

But he doesn't stop.

He doesn't even *pause.*

The second orgasm crashes into her too quickly, too forcefully, and she thrashes, her restraints rattling with each desperate cry.

"Green!" she gasps. "Green!"

She's begging for more.

And fuck, he gives it to her.

One of his hands slides between her legs.

I feel it. I swear to God, I *feel* the moment his fingers push inside her because my clit throbs in response. My panties are soaked. My breath is locked in my throat, champagne flute forgotten in my grip.

It's a spell. A fucking curse.

I can't look away.

Won't look away.

Then, he lifts his head, mask sliding back into place, hiding his face from me.

My stomach clenches.

The mask. *His mask.* The one I've heard whispers about. The one the club reveres.

The Devil's mask.

And the moment his dark gaze locks onto mine, *I whimper.*

His tongue sweeps over his lower lip, tasting the woman on his mouth. His hand drops to the bulge in his pants, gripping himself through the black leather.

God, I might come just from watching this.

Three fingers dip into his mouth as he licks himself clean and my lips part.

Heat burns through me, from the tips of my ears to the insides of my thighs.

He steps aside, pressing a button on the platform's frame, lowering the bound woman to the level of his cock.

He's going to fuck her.

And I've never wanted to switch places with someone more in my life.

Slowly, deliberately, he unzips himself. The motion is

unhurried, taunting, revealing the barest glimpse of tanned skin, dark curls at the base of his shaft.

I don't realize I'm *staring* until his fingers wrap around his dick, stroking once, the muscles in his forearm flexing as he tightens his grip.

Something in my chest *flutters.*

A dark thrill. A sick longing.

He knows I'm watching. *Wants* me to watch.

And fuck, I do.

The flash of gold catches my eye first. A foil-wrapped condom in his other hand.

He tears the corner open with his teeth, turning slightly to spit the piece onto the floor, and then—without breaking eye contact—he rolls it down the length of his cock.

I squeeze my thighs together. Hard.

He presses a hand to the woman's stomach, his fingers dragging upward, stroking between the valley of her breasts. He cups one, squeezing possessively before pinching her nipple between two fingers, rolling it until she gasps.

Then he grips her shoulder and positions his cock at her entrance.

And *slams* into her.

A choked sound leaves my throat.

His stomach flexes with each roll of his hips, his thrusts powerful and unrelenting, using the motion of the suspended frame to push deeper, harder.

I think I *might* be shaking.

His eyes never leave mine.

She gasps out a name and I wonder if it's his. It's not.

A man steps forward, responding to her call. He

approaches, adjusting the woman's headrest, tipping it back until her mouth is open, waiting.

The new man pulls out his cock, and she takes him eagerly.

The Devil *watches me* as he fucks her, as she moans around the other man's cock, as the two of them work her over in perfect, ruthless synchronization.

"There you are!"

I nearly *jump* at the sound of Eve's voice, the world snapping back into focus.

My skin is *on fire*, my pulse frantic, my panties–fucking ruined.

"We've got to get you newbies home before bedtime."

Eve is speaking to the other recruits, but I barely register it.

Because when I turn back—*he's still looking at me.*

The elevator chimes, signaling our departure, but I *can't move.*

Even as I step backward into the rising lift, as the doors close, I *don't break eye contact.*

Neither does he.

And right before the doors fully seal—

He smirks.

Chapter 7
Lucian

Two weeks.

Two fucking weeks of putting out fires and breaking necks to keep everything running smoothly.

You'd think by now, with the systems I have in place—the rules, the structure, the people trained to handle everything—I could take a goddamn breath without the world lighting itself on fire.

Apparently not.

The first week was simple enough. One of our Paris clients got caught getting handsy with a Companion in public. I sent him a warning. He thought that meant I was bluffing. He doesn't think that anymore.

The second week? That's when the real shit hit the fan.

A client went rogue. Not just boundary-pushing. Not just breaking a contract.

He kidnapped one of my girls.

Used her as a human shield while trying to escape some debt he owed.

He was able to hide for three days before I tracked him down.

My girl's safe. He's not breathing anymore.

I made sure of that.

Because no one touches what's mine.

And every woman under my protection—every contract, every Companion—is *mine*.

So now I'm back.

Back in the city. Back in control.

Back to *my empire*.

The Black Ledger is where it belongs—at the center of power. Silent. Discreet. Unshakable.

And last night, I needed a release. An outlet.

I needed the rush. The surrender. The kind of night that wrings the tension out of your bones and leaves you drunk on control.

The Devil walked the halls of the Masquerade and found plenty to play with.

And it should've worked.

It always does.

Except last night, it didn't.

Not the way it usually does.

I knew a new batch of recruits was set to begin orientation. I make a point to introduce myself, at least once. A presence check. It matters.

But I didn't.

Two weeks of back-to-back fires—violent, bloody, reputation-shaking messes—kept my attention off the books and squarely on the men trying to bleed me dry.

Eve can handle the orientation. I trust her with everything. But *The Ledger* isn't just a business. It's not some faceless corporation.

It's my empire. My name. My legacy.

Everyone in it is family. Everyone in it is mine to protect.

Apparently that now includes *her*.

The woman from the rooftop party.

I gave her a card. I don't usually do that. In fact, I haven't done it in years. It was a rash decision, one I made before I had time to think better of it.

And if I'm being honest—I still don't know why I did it.

She wasn't throwing herself at me. She wasn't even trying to impress anyone.

But the way she stood up to that prick—defiant, unafraid, mouth sharp as a blade—and the way she didn't flinch when I made sure he'd never try that shit again...

There was something there.

Something in her eyes that told me she wasn't weak. That under the shock and nerves, under the cocktail dress and too-honest laugh, there was someone who could hold her own in this world. Maybe even thrive in it.

I gave her the card, assuming she'd toss it.

Most do.

Women like her don't usually follow through. Not because they can't—but because they don't believe they belong here.

But then... she showed up.

She put on black and walked into my club like prey ripe for the taking.

And last night, she watched me.

Not from behind a screen. Not from the safe shadows.

She stood on the edge of The Devil's Playground and looked me dead in the eye.

I don't get involved with recruits. That's not a rule—it's law.

But this girl?

This girl I barely know...

She's already broken a rule just by *making me notice.*

"Knock, knock!" Eve raps her knuckles twice on my open door before walking in, a black folder tucked beneath her arm like it holds state secrets. "Is it my turn to face the gauntlet?"

I huff a quiet laugh, already rising to my feet with a stretch. "Espresso?"

"God, yes." She makes herself at home in the sitting area —in my chair, of course—crossing one leg over the other as she sets her notepad down.

I move to the coffee bar, the familiar routine of grinding beans and fitting the portafilter into place settling the tension still clinging to my shoulders. The hiss of steam cuts through the quiet as I pour two shots into warmed cups.

"Long night?" she asks, pulling out her pen.

"Could've been longer," I say, setting a cup down in front of her.

She lifts it like a toast. "You should try being the one wrangling over a dozen barely-trained women through nine floors of organized depravity. The Devil might run the club, but I'm the poor soul stuck babysitting the damned."

"Poor soul," I echo dryly, lifting my own cup.

I settle into the armchair opposite her, watching as she flips open the folder.

"Noticed you took the recruits home early last night," I say casually. "Someone couldn't handle it?"

She shakes her head. "No one bailed, surprisingly. We usually lose at least one to the sensory overload, but this group?" She sips. "Seems set on sticking it out."

That earns a slow nod from me.

"Interesting."

"Mm," Eve hums, flipping a page. "Very."

She pulls out a printed list, shuffling it neatly on her lap like she always does.

"I'm going alphabetically," she says. "Easier that way."

I nod, grabbing my tablet from the end table beside me and unlocking it with a swipe. The new recruits' profiles are already loaded, thumbnails lined in neat rows. Faces, names, stats.

I scroll slowly, skimming like I always do. I don't need every detail—just enough to know what I'm working with.

"Two of them advanced to Companion status already," Eve starts, scanning her own notes. "Both were scouted previously, just needed orientation to meet the standards."

"The fast-tracked ones?"

"Mm-hmm. Already had soft contracts waiting for them. A few left during the second week. One after waxing day. Couldn't handle the vulnerability, I think."

I don't comment. Some women romanticize this life.

Others crumble under the pressure the moment it stops being a fantasy.

"Fifteen are left," she continues, shifting in the chair. "But we'll see who sticks around after the first Sponsor week."

I nod again, scrolling through faces as she talks. Notes on etiquette training, style consultations, sexual boundaries. My eyes catch a flash of platinum blonde, then another with a sharp red bob.

Then—

Auburn.

Rich and full, the same way I remember it from the rooftop. The same hair I spotted across the Devil's Playground last night, paired with a black bunny mask and eyes wide with want. Even in a two-inch thumbnail photo, she stands out. Like a flare in a dark forest.

Sienna Knight.

The woman in red.

The little rabbit who wandered straight into the wolves' den.

And didn't run.

Twenty-four years old. College graduate. Working—well—worked, in some go-nowhere corporate job when her degree would have taken her so much farther.

My thumb pauses just above her profile.

Eve doesn't miss it.

"Oh yes. Your little protégé," she says smoothly, tapping her pen against her clipboard. "I can see why you're interested in her."

"I'm not interested," I say, enunciating the word like it offends me.

Eve snorts. "Riiight. And I'm a virgin."

I lift a brow but don't rise to the bait.

She leans back into her chair, one leg crossing over the other. "She's doing well," she adds after a beat, the smirk giving way to something more thoughtful. "Green in some ways, sure. Definitely inexperienced, especially sexually. But she's observant. Composed when she wants to be. Smart. Determined. One of the few I think will graduate to sponsorship."

I nod once, shifting the conversation. "What clients stepped forward?"

"The list just closed this morning. Mixer's tomorrow night."

I swipe back to the dashboard and pull up the pre-approved sponsor slate for this batch. Fifteen high-net-worth clients—curated, vetted, and aligned with our standards. All of them with experience in mentoring new recruits. All of them personally cleared by me weeks ago.

I find no fault in any of them. I wouldn't have approved them if there was.

"As usual," Eve continues, "they'll meet the girls, bid on the ones they want to sponsor. Highest bid wins."

Once the recruits make it past their initial training and assessments, they'll divide their time between Ledger training and shadowing their sponsors. Clients that teach them the ropes in real-world settings. Personalized guidance. One-on-one mentorship.

And then graduation.

A mutual agreement between client and recruit. When the girls are ready, they sign off. The recruit becomes a Companion moves on to contract work.

I glance through the sponsor list again, though I'm barely registering the names. I know who they are. I know what they want.

My thumb hovers once more—this time over her name.

I should close the file.

"Who do you think the sponsors will want to match with?" I ask instead.

Eve shrugs, feigning indifference. "We'll see who's interested in sponsoring her tomorrow."

"I wasn't just talking about her."

She smiles without looking up. "Sure, boss. Whatever you say."

I don't dignify it with a reply. I set my tablet down, walk back to my desk, and lock up the files before I leave for my next meeting—one I'm not fucking looking forward to.

I smooth my sleeves, adjust my cuffs, and grab my jacket from the hook.

As I step past her, I speak without looking back.

"Keep me updated."

Eve's voice follows, low and knowing. "Of course. About just her or—"

"Watch it," I call over my shoulder.

I don't wait for her laugh, even though I hear it anyway.

By the time the elevator doors close, I've shut the file in my mind too. Locked tight.

Because where I'm going next?

There's no room for distractions.

Chapter 8

Sienna

The smell of soy sauce and sesame oil fills the room as I dig my chopsticks into a carton of lo mein, sitting cross-legged on the plush white rug in the middle of my very-not-Ben apartment.

The new cream sectional behind me is wide and welcoming, with tufted cushions and cozy throw pillows in pale blush and soft sage green. A fluffy knit blanket is draped over the arm, and I've added gold-framed art prints above it—delicate sketches of flowers and abstract shapes that make me feel calm. Feminine. Soft. Like I finally get to breathe in my own space.

My Pinterest board has officially come to life.

"You've got good taste," Harper says between bites of orange chicken, her takeout box resting on her thigh. "It looks like one of those dream apartments on Instagram. All you need is a dog named Maple and a coffee machine that costs more than your rent."

I grin around a mouthful of noodles. "Wait till I pay off those last two credit cards and I'll consider both."

Harper hums approvingly, nudging her foot against mine. "Well, you're definitely not getting fired this time. Unlike some people..."

I raise a brow. "Oh?"

She sets her box aside, leans back on her elbows, and gives me a look. "You didn't hear this from me, but apparently Steve tried to play the whole thing off like *you* attacked him."

I blink. "You're kidding."

"Nope. But turns out, you weren't the only one who saw him get decked at the party." She grins. "Some intern from the finance team reported the whole thing—said she overheard him being a total creep and saw everything."

I let out a disbelieving laugh. "So they believed her?"

"Oh, they didn't have a choice once they got a call from some hotshot lawyer from The Masquerade." Harper pops a piece of chicken in her mouth, clearly enjoying the gossip. "Apparently, they were going to press charges if he wasn't *dealt with* properly. They marched him out of the building by lunch. Security escort and everything."

My jaw drops. "You're serious?"

"Dead." She grins. "They even sent out one of those vague internal memos about 'upholding workplace values.' I almost framed it."

I laugh, the kind of deep, cathartic laugh that only comes after too much stress and too many "what ifs."

"He cried too. It was glorious."

Oddly that makes me feel a lot better, knowing he got what was coming to him.

It seems lately the men around me are the only ones getting their dream life and dammit, it feels like it should be my turn now.

I glance around the apartment again, my heart giving a little flutter at how different it feels now. How much lighter.

Every piece I've added since Ben left has been a quiet little rebellion. A small declaration of independence.

But as much as decorating has distracted my mind all day, there is nothing to stop me from thinking about the Sponsor Mixer tomorrow night.

The nerves start to tingle again in my chest, but Harper bumps her shoulder against mine, pulling me back to the moment.

"You're going to kill it," she says, somehow always knowing what's going on in my mind.

Harper stretches her legs out, flexing her toes as she grabs another dumpling from the container between us. "Alright, enough about work. Let's get to the real topic of interest here."

I arch a brow, popping a piece of broccoli into my mouth. "And what would that be?"

She rolls her eyes, exasperated. "Oh, I don't know— maybe the fact that you spent last night in a nine-story sex club? You've been suspiciously quiet about that, and I do *not* appreciate the lack of details."

My face heats instantly, and I shove another bite of food into my mouth just to avoid answering.

Harper is undeterred. "Come *on*, Sienna. You went to *The*

Masquerade as a Black Mask. You had full access. I need details."

I chew, I swallow, because what the hell am I supposed to say?

That I stood in *Wrath*, surrounded by power and depravity, and *liked* the way men looked at me? That I walked into *The Devil's Playground* and watched as the man in the devil mask devoured a woman like she was his last meal?

That he locked eyes with me and somehow fucked my soul.

That even now, just thinking about it, my thighs squeeze together, and my breath comes a little *too* fast?

Yeah. No.

I clear my throat. "It was... a lot."

Harper snorts. "Yeah, no shit. Give me something better."

I exhale slowly, staring at my takeout box. "I—I liked watching."

Harper stills, then grins like a cat who just found a whole flock of canaries. "Oh? *Oh!?* Is my baby girl entering her hoe-era?"

"Oh, shut up." I swat at her but she just dodges.

Harper cackles. "God, I *love* this for you. I mean, obviously. Have you *seen* the men at that club? Of course, you liked watching."

"I also liked, um—" I gnaw the inside of my lip. "—being watched?" I turn the words up on the end as if I'm posing a question.

"Bitch." Harper is practically levitating off the floor in anticipation. "Did you get run through like a New York subway and didn't immediately call me? I could have taken your picture like a proud mom on her kids first day of school."

"You're ridiculous." I stand, grabbing the empty containers and heading for the kitchen.

Harper heads for a bottle of wine.

"And no. We weren't allowed to be touched but I sort of went up to..."

"Oh, my god you went to the Devil's Playground."

I wince, nodding.

"And I kind of watched... the Devil fuck the brains out of this woman." I cover my face with my hands knowing I look like a God damn cherry tomato. "And he kind of... watched me."

I pause.

Harper is nearly drooling.

"The entire time."

Harper's practically vibrating, wine glass in hand, eyes sparkling with enough mischief to light up Manhattan.

"Holy shit," she whispers, like we're teenagers gossiping about our first kisses. "That's better than any porn plot I've ever heard. And he just... watched you the whole time?"

I nod slowly. "The entire time." I say it again, softer this time, letting it settle between us.

Harper takes a sip, studying me. "And how did it make you feel?"

I sink back onto the couch, drawing my knees up to my chest. "Exposed."

Her brows rise in surprise—not judgmental, just curious.

"Not just, like, oh-my-God-he's-hot-and-staring-at-me exposed." I glance at her, then away again. "But like... he could see something in me that I haven't even admitted to myself yet. Like I walked in wearing a mask and he already knew what was underneath it."

Harper stays quiet for a beat. Letting me talk. Letting me feel it.

"I don't know how to feel about it." My voice is barely above a whisper. "I think it should have disgusted me. It should have scared me."

"But?" she prompts, already knowing the answer.

"But I couldn't stop watching," I admit. "And he wouldn't stop looking at me. Like..." I trail off, the words too heavy to finish.

"Like he already knew what you were thinking?" Harper fills in, softly.

I look down at my wineglass, then give the smallest nod.

"Babe," she says gently, "you're allowed to feel that. All of it."

I sigh, leaning back against the new cushions. It's the kind of couch Pinterest dreams are made of, and it's mine. But I still feel like I don't belong in it. Like I'm pretending to be someone I'm not.

"What if this isn't me, Harp?" I ask quietly. "What if I'm just a normal girl playing dress-up in a world that's going to swallow me whole?"

Harper scoots closer, bumping her shoulder against mine again. "Sienna, babe, this world doesn't make you bad. Wanting things—desire—doesn't make you bad."

I swallow, hard.

"You went to a sex club and liked what you saw. That's not some earth-shattering crime. It just means you're discovering what you actually want. And that's a *good* thing."

"I'm scared," I admit, the words raw and unfiltered. "What if I'm making a mistake by staying?"

Harper nudges me again, this time gentler. "Then you'll walk away."

I blink at her.

"If you don't like it, walk away," she repeats. "But if you do? Own it."

I laugh—nervous and shaky. "You make it sound so simple."

She shrugs, sipping her wine. "It *is* simple. You don't have to be scared of what you want. No one can control you unless you let them."

Her words settle in my chest like an anchor. Heavy, grounding.

I glance around the apartment. The new couch. The fresh art prints. The soft cream throw I bought on sale last week, now folded perfectly on the armrest. My life is changing. Quietly, but undeniably.

Maybe I am too.

Maybe that's okay.

Chapter 9

Lucian

It's late.

Rain clings to the windshield in silver rivulets, catching the dull amber glow of the overhead streetlight like veins of gold. The engine idles for a moment before I kill it, leaving nothing but the soft patter of droplets on metal and the ticking cool-down of the car's frame.

The road is slick, black as oil, reflecting the halo of the lamplight in puddles along the curb.

I don't get out.

Not yet.

My fingers rest loosely on the steering wheel, tapping once—twice—before I catch myself. It's a twitch I thought I broke years ago. One that comes back on occasion.

This place hasn't changed. Same cracked asphalt. Same rusted-out signage above the old freight entrance. Same scent of oil, rain, and cigarette smoke clinging to the concrete bones of the building. If ghosts exist, this place is full of them.

I haven't been here in years.

Not since the night I told Lorenzo I was out.

The night I walked away from the family and everything it meant.

And now... here I am again.

Back at the warehouse. Back at the beginning.

Only this time, it's not loyalty I'm questioning—it's peace. And whether men like us ever really get to have it.

I grab the bottle of whiskey sitting in the seat next to me.

Dalmore 25.

It's the one Lorenzo and I used to drink after deals went clean—after bodies were buried and the books balanced in our favor. Top shelf. Aged twelve years longer than most men survive in this business.

We always said it was the kind of thing meant to be savored slowly. Something for victories.

But this isn't a victory.

Not now.

Not after what I did.

They're watching. I know that much. Always eyes here. Perched in corners, behind tinted glass. Probably a sniper two rooftops over, just in case I came looking for blood instead of peace.

But that's not what I'm here for.

I didn't come to reignite old wars.

I came to make sure a new one doesn't start.

Because if it does—if it's him versus me—there won't be a city left when it's over.

I walk forward, my footsteps loud against the wet gravel, and stop in front of the metal door.

My fist clenches once around the bottle's neck before I knock. Two sharp raps.

Then I wait.

A breath. Another.

The door creaks open.

The man standing behind it isn't familiar. Tall, broad-shouldered, all quiet menace wrapped in a black jacket. He doesn't speak but he doesn't need to.

He's not supposed to know me. And I'm not here to make introductions.

I step inside, keeping my posture relaxed but my eyes sharp, skimming the corners and shadows. Watching for movement. Watching for tells.

I'm in the lion's den again.

Only this time, I'm not walking in as a brother.

I'm walking in as the man who murdered his.

They pat me down before I take another step inside.

I raise my arms without a word, letting the two soldiers do their job. They're thorough—checking boots, waistband, even the inside of my jacket lining. One gives me a look like he hopes I brought something, just to give him an excuse to throw a punch. I don't.

I'm not here for a fight.

Doesn't mean I'm not ready for one.

I clock ten bodies scattered across the warehouse—two near the doors, three on the upper-level catwalk, the rest posted in shadows. That means, conservatively, I'm staring down the barrels of at least twenty guns.

And I walked in with nothing but a bottle of whiskey.

It's still in my hand when I see Lorenzo.

Sitting at a long metal table, one leg crossed over the other like he's holding court. A cigar glows between his fingers, the cut slow and deliberate. He doesn't look up—not yet. Just rolls the flame from a silver lighter over the end, inhaling until the tip burns orange and ash starts to form.

I haven't seen him in years, but nothing about him surprises me. Still wears those expensive suits with the Italian cut and the dark ties. Still has that ring on his pinkie finger—his father's. A ring that marks him as the head of his organization.

Still looks like the devil with charm to burn.

I step forward and take the chair across from him, placing the bottle on the table between us. I don't say a word.

He finally looks at it. Not me. Just the bottle.

His lips curl slightly around the cigar, but it's not a smile. Not even close. He flicks ash into a tray near his elbow, then leans back in his chair, one arm slung casually along the backrest.

"Took you long enough," he says. Voice like gravel.

I settle deeper into my chair, resting one forearm on the table. "You're hard to catch when you're pissed."

He laughs—one sharp breath through his nose. No amusement in it.

"Harder when I'm grieving."

The words land heavy between us.

I nod once. "I know."

His eyes flick to mine for the first time. Cold. Cautious.

"No apology?" he asks.

"I didn't come to apologize."

He hums like that answer doesn't surprise him.

"Then why are you here?"

I nudge the bottle forward.

The glass scrapes across steel.

He watches it with the same dead expression he used to give corpses we dumped in the river.

Then—finally—he cuts his gaze up to me.

Silent. Waiting.

I look him in the eye.

"Enrico crossed a line."

Lorenzo's expression doesn't change. Not yet. But I see the pressure building behind his eyes.

"He used one of my girls as a fucking shield," I continue, tone even. Controlled. "Owed money to men too dangerous to default on, and instead of taking the hit like a man, he threw a civilian in front of the bullet."

Lorenzo doesn't blink. But the muscle in his jaw jumps.

"He laid hands on her," I say, voice dropping. "Split her lip. Bruised her ribs. And all while screaming about how his family would protect him."

I pause.

"You and I both know what happens to a man who uses that name to justify cowardice."

The table shakes.

Lorenzo's fist slams down like thunder, and the bottle between us rattles violently. His cigar jumps, rolls, and sears a black scorch mark across the surface before settling.

"You think I don't fucking know that?" he roars.

The room shifts around us. Every man present goes still —fingers twitching near triggers. I don't move.

He glares at me across the table, eyes burning with grief and fury.

"I taught him better," he growls. "I raised him better."

"I know you did."

"You think I wanted this? You think I'd want my brother to die over some goddamn—"

"Careful," I cut in, my tone sharp enough to slice through the storm building between us. "She's not some goddamn anything. She's Ledger. She's mine. And your brother knew the rules."

He breathes hard through his nose, fists clenched on the table, but I see it—under the rage, under the hurt—he knows I'm right.

If someone had laid hands on one of his, he'd have done the same.

He just didn't think I would have the balls to do it to his brother.

But he forgets—we wrote these fucking rules together.

And I never forget a debt.

No matter who owes it.

"You jumped the fucking gun," Lorenzo snaps, voice still ragged from the outburst. "We were working on settling the debt. He was going to make it right."

I shake my head slowly, evenly. "Bullshit."

His eyes flash.

"You and I both know," I say, voice low but firm, "once a hit goes out from *that* family—the Irish–there's no settling. No pulling it back. Not unless the other side's already dead."

Lorenzo leans forward, bracing his forearms on the table, his voice turning cold. "He was mine to handle."

"And you didn't handle him," I fire back. "So I did."

Silence stretches thick between us.

"I won't apologize for it," I continue. "I don't regret it. What I did had to be done."

He looks away for a beat, jaw tight, but I keep going.

"I came here for peace. I want your word—on the code. No retaliation. We bury it. You grieve your brother, I move on. We end it here."

But then something shifts.

That coldness in his face curdles into something darker. More twisted. He turns back toward me, slow, a new gleam in his eye—something poisonous.

A smile that doesn't touch his mouth curls there, followed by a thick stream of spit he lets fall to the concrete floor.

Then, in a tone that scrapes bone:

"A pound of flesh for a pound of flesh," he says, venomous. "Your whore gave a pound of flesh. My brother gave his life. There's no universe where that balances on the scales."

I don't flinch. But I hear the scrape of footsteps. Two of his men take a step closer—subtle, but not subtle enough.

My gaze cuts to them, then back to him.

He knows better.

But rage makes men stupid.

Lorenzo leans back, tossing the cigar from his fingers like he's throwing away the last shred of civility.

"Get the fuck out of my warehouse, Lucian."

I don't move right away.

The silence stretches. Heavy. Final.

Then slowly, I rise. No sudden movements. No retreat.

My eyes stay locked on his, steady and unreadable.

The weight of what we've become settles between us—no longer brothers, just two predators with a body between them.

I fix my cuffs, smooth my jacket. My voice is even when it comes.

"You're supposed to be better than this, Lorenzo."

My old friend's jaw ticks. His eyes burn.

As I turn, he throws his last shot after me, voice laced with venom.

"You would do best to keep your head down. Because when I come collecting... I won't miss."

I pause at the threshold, one hand on the steel door.

"I'll see you around Lo."

And I walk out, leaving the bottle of whiskey on the table where it sits—untouched.

A peace offering refused.

A warning ignored.

And now a war about to be written in fucking blood.

Chapter 10

Sienna

The hum of curling irons and the soft hiss of hair spray fill the air as stylists and makeup artists work their magic. The room smells like roses and heated ceramic. There's music playing low—some sexy, thumping track that's clearly meant to set a confident tone —but my nerves are louder.

Most of the girls went with little black dresses. Classic. Timeless. Safe.

I went the other direction.

Bone-white.

Short.

Fitted.

Deliberately bold against my skin.

A statement.

I catch my reflection in the mirror. My auburn hair tumbles in waves, and my makeup is flawless—soft, glowing, and not too sultry. The dress hugs every curve, skimming high on the thigh and dipping just low enough to earn a second glance.

If nothing else, I look like I belong here tonight.

Even if I'm not sure I feel like it yet.

The girl beside me is pale. Her stylist moves to grab more setting powder, and she clutches her clutch like it's a lifeline. Her hands are trembling.

I lean over just slightly, offering a smile. "You look stunning. That neckline? Showstopper."

She exhales a shaky breath, smiling back. "Thank you. I feel like I'm gonna pass out."

"Then make sure you do it gracefully," I tease gently. "Preferably onto someone rich."

She laughs, tension bleeding from her shoulders. "Noted."

I hope it helped. I really do. Because I get it.

The nerves. The unknown. The sick tangle of excitement and dread.

Tonight is the *Mixer*. The moment all of this—the training, the NDA, the whispered promises—gets real. Billionaires, CEOs, politicians... men with too much money and too little time will walk onto the rooftop patio tonight looking to sponsor their next Ledger Companion.

And we're the inventory.

It's not a transaction—not exactly.

We've already set our limits.

We get to say no.

But still... we're the ones being chosen.

It's all starting to feel painfully real now.

What if no one bids on me?

Does someone... pity-pick the leftovers?

Is there a consolation sponsor for the girls who aren't anyone's first choice?

Or worse—do they cut you loose?

Toss you out of the Ledger and wish you luck?

The thought tightens around my lungs.

I've been applying for jobs outside of this, submitting resumes, sitting through interviews that all blend together. Nothing's landed yet. And if this doesn't work out...

I don't let myself finish the thought.

I adjust the hem of my dress and glance around for someone to ask. Maybe one of the assistants. But before I can move, a familiar voice rings out.

"Ladies," Eve says, stepping through the door in a tailored black suit and stiletto heels that could draw blood. Her dark hair is swept back in a sleek knot, and her signature red lipstick looks like war paint.

All conversation stops.

Every stylist freezes mid-sweep. Every girl lifts her chin.

Eve smiles, and it's sharp enough to cut glass.

"Showtime."

The rooftop patio glows under the fading warmth of sunset, the sky painted in brushstrokes of lavender and gold. Delicate strings of lights crisscross above us like constellations, twinkling against the evening sky.

Sculpted hedges and glass railings line the edges of the

terrace, framing a panoramic view of the skyline below. But no one's looking out.

All eyes are on us.

The recruits.

I grip my champagne glass a little tighter, the chilled flute dampening my fingertips as I force a breath past the tension building in my chest. The patio is overflowing with power. You can feel it pressing against your skin like static.

Suits that cost more than my rent. Smiles that don't reach their eyes. Watches that gleam beneath cufflinks and perfectly tailored sleeves.

They're not all men. A handful of women linger in the mix too—sharp, composed, commanding. Ledger Companions and prospective clients alike.

I spot two of the senior Companions weaving through the space—effortless, radiant, magnetic. They greet sponsors with kisses on cheeks and sly smirks, pausing to speak to the girls and subtly steer conversations.

They're not here for contracts tonight.

They're here to help us.

Thank God.

I've made it through my first three conversations without spilling a drink or saying anything humiliating. I'm counting that as a win.

The first was with a man who runs a global logistics empire. Kind, in a calculating way. He asked me what I thought of the *Ledger's mission*. I said something about confidence, trust, curated companionship—at least I hope I did. My mouth was dry and my mind was racing but he nodded, intrigued.

The second was an author.

Famous, apparently.

He was surprisingly charming—eccentric in a genius sort of way—and far more interested in me than I expected.

The third was... odd.

Too charming. Too polished.

Like a veneer over something rotting underneath.

A senior Companion named Bianca stepped in halfway through the conversation with a gentle hand on my arm and a subtle redirect. I don't know what she saw, but I was grateful all the same.

It's been just over an hour. My cheeks hurt from smiling. My heart is still racing.

But I'm doing it.

I'm remembering what Eve told us: *Eye contact, good posture, curious but not overeager. You're not selling yourself. You're showing them what they could never afford anywhere else.*

So, I stand a little taller. Keep my chin up. My shoulders back. I sip slowly and move deliberately—like I've been doing this forever.

But the truth is?

I'm still just the girl who's still paying off credit card debt.

Still looking for another job.

Still deciding who she is.

And right now?

She's a woman in bone-white, walking among wolves—and holding her own.

At least, that's what I tell myself as I reach for another flute of champagne from a passing tray, hoping the bubbles will do something to loosen the tight coil in my chest.

And then the air shifts.

Like a breeze cutting through velvet, so subtle and sharp it makes the hairs on my arms rise.

A hush spreads—not obvious, but present. A subtle recalibration in the room, like every man just straightened his posture. Like every Companion turned her head in unspoken recognition.

I don't have to look to know he's here.

Lucian Vale.

My fingers tighten around the delicate stem of my glass. My breath stalls.

He steps into the space like it belongs to him—and it does. Black suit. Crisp white shirt. No tie. The top buttons undone just enough to hint at something dangerous beneath the surface. Everything about him is clean, restrained, and devastating.

Controlled.

Untouchable.

He moves like a man who doesn't chase power because power follows him.

For a beat, I forget the conversations around me, the sponsors milling about, the other girls smiling and laughing on cue. My focus narrows to one man.

Lucian.

It's the first time I've seen him since the rooftop of The Masquerade. Since the night he broke my manager's face and handed me the key to a life I didn't even know I could want.

And now he's here.

My pulse skips, quickens. My skin flushes, and suddenly the patio feels too warm.

I catch glimpses of him through the crowd—moving slowly, greeting a few high-rolling sponsors, exchanging brief words with senior Companions. Nothing over the top. Just enough to remind everyone who runs this empire.

And I can't stop looking for him.

I try to focus on the conversation I'm in, nodding along as a kind older man compliments the structure of the mixer and asks polite questions about how training has gone so far. I give thoughtful answers. I remember my posture. I smile like Eve taught.

This is the job.

Mingle with the sponsors. Engage. Impress.

And I'm doing it. I am.

But it's hard to stay present when I can feel him behind me. Not literally—he hasn't come near me. But the awareness of him, of where he is in the room, is magnetic.

I track him without trying to. His broad frame leans in to speak with one of the senior Companions, the deep timbre of his voice cutting through the hum of polite conversation. He speaks low, controlled—but it carries, just enough to stand out.

Like him.

I tell myself not to look. To focus. To keep my eyes on the man in front of me. But every time Lucian moves into my periphery, I feel it.

And every time I chance a glance—he's already looking away.

My skin prickles. My mind spins.

Eventually, I slip away to the bar and set down my half-finished champagne. "Club soda with lime," I tell the bartender, needing the grounding of something cold and sober.

Bubbles rise in the glass, and I take a slow sip, exhaling as I turn back to the crowd.

He shouldn't be the distraction. He's the damn owner. He's off-limits. I'm pretty sure even thinking about him like this is against some unspoken rule. Maybe an actual one.

But the more I try to push him out of my mind... the more it feels like he's already there.

Because he is.

I feel it before I see it. That electric awareness that prickles up the back of my neck like a warning.

His gaze is on me.

My fingers tighten around the glass as I slowly scan the room—just in time to catch him walking directly toward me.

It's like watching a storm cross calm waters. Controlled power. Quiet menace. He's not hurrying. He doesn't need to. The space clears around him as if the room parts to make way for the man who owns it.

And somehow, I don't move.

My breath stalls, but I lift my chin, meeting him head-on as he reaches me at the bar.

"Miss Knight," he says, voice low and smooth like aged whiskey. "Enjoying the evening?"

I blink once. Of course he already knows my name.

I hope I'm hiding how much that affects me.

"Mr. Vale," I nod, willing my voice to stay steady. "I am. It's... a lot to take in."

A faint smile touches the corner of his mouth. It's barely there. "That's the point."

He pauses, his gaze sliding over me—not in a way that feels lecherous, but like he's reading something between the lines of my expression. Maybe even beneath my skin.

"You surprised me," he says.

I arch a brow, caught off guard. "How so?"

His eyes don't waver. "Didn't think you'd actually come."

That lands. Harder than it should.

I reach for my glass, giving myself a second before I answer. "Then why give me the card?"

Lucian studies me for a long moment, the weight of his gaze a pressure I feel in my chest, my spine, my pulse.

"That's a question," he says finally, "you'll answer over time."

His tone is unreadable. Smooth. Dismissive, maybe. Or patient.

"Or you won't," he adds simply.

I swallow, unsure whether it was a challenge, or something else entirely.

But I can't stop myself.

"Well, you're the expert. How am I doing so far?" I ask, careful to keep my tone even, even as something inside me twists with the question.

Lucian doesn't answer right away.

He just looks at me.

And not the way most men do. He's not undressing me

with his eyes or cataloging my features. He's reading something deeper. Searching for something I don't even know if I'm showing.

My stomach tightens under the weight of it.

Then—he moves.

One step closer. His hand settles lightly at the small of my back. Not inappropriate. Not even intimate. But I feel it like a brand. A press of awareness against my body that makes my breath catch.

He leans in, his lips brushing near my ear as he gently turns me by the waist, angling me toward another conversation across the room.

"Watch her," he murmurs.

I do.

A stunning brunette in a tight navy dress is engaged with a man who looks like he could buy half the city. She's smiling, laughing softly, touching his forearm every chance she gets.

She's perfect. Effortless.

Until Lucian speaks again.

"See how she forces the conversation? How she leans in too much?" His voice is low. Private. Every word slides down my spine like silk wrapped around steel. "Desperation isn't enticing."

The air leaves my lungs. I'm clenching around nothing, and my knees press slightly together before I can stop them.

God. His voice alone shouldn't make me this hot. But it does.

Lucian steps back, just enough to release the warmth of his presence, and straightens his cuffs with unhurried ease.

Then he meets my eyes.

"Don't do what she did," he says softly. "Be better."

Lucian's eyes flick to something behind me—someone else, maybe—and he gives the faintest nod. Then his eyes are back on mine.

"Show me."

Then he steps back, that cool, controlled presence folding into the crowd once again like smoke in the air. Leaving me breathless.

And burning.

Chapter 11

The rain's long gone, but the city still feels wet—like it's holding its breath.

Up in the main conference room of The Ledger, the table is sleek, the chairs are filled, and every man here knows exactly why we're meeting. No one's wasting time.

I pull out the file I prepared at five this morning and slide it to the center of the table.

Lorenzo DeLuca.

Three sets of eyes lock on the name. No one flinches. That's why they're in this room.

"He'll retaliate," I say plainly. "We all know it. He lost a brother. His pride. He'll want blood for both."

Rian, head of personal security, nods once. "So far he's keeping it quiet. But we've got eyes near the docks and his warehouses. Traffic's up."

"He'll test the waters." My fingers tap twice on the folder. "Look for cracks."

I lean back, lacing my hands in front of me. "There can't be any."

No one answers. They know better.

I shift the conversation. "Until he shows his hand, I want protection increased around all high-profile companions. Start with Sera."

A few glances pass. Everyone knows why.

"She's the reason Enrico got himself killed," I say flatly. "And now she's vulnerable. Lorenzo's not in his right mind, and I'm not taking chances with someone who's already been through hell."

Killian steps forward without hesitation. "I'll see to her myself."

"Good." I meet his eyes. "She doesn't need to know the details. Just keep her safe."

He nods. "Understood."

I rise from my chair, the room going still.

"The next time someone so much as breathes wrong in my direction…"

I sweep a glance over the table.

"…I expect a name on my desk before the body goes cold."

They all nod once. They know the drill but Rian answers for all of them.

"Clear, boss."

Downstairs in my office, I pick up my espresso cup—the second of the morning—and it's barely eight.

The flavor is bitter, sharp. I welcome it.

On my screen, the sponsor bids for this season's recruits load in a neat column. I intend to skim through them with the same clinical precision I apply to everything else.

Until I see her name right at the top of the fucking list.

Sienna Knight.

I didn't need to search for her. She's the name already highlighted, bold and glowing with more bids than any other recruit in this class.

Of course she is.

I sit back, jaw tight.

It's not just her looks. The Ledger sees beautiful women walk through its doors every week. Polished. Poised. Professionally seductive. I've seen thousands. I've forgotten most of their names.

But Sienna?

There's something raw in her. Something unshaped.

She doesn't even realize how enticing she is.

That makes her dangerous.

Her lack of experience isn't a liability—it's a fucking selling point. The sponsors don't just want to guide her... they want to mold her. Shape her. Break her in. Claim her as their own.

The thought sits like a shard of glass in my gut.

I push the espresso aside, suddenly uninterested.

Curious. Eager. Defiant.

That's what I saw the night she stood on that rooftop, face-to-face with a man who thought he could intimidate her. She didn't back down then—and she hasn't since.

The sponsors see it. They want it.

And I don't like it.

Not one damn bit.

I tap a finger against the screen, then slide open the document with her post-mixer notes. Standard protocol—each recruit ranks their sponsor interactions. Comments, impressions, preferences.

Sienna's are… brief. Polite. Noncommittal.

She liked several. Admired a few. Thought one or two seemed "interesting."

But she didn't pick one.

Not yet.

She's waiting.

Or hesitating.

And she has every right to. The top girl always gets her pick. It's how we've always done it.

But Sienna Knight isn't like the others.

She's too new. Too raw. Still full of bright edges and nervous smiles. The kind of recruit who doesn't know what the wrong choice could cost her.

And I've seen what the wrong sponsor can do.

It starts with overconfidence. A client who thinks he can reshape her faster than she's ready for. Push her too far, too fast. They think if she crumbles, they'll rebuild her stronger.

But they never do.

They just break her.

My jaw ticks as I scroll through the approved sponsor list, reading with a narrowed eye. I vetted these men myself. I know their preferences. Their patterns. Their reputations.

None of them are right for her.

Not really.

She needs structure. Patience. A steady hand and

someone who will know when to pull back, not just how to push forward.

That's why I'm looking into this.

Not because I want her.

Not because her auburn hair has been crawling under my skin since that rooftop party.

Not because I watched her watch me last night. Or because I've imagined her bound in leather and writhing in my hands no less than two dozen times since we locked eyes in the Devil's Playground.

No.

It's because no one else will handle her correctly.

That's all.

That's the only reason I'm doing this.

And I tell myself that lie again as I pull up her file, slide my finger over to the "sponsor override" tab...

And then I page Eve.

I've checked the time so many times I might as well just tattoo it on my wrist.

8:57 AM.

Still no Eve.

I sit in the third row—not too close to the front to seem overeager, not in the back like I'm hiding. It feels like the Goldilocks of seating choices, and yet somehow it still doesn't feel right.

I tuck my phone into my lap and glance around. Everyone's dressed up again. Polished. Quiet. The air hums with nerves, and I'm no exception.

My leg is bouncing, hands wringing in my lap before I force myself to stop. I can't look like I'm falling apart. I have to appear collected. Graceful. Poised.

Like I belong here.

I replay the conversations from last night in my head like a mental montage on repeat.

The charming man who smelled like cedar wood and asked intelligent questions.

The silent one with the cold smile and assessing gaze that made me feel like I was being dissected.

The older gentleman who made me laugh with a terrible dad joke and genuinely seemed to care if I was comfortable.

And then... Lucian.

His challenge still lingers like a ghost. *Don't do what she did. Be better. Show me.*

I *did* try. I *was* better. I think. God, what if I overdid it? What if they all saw right through me and thought I was trying too hard?

I slide my purse off my shoulder and set it carefully on my chair, along with my blazer. Then I make a beeline for the coffee station in the back of the room.

I don't even care if the caffeine makes my heart race more—at least it'll give my hands something to hold.

The coffee's lukewarm and bitter, but it gives me something to focus on.

9:12.

Still no Eve.

Conversations are starting to hum among the other recruits. Nervous laughter. Whispered speculation. I return to my seat and scroll through my inbox, as if a job offer might magically appear and make all of this irrelevant.

It doesn't.

9:24.

I'm just about to start spiraling again when my phone buzzes.

HARPER: 💅 🔥 🏆 Don't forget you're *the* moment today. They're lucky to breathe your air.

I smile, immediately typing back.

ME: More like *panic in human form* with killer lipstick. But thank you.

HARPER: Panic is sexy if you accessorize it right. Also, you wore white. You're the sacrificial virgin in a room full of horny vampires. I'm sure they ate it up.

I choke on my coffee.

ME: Helpful as always.

HARPER: Text me the second you know who won you. Or I riot.

9:45.

At last, the doors at the front of the room open and Eve walks in, a black folder in one hand and her hair in a slick, perfect bun. She doesn't look flustered, but the quickness of her steps gives her away.

"Sorry, darlings," she says as she makes it to the front. "Minor chaos upstairs. But I have your placements."

All the air seems to suck out of the room. My heart hammers behind my ribs. I sit up straighter, clutching my cup like it might anchor me.

This is it.

This is the moment that decides everything.

And I'm not sure if I'm ready.

I take another sip of my now-cold coffee, willing it to settle the storm building in my stomach. It doesn't.

The room is buzzing with soft chatter and barely-contained anticipation. Girls sit in tidy rows, hair and makeup still perfect from the early morning prep session.

Some bounce their legs. Some chew the inside of their cheeks. Me? I can't feel my hands.

Eve steps to the front of the room, a thick stack of black folders in hand. She doesn't waste time.

"Alright, ladies," she says with a bright, confident smile. "You all survived the first phase of training, which is no small feat. And I'm proud of every single one of you. But today... today is the next step."

A hush falls over the room.

"The highest bid in this batch goes to..." She flips open the first folder. "Mila Rosenthal."

Mila gasps, her perfectly manicured hands flying to her mouth. She turns, wide-eyed, as the other girls clap politely.

"Your sponsor was impressed with your poise, your warmth, and the way you handled difficult questions with a smile." Eve hands her the folder. "You'll be meeting with him shortly."

Hm, I thought the top girl got to pick her sponsor. I wonder why it was switched up.

Mila beams and glides out of the room with a confidence I can't muster.

I swallow around the lump in my throat, trying not to feel the sharp pinch of disappointment. I didn't think I'd be the top girl, but... hearing someone else's name stings more than I expected.

Eve continues down the list, calling name after name.

"Bianca Monty."

"Nicole Parks."

"Addison Voss."

Each girl receives her folder and exits the room with a

mix of nerves and excitement, disappearing into whatever future they've just been handed. Their heels tap against the floor. Their giggles and relieved laughter linger in the air.

And I sit. Smile glued in place. Palms sweaty. Heart pounding.

It's fine. Totally fine. I probably just wasn't in the top half. Maybe I'm later on the list. Maybe she's going alphabetically in reverse and I'm just low down on the order.

Another name. Another girl leaves.

One by one, the seats around me empty.

It's not fine.

It's getting harder to breathe.

My fingers twitch against my thighs. My vision flicks to the clock.

9:53.

Eve calls another name. Another girl squeals, hugging her seat mate before grabbing her folder and leaving.

I smile with her. Nod. Pretend I'm not dying inside.

My legs bounce now. I can't stop them. I pinch my thumb and index finger together, a grounding trick I saw on TikTok.

It doesn't work.

"Clara Jennings."

Clara leaves.

Then there were two.

And then just me.

The room is silent now. The buzz is gone. All the laughter, the chatter, the electricity—it left with the others.

Eve doesn't say anything at first. She just stands at the

front of the room and clasps her hands together. Because she is all out of folders.

Her gaze lifts and lands on me.

My stomach plummets when she gives me a sympathetic smile.

Because now I know.

No one bid on me.

I wasn't picked.

My heart thuds in my ears. Loud. Heavy. Final.

I told myself I wouldn't let this define me. That if it didn't work out, I'd move on. That this was just a steppingstone.

But even though I've been applying for other jobs, I've been *here*. Focused. Trying.

And it still wasn't enough.

I bite the inside of my cheek hard, trying to will the tears away.

Because when you're the last girl sitting in a room full of empty chairs?

You don't need anyone to tell you you've failed.

You already know.

Eve's expression is unreadable as she crosses the room. Each step across the marble floor hits like a judge's gavel hammering in my verdict.

She stops directly in front of me.

My breath stutters.

"Come with me, Sienna."

That's all she says.

No folder. No sponsor's name. No smile.

Just four words.

I nod numbly and stand, my legs stiff and unsteady beneath me. I gather my things with mechanical precision, following her like I'm headed to an execution.

Because I am, aren't I?

She's taking me to sign a final form. To be walked out the back door of The Ledger with polite apologies and a folder that says *Not a Good Fit* in bold letters across the top.

I should ask her.

Should say something. Ask why but I don't.

I'm not sure I want to know the reasons.

The hallway is too quiet. Too clean. Every soft step feels like a nail hammered into my coffin. My pulse beats in my throat, my ears, my wrists.

The elevator heads up to the topmost floor. We don't take the path the other girls did when they went off to meet their sponsors.

Oh, God. Maybe they throw the undesirables from the rooftop like discarded dreams.

We exit the elevator and descend down a corridor I haven't been in before. The walls are lined with black marble, threaded with veins of gold. Opulent. Stark. Intimidating.

Just like this place.

Just like the rejection I know is coming.

Finally, Eve stops in front of a large, closed door.

It's beautiful—sleek black wood, carved with ornate gold filigree that glints in the soft lighting. A polished brass handle gleams like it's never been touched.

This is... not the exit.

I frown, confused, my brows pulling together as I look between the door and her.

"Where are we—?"

Eve turns to me, one brow arched with infuriating calm.

And then she smirks.

Not smug. Not cruel. Just... knowing.

"Your sponsor," she says simply, gesturing toward the door. "Enjoy your training."

I blink.

My lips part.

"What?"

But she's already stepping back. Her steps retreating down the hallway. Gone without another word.

I stand frozen, that single phrase ringing in my ears like it's been shouted through a megaphone.

Your sponsor.

I have a sponsor.

I'm not being fired.

My heart stutters. Skips. Lurches.

I *have a sponsor.*

But no folder. No name.

No information at all.

Just this door.

My palm presses flat against the cool surface before I realize I've even moved.

Then—one slow breath later—I turn the handle.

And step inside and in an instant, I'm frozen.

Lucian *fucking* Vale.

Standing in front of a sleek black desk, leaned casually

against it like he has all the time in the world. His gray eyes are already on me, unreadable, unflinching. Like he's been waiting.

Like this was always part of his plan.

The door shuts behind me with an ominous *click*.

My breath catches so hard it burns.

No.

No. No. *No.*

Not him.

Anyone but him.

I take one slow step inside, heart pounding like war drums in my ears. My eyes flick over him instinctively—black suit, dark shirt, the collar open just enough to feel indecent, his sleeves rolled back to reveal tattooed forearms.

He doesn't speak.

Just watches.

Waiting.

The silence stretches until it strangles me, a knot twisting tight in my chest.

He knew.

He *knew* I was sitting in that room, watching every other girl walk out with a folder and a smile while I convinced myself I was about to be fired.

And this bastard said *nothing.*

Heat floods through me—rage, humiliation, disbelief—all colliding like lightning in my chest. My hands curl into fists at my sides.

"You—" I exhale, sharp and venomous. "Are you *fucking* kidding me?"

His brow lifts. Just slightly. Unimpressed. Unbothered.

"Careful."

One word. Cool and smooth like poured ice.

Oh, I see how this is going to be.

He looks at me like I'm just a piece in his game. Like none of it mattered—the waiting, the anxiety, the sheer panic that made me question *everything*.

And now I'm supposed to what? Smile? Thank him?

Fuck. That.

"You let me sit there," I spit. "Alone. While every other girl walked out with her folder like a damn graduation ceremony—thinking I failed. That no one wanted me. That I wasn't *good enough*."

He doesn't flinch. Doesn't move. Just watches.

My voice shakes with the force of it. "Was that fun for you? Was it *satisfying* to sit up here while I practically had a heart attack downstairs?"

His head tilts, expression still unreadable. "It was necessary."

"Oh, *necessary*," I echo with a bitter laugh, pacing a short line in front of his desk. "You're unbelievable."

"You'll find I'm a lot of things," he says simply, "but unbelievable isn't one of them."

God, he's infuriating.

And the worst part?

He's still the most attractive man I've ever seen.

That voice. That calm control. That maddening confidence that only makes me want to *bite* him.

I plant my hands on my hips, leveling him with a glare. "Well, congratulations. I'm here. So now what?"

His eyes flick down, then back up. Slow. Deliberate.

Now?

Now the real game begins.

Chapter 13

She walks in at exactly eight o'clock.

Which would be acceptable—if she were the client.

But she's not.

"You're late," I say, not looking up from the file I'm reviewing.

There's a pause. Then the quiet shuffle of her boots as she takes a few more steps inside.

"I thought I was on time," she says carefully.

"You arrived at eight. My appointments begin at eight. Which means now we're behind."

A beat of silence. Then—she takes a subtle breath and lifts her chin. No protest. Just that small flick of her eyes to the ceiling, almost like she's recalibrating.

A tic of rebellion. A small one but still, I mentally catalog it.

Before I can say anything further, the intercom buzzes.

"Mr. Vale, Jaxon Kane is here for you."

"Send him in." I glance at Sienna and nod toward the seating area near the window. "Sit."

She hesitates for just half a second. Then moves.

Her footsteps are soft on the hardwood, and I note the way she chooses the chair furthest from my desk. Composed. Controlled. But the way she fidgets in the chair before her hands smooth over her skirt before she sits isn't lost on me.

She's nervous.

The door opens behind me, and Jaxon strolls in like he's walking into his mother's house.

"Took your time," I say without looking up.

"You try parking in Midtown with a matte black McLaren."

"Use the valet." I shake my head. I don't know why he insists on complaining about the crowd he draws when he drives his flashy cars around town.

Cocky asshole.

He drops into the chair opposite me with a smirk when he cuts his eyes at Sienna with that question lingering in his gaze. One I won't answer because I'm not introducing her.

She's not ready to meet someone like Jaxon.

Not until she learns how to sit still.

"How's the right hook?" Jaxon asks as a stick of spearmint gum disappears into his mouth.

I arch a brow, amused. "Ask your jaw."

He rolls his eyes and nods to my monitor. It blazes to life when I hit the power button, and Jaxon's interface takes over the entire display.

"Twelve hours," he says casually, tapping twice to bring

up a wall of code so dense it looks like a foreign language to most. "That's how long it took me to get into the center of your system."

I narrow my eyes. "You hacked into The Ledger?"

"Technically? Yeah. But don't worry. It was just me. A standard hacker?" He leans back, stretches his arms behind his head, his biceps flexing beneath the sleeves of his black henley. "Two to four weeks. Minimum. And that's assuming they're good."

I don't like that. I don't like that even a theoretical breach is possible.

Jaxon catches the shift in my expression and grins around his gum. "Told you, you should've hired me to build your infrastructure from the beginning."

"You would've been ten years old."

"Oh, right." He blinks, then shrugs. "Well, I'm fixing it now. This shit's child's play."

"Lay it out."

He launches into it without missing a beat. Server vulnerabilities. Contract routing logic gaps. Firewalls with outdated firmware. He pulls up a visual model—my entire empire in blueprint form—and picks it apart with precision.

It'll cost millions.

That's not what gives me pause.

It's the time.

"How long?" I ask, my voice like flint.

He doesn't answer right away, just flicks another screen up—a projected rollout timeline, months in length.

"I want it locked down today."

"Hold your horses, O Great and Powerful Ledger Lord,"

Jaxon says with a snort, kicking his feet up on the edge of my desk like he doesn't have a care in the goddamn world.

"You're asking me to build an entirely new and secure server farm. Not just mirrored backups—but real, deep redundancies. Multiple disaster recovery sites, all with layered encryption and biometric access protocols. We're talking about locking down every girl, every contract, every client from every direction."

"And?" I prompt.

He pops his gum. "Give me a month."

I exhale slowly through my nose, not liking it. Lorenzo hasn't made a move yet. But it's coming. I can feel it in my bones. And when he does, he'll come hard.

Jaxon seems to sense my unease. "It'll be bulletproof, man. If I'm building it, they won't even know where to start looking."

I nod once, then glance toward the corner of the room.

Sienna hasn't moved.

Her legs are still crossed, her hands folded neatly in her lap. She's learning when to fade into the background. Not successfully yet, but at least she understands that it's needed—without having to be told.

A promising start.

Jaxon wraps up his updates, grabs his laptop, and mutters a goodbye on his way out. I nod once but keep my eyes on her. She shifts as the door clicks shut. Not much. Just a slight adjustment of her spine.

She's preparing for what will come next. Likely assuming I'll launch into some sort of lesson.

The moment stretches and she draws a breath like she's about to speak.

Though–she doesn't.

Instead, she clenches her jaw and keeps her eyes on her lap.

She fidgets.

Almost says something another two times while I keep writing notes on my tablet, adding follow ups to my calendar for progress checks with Jaxon.

I set down the pen in my hand and lean back in my chair, fingers steepled beneath my chin. She avoids looking at me as I give her a long inspection up and down. Cataloging her nervous movement and squirming.

"A good Companion knows how to be present," I say, voice even, "without demanding attention."

Her eyes finally dart toward me, but she doesn't respond. Not verbally. The twitch in her posture is enough. She's still expecting more.

She doesn't understand this yet—what I'm doing.

Sienna came in expecting seduction lessons. Teasing. Flirty smiles in a mirror. That's what most of them expect.

But that's not what she needs.

She needs silence. Stillness. Discipline.

She needs to unlearn the things she thinks give her power... so she can learn the things that actually do.

Stillness is strength. Presence is a weapon. And patience? Patience is the most lethal blade in her arsenal.

But she isn't there yet.

She exhales—just a little too loudly. Her foot taps a few times, before she stops it. Her hands tighten in her lap.

Then, finally she can't handle the stillness.

"Are we going to begin training soon?"

I don't look up from my paperwork. "You've been in training since the moment you walked in here."

"I mean... do... something."

"You're doing something now."

I can nearly feel the weight of her eyeroll.

"I'm sitting here like a glorified chair decoration. That's such a great use of my time."

Finally I look at her, holding her stare and letting the weight of my attention sink into her.

"It is if that's what your contract is asking you to do."

I watch the flicker of frustration in her eyes. The way she squares her shoulders like she's gearing up for battle. But she says nothing more. Not yet.

"Sit. Be quiet. That's it."

She looks away this time staring out the window at nothing.

Another lesson: Not everything requires a response.

The room falls into silence again. I take a few calls. Skim a few reports. Send a few messages. She doesn't interrupt. But I can feel her presence like a pressure point behind my left eye.

A low growl breaks the stillness of the room as her stomach rumbles.

She freezes like she's afraid I heard it.

I did.

Her stomach growls again, and she shifts—just slightly —trying to muffle it with her movement. She folds her hands in her lap over and over, likely tensing before her stomach protests her hunger again.

It's barely eleven. Another hour and a half before the recruits head down for lunch and afternoon training with Eve. She won't make it that long. And I know she won't ask.

So I type out a message to my assistant.

A tray arrives minutes later—set quietly on the table in front of her

Diced fruit, soft cheeses, fig and honey jam with crackers, mini strawberry danishes, a carafe of hot coffee, and two bottles of still water.

Sienna looks at it but doesn't move toward the tray. Doesn't reach for the food.

Good.

She knows to wait.

I stand, slipping my watch back onto my wrist.

"I'll be back in thirty minutes," I tell her, buttoning my jacket.

She blinks up at me.

"Stay here. Help yourself."

And then I leave—closing the door behind me.

<hr>

I didn't actually have anything that required me to leave the office.

No meetings. No calls that couldn't wait. No urgent fire to put out.

So I take the elevator down to the fifteenth floor terrace, the one still scented faintly with perfume and cigar smoke from the recent night's mixer. The space is empty now, but I can still hear the echoes of clinking glasses and forced laughter in my mind.

I pull my phone out of my pocket.

And for thirty minutes, I scroll through Sienna's Instagram.

She doesn't post often. A few shots of latte art, a blurry concert photo from last year, a carousel of fall leaves and cozy knits. But there's a selfie tucked between them—her in oversized sunglasses, hair up in a claw clip, lips puckered around a boba straw. The caption says nothing but a bunny emoji.

Of course.

Looks like the little rabbit has a theme going on.

I tilt the phone and study the image a beat longer than necessary.

Then I lock the screen and head back upstairs.

When I return to the office, Sienna is exactly where I left her.

The tray's been touched. At least half the food is gone—two crackers stacked on her plate, the fruit rearranged, the coffee carafe mostly full but one of the water bottles nearly empty. The other untouched.

She saved it for me.

I sit across from her and let my gaze linger on the plate.

"You didn't wait to be served."

Her eyes widen. Her spine straightens like a wire being pulled taut.

Panic blooms just behind her expression. Her lips part.

"Good," I say calmly, leaning back in my chair. "You understood the more important rule. You weren't greedy."

Her shoulders ease just slightly.

"You were thinking of your contract even when it wasn't expected. As a Companion, you must always be thinking ahead."

She nods, a slow, tentative dip of her chin.

I reach for the tray, select a slice of papaya, and spear it with the small silver fork. Her gaze flicks to the movement, just for a second, and then snaps back up as if caught.

I smirk.

"They'll pay for your attention," I say, placing the fruit between my teeth. "Your silence. Your presence. If they want noise, they'll ask for it."

Another pause.

"Until then, learn how to exist without demanding anything."

The lesson hangs in the air between us, weighty and exacting.

Sienna nods again. This one firmer. A small effort to regain ground.

I let the silence stretch, my eyebrows raising expectantly.

"Yes." She affirms.

Then finally, "Yes, sir."

Good girl.

Finally—calmly—I push my chair back and rise.

"Come back tomorrow."

She gathers her things, quietly.

My hand wraps around the untouched water bottle she left for me and I head back to my desk.

"And Sienna?" I add, just before she opens the door.

She glances back, her expression neutral but eyes too alert.

"Don't be late again."

She nods and slips out the door.

I don't tell her I'll be watching but she should know—I always am.

Chapter 14

Sienna

Two weeks. Fourteen days. One hundred and twelve hours spent either sitting silently in Lucian Vale's office or running the world's most unimportant errands.

I swear I've been more houseplant than person lately. Some mornings, he barely even looks at me. Other times, he barks a single word—*Sit*—like I'm some sort of glorified show dog.

And his little *assignments* are pissing me off.

Yesterday, I stood in line at a boutique patisserie for *exactly* four vanilla bean macarons. Not five. Not a variety box. Four.

Earlier this week, I hand-delivered a custom engraved fountain pen to a man who said *thank you* by staring at my chest for a full ten seconds. Lucian's assistant asked me how things were going and I told her.

Lucian must has been told because the man's contract was canceled the next day.

Today, I spent forty-five minutes hand-selecting new silk pocket squares for Lucian's personal collection, all in his preferred shades of charcoal and black. Because apparently his assistant "folds them wrong," and this was a task better suited for me.

I think my eyeballs almost detached from the force of my internal screaming.

Now, as I finally leave his office, I feel his presence behind me like a second shadow. His scent lingers in the air —a subtle blend of expensive cologne, leather, and something warm and masculine I can't quite place. Like cedar and sin.

He never wears a tie. Never. Just crisp shirts that mold to his frame and leave the top button open like an invitation I'm not allowed to answer.

Today, that damn collar gaped just enough to show the edge of one tattoo. Black ink, curved and sharp against his tan skin. I'd spent the better part of an hour trying not to look at it. Not to wonder how far it went. Not to imagine tracing it with my fingers, my tongue.

His sleeves are always rolled up to his forearms, and every time his hand tightens into a fist—usually in response to something *I* do—I catch the flex of his forearm muscles. The way his veins pop just slightly. The hint of another tattoo curling toward his elbow.

It's torture.

And that's not even the worst of it.

At the end of each day, he sits with me and tells me what I did well. Not kindly, not gently—but directly. Specifically. Thoughtfully.

Like he sees me.

And it's pathetic, but I *live* for those few minutes. The moment his eyes actually lock onto mine. When his voice drops, low and steady, as he delivers his verdict.

"Good instincts."

"Well done today."

"You're learning."

He probably doesn't even realize it, but it lights something up inside me every time. A spark I try so hard to douse because I know better.

But today? I nearly short-circuited.

I caught myself watching his mouth as he sipped his espresso, completely tuned out to the rest of the world.

What would it feel like to have that mouth on mine?

Or elsewhere.

I shake the thought loose as I step into the elevator, pressing the button for the lobby with more force than necessary.

It's not even frustration anymore—it's desperation.

Lucian didn't even look up when he released me. Just that quiet, firm, *"You're dismissed for the day."* Like I was one of his meetings. One of his checklists.

Like I didn't just spend six hours playing statue.

With my earbuds in place, I pull out my phone and dial the one person who'll understand exactly how maddening this is.

"Tell me you've either stabbed him or kissed him," Harper answers on the first ring, no greeting required.

"I've done neither," I mutter.

I shift my bag to the other shoulder as I dodge around a

stalled food cart. "I swear to God, Harper, if I have to run one more errand that involves dry cleaning, espresso orders, or picking up cufflinks from some boutique I can't even afford to breathe in—"

Harper's laugh rings through the speaker. "Oh no. Not the sacred cufflinks. How dare he."

"I'm not joking," I mutter. "He sent me to pick up these custom-made ones from this appointment-only place in SoHo. The guy at the counter looked at me like I was either a sugar baby or a thief."

"Oh. Maybe both. I love role playing." Harper chirps. "Honestly, though? If the man sent you to SoHo, the least he could do is take you to dinner after. Feed you. Rub your feet. Apologize for being a control-freak daddy dom in denial."

I roll my eyes, ducking into the stairwell leading to the downtown platform. "Don't start."

"I'm not starting, I'm helping. Sienna. Babe."

"I'm not—"

"Here's how you solve this. Push him back on his desk and ruin his entire day," Harper cuts in, matter-of-fact like it's a viable item on my to-do list.

I snort, descending the last step. The platform is busy but not packed. It smells like heat and metal and faintly like pretzels. "Harper!"

"I'm serious. One shove, straddle him like a goddess, and just grind until he breaks."

"You've thought about this way too much."

"Oh, I have. Many times. In vivid detail. Pull his tie and—"

"He doesn't wear a tie," I mutter under my breath, scanning the arrivals board.

"Ugh. Of course he doesn't." Harper groans. "That's how the truly dangerous ones get you. Open collar. Barely-there smirk. Forearm porn. You're doomed, babe."

I open my mouth, but I'm distracted by a man standing a few feet away. Early-thirties maybe. Tall. Watching me with interest that's not subtle in the slightest. His gaze drags slowly down my legs, back up to my face, and he smiles like he's just seen something worth his time.

"Hey," he says smoothly, stepping closer.

"Not in your dreams, honey," I say, not even slowing my step as I move to the opposite end of the platform.

Harper cackles in my ear. "Oh my God. You didn't even let him finish!"

"If he had, I might've been forced to pull out pepper spray."

"God, I love this new energy. You're glowing. Like, dangerous glowing. Like 'I've-been-simmering-too-long-under-Lucion's-stupid-sexy-glare' glowing."

I pinch the bridge of my nose, slipping into an empty spot near a pillar as the faint rumble of the train begins to echo through the tunnel. "Harper."

"You need to let it out."

"I know," I mutter. "But I don't even know what *it* is. I sit in that damn office, day after day, doing nothing except whatever chore he tosses my way. He barely looks at me. Doesn't talk unless it's to give me some cryptic feedback at the end of the day like I'm in some twisted episode of *America's Next Top Companion*."

"Next week on *The Black Ledger's Got Talent*," Harper drawls, "Sienna breathes too loudly and gets told to sit in the corner and manifest silence."

I exhale a laugh, pressing my free hand against the pillar. The train is getting closer now. "I feel like I'm going insane."

"You just need a release. Like—punch a pillow. Or his face. Or, you know, skip on over to the Masq and ride the Devil into the abyss."

"Harper."

"I'm just saying, Lucian's clearly working out his issues with God or whatever, but the Devil? The Devil would know *exactly* what to do with all that energy."

"We're still meeting for hot wings tomorrow night, right?" I interrupt, deadpan.

She sighs. "You're no fun."

"I'm fun. I'm just not... sex club punch card fun."

"Give it time."

I hear the screech of brakes as the train barrels around the corner, slowing.

"Gotta go," I say. "Train's here and you know I get zero reception in the tunnels."

"Fine," she relents, dramatic as ever. "But mark my words—by next week you're either solving your Lucian frustration or letting the Devil rail you into next Thursday. Honestly, go for both. Split the difference. One at each end."

I bark out a laugh. "Bye, Harp."

"The Devil would totally get the caboose. You *know* he's an ass man."

"You're horrible. I love you."

"Love you too, baby girl. Text me when you're free."

I hang up as the doors slide open and step inside, still grinning.

God help me, she might be right.

The Devil probably *is* an ass man.

The train ride is a blur. So is the walk from the station to my building, my heels snapping against the pavement, every step rattling with residual irritation—and something else simmering beneath my skin. Not anger. Not really.

Tension. That's what it is. A slow, constant hum beneath my skin, sparking in my blood like a fuse that refuses to burn out.

My apartment is quiet when I step inside, the late afternoon light spilling through the gauzy curtains. It's warm. Peaceful. Soft. The creams and dusty rose tones I picked for the decor hug me like a favorite sweater. It should settle me.

It doesn't.

I drop my bag by the entryway and head to my bedroom, but I don't begin changing my clothes. Not yet. My short black dress hugs my thighs and still clings with the faintest imprint of my body heat. My sheer hose—gartered beneath —give the illusion of innocence and sin stitched into one as my heels lengthen my legs.

I collapse backward onto the bed, my arms spread wide, staring up at the ceiling.

His voice rings in my ears.

Sit.

Eat.

His voice is a command. Always is. But when it turns soft?

Good.

You did well.

Those words—low and gruff, shaped by that perfect mouth—slip into the silence and turn molten inside me.

God, I want to hear him say that with his lips against my skin. Right behind my ear, where it's most sensitive. I want to feel the scrape of his stubble along the base of my neck. His hands—big and rough, so different from mine—sliding down my bare back. I want to feel those calluses dragging across smooth skin.

My own fingers run up my stomach. Around the curve of my breasts over my clothes.

Chills run up my arms as the thoughts deepen. The images become clearer.

I sit up slowly, breath catching in my throat.

My fingers close around the cool knob of my bedside drawer and grip the matte handle of my vibrator. I pull it out and stare at it for a moment, my pulse ticking in my throat.

I'm still in my work clothes.

Short black dress. Sheer stockings suspended by delicate straps that hook onto lace. No one knows what's underneath. No one but me.

Except now, in my mind—he does too.

Lucian Vale stands behind me, pressing me forward over the edge of his big desk. My hands brace against it, fingers splayed wide, heart pounding.

I walk to the bed and bend slightly, just enough to lean forward, placing one palm on the mattress. I close my eyes and lose myself in the fantasy.

He'd come up behind me. One hand sliding around my

waist, firm and sure. The other gently brushing my hair aside, revealing my neck for his mouth.

"You've been such a good girl this week," he'd whisper —rough and deep, all scruff and sin. The kind of praise that burns.

The sound of it in my head makes me shiver.

I click the vibrator on.

Slow at first. Teasing. I slip it beneath my dress, up along the edge of my stocking. I imagine it's his hand. The low growl he'd let out when he discovers the suspenders, the lace, the heat.

His palm would drag along my thigh. Fingers push aside the thin fabric of my panties and find me already wanting.

"*So wet,*" he'd murmur against my skin, voice reverent. Like he's in awe. Like he wants to devour me for it.

My mouth parts at the image. I work the toy in slow, deliberate circles over my clit, my hips rocking on instinct.

I smell him. His cologne—smoke and spice and desire— clings to my imagination like a second skin. I *feel* him, too. The weight of his presence behind me. Not touching. Just there. Always there.

Silent. Watching.

"You're doing so well... just like that."

My breath catches as I press the toy more firmly against myself, the pulsing vibrations syncing with the throb building inside me. My legs part a little wider. My back arches.

The movement is instinctual, involuntary.

"That's it, beautiful. Let me see how pretty you play with my pussy."

A whimper escapes me at the thoughts I'm putting into my own mind.

How he would talk to me. How he would talk me through playing with myself. Making myself come simply for the pleasure of him watching me.

I roll my hips in slow, steady circles, dragging the pressure along the place I need it most. Every nerve in my body feels wound tight, every stroke drawing me closer. Closer.

"Such a good girl. You always obey when it matters."

My mouth parts as I moan. Louder this time, not holding back the pleasure warming my body.

I imagine his breath on my neck.

The warmth of his body behind mine.

The rasp of his voice, low and commanding—so close, I could feel the words slide across my skin.

"Come for me. Right here, in my hands. Show me who you belong to."

The line hits like a spark to dry kindling.

My body tenses—pleasure coiling, tightening, ready to explode.

"I want to feel you fall apart—so do it. Come for me, beautiful."

The thought sends me over the edge.

My orgasm rushes through me like a wave I didn't see coming. It punches the breath from my lungs, makes my knees tremble, forces my mouth open on a soft, broken moan. His name dances on the edge of my tongue—but I don't say it.

Not out loud.

My body melts forward, chest pressing to the comforter as the last aftershocks ripple through me.

But I'm not done.

Because now I imagine his voice again, softer this time.

"That's it," he says, *"but I'm not finished with you yet."*

Sitting up, I put one foot on the edge of the bed and hook my panties aside with my finger. I run the toy down my pussy, gathering the slickness on the head of the vibrator.

"Such a filthy little thing... wanting more."

It's not Lucian in my head anymore.

It's *the Devil.*

Dark mask. Hard hands. Warm breath that runs down my neck as he breathes me in.

"Look at you—dripping. Beautiful. You want the Devil to ruin you, don't you?"

I release a shuttered breath in response to the man in my imagination.

Mouth wet and hungry as he drops to his knees in front of me.

"I bet your sweet cunt is clenching so tight right now—wishing it was my cock."

The pressure in my core tightens again, fast and sharp. I rub the toy in tight, rhythmic strokes and grind against it, chasing that second high with abandon.

"Keep rubbing that pretty clit for me. Just like that. Don't you dare stop."

I picture him moving my hand out of the way—slowly, deliberately—claiming me with his mouth.

Tasting me like he's starved.

Like he's waited for this moment. For me.

I've never felt that before.

Never had someone want me like that. Not like that.

My ex wouldn't even try. Always had an excuse, a complaint.

But the Devil?

He devoured that woman like worship. Like sin. Like pleasure was his only god.

And now I want to know what it feels like to be opened up like that. Ruined by a tongue and a growl and the weight of him holding me still while I come undone.

"This mouth was made to taste you, little one. So let me."

I imagine it—the warmth of his breath, the scrape of his stubble. What his hot tongue would feel like swirling around my clit, sucking the pleasure from me as his rough voice like a caress, just before he wrecked me.

"Come for me, little one. Right here, right now—make the Devil proud."

And then I'm gone again—head thrown back, mouth open, hips moving shamelessly, legs shaking as the orgasm crashes into me like a wave breaking against rock.

It takes everything in me to stay upright until the last of the waves subside.

My fingers tremble as I turn off the toy and toss it to the bed beside me. I collapse back into the pillows, breath ragged, heart still stuttering in my chest.

God.

I stare at the ceiling.

What the hell is happening to me?

I grab a tissue to clean off the vibrator, and carry it to the bathroom to rinse. My legs are still shaky but that was fucking amazing.

It's the best orgasm I've ever had, and it was only to thoughts of what these two men could do to me.

Fuck.

I need a cold shower.

And probably an exorcism.

Definitely some holy water. But maybe I'll just pour myself a large glass of wine.

Maybe two.

Maybe... one for me and one for the Devil.

The clock on the corner of my screen reads 8:02 AM.

I check my watch to confirm it's right, a hot coil of irritation already forming beneath my ribs. She's late. It's just two minutes—but two minutes late for a client who pays millions could end a contract in a heartbeat. It's unacceptable.

And she knows better.

Sienna's been under my sponsorship for a month, and we still haven't moved past the first goddamn lesson: *You can't control a room if you can't control yourself first.*

She wants reasons, explanations for everything I ask her to do. It's exhausting. I understand the reason behind it— she's mistrustful by nature, wary of the unknown. Useful qualities, but dangerous if not honed correctly.

That mistrust needs to become intuition. She needs to be able to anticipate and deliver without question. Without hesitation.

But we aren't there yet.

She isn't there yet.

I drum my fingers once on the desktop, teeth clenching together. I'm not accustomed to waiting on anyone. The fact that it's her makes it even worse.

Sienna's outward signs of frustration have become bolder, harder to ignore. It tests my patience, makes my palm itch with the urge to bend her over this desk and correct the brattiness out of her—the way I would at The Devil's Playground.

The way she needs.

But I can't.

So instead, I ball my hand into a tight fist, breathing through the steady, building heat beneath my skin.

The door finally opens. 8:03 AM.

Sienna rushes in, the clack of her heels sharp against the marble floors, auburn hair wild around her shoulders.

She's agitated.

Flushed.

She drops her bag onto the chair beside her without looking up, and when she does finally glance at me, the tension in the room spikes immediately.

I don't return her gaze. Instead, I turn a page in the stack of reports on my desk, my voice cold and steady.

"You're late."

Her lips part. She exhales audibly, frustration evident in her tone even before the words leave her mouth. "The subway was down. I can't exactly control public transportation."

I flick my gaze up to meet hers then, letting the weight

of my displeasure linger in the heavy silence. She holds it for two seconds before looking away.

Barely.

But she rolls her eyes on the way down, and the palm at my side twitches again.

She has no idea how thin my patience is wearing—or what it's costing me to hold myself back.

Three minutes. An eye roll. A sarcastic remark.

I won't let it slide. Not this time.

But the intercom on my desk buzzes, interrupting before I can address it. "Mr. Vale? Jaxon Kane is here to see you."

"Send him in," I say without breaking my stare.

Sienna settles into her chair, clearly sensing my mood.

I straighten, pulling my cuffs into place, watching as Jaxon strolls through the door with his usual laid-back confidence.

I would invite her to join the meeting if she could get past this first fucking lesson.

But I won't.

Not until she learns how to sit still.

Not until she learns how to control herself.

Jaxon smirks at me, amusement in his eyes as he clocks my mood instantly. He tosses a small device on my desk and settles in the chair across from me.

He gives me a mock two-finger salute in greeting.

"What the fuck is this?" I bark out the question and immediately glower at Sienna.

She's not looking at us but Jaxon sees it.

His cocking fucking grin widening. "So, I take it I'll be seeing you at the gym tonight then."

I pinch the bridge of my nose. "Move it along Jax. I have more appointments."

"An untraceable tracker for your girls," Jaxon explains casually, leaning back and threading his hands behind his head. "Just tack it down with a bit of nail glue and paint over it with nail polish. If your girls pass through security scanners—even the handheld wands—they shouldn't detect it."

I pick up the baggie, examining the small metallic device carefully between my fingers. It's barely bigger than a fleck of glitter. "How long does it last?"

I notice Sienna perk up slightly. Her curiosity getting the better of her but she corrects herself quickly.

Jaxon shrugs, adjusting the cuff of his sleeve to reveal heavy ink across his wrist. "Month, maybe two, depending on wear and tear."

He leans forward, grabbing the wireless keyboard from the corner of my desk.

With a few fast keystrokes my desktop monitor flickers to life. I watch as he navigates into the updated Ledger Companion app, entering an admin login that immediately brings up a city map.

At the center, a green dot pulses steadily over the Ledger skyrise.

I raise an eyebrow, impressed despite myself. "This is live?"

"Real-time," he confirms, nodding slowly. "Instantaneous updates. Encrypted end-to-end, completely anonymous and private. You've got eyes everywhere without anyone knowing."

"How many of these do you have?"

"Just the prototype." Jaxon shoots me a knowing look, a smug smirk playing on his lips. "Thought you might want to test it out before we manufacture more."

Instinctively, my gaze slides toward Sienna, still sitting quietly in the corner.

She's pretending not to listen, staring straight ahead with that carefully practiced neutral expression—except for the slightest roll of her eyes as she releases an irritated sigh.

My jaw clenches. She's walking a dangerous fucking line today.

"Sienna," I say, forcing calmness into my voice even as irritation threads through it.

She lifts her head, turning toward me slowly.

A defiant spark flashes in those bright blue eyes as she meets mine head-on. "Lucian," she replies evenly, matching my patience with her carefully controlled tone.

Jaxon fucking gleams at the interaction.

I pick up the baggie, placing it pointedly at the edge of the desk nearest her. "How about you run down to the spa and get your nails done."

After a pause. "Red, of course."

Her gaze flares again, but she quickly reins herself back in, lips pressing into a thin line as she stands, gracefully retrieving the small plastic bag without another word. "Of course," she answers tightly, turning swiftly on her heel and heading for the door.

Her hair brushes along her back with each irritated step, until her steps fade into silence.

I exhale slowly as the door shuts behind her, leaning back in my chair and pinching the bridge of my nose again.

Jaxon lets out a low whistle, amusement radiating off him in waves.

"Don't fucking start, Jax," I warn him, narrowing my eyes. "Just tell me how long it'll take to make more."

Jaxon's grin is back, wider this time, as he leans deeper into the chair. "You know, Luc, if you actually told me what we're protecting against, I could probably be more helpful."

I narrow my eyes, but say nothing as I rise from my seat and head over to the espresso machine tucked into the custom cabinetry behind my desk.

The familiar routine settles me, grounds my scattered thoughts. I pull two small white porcelain cups from the overhead shelf and position them beneath the machine, the strong, rich aroma of espresso quickly filling the air.

"I've told you what you need to know," I reply carefully, not turning around as I speak. "There's a potential threat against my business. Specifically my girls."

"Potential." Jaxon snorts softly, the skepticism thick in his voice. "Come on. You called me in, rushed a complete overhaul of your systems, and just ordered your star recruit to put a tracker on herself. That doesn't sound 'potential.' It sounds inevitable."

The machine hums softly, and two perfect shots of espresso drip steadily into the waiting cups. I take a slow breath before responding, turning to glance at Jaxon over my shoulder. His expression is curious, sharp, intelligent—like always.

But beneath that, I see genuine concern.

"I'm being careful," I finally say, choosing each word with precision. "We've had threats before, but this one's different. Personal."

Jaxon's eyes narrow slightly, picking up on the undertone immediately. "Personal how?"

"An old acquaintance," I explain carefully, lifting the cups from the machine and placing them onto matching saucers. "One who's decided to make his problems mine."

I cross the office, setting one cup on the desk in front of Jaxon and taking a slow sip of my own. The espresso slides down my throat, hot and dark, sharpening my senses. Jaxon's fingers curl around his cup, but he doesn't lift it yet, his gaze thoughtful as he studies me.

He raises one brow. "Organized?"

I don't confirm or deny it outright, just offer a subtle nod. "Enough to warrant caution. Enough to justify locking down every system I have."

Jaxon finally takes a sip, eyes assessing. "Fair enough. But if this gets bigger than tech—"

"I have security already in place for that," I interrupt quietly, knowing exactly where his thoughts are headed. "I appreciate it, Jax, but I need you focused solely on the infrastructure."

He nods slowly, clearly dissatisfied with my limited disclosure but knowing better than to push me further.

"Then I'll have your new servers delivered by next week, backups running immediately after that. The rest will take time, but it'll be impenetrable when it's done."

I give a small, satisfied nod. "Good."

Jaxon finishes the espresso, sets down his cup, and rises

from the chair. He pauses by the door, turning back with his usual cocky smirk. "By the way—your recruit is cute."

I glare at him, but he holds up his hands, surrendering with a laugh. "Relax, boss. I'm not suicidal."

He's still chuckling when the door clicks shut behind him.

Nearly an hour later, Sienna returns, stepping into my office quietly. She lingers just inside the doorway, freshly painted nails a vibrant, deep red that catches the afternoon sunlight. My gaze narrows slightly, tracing the vivid hue on her fingertips. I half-expected defiance—an act of subtle rebellion to test me—but she's done exactly as she was told.

I'm irritated that she didn't disobey...and strangely disappointed that she listened.

But her obedience deserves a reward, at least for now.

"Good," I say smoothly, leaning back in my chair. Her eyes lift sharply to mine, wary but brightening slightly at my praise. I allow a measured pause before continuing, "I've got a job for you."

Interest flickers openly across her expression, and for a split second, she's nearly giddy before quickly schooling her features. The determination to hide her eagerness amuses me, but I don't let it show.

"My next appointment is a long-standing client who's indicated he wants to close his Ledger account," I explain, watching her closely. "I want you to entice him to reconsider."

Her brow furrows delicately, confusion mixed with genuine concern. "How exactly am I supposed to do that?"

Before I can answer, my assistant's voice crackles over the intercom. "Mr. Vale, your next appointment is here."

Perfect timing.

I rise smoothly from my chair, buttoning the top button of my jacket as I cross the room. "Convince him to stay with only your presence." Pausing near her, I lower my voice, the command slipping from me effortlessly. "Don't say a single word to him the entire time."

She blinks, clearly startled, lips parting to argue—but the door opens, cutting off any further protest.

Long time vendor and client of The Ledger, Mateo Calderón steps into my office with an ease that belies the tension beneath his careful smile. He reaches forward, his grip firm as we shake hands.

"Lucian," Mateo says warmly, though the warmth doesn't quite touch his eyes. "It's been a while."

"Mateo," I return evenly, gesturing toward the plush seating area opposite my desk. "Good to see you. Please, sit."

He nods, settling onto one of the leather chairs with practiced casualness.

My hand moves to the small of Sienna's back as I guide her away from my desk, toward the sitting area with us. Mateo follows her every step as she crosses in front of me to take the seat next to me.

His gaze drags slowly over her, openly possessive. It's

subtle enough that someone less attuned wouldn't notice, but my jaw tightens at the implication.

It irritates me—and something darker coils deep in my gut. Protectiveness flares unexpectedly, making my muscles tense.

"Lucian. I appreciate you seeing me so promptly."

"Of course," I reply evenly, leaning back against the leather sofa, one arm casually over the back. "Though, I'm surprised at your request. You've been in good standing with the Ledger since the beginning."

Mateo shifts slightly, clearly uncomfortable. "It's not personal, Lucian. But... certain complications have arisen."

"Complications," I repeat slowly, tilting my head in faux-curiosity. "Care to elaborate?"

His eyes flick briefly to Sienna again, lingering far too long before returning to mine. I suppress the immediate urge to wrap my arm around her shoulders and pull her next to me. Mateo clears his throat, clearly struggling to maintain focus.

"You understand I do business with a *variety* of clients," he says carefully, gaze lowering as he chooses his words. "There's pressure building from DeLuca. Rumors of...tension between you."

My shoulders tighten imperceptibly. So, Lorenzo is finally making moves.

It's about fucking time.

Chapter 16
Lucian

"And?" I press, voice calm, betraying none of the adrenaline now rushing through my veins.

Mateo's voice lowers, a subtle warning threaded in his words. "I have no desire to be caught in the crossfire between you two. Removing myself from your... *ledger* seemed wise."

I nod slowly, considering his words. He isn't wrong to be cautious. But I won't let fear of Lorenzo unravel my enterprise. "I can assure you, Mateo, the situation with DeLuca will be contained. The Ledger always protects its own."

Mateo shifts again, clearly uncomfortable. His eyes slip toward Sienna, as if weighing what to share in her presence.

She adjusts the hem of her dress casually, but there's something deliberate in the way her fingertips trace down her thigh. Mateo's focus zeroes in immediately, distracted by the subtle, calculated movement.

My irritation rises sharply.

"Was there more, Mateo?" I tap my finger on my knee

twice, stopping myself but I couldn't hold back the irritation in my tone that time.

He fumbles, words trailing off, eyes flicking briefly to me as if realizing he's been caught. Clearing his throat, he tries to continue. "Lucian, I appreciate your assurances, but—"

Sienna's gaze flicks toward me, sensing the shift in my mood. Her eyes hold mine steadily, softening slightly—a quiet reassurance. *It's okay.* I read her easily, the unspoken words nearly audible.

She places her hand over mine with a soft squeeze before she rises gracefully.

I ignore the jolt that zap through me at the feel of her skin on mine.

Mateo tracks her every movement, unable to look away. My jaw clenches harder, but outwardly I remain utterly indifferent.

"Let me see if I can convince you, old friend."

My fingers tap rhythmically on my knee, irritation pulsing beneath my skin as I launch into a few pre-planned incentives. Exclusive contracts at my most lucrative clubs, a higher kickback for first pick of the day's selections, among other things.

Mateo owns a luxury food and wine distribution company. Having first selection of the freshest produce and fish of the day is very valuable to the high-end establishments I own.

But Mateo dips out of both ends.

His refrigerated trucks perfect front for smuggling weapons, designer drugs, or laundered cash and Lorenzo is one of his top clients.

However, he's also been a long-time client of The Ledger. He prefers softer Companions. Quiet ones.

And right now, he's not listening to a fucking word I say because he's wholly engrossed in Sienna as she makes her way across the office to my espresso bar.

I run my tongue along my bottom lip, suddenly needing that burn to squash the annoyance boiling within me.

Mateo's gaze lingers on the subtle sway of her hips as she moves with practiced ease. The way she stands at the counter. Her weight on one leg, the other shifted slightly out, accentuating the curve on her hip.

Possessiveness flares again, stronger this time.

I want to stand up and grab Mateo's face between my fingers and force him to turn away from her. I want to tell him if I catch his eyes on her again, he's going to lose them.

What the fuck is wrong with me?

This was my idea. I told her to do this and I'm not about to lose control over my own fucking assignment.

She returns a moment later, espresso cup delicately in hand. She bends at the waist more than needed, setting it before me silently.

Her eyes were locked onto me the entire time. A slight curve to her mouth as if the two of us are sharing a joke only we know.

She prepared it perfectly. She's paying attention—to everything.

But so am I.

Mateo's eyes darken appreciatively, and I suppress a growl. This is how I wanted him to react.

He wants her.

So, I'll show him exactly what doesn't belong to him.

I straighten slowly, an idea forming—one that risks my control, but feels oddly satisfying in the moment. I reach for Sienna's hip, gently tugging her into my lap.

She stiffens momentarily, surprise rippling through her body, but she settles quickly, gracefully crossing her stocking-clad leg over the other. Mateo's eyes widen hungrily, fixated, exactly as I knew they would be.

And then my fingers brush along her thigh, tracing the delicate fabric, feeling the silkiness give way to smooth, bare skin.

Her breath catches so softly I almost miss it, but I don't. The faintest shiver works through her body, barely visible, but I feel it beneath my palm—the quickening of her pulse, the subtle tension of her muscles beneath my touch.

Heat gathers low in my stomach in response, my body tightening sharply, a sudden rush of desire I hadn't expected. My grip tightens fractionally, possessively, before I trace the line of her gartered stocking tenderly with the tip of my finger.

Her thigh shifts almost imperceptibly, pressing just slightly into my hand—a reflexive response she immediately tries to suppress.

But it's too late.

I felt it. And now I can't stop feeling it, my body responding against my will.

How easy it would be to kick Mateo out of my office and pull her tight ass onto my lap fully, straddling me. Letting me push this fucking dress up and squeeze my hands around both firm globes.

To rip her wet panties off and watch my cock slide into her sweet cunt.

And that is a dangerous fucking thought.

Mateo swallows audibly, his gaze locked on my hand resting against Sienna's leg. Desire flares unmistakably in his eyes, and I know I've won.

Checkmate.

"So, Mateo," I say calmly, taking a slow sip of the espresso. "Do you really want to leave The Ledger?"

He hesitates, eyes never leaving Sienna. His throat works, struggling to form a coherent response. "Perhaps," he finally concedes softly, "we can reconsider."

"Mateo rises from his seat slowly, clearly reluctant to leave, his gaze lingering on Sienna. He straightens his suit jacket, smoothing it down as if needing something to occupy his restless hands.

"I'll see you out," I say firmly, dismissing him.

Sienna immediately takes the cue, sliding gracefully off my lap.

Turning toward her, Mateo extends his hand, eyes locked onto her as if she were the prize he truly came here for.

"And your name is?"

Her answer is simple, controlled. "Sienna."

I hear the allure in it and stretch my neck to one side, alleviating some of the pressure within me as it cracks twice.

Mateo takes her hand and brings it to his lips, pressing a lingering kiss to her knuckles. She smiles coyly, the perfect Companion, her act flawless.

I motion Mateo toward the fucking door and he goes.

Sienna moves to stand at the side of my desk, composed, waiting silently, her posture impeccable. Mateo spares her one last lingering glance before shaking my hand and I shut the door firmly behind him.

I pause, staring at the wood grain of the closed door, attempting to regain some semblance of self-control. I flex my fingers slowly, the impulse to spank her—to teach her exactly who's in charge—so intense it borders on painful.

"Well?" Her voice breaks the silence, curious but edged with something else—impatience, maybe. "How did I do?"

I turn slowly, my gaze sharp, unyielding. Her confidence falters, just slightly, under my scrutiny.

"Turn around." My tone is cold, clipped. "Hands on the desk."

She blinks rapidly, shock giving way to irritation. "Excuse me?"

It grates on my nerves, that defiant spark. Every part of me wants to bend her over my desk, strip away that stubborn attitude.

"Turn around," I repeat, voice lethal in its softness. "Hands on the desk."

I watch as a flush spreads across her cheeks, her breathing quickening as realization sets in. Her pupils dilate, betraying the surge of desire she tries to conceal.

Good.

Let her feel the danger of her own game.

Slowly, deliberately, she obeys—though her compliance is minimal. Her fingers barely touch the edge of the desk, her legs pressed tightly together.

That won't do.

I step close, just behind her, feeling the warmth radiating from her skin. I run both hands down her shoulders, over her arms, all the way down to her wrists, feeling her shudder beneath my touch.

Without hesitation, I adjust her stance, spreading her palms flat against the wood, pushing them farther apart until she's exactly where I want her.

"Why did he change his mind, Sienna?" My voice is a dangerous murmur against her ear.

She visibly trembles, her breath hitching audibly. "I—I don't know," she whispers, nearly breathless.

Lies. And we both know it.

I nudge her feet wider apart with my own, the sudden movement drawing a gasp from her lips.

"I think you do know." My hands slide deliberately down the length of her spine, savoring the subtle way she arches into my touch. The silent defiance of that movement alone deserves punishment.

But not yet.

Grasping her hips firmly, I pull her back, aligning her body precisely how I want it, every curve pressed intimately against me. She inhales sharply, the sound going straight to my cock, threatening my already tenuous control.

"Tell me," I demand softly, my voice edged with the promise of retribution. "Why did he reconsider?"

She swallows audibly, her voice a heated whisper. "Because he saw something he wanted."

My fingers tighten possessively, satisfaction burning fiercely in my chest. "Exactly. And do you know why he couldn't have it?"

She hesitates, breathing heavily, desire and defiance warring within her. "Why?"

I lean closer, my lips brushing her hair. "Because it already belongs to me."

"Desire doesn't live in what you give your contract—it lives in what they didn't know they wanted until you offered it," I whisper quietly against her ear. "You made him desire you. How?"

My hand moves deliberately down the curve of her ass, slipping beneath the hem of her dress, tracing the line of her stocking where it ends on her thigh.

Her breathing is heavy, nervous yet unmistakably excited. She licks her lips before answering softly, "He wanted to be you."

A swell of pride mixes with my possessiveness. "Very good," I murmur approvingly before stepping back.

She moves as if to straighten up. "Don't move," I command sharply.

I retrieve my espresso, moving behind her to lean casually against the coffee bar, observing her. "Not only did you control the room with just your presence, but you anticipated what would change his mind. He thought, if he stayed, he might become me—with *you* sitting on *his* lap."

Her back straightens slightly at the praise, but I'm not finished.

"But even though you did well, you still failed."

She jolts, nearly standing upright. "Ah uh. Stay put."

Frustration and embarrassment flash across her face, but she returns to position—legs apart, palms flat, hips pushed out. My hand clenches inside my pocket, restraining myself from touching her again.

"I said not to say a word to him the entire time. You told him your name."

She opens her mouth to protest, but I silence her swiftly. "Not a word means exactly that."

The silence hangs heavily between us. Her fingers flex impatiently against the desk, waiting for correction she undeniably craves.

She can't sit still. Anticipating what may come next. Scared of it. Wanting it.

I glance at my watch. "Three minutes are up. You're dismissed for the day."

She bolts upright, nearly stomping out before I call her back. "And Sienna?"

She pauses, fists clenched, turning slowly with fire in her eyes.

Her thighs press together subtly, and satisfaction curls through me. Let her ache. Let her wonder what would've happened if she disobeyed—or if I'd followed through.

"Don't be late again."

She storms out without another word.

Hours later, I stand alone in my office, adjusting the cuffs of my shirt and looking at the busy city as the sun sets and New York comes to life for the nighttime. A veil of darkness draping over the city that begs for its citizens to come explore it.

Sienna's perfume still lingers, intoxicating and tempting.

I can't get the feel of her out of my mind, and I need to fucking do something about it.

I've killed men for breaking my laws and here I am, a fucking hypocrite putting my hands on my own merchandise and loving it. Fucking wanting more of it.

But I'm starting to not care.

I'm starting to want to rewrite those fucking laws so I can have what I want.

She pushes me, challenges me in ways no other Ledger girl has dared. And fuck if I don't want to rise to every single challenge she throws my way—to teach her, correct her, and bend her to my will.

She's going to test every boundary I have. And when she finally breaks one... a slow smirk crosses my lips as I unlock my phone and open the Ledger app.

...I'll make her beg for the consequences.

I navigate to the new tracker page. The chip buried under the polish of Sienna's freshly manicured nails is working. The marker is stationary and blinking inside an apartment building about thirty minutes from here.

My smirk widens to a grin as I look at the route she took home. Careful to go up and down cross streets, Sienna spelled out two letters clearly with the path she took:

"F" and "U."

I chuckle darkly.

"Oh, I'm going to enjoy taming the brat out of you, little rabbit."

Chapter 17
Sienna

Maybe telling Lucian to go fuck himself via the tracking device wasn't my brightest idea, but in my defense, I was too pissed off to think clearly.

Today was the worst. Then briefly the best, then rapidly back to the worst.

Yes, I woke up a bit late—but only a bit. The subway decided today was the perfect day to malfunction. Cabs were impossible, buses overcrowded and crawling at a snail's pace because apparently, the subway outage inspired everyone in New York to flood the streets.

Three minutes. Just three measly fucking minutes late, and Lucian—Mr. Control-Freak of the Millennium— couldn't let it slide this one time. Four weeks straight of punctuality, and today he decides to humiliate me for being slightly behind schedule?

Whatever.

The Ledger spa appointment afterward was a saving

grace, at least. The manicure, pedicure, and those heavenly massage chairs melted some of my frustration away. I almost forgot my morning from Hell entirely by the time I was summoned back to Lucian's office.

I had been so excited when he told me about something new. Christ, I'd practically jumped into his arms like an idiot. I nailed it, though—played my part perfectly.

But I wasn't prepared for Lucian to pull me onto his lap, toying with the lace edge of my stocking, discovering the stirrups beneath my dress. He was staking his claim, showing me that he knew exactly what lay underneath.

If my ass hadn't been on his thigh, I'm sure I would've felt his dick hardening beneath his slacks.

But Jesus Christ, bending me over that desk.

The fantasy I'd replayed in my head countless times felt dangerously close to reality. His hands on my body, positioning me exactly as he wanted, almost pushed me to the brink right there.

I swear I nearly came from anticipation alone.

I was certain he'd spank me. The thought made my knees weak, my body craving his discipline so intensely it scared me.

But the blow never came.

And when he dismissed me, frustration and humiliation battled inside me. It wasn't just embarrassment at being scolded or put in place. It was disappointment that he didn't follow through.

He had brought me right to the edge, so close to crossing a boundary we've both skirted around. And I wanted it— God, did I want it.

I wanted him to break, to put his hand on my ass and admit, through every stern touch, how thoroughly I've invaded his carefully controlled world.

But he held back, as always. And now, all I can think about is how close I came—and wonder just how close Lucian is to breaking his own rules.

Another thing I'm wondering about is who this woman is staring back at me in the mirror.

My eyes run down my body and I barely recognize her.

Harper called after work, practically begging me again to join her and Adriano at The Masquerade. She still refuses to call him her boyfriend, despite the fact he's basically been living at her place—or she's been at his—every single night this week.

It's cute, really. Harper deserves someone who lights her fire even brighter than it already burns. That's exactly why I finally agreed to go out tonight.

I want to feel that fire myself—the kind Lucian ignites every time he pisses me off, every time my mind drifts back to that first night at the club, watching the Devil himself fuck a woman into oblivion.

The dress I chose for tonight is black leather, fitting me like a fucking glove.

It looks like thick bands of leather wrapped around my body, barely confining my tits, with a dangerously short hem.

My heels are high, my lipstick matches my nails, and I'm ready for a night of...what exactly, I'm not sure.

Harper bursts into my apartment without knocking,

Adriano and another guy trailing behind her. She whistles appreciatively.

"Damn, Sienna. Planning to break hearts or laws tonight?"

I smirk, grabbing my clutch. "Why choose? Let's do both."

Harper laughs and nudges Adriano, who wraps an arm around her waist possessively. "This is Roman," she announces, indicating the friend who's currently eyeing me up and down.

Roman is handsome, I'll give Harper that—tall, sharp jaw, striking features—but the way he looks at me screams he only wants one thing, and for some reason, it doesn't appeal to me at all tonight.

The club is bustling when we arrive.

Harper and Adriano immediately snag white masks, heading into level 2, Lust, eager for their night ahead. I slip on my black rabbit mask, feeling powerful and anonymous.

Roman chooses a white mask as well, sticking close to me near the entrance. The safe zone—where the rules of looking without touching are more my speed right now.

"So," Roman begins, leaning slightly toward me. "Have you been here before?"

I nod, my gaze roaming lazily around the room, taking in the glances sliding over me. The allure of my black mask— the woman who wears the Devil's invitation—is thrilling, intoxicating.

"Once," I reply casually.

He steps closer, his voice dropping. "You know, Harper's talked you up a lot. Says you're something special."

I smile politely, deliberately not looking at him, maintaining control. "Harper's known to exaggerate." Making him want what I'm not giving him.

My attention.

Roman chuckles softly, undeterred. "Maybe, but looking at you tonight, I don't think she's wrong."

I glance up at him coyly through my lashes, letting a teasing smirk curl my lips. It's amusing, really—he thinks he's seducing me, yet he's completely unaware I'm guiding this interaction. My Ledger training is coming in handy already.

"Careful," I say, tilting my head slightly, voice playful but authoritative. "Flattery will get you everywhere and nowhere at the same time."

Roman's flirting is not selling me. I know he only wants to use cheesy lines to try and get me in the sack.

He probably says a lot of the same stuff to girls, leading them on with the promise he's actually interested but really, he just wants to fuck and doesn't really have many standards on who it is.

As I think of these things, I surprise myself.

The old me, the one that pined after Boring-Ben would have been all over this. Craving any kind of attention and believing it instantly.

These words would have likely worked before.

But not now.

There is not a single cell in my body aroused by Roman, the bedroom eyes he's giving me or the prospect of fucking him.

Because I'm in the Devil's territory.

And knowing he's probably just a few floors above gives me chills. Wondering if he has a toy to play with yet.

If his tongue would feel as amazing on me in person as it does in my fantasies.

That is what sends a rush of heat across my chest and up my throat.

What flutters my pulse and makes me clinch my thighs together as my panties grow wetter.

I down the rest of my chardonnay and signal for another. Roman's eyes flash with intrigue, clearly enjoying the thought that I'm just loosening up for a night of lust.

"I've been trying to find out a bit about you from Harper but she's keeping any details about you a mystery."

"Is that so?" I give a polite smile to the server as I take a new glass of wine from their tray.

"You snooping around on me, Roman?"

I let my voice drip with flirtation and watch as it pulls him right in.

So easy.

"When I find something that intrigues me, I go after it."

Lame.

"So, what exactly do you do for a living, mysterious Sienna?"

I look at my wine and smile. I hadn't anticipated this question and I'm not really sure how to answer.

Oh, I'm training to be an escort to billionaires.

Or maybe, *I'm a paid houseplant in my boss's office who I think of every night when I come on my vibrator.*

I probably shouldn't use either of those. Especially the second one.

"Maybe she's one of the Devil's playthings." A woman whispers to her partner quietly as they pass us by.

I turn my head following them. All thoughts going back up to the ninth floor and wondering if the Devil is walking the halls of Hell tonight.

"Will you excuse me?" I take a big gulp of wine—for courage. "I need to use the bathroom."

I don't wait for Roman's answer as I turn, heading straight to the elevator.

Before I can talk myself out of it, I push the button for the Devil's Playground.

Chapter 18
Sienna

My heart pounds relentlessly as the elevator ascends to the top floor. This is reckless—borderline stupid—but I'm drawn to him in a way I can't resist.

The doors slide open, and my breath catches. There, seated regally on his throne, is the Devil himself. Black pants, no shirt, his powerful chest and sculpted abs proudly on display.

His face is hidden behind the familiar black mask, making him even more dangerously magnetic.

Our eyes lock instantly, and what truly takes my breath away is the intensity of his gaze, the way his eyes burn into mine, almost possessively.

Still clutching my wine glass, I step out of the elevator. But instead of walking directly toward him, I pause, realizing for the first time that he's seated in a large, recessed pit.

His throne is perfectly centered at the farthest edge,

allowing him to see everything and everyone to see him. It's an exhibition, a display of power and control.

Slowly, confidently, I begin to circle the perimeter of the pit, moving at a deliberately torturous pace. He tracks every step I take, watching me closely, predator to prey.

I secretly hope he's hunting me.

It's exhilarating, arousing beyond anything I've ever experienced.

It takes every ounce of my self-control to tear my gaze away from his. Facing forward, I take a sip of my wine and allow my attention to drift to the spectacle unfolding around me.

The woman from the first night—the one whose pleasure he'd claimed for everyone to see—is back, wearing a black fox mask.

Another woman, also masked in a fox disguise, is seated in a chair clearly designed for maximum exposure and pleasure, her legs parted wide, fully on display.

The first woman kneels between the other's thighs, skillfully pleasuring her with her mouth. The seated woman's head is thrown back in sheer ecstasy, hands gripping the chair's arms desperately.

But there's more—far more.

A man lies flat on the cushioned floor, driving into the fox I recognize from below. Behind, another man presses into her ass, matching the first man's rhythm perfectly.

A sharp clench seizes my stomach, sending a rush of butterflies cascading through me. The erotic choreography is mesmerizing. Sensual, rhythmic, all four of them moving in perfect harmony, driving each other toward a shared climax.

The hairs on the back of my neck prickle as I sense the weight of someone else's awareness pressing upon me.

And I know who it is.

Unable to resist any longer, I glance back toward the Devil. His eyes are still locked on me, fierce and possessive. The heat of his stare warms me from within, igniting the fire I'd been craving all night.

For weeks.

Since the first night I was here.

Or perhaps, the night I met Lucian on the rooftop lounge.

I keep walking, my pacing slow and steady. He tracks me, then, unhurriedly, deliberately, he raises a finger, beckoning me with two sharp, commanding gestures.

My heart skips a beat, and I stop my path. My body turns toward him and I tip my head to the side, before taking the last sip of my wine.

A server must have been waiting nearby, because a gloved hand was there instantly, offering to take it from me.

With both hands at my side, my pulse galloping, I move toward him. Each slow step down the two stairs into the pit amplifies my anticipation.

My senses are overwhelmed—the low hum of music vibrating through my bones, the mingling scent of expensive cologne and sweat, and the sight of bodies moving passionately around me.

He rises from his throne, descending one step, then another, his strides patient yet commanding. As I approach,

I realize he's taller than I'd thought, more imposing, more powerful. My breath quickens.

We meet midway, standing beside a dark wooden table. Up close, I see that his mask isn't simply black—it's deep red, layered beneath black, glimpses of crimson peeking through.

It covers his entire face, leaving only his strong jaw and sensual mouth visible. The top encases his hair, two horns curling back magnificently.

I imagine gripping those horns, pulling him down between my thighs, feeling their cool, smooth edges grazing my sensitive skin as he tastes me for the first time.

My cheeks flush hot at the thought.

Intricate tattoos trace up from his forearms, weaving across his defined chest, edging slightly up his neck, then disappearing behind him. My fingers twitch with the urge to touch him, trace every inked line, but I hold back, my breathing shallow and heated.

Suddenly, he places a firm hand on the small of my back, pulling me against him.

The unexpected contact rips a surprised gasp from my lips, and I see the corner of his mouth lift into a smirk.

His warmth surrounds me, his cologne intoxicating. I fight to keep my hands by my sides, desperate to touch him yet restraining myself.

He guides me backward until I'm pressed against the table, gripping it behind me to steady myself. He leans close, his breath ghosting over my ear.

"Tell me, little rabbit," he murmurs, his deep voice sending a ripple of relief through me, unraveling some of the tension that had coiled tightly within, "what are you looking for?"

I try to mask my nerves, responding quietly, "I'm not looking for anything." I congratulate myself for even remembering how to speak.

The Devil chuckles—low, deep, knowing—and then moves swiftly. He grips my thigh, effortlessly lifting me onto the table. Instinctively, one of my hands wraps around his neck, the other bracing myself behind me.

He pulls my leg to his side, his other hand gliding slowly down my hip and thigh, pulling my other leg open until I'm pressed flush against him. I feel how hard he is and, without thinking, grind against him, my mouth falling open at the sensation.

My head tips back, exposing my neck. He seizes the moment, running his nose along the sensitive skin, inhaling deeply. I bite my lip, stifling another moan.

His mouth brush against my ear as he calls my bluff. "Liar." He pulls back slightly, meeting my eyes. "You're out of your league."

"I am not," I protest weakly, not even convincing myself.

In another swift motion, he spins me around, pressing me forward onto the table. His hand travels up my back, holding me firmly down. I watch our reflection in the aged mirror ahead, my stomach tightening with desire.

His exploring hand ignites trails of fire along my hip and ass, slipping inward along my thigh. He growls softly, pressing his erection firmly against me, teasing me.

"You did come here looking for something, didn't you, little rabbit?"

I shudder, every muscle in my body coiled with anticipation. His touch is slow, deliberate torment, grazing the sensitive junction where my thigh meets my pelvis, hovering there, just out of reach.

I hold my breath, desperate for more, aching for him to claim me.

He grips my thigh firmly, pulling my hair back sharply with his other hand, forcing me to watch our reflection in the mirror. My eyes widen, mesmerized by the raw, erotic image.

His lips brush lightly against my ear, voice dripping with sensual menace. "You're a scared little rabbit," he murmurs, pausing to drag out my torment.

I squirm beneath him, craving contact, silently begging him to end the exquisite torture.

"And if you're not careful, you'll get eaten alive."

He pulls me upright, releasing my hair, and turns me to face him without allowing any distance between us. One hand circles my throat possessively, while the other deliberately pulls down the hem of my dress.

Anger flashes through me, knowing he's only played with me, teasing me without intent to fulfill.

"Go," he commands, stepping back.

Cold.

Dismissive.

My body stiffens, pride burning hotly beneath my skin.

I watch as he backs away, muscles flexing beautifully with each deliberate step up to his throne. He turns back, towering over me, watching silently as I remain standing there—aroused, angry, and utterly at his mercy.

It infuriates me. The Devil's playground is his domain—his rules absolute, just like Lucian at the Ledger. And tonight, I'm just another piece on the board.

With my jaw clenched tight, I turn and leave. But not without making a promise to myself.

I'll come back. And next time, he won't turn me away.

Chapter 19
Lucian

Evening settles heavily over the city, deep shadows stretching across my office.

I glance at my watch, the time ticking steadily toward the gala. Sienna's had the day off, though she probably didn't realize it was intentional. The event tonight would be demanding enough, a new challenge I know she'll be eager for.

My shoes echo softly on the polished marble as I head down to the Ledger spa. Anticipation coils low in my stomach. I sent her a dress earlier today—Ledger red, provocative, perfectly tailored. But something tells me she won't have worn it.

I'm counting on that defiance, in fact.

She *should* push me on this.

Entering the spa, the soothing scents of lavender and eucalyptus fill the air. The attendants immediately quiet, stepping aside respectfully as I approach the private lounge where Sienna waits.

My heart picks up pace just slightly.

When I open the door, my suspicion is confirmed. There she stands, breathtakingly beautiful but definitely not wearing the dress I sent. Instead, she's chosen a classic little black number that hugs every curve of her body perfectly.

Her hair cascades over her shoulders, styled loosely, effortlessly elegant. Her eyes snap to mine immediately, challenging and slightly defiant beneath her careful composure.

I arch a brow, letting my eyes trail slowly down her figure before returning to meet her gaze directly.

"Interesting choice," I say coolly, leaning casually against the doorframe. "Care to explain why you chose to ignore my instructions?"

She lifts her chin slightly, clearly prepared for this question. I watch with interest as she smooths down the fabric of her dress, gathering herself.

"I looked up tonight's exhibit," she begins confidently, holding my gaze steadily.

"The artist specializes in black and white paintings, with red as the only accent color. Wearing the dress you chose would have competed with the artwork. I didn't want to offend the artist by clashing with the pieces she's worked so hard to create."

Her explanation is perfect, considerate, and impressively thoughtful. She passes the test without even realizing she's taken one.

A corner of my mouth threatens to twitch upward, but I suppress it, maintaining my neutral expression.

"You're thinking like a Companion. Every detail matters

and it will be your job to make sure it goes smoothly. Well done"

Like aways, she hangs on that small compliment. She tucks her bottom lip between her teeth nervously trying to hide the joy she gets when I tell her she's done something right.

It's a tick I want to punish her for. Take that lip between my teeth and teach her I'm the only one that's allowed to bite it.

Except I'm not. She's off limits.

I finally concede, straightening from the doorframe. "Shall we?"

In the limo, silence settles between us comfortably at first, the low hum of tires over pavement filling the space. I finally break it, my tone measured. "Tonight, you'll be surrounded by money—prospective clients eager for an opportunity to meet a Ledger Companion."

Sienna's eyes flicker toward me, curiosity evident in their blue depths. "Anything specific I should do?"

"Simply mix and mingle," I reply evenly, adjusting my cufflinks. "Enjoy the art, the company. But keep in mind—for some of these prospects, you are the art they'll be admiring tonight, the masterpiece they'll be vying to purchase."

Her gaze sharpens, understanding blooming behind her eyes as she absorbs my words. "Understood."

"Good." I relax slightly into my seat, studying her quietly as the city lights blur by outside the tinted windows.

We arrive at the gallery to find the party already in full swing, elegantly dressed guests mingling beneath the soft glow of strategically placed lights. I step out first, offering my hand to help Sienna from the limo. She takes it, her fingers trembling slightly with excitement or nerves—perhaps both.

I tuck it into the crook of my elbow and she slides closer to me.

It's immediately obvious she's never attended an event quite like this, though she's doing an admirable job masking her curiosity beneath practiced composure.

Heads subtly turn as we enter, conversations quieting momentarily. I'm accustomed to it—the subtle recognition, the intrigue of the Ledger—and tonight is no exception. But tonight, the attention also lands squarely on Sienna, as it should.

The woman of the hour notices our arrival immediately. She strides toward us, a vision in a sleek red dress designed to match the vivid accents in her art.

Tall, strikingly beautiful, and effortlessly confident, she smiles warmly as she approaches.

I lean forward slightly, kissing my old friend's cheek. "Clara," I greet her warmly, feeling Sienna tense beside me before stepping away when Clara smoothly takes my arm, standing intimately close.

"Lucian," Clara purrs, "always a pleasure."

I see Sienna's throat move as she swallows down a flash of jealousy, exactly as I expected she might. A lesson she must learn, though I'd be lying if I said I didn't enjoy seeing it bother her.

"Sienna," I say, gently drawing her attention, "this is Clara, tonight's featured artist—and a former Ledger

Companion. One of the first, actually."

Sienna's expression shifts ever so slightly, a mixture of surprise and insecurity quickly masked. She studies Clara briefly, clearly measuring herself against the other woman.

Another important lesson—there's no room for insecurity in a space where each Companion is a masterpiece in her own right.

Clara gives me a quick rundown of the viewing order for the gallery, thanking me repeatedly for my patronage and support. She touches my arm again lightly before rushing off eagerly to greet other guests.

Sienna tries to step away as well, but I reach out, capturing her wrist gently yet firmly, keeping her close.

I lean in slightly, my mouth close to her ear. "Your first failure tonight," I murmur softly. "Jealousy and competition are beneath a Ledger Companion."

She pulls her wrist away sharply, sparks lighting in her eyes. "Jealous? Hardly," she says smoothly, composing herself quickly. "I was just daydreaming about being taller. Is that a crime?"

My eyes narrow slightly, though amusement threatens at her defiance. "Be careful, Sienna," I warn quietly. "I'll be watching closely tonight."

I step back, giving her space to mingle.

Over the next hour, she moves gracefully through the gallery, her presence magnetic. Even as I attempt to engage politely with acquaintances, my awareness never fully leaves her.

The soft glow of the low lights catches her auburn hair,

reminding me vividly of how it felt wrapped tightly around my fist last night.

I half-listen to Adam, an investor I've known for years, as he drones on about his latest ventures. "Odd about Mateo," he muses quietly, swirling his drink thoughtfully. "Not like him to take a day off. The man even worked the day his first son was born, for God's sake."

I hum dismissively, eyes narrowing as I track Sienna again.

Adam seems oblivious to my distraction, continuing to speculate aloud.

But something else is demanding my attention. An instinct that sends alarms through me when I notice a man lingering nearby, his attention fixed unwaveringly on Sienna.

He already approached her.

Twice.

The first time, she did what she should have and engaged him like a Companion. Enticing him with what she withholds, making him want to become a member for a chance.

The second time, it was short. She didn't hold eye contact, instead focusing forward on the art. A believable distraction.

But now he's back. Positioned closely behind her, eyes lingering in a manner that sparks possessive anger within me.

My knuckles flex subtly, tension coiling tight within my chest. I don't like the way he's looking at her—not one fucking bit.

She dismisses herself from her current conversation, pausing before a large, evocative painting. The art is raw, passionate—two figures entwined in black, accented only by bold, violent streaks of red. A hand grips a throat, both threatening and protective.

My steps are quiet as I approach, sliding my palm possessively over her back, gripping her hip firmly.

She gasps softly, body stiffening, then subtly relaxes into my touch. The man who'd been lurking behind her retreats immediately, understanding my silent claim.

"What do you see?" I ask softly.

She hesitates, then quietly answers, "Trust. She trusts him to protect and pleasure her, even though he has the power to hurt her. But he won't—unless she asks him to."

That last part she says with a daring coyness in her eyes.

I'm momentarily stunned by the depth of her insight. It's exactly what I feel every time I'm near her, this over-whelming need to protect and dominate simultaneously.

And it's driving me fucking crazy.

"Exactly," I murmur, impressed.

Her cheeks flush delicately, and I tighten my hold on her hip, before I remember I don't need to piss a circle around her and ward off that dickhead.

I decide to walk with Sienna for a few more paintings.

When she's not actively trying to make my head explode, she's quite enjoyable—for reasons other than my urge to rub my hands over her smooth ass.

I barely allowed myself a teasing touch last night, and it took all my strength and patience to pull away from her, not to rip her panties off and sink deep into her.

God, I deserve an award for the restraint I showed. She wanted it—badly—but she's not ready yet.

While moving gracefully through the gallery, Sienna's presence is magnetic. But my attention shifts sharply as a known troublemaker, approaches. An arrogant trust-fund schmuck that thinks he can buy his way into anything.

Except the Ledger, you prick.

"Lucian Vale," Thomas says smoothly, his gaze sliding suggestively toward Sienna. "I'm surprised to see you here tonight, given the recent...disturbances in certain circles. People are talking, you know."

I stiffen, tension rippling through me instantly.

Thomas knows exactly what he's doing—hinting at things he shouldn't know about. Sienna picks up on the subtle implications immediately; her eyes flick toward me, cautious yet curious.

My hand moves instinctively, capturing her wrist, pulling her just slightly behind me. She doesn't protest, and a quiet satisfaction fills me.

She may battle me on training, but she recognizes when a situation requires caution. I stand taller, feeling the trust she's silently placed in me.

I lean forward, my voice dropping low and dangerous. "Be careful, Thomas. Certain topics are best left unspoken—especially when they don't concern you."

Thomas's smirk fades under my menacing gaze, understanding my implicit threat. He steps back, nodding stiffly before turning away.

Once he's gone, Sienna steps from behind me, her eyes sharp with accusation. "What was that about?"

My response comes out sharper than intended. "Nothing that concerns you."

The defiant veil drops instantly over her features, eyebrow cocked in challenge.

"Fine. You know everyone talked about you disappearing for weeks knee-deep in a bloodbath. Then you come back, putting tracking devices on me, clients bailing on their accounts, and you really want to pretend everything's fine? Go ahead. But don't pretend I'm stupid or that I should turn a blind eye if I might be in danger."

I open my mouth to tell her to watch it. That I would never let anything happen to my girls, but she doesn't wait for an answer.

Turning abruptly and placing her drink on a server's tray before she storms off toward the hallway leading to the bathroom.

I watch her until I can't see her anymore. My palm twitching at my side.

With a deep huff, I rake my hands through my hair.

Taking in the space, the crowd is beginning to clear out and Clara seems to finally have a moment to herself.

While Sienna is in the restroom, I finalize my purchase of one of Clara's paintings—the large one Sienna admired earlier.

Clara gives me a resigned smile, gratitude clear in her eyes. "Thank you, Lucian. Your support—means everything."

"You did wonderfully," I tell her genuinely. "I'm proud of you."

Glancing around, I realize Sienna hasn't returned. A jolt

of unease hits when I also don't see the creep who had been eyeing her all evening.

Excusing myself swiftly, I hand Clara my whiskey glass and stride purposefully toward the hallway.

Something inside me tells me that son-of-a-bitch is going to be here.

My anger ignites instantly when I see him cornering Sienna against the wall near the restroom entrance. She's visibly tense, her eyes blazing, but she hasn't yet called out.

I'm a storm down that fucking hallway, my steps silent, my fists balled, he doesn't even hear me coming.

Sienna spots me approaching, relief flooding her expression, and something possessive flares hot inside me.

Before the man fully registers my presence, I seize him, turning him abruptly and striking him squarely across the face with calculated precision. Grabbing his shirt, I headbutt him sharply before smashing his face into the drywall, the impact brutally satisfying.

"Lucian!" Sienna gasps, startled.

The man collapses, groaning weakly, blood streaming from his nose. My breath comes in controlled bursts, adrenaline surging, yet my rage remains icy cold, tightly coiled beneath my composed exterior.

The image of Sienna trapped, vulnerable, sends a fresh wave of fury through me. Coldly, deliberately, I step over him, reaching for Sienna's hand and pulling her protectively close.

Her safety matters above all else.

"Let me see." I quickly inspect her for injury, my jaw

tight with tension and a fierce need to shelter her from harm. "You're okay?"

"I'm fine," she assures me, voice steady despite the lingering tension in her body.

"Fucking asshole. Did he touch you?" I look back at the piece of shit, tempted to kick the piss out of him for good measure.

"Lucian." Sienna's voice pulls me back with a tug on my arm. "I'm okay."

My chest tightens, her courage both admirable and frustrating. I should never have allowed this situation to unfold.

"Let's get out of here," I murmur softly, guiding Sienna away, my pulse still pounding from a potent blend of anger, protectiveness, and an unsettling tenderness I'm not ready to acknowledge.

As soon as we emerge from the hallway, I spot a member of Ledger Security—a man from my detail, off-duty tonight but immediately attentive.

"Take care of that," I command quietly, nodding toward the crumpled figure behind me. He complies without question.

Sienna stays close as I lead her toward the gallery exit, her hand still firmly clasped in mine. The possessiveness and fury in my veins refuse to fade, my jaw clenched tightly as I guide her toward the waiting limo.

The night air hits us sharply, a cold contrast to the heated violence we've just left behind.

She glances up at me, questions swimming silently in her gaze. Questions I know I owe her answers to—but not yet. Not here.

I help her into the limo, my hand lingering protectively at the small of her back, sensing the slight tremble she tries so hard to hide. I slide in beside her, shutting the door with a firm, controlled click.

As the car pulls away from the curb, tension still coils tightly within me. Because tonight confirmed something I can't deny, something dangerous and consuming:

Sienna isn't just a Companion I'm responsible for.

She's mine.

Chapter 20
Sienna

The silence in the limo feels thick and suffocating, pressing down heavily between us. Lucian sits rigidly at my side, his jaw clenched so tightly that I can practically hear his teeth grinding.

His gaze is fixed straight ahead, eyes distant yet smoldering with barely-contained fury. He's nearly shaking with it, his breathing measured in careful, controlled breaths.

I stare down at my hands, shoulders tense, still replaying the incident in my mind. Seeing Lucian move like that—swift, brutal, precise—made it clear this wasn't new to him.

This isn't something he learned just to protect his companions. He's done worse. Probably killed before.

And yet, despite knowing that, I can't deny the unsettling rush of attraction that surged through me when I watched him handle that asshole.

It's insane. Completely irrational. But I've never felt safer than I do right now, sitting next to Lucian Vale.

I glance toward him subtly, noticing the way his fists rest clenched in his lap. There's blood smeared across his knuckles, a jagged line split open from striking that asshole's jaw.

Without thinking, I lean closer, concern tightening in my chest.

"You're hurt," I murmur softly, reaching instinctively toward his hand.

He barely registers my voice, eyes flicking to me only after I've moved.

He glances down at his knuckle like he'd almost forgotten it was there, but his expression remains impassive, betraying nothing.

"Dammit, Lucian," I mutter, scooting forward quickly toward the small built-in bar across from us. I snatch up a napkin, pressing it gently to the bloody gash on his knuckle.

My touch is cautious, hesitant, but his hand remains perfectly still beneath mine.

"You shouldn't have fought him," I scold quietly, pressing lightly on the wound. I glance up and immediately frown when I see amusement flickering in his eyes.

"You find this funny?"

"Not funny," he replies evenly, his voice low and smooth —infuriatingly calm compared to my own anxiety. "But your sudden concern is rather charming."

I huff out a breath, irritation flaring. He's humored by my worry—of course he is. But despite the annoyance, I keep tending to his hand.

He doesn't pull away, even though part of me fully expected him to brush off my attempt and do it himself.

I don't know why he's letting me help, but I can't deny the warmth blossoming in my chest at the simple intimacy. My fingertips linger on his skin longer than necessary, my pulse quickening slightly at the roughness of his hands, the strength beneath.

He watches silently, carefully studying every movement as if memorizing them.

I set the bloodied napkin aside and grab a fresh cloth one, scooping a handful of ice cubes from the bucket. Wrapping it neatly, I gently press the cold bundle to his knuckle.

"You seem to have a lot of drama and crisis in your life." I look from the napkin to him and maybe shouldn't have. There's an intensity in his gaze, dark and so close—much closer than I realized.

"Y–you should have a Crisis and PR department at the Ledger. Let them handle these things for you."

A hint of amusement flickers in his eyes, breaking through some of the lingering tension. "You think my problems can be solved with a press release?"

I shrug, fighting a smile. "I don't know. Have you tried solving things without punching someone?"

Lucian tilts his head slightly, studying me with renewed curiosity. "You have a better idea, then?"

"Maybe," I tease lightly, dabbing the ice carefully against his knuckles. "Why solve problems yourself when you can pay someone else to make them disappear?"

He chuckles softly, the deep, rich sound resonating through the enclosed space, sending warmth pooling in my stomach. His gaze softens just enough to make my breath hitch.

"If you're so good at crisis management, why didn't you go into PR when you graduated? You're smart. You certainly could have."

I huff out a breath, rolling my eyes instinctively. His palm twitches beneath my touch, fingers curling into a tight fist again, and a thrill of satisfaction ripples through me.

I love getting that reaction from him.

But I answer plainly, quietly, deciding suddenly that honesty feels safer than playing games.

"My ex-boyfriend," I say simply, eyes trained on his hand, avoiding his gaze. "He didn't exactly encourage ambition."

Lucian's posture shifts subtly. His hand tightens once more, knuckles whitening, before he forces it to relax again. He turns his face toward the window, the muscle in his jaw twitching.

I bite back a satisfied smirk at his reaction, enjoying it far more than I should.

The limo fills with silence, tense and charged, before he finally speaks again, voice deceptively calm.

"This ex," he murmurs carefully, still staring out the window. "It was serious, then?"

I swallow, suddenly aware of the heat radiating from him, how close we're sitting, our knees almost brushing. My heart pounds harder in my chest. "We dated since high school. He was the first—the only—boy I ever loved."

I allow myself to lean in slightly, savoring the faint tremble of tension rolling off him.

Inspecting the cut, I press the ice more gently now, my

voice dropping as I concentrate. "Hell, he's the only boy I've ever even kissed."

His head snaps back around, eyes blazing fiercely into mine, the possessiveness clear and unguarded for one brief, heated moment.

This time I don't hide my smirk, a small thrill racing through me at his jealousy.

Good. Let him think about that.

If only he knew how many other firsts I've yet to experience. Like oral.

I'm no virgin. Ben and I had sex plenty of times since we were seventeen. I learned how to suck dick, testing things out on him. But he would never go down on me. No matter how much I showered or shaved. If the room was dark. Nothing.

Hell, I could've jumped clean off a bar of soap, ready to be devoured, and he still would've told me he couldn't do it.

I wonder what Lucian would do if he knew. Would he lay me down, pull my panties to the side, and give me a long, slow lick?

Jesus.

This line of thinking is dangerous, especially since I'm currently holding Lucian's hand in my lap. It would be so easy to spread my legs just a bit, guiding his hand between them, letting him feel how wet I am just imagining his mouth there.

Thankfully, the limo slows to a stop in front of my building, dragging me out of my fantasy.

Lucian gently slips his hand from mine, stepping out first. He straightens, gaze sharp as it scans my building, the street, and the shadowed corners nearby. Even now, he's alert, protective. It sends warmth curling through me again, though in a different way than moments ago.

When he's apparently satisfied we're safe, he extends his hand, helping me out of the limo. His touch remains firm, possessive even, as he guides me toward my door.

"You don't have to walk me up," I murmur softly, suddenly shy beneath his intense scrutiny.

"I'm walking you up," he replies firmly, leaving no room for argument.

Okay.

We enter the building, stopping at the elevator. The silence settles over us again, punctuated only by the soft hum of machinery.

Lucian finally breaks it, voice low and carefully neutral. "Your ex. He still bother you?"

I shake my head, shrugging slightly. "No. Not exactly. He just—he still has a key to my apartment. It weirds me out sometimes, but the landlord refuses to change the locks."

Lucian's entire body stiffens beside me, his jaw tightening again into that now-familiar scowl. Clearly, he doesn't like that one bit.

"That's unacceptable," he says coldly, anger barely concealed. "You shouldn't have to worry about your own safety."

"I don't think Ben would ever—"

"Doesn't matter," he cuts in sharply. "You shouldn't have to question it. Ever."

I swallow, heat rising in my cheeks as we step onto the elevator, tension heavy between us. When we reach my floor, he insists on walking me right to my door, clearly still bothered.

"Thanks for tonight," I whisper softly, fumbling with my keys, certain he's about to turn and leave now that I'm safely home.

He doesn't move. Instead, he looks down at his injured knuckle again, flexing his hand briefly before looking up, voice unexpectedly gentle.

"You wouldn't have a band-aid, would you?"

My heart skips a beat, warmth spreading through my chest at the quiet intimacy in his request.

"Yeah," I reply softly, stepping aside and opening the door wider. "Come on in."

The moment we cross the threshold into my apartment, something shifts in me. Lucian's presence here feels startlingly intimate—maybe even invasive—and my heart pounds unevenly in response.

A flush of self-consciousness overtakes me as I glance quickly around the room, suddenly seeing everything through his eyes.

Is it too messy? Too small?

Does he think it's childish or pathetic?

Lucian remains quiet as he enters, glancing around discreetly, clearly trying not to make it obvious he's checking my apartment for threats.

The gesture should annoy me, but instead, it sends another wave of heat rushing beneath my skin. Still, I roll my eyes slightly and say,

"If you want to make sure there are no boogeymen lurking around, feel free to look."

He pauses, a brief smirk touching his lips before he abandons the pretense entirely, stalking quietly through my home. He flips on lights, looking inside closets and behind doors, meticulously ensuring everything is safe.

It's oddly comforting, watching him prowl like that—protective, thorough, his powerful frame moving with calm, controlled purpose.

But my blood freezes in my veins when he reaches my bedroom doorway and stops abruptly, body going tense. My stomach drops.

Oh no.

I'd completely forgotten my vibrator was still sitting boldly on the nightstand, charging.

After last night's stunt with Lucian's *"hands on the desk"* command, followed by the Devil pinning me possessively at The Masquerade, I'd practically burned the thing out trying to find release.

For a full, agonizing minute, Lucian doesn't move.

He simply stares at the nightstand, unmoving, before finally walking into the bedroom, checking the rest of the space. Heat surges over my entire body, embarrassment mingled with a perverse thrill that he now knows exactly what he does to me.

He finishes quickly, inspecting my bathroom, closet, and the balcony, carefully checking the locks. I remain rooted in place by the kitchen counter, hands flat on the cool surface, heart hammering so loudly he can probably hear it.

When Lucian returns to the living room, he stands there silently, tall and devastatingly attractive, hands planted firmly on his hips as he slowly sweeps his gaze around my apartment again.

Watching him like this, all lethal intensity and restrained strength, sends desire coiling low and tight in my belly.

"Can I get you—"

"You should get an alarm system," he cuts me off firmly, meeting my eyes with fierce seriousness.

I press my lips together, fighting off a smirk that I'm sure shows anyway. "Okay."

He studies me silently for another beat, tension flickering between us before he takes a deep breath, straightening. "I should go."

My throat feels dry, and my heart sinks at the idea of him leaving, but I force a small smile. "Right. I'll see you tomorrow."

Lucian gives me a final, lingering glance that sends chills dancing over my skin, then turns and quietly lets himself out.

I exhale shakily as the door clicks shut behind him, unable to deny the burning ache still pulsing steadily between my legs—or the realization that Lucian Vale, in my home, feels far more dangerous to me than any threat he just checked for.

I wake up feeling... weirdly amazing.

The kind of sleep that settles deep into your bones and doesn't let go until morning. I blink slowly at the ceiling, stretched comfortably in my sheets, and let out a little sigh of satisfaction.

Must've been the combination of three toe-curling orgasms—thank you, newly-charged vibrator—and the residual adrenaline from watching Lucian beat the ever-loving shit out of a creep in a tailored suit.

Apparently violence and orgasms are the key to restful slumber. Who knew?

By the time I'm showered, dressed, and out of my robe, the apartment smells like toasted bagel and fresh coffee. I spread my favorite honey-walnut schmear over the warm bread, humming softly, when a sharp knock at the door makes me pause.

I glance at the clock, frowning. It's still early. Too early for unexpected visitors.

I peek through the peephole and immediately groan.

Great. My landlord.

Mr. Jenkins stands in the hall, arms crossed and mouth turned downward in his usual disapproving way. He always looks like a pissed-off rat with an oily comb-over and a vendetta against joy.

I open the door cautiously. "Morning?"

"There's a locksmith here," he grumbles. "Needs about fifteen minutes. Says he's here to change your locks."

I blink, stunned. "Wait—what?"

Before I can even gather my thoughts, he shoves a glossy packet into my hands. "And this too. Security alarm's been activated. You just gotta set the code."

I stare at the pamphlet and know without a shadow of doubt who did this.

Of course.

Lucian.

My shock gives way to hot, bubbling irritation. My blood starts to simmer.

Oh, he did not.

He did not go over my head, tangle up my already miserable landlord, and take control of my apartment without saying a damn word.

If he gets me evicted for violating some weird clause in my lease, I will skin him alive.

Mr. Jenkins is already walking away by the time I manage a strained, "Thanks, I guess."

I let the locksmith in. He's polite, quiet, and disturbingly fast, installing a shiny new electronic deadbolt in record time. When he hands me two fresh keys and tells me the system is ready to program, I give him a tight smile while fantasizing about throttling a certain steel-eyed control freak.

By the time everything's finished, I check the time and nearly scream. I'm going to be late.

Fucking fantastic.

No doubt Lucian will use it as an excuse to sentence me to another humiliating stand-off in "time out" at his desk—like a misbehaving toddler in need of public shaming.

And it'll be his fault. But that won't matter.

I glance longingly at my untouched bagel, now slightly cold on the counter. I'm too pissed to eat it. I shove it into a napkin, toss it into my purse, and slam the door behind me after punching in the new alarm code.

Letting out a deep breath, I storm through the lobby,

fuming, heels clicking with purpose. I'm ready to let Lucian Vale have it.

But the moment I push open the front doors, a man in a black suit steps forward from the sidewalk.

"Sienna Knight?"

My shoulders sag as I catch sight of the sleek black SUV parked behind him, polished to perfection. And then I see the logo—etched in gold, small and subtle on the rear passenger window.

BL.

Ledger transport.

Of course he sent a car.

The driver opens the door smoothly, offering me a respectful nod. "I'll be driving you to work, ma'am."

I stare at him for a second, debating whether to launch into a tirade here and now. But... fine. This guy is an innocent bystander.

And at least this way I might actually get to The Ledger on time and spare myself whatever demeaning punishment Lucian's cooked up for tardiness.

With a huff and a dramatic eye roll, I climb into the backseat.

He thinks he's clever.

Let's see how he likes getting a taste of his own medicine.

Chapter 21
Lucian

How many times can a boss think about getting their employee off with a purple vibrator before it becomes unhealthy?

Two? Three?

How many times can that same boss jerk off to the image of her thighs spread wide, soaked and shaking, while she comes all over his tongue—before HR should be notified?

Because if the limit is three, then I hit that somewhere between last night and this morning.

And that's not even counting when she showed up at The Masquerade in that black dress, all curves and fire, practically begging for trouble. Or when she sat on my lap—smug and sweet—and I got a feel of those fucking stirrups holding up her stockings.

I still haven't recovered from that.

I release another deep breath, irritation curling under

my skin as I stare blankly out the window of my office. The city looks deceptively calm this morning.

Shame I'm not.

Because when I think about my finger toying with those stockings I remember Mateo saw her first.

The thought alone is enough to make my grip tighten into a fist. Even for a second—before I had a chance to really see her, to touch those legs—he got a glimpse.

And that pisses me off more than it should.

But I got my first real taste when I bent her over my desk.

Correction—when I *made* her bend.

Teaching her the position I like. The one she'll need to remember for the punishments I know are coming. Because she'll earn them. She wants to.

That look she gives me from behind the Devil's mask at the club—curious and daring. That fucking look that dares me to lose control.

The way she mouths off, pushes buttons, tracks my movements like she's studying the exact moment I'll snap. Watching for the tension in my fists, like it turns her on to see me restrain myself.

Spoiler: It does.

And now I'm thinking about spanking her.

Great.

My cock's already hard—again.

It's like my brain tries to run damage control while my body's already halfway to pressing her over the nearest flat surface and showing her exactly what happens to bad little rabbits.

Her ass would be beet red. Warm under my palm. My hand stinging from every delicious impact. Her breath hitching. Her back arching. Her thighs slick.

I shift against the counter and mutter, *Jesus Christ*, under my breath.

I need caffeine. Strong, black, and distracting.

I finish making the espresso, fixing it just the way I like it, and not a second too soon. Because I can feel her the moment she steps into the building.

She's pissed.

Good.

The rush of her footsteps echoes sharply down the corridor. Her presence is electric. Hot. Furious.

Right on schedule.

I school the smirk tugging at my mouth, turning just in time as she storms through the door of my office like a goddamn hurricane.

I lift the delicate porcelain saucer and cup, perfectly calm, my expression schooled into smooth indifference. The scent of dark roast wafts between us as I take a sip.

"Congratulations on being on time today," I say, cocking a brow as the heat from my coffee rolls across my tongue. "I almost thought I'd have to start without you."

"Start what? Being an overbearing jerk?" she snaps, her voice tight and biting.

Her eyes blaze—stormy, furious, beautiful. That sharp, blue fire burns through me more effectively than the espresso sliding down my throat.

I set the cup down slowly, carefully, because if I'm not

deliberate, I might break something. Or worse—pull her over the desk and end this argument the way I *want* to.

"You had no right," she grits out. "No right to interfere in my personal life. Invading my space like that—"

I let her finish, because watching her come undone is almost better than touching her. *Almost.*

When she finally draws breath again, I speak with practiced calm. "Your safety *is* my business, Sienna. Because *you* are my business."

She rolls her eyes and throws her hands up. "Don't give me that bullshit. You don't get to toss around that line like it justifies everything. I didn't ask you to protect me."

"No," I agree, stepping closer, "you didn't. But you also didn't stop to think that someone might need to."

"I can take care of myself," she shoots back.

My mouth tilts into something that's not quite a smile. "Can you? With an ex who still has a key to your apartment? A building with no security? A landlord who doesn't give a fuck?"

"You can't just go around doing whatever you want," she says, her voice rising, every word dripping with frustration. "Sending people to my apartment? Having work done without permission?"

"I can," I interrupt smoothly. "And I will."

She stares at me like I've grown a second head. "You *will?*"

I nod once, unapologetic. "I did."

Her jaw clenches as she steps forward, eyes blazing with disbelief. "Stay out of my building, Lucian."

And now I really do smile.

"I bought it," I say, letting the words settle between us like a slow-burning fuse. "So technically, it *is* my building now."

She goes still.

I watch the exact moment her brain stalls out. The wheels are turning, trying to process whether I'm bluffing.

I'm not.

I never bluff.

"It pays to have friends in the right places," I continue, casually walking back around to my desk. "Friends who owe you favors. One call to the right person, and by dawn, I owned the building."

Her lips part, stunned.

"Within fifteen minutes, the locksmith was en route," I add. "And another fifteen after that, your piece-of-shit land-lord found out who his new boss is."

I sit back in my chair, steepling my fingers in front of me, gaze locked on hers.

"I expect Mr. Jenkins will be much more... *amicable* to tenant needs going forward."

Sienna just stares at me, silent, blue eyes wide with stunned fury.

And fuck, I want to see what she does next.

And soon I will.

Because the new lock and security monitoring?

That's not the only change happening in her apartment today.

No less than a dozen cameras are being installed— discreet, invisible to the untrained eye. Jaxon's tech. His best work. Firewalled, encrypted, completely secure.

No creeps. No risks. No chance of some perverted fuck hacking into the feed and watching what belongs to me.

I'll get alerts when she leaves. When she gets home. When she's in the shower or curled up on her couch or asleep in bed with that damn plush blanket pulled up to her chin like she's not the most temptable thing I've ever seen.

And when she touches herself—when she spreads those pretty thighs and plays with her tight little pussy and that goddamn purple vibrator—I'll be able to hear the breathless sound of my name fall from her lips as she comes around it.

Because she will.

She already does.

I clench my fists beneath the desk, dragging in a slow breath as I try to push the thought away, but it's no use. My cock's already hard again, straining against the confines of my pants like it's just as obsessed with her as I am.

Fuck.

I have to stop.

If I let these thoughts keep spiraling, there won't be a single drop of blood left in my brain to keep me sane. It's all going to rush to my dick.

Sienna doesn't stay quiet long.

Her mouth parts like she's about to launch another tirade—probably something about boundaries, privacy, or how I'm violating every line in some imaginary rulebook she thinks applies to me.

But I've had enough.

"Drop it, Sienna."

My voice is low. Firm. Final.

Her eyes flash with defiance, but she hears the edge in

my tone. The warning. She huffs, arms crossing over her chest in a petulant gesture that makes my cock twitch again.

I record the look for later—burn it into memory.

That's three spankings now: one for the mouth, one for the attitude, and one just because I want to feel her writhing under my hand.

Soon.

But for now, there's work to do.

Half an hour later, we're in the training room.

The girls are seated in a semi-circle, a sleek black monitor mounted behind me, ready to light up. I stand in front of them, hands loose at my sides, watching each face with calculated ease.

Some of them fidget.

Some look too confident.

Sienna—she's fighting not to glare at me, but her curiosity is winning out.

I press the remote and the screen flares to life.

"This exercise," I begin, voice even and clipped, "is about reading what isn't being said."

The remote clicks, revealing a picture of a man—mid-forties, expensive suit, thin smile, tired eyes.

"Your job is to match this face to the right client profile in your Ledgers. You'll each receive the same set of possibilities. You have one minute to decide."

A few girls shift in their seats, murmuring softly.

"Your entire profession," I continue, "relies on your

ability to understand people before they open their mouths. Before they tell you what they want. Sometimes they don't even know what they want."

Another click. Another photo. A younger man this time. Arrogant smirk. Slightly askew tie. Restless energy in his posture.

"Your contract may arrive in a good mood and leave dangerous. Or they may arrive calm and stable—but are carrying a ticking time bomb in their chest."

I let that hang there, sweeping my gaze across them.

"Profiling matters. Recognizing tension in a jaw. A twitch in the hand. A dullness in the eyes. All of it tells you something. And if you're good—if you're *really* good—it could mean the difference between a satisfying night and a dangerous one."

I glance toward Sienna.

Her lips are pursed, her posture tight. But she's listening.

She always listens when it counts, even if she's looking at me like she wants to bust my balls.

"Let's begin."

An hour into the exercise I click to the next image: a woman this time. Mid-thirties, elegant but closed-off, with sharp eyes and a perfectly neutral expression.

"Take sixty seconds," I instruct. "Then tell me which of the four profiles you believe fits. And why."

The room settles into thoughtful hum of low conversation as girls tap their manicured fingers against tablet screens and whisper to each other. I scan them all, but I'm watching Sienna the closest.

She looked at her screen about ten seconds and is not

sitting, tapping her pen against her lower lip—absently, like she has somewhere better to be. Then, as if feeling my eyes on her, she flicks her gaze up to meet mine.

And smirks.

Not subtle. Not sweet.

Smug.

"Got something to share, Miss Knight?" I ask coolly.

She blinks innocently. "No, sir. Just waiting for my turn to be right. Again."

A soft giggle escapes one of the other girls—Gia, a petite redhead with a sharp tongue. "She's not wrong. She's nailed, like, every single one."

"Don't inflate her ego," mutters Nika, flipping her long braid over her shoulder. "It's already spilling into my personal space."

Sienna just beams at them like she's being serenaded.

I arch a brow. "Confidence is encouraged. Smugness gets you nowhere."

"Then it's a good thing I'm not aiming for nowhere," she shoots back sweetly, crossing one leg over the other in a slow, deliberate motion like she wants to drag my attention straight to her thighs.

She knows I'm going to fucking take that bait.

Careful, my gaze tells her. *You're pushing.*

She lifts her chin, reading it perfectly.

Good, her expression says back. *Because I'm not done yet.*

Someone finally blurts out an answer. Incorrect but the logic wasn't terrible. Someone else delivers the right answer and in return I click to the next profile.

When I walk behind the row of chairs, I slow deliberately as I pass her. I feel her straighten slightly as I near—waiting. Testing.

I lean close enough for my voice to hit only her ears.

"Keep it up," I murmur. "See what that confidence earns you."

She doesn't flinch. Doesn't even blink. Just turns her head slightly and whispers back.

"Oh, I *hope* it earns me a restraining order against my nosey boss."

My pulse spikes. My hand grips her chair harder.

Nika clears her throat. "I think it's Profile C—guy looks like he drinks top-shelf whiskey and cheats on his wife with yoga instructors."

Gia hums. "Profile A. Divorcee. Wants validation from pretty women and to feel interesting again."

I nod once. "Good. You're learning to look deeper than the surface."

My gaze flicks back to Sienna.

She's still smiling. Still smug.

And still completely determined to cross whatever line I draw—just so she can watch what I do when she does.

I hope she fucking likes what she's begging for.

Chapter 22

Sienna

After everything he did—the lock, the alarm, buying the fucking building—I made it my mission this week to make Lucian's life hell.

And God, I've done a damn good job.

I ignore his instructions.

Roll my eyes when he corrects me.

Smirk when I catch him looking.

I challenge him in ways the other girls wouldn't *dare.* Because I know he's letting me push. Letting me dig my own grave.

And I can't help it—I *want* to see how deep I can go.

I want to be reckless. To crack that carefully constructed armor of his and see what's underneath. He crosses lines? So can I. And I'll do it with a smile.

But every time I toe the edge, he doesn't snap.

He watches. He waits.

And it makes me angrier.

It's another training day. Another afternoon where Eve is off on a contract, so Lucian steps in—filling her role in the most uncomfortable way possible.

Today, he has us all in his office. Tea and coffee on polished trays. Everything just so, like always. Except nothing about this feels professional.

Because the other girls are acting like we're on some delusional speed-dating episode of *The Billionaire Jerk-face Bachelor.*

Gia leans forward too far when she talks, hoping he'll glance down her blouse. Nika plays with her straw like she's trying to jack it off. Every question that gets tossed his way sounds like a pickup line, thinly veiled with curiosity of how big his dick is.

"What's your favorite city to travel to?"

"Do you ever go to the beach?"

"Are you *seeing* anyone?"

Jesus Christ.

They have a chance to ask the most powerful man in this entire company anything—and *this* is what they do with it?

I sip my coffee and roll my eyes so hard it's a miracle they don't get stuck there.

I prefer this office when it's just us. When I can smell his cologne drifting in the air, mix it with the dark, bitter scent of espresso.

When he says my name low and quiet, in that voice that scrapes against my spine like a secret he wants to keep.

But right now? I'm over it.

Another girl—Tasha, maybe—leans toward me, all

glossy lips and perfectly curled hair, and whispers behind her manicured hand, "These questions are so lame. I feel like we're in a group date from Hell."

I smirk, keeping my gaze forward, but my voice carries just enough Lucian hears it.

"Yeah, all we're missing is a rose ceremony and matching bikinis."

A few girls stifle awkward laughter. One lets out a choked snort. Tasha covers her mouth like *she* didn't just start it.

Lucian turns his head slowly. That calm, collected mask he wears so well? Slipping.

Just a little.

Enough.

"Dismissed," he says, low and clipped.

Chairs scrape and tea cups clink against saucers as the girls scramble out, tripping over themselves to avoid the sudden shift in the atmosphere.

I stand, smug. Victorious.

And then his voice slices through the room again.

"Not you."

I freeze.

A thrill of heat runs down my spine. I'm not afraid.

But I probably should be.

The door closes behind the last girl with a soft *click*. The silence that follows is deafening—*dangerous*. I don't move. Don't breathe.

Lucian doesn't yell.

He doesn't snap.

He simply straightens his cuffs.

Then he circles.

Slow. Measured. Predatory.

Every step feels like it echoes inside me. He's not just walking—he's *stalking,* and I'm his prey. The heat I was riding so confidently moments ago is already shifting—turning molten, disorienting.

"So," he says finally, voice smooth as his espresso, "care to explain your little outburst?"

I try to roll my eyes. Try to summon the fire I felt just minutes ago.

But my mouth is dry. My heart won't stop thudding.

I swallow, forcing the words past lips that suddenly don't feel so smug. "It was... ridiculous. The flirting. The questions. I just—someone had to say something."

He hums low, like he's considering that answer. He's standing behind me now—I can feel him, close enough that the heat of his body kisses my spine.

"And of course," he murmurs, "that *someone* had to be you."

I don't answer.

Because yes. It did.

Because I wanted to get under his skin.

I wanted him to lose control.

And now that he's not? It's somehow *so much worse.*

I hear the rustle of his jacket as he steps closer, feel the shift in the air as he lowers his voice to a deadly whisper.

"You've been pushing me all week, Sienna."

My breath hitches.

"And now that you've woken the devil," he continues, "what exactly do you plan to do with him?"

I don't know.

God help me, I *don't* know.

But I sure as hell can't back down now.

I lift my chin, even though my voice isn't nearly as steady as I want it to be. "I'm not afraid of you."

He doesn't laugh.

He doesn't move.

He just speaks—low, lethal, final.

"Let's see if that's true."

Lucian slips off his jacket with a fluid motion, the expensive fabric whispering against itself as he hangs it neatly on the coat rack in the corner of his office.

"Hands on the desk."

"You can't be serious." My voice is breathless. Barely a whisper.

But he is.

He doesn't answer—not with words. Just steps toward the desk, his movements precise, calculated. He removes his cufflinks—the same ones I picked up from the jeweler two weeks ago, the ones I remember being heavy and sharp in my hand—and places them gently on the wood surface, one by one.

Then, slowly, he rolls his sleeve. Not rushed. Not rough.

Deliberate.

Revealing bronzed skin, thick forearms roped with strength and veins that make my pulse skip.

"You're about to learn exactly how serious I am," he

says, voice low and even. He starts on the second sleeve, rolling it to match the first.

"Hands—on—the—desk."

Each word lands like a promise.

I move. Hesitant. Not because I don't want this, but because suddenly I *do*.

And that's more terrifying than anything.

I walk to the desk, walking softly across the polished floor. My fingers touch the surface first, then my palms.

I bend forward, mimicking the position he had me in the other day—but not quite. My stance is off. Elbows too tight. Back not arched. Feet not wide enough apart.

Part of me does it on purpose.

Part of me doesn't know what the hell I'm doing anymore.

Lucian follows—quiet, patient.

I don't hear him move. I *feel* him behind me.

And then his hands are on me.

Not rough. Not fast.

Just... *firm*. Controlled.

He adjusts my hips with a touch that lingers too long. Smooth palms sliding down my sides, pressing one hand between my shoulders until I sink deeper into the position he wants.

It's humiliating. It's thrilling.

It's everything I didn't realize I needed because I feel electrified inside and it's flowing straight to my pussy.

This feels like foreplay and just this thirty seconds of interaction has me soaking fucking wet. So much more so than Ben was ever capable of.

Lucian's voice slides over me like smoke. "You've been very naughty, Sienna. Rolling your eyes. Talking back. Pushing."

Oh my God. I swallow. My fingers flex against the desk.

"The point of today's exercise," he continues, his tone calm and almost... instructional, "was to teach you the art of conversation. How to read a client. Engage. Anticipate. Not flirt. Not pout. Not compete for attention like it's some game."

"They all failed today." Lucian says, his voice a murmur near the base of my neck.

His hand glides over my spine again, slow and deliberate.

"But so did you."

My breath catches, my cheek pressed to the cool wood of his desk. The contrast of temperature sends a chill through my body—one that's chased away the moment his warmth crowds in behind me again.

I should be ashamed.

But I'm not.

Because I *like* the way he touches me. The way his hands smooth down my hips, firm and sure. The way he molds me into position without resistance. I could fight it—but I don't want to.

I *want* to know what happens next.

His foot nudges mine, gently spreading my stance even wider. The movement feels functional, calculated... but it's also intimate in a way that steals the air from my lungs.

He's preparing me.

For what, I don't know.

One of his hands settles on my hip, grounding me. The other slides up the line of my spine, his palm wide, warm, and unhurried. When he reaches the space between my shoulder blades, he applies the slightest pressure—pressing me forward until my chest brushes the polished desk.

"Good girl, Sienna." he says softly, like the words are just for him. "Just like this. Every time."

My breath stutters. My heart is thundering so loud I'm certain he can hear it.

"You act like you want control," he murmurs, his voice low and sharp and devastating, "but what you really want is to give it up."

Both of his hands slide down then, leisurely, like he has all the time in the world. He palms the curve of my ass, squeezing gently, like he's testing the tension beneath my skin.

"You want someone to take it from you," he continues. "To *know* what you need... before you ever say the words."

My eyes flutter shut. My body feels molten. Wrecked without even being touched properly.

I hear the sound of fabric shifting—and then feel the cool air kiss my thighs as he pushes my dress up.

My breath hitches, my thighs clenching involuntarily as I'm fully exposed—my lacy black panties stretched over the curve of my ass, the black garters and stirrups hugging the tops of my sheer stockings.

A low rumble sounds in his throat.

It's not a growl. Not quite.

But it's *dangerous*. Deep. Primal.

His fingers slide reverently back down the globes of my ass, slow and steady.

"You wore these for me," he says darkly. "Don't lie."

I swallow hard, my cheek still pressed to the desk, my fingers curled into the wood.

"You've been begging for this. Every bratty look. Every smart little comment. Every time you opened that mouth, you were asking for this."

I can't speak.

I don't *want* to.

Because he's right.

And I don't want him to stop.

"Now, answer me, Sienna."

His voice is low—coiled restraint stretched thin and fraying.

I feel him press forward and *moan*, deep and unguarded, as the thick line of his erection grinds against the swell of my ass. My cunt clenches involuntarily, the air punched from my lungs at the sound he makes.

That fucking sound.

His hand finds my hip again, squeezing hard enough to make me whimper. The other drifts up—palming my ass, sliding slowly along the curve of my lower back, then up my spine.

When he reaches my shoulder, he doesn't grip—he massages. Deep, slow, tender. His fingers dig into the tension I'm holding like he knows every tight, anxious place inside me.

"Answer me, Sienna," he repeats, his breath warm at my ear. "You wore these for me. Didn't you, *Angel?*"

My name on his lips is sinful. But *Angel?* It melts me.

I push back into him—pressing my ass into the thick ridge of his cock, wordless and needy, desperate for more than the teasing brush he keeps giving.

But the moment I do, he pulls away.

A strangled sound slips from my throat. When I relax in disappointment, he presses forward again—grinding into me just enough to make my knees weak.

He's toying with me.

Ruining me.

Making me desperate for him.

"Yes," I breathe. It's a moan. A confession. A *beg.*

And then—

A rush of cool air.

SMACK.

I cry out, startled, the sharp sting lighting across my ass as my body jerks in shock. I try to lift up, instinctively, but his hand presses firmly to the center of my back, keeping me down with terrifying ease.

"Yes, what?" he asks.

His tone is lethal. Quiet and cold.

I stammer, still dazed. "I—I—"

SMACK.

Another slap. Harder this time. The sound echoes off the walls, heat blooming beneath my skin as I gasp.

"Yes, *sir!*" I blurt, trembling. "Yes, sir—I wore them for you!"

The silence that follows is thick. Tense. Electric.

And Lucian?

He finally smiles.

I can feel it in the air between us.

"I knew you could be a good girl," he murmurs, the words curling down my spine like silk laced with smoke.

And then his hand lifts.

Crack.

I suck in a gasp as the slap lands harder this time. Sharp. Stinging. My body jolts, a whimper escaping before I can catch it.

His palm glides over the spot he just struck—slow, cruel, *teasing*. He massages the sting like he's soothing a wound and branding me all at once. The friction lights up my skin, making my core throb with need.

"You want to act like a brat, Sienna?" His voice is so calm. Deep. Patient, like he's explaining math.

Another hit.

"Then you'll be treated like one."

My eyes burn. I'm humiliated—laid out across his desk like a disobedient schoolgirl. My ass bare, dress bunched at my waist.

But worse than the shame?

Is the *heat*.

The pleasure-pain that pulses from every spank, ricocheting straight to my clit. It buzzes there—taunting. Torturing. Every hit *hurts*, but somehow, it makes me wetter. Makes me ache harder.

Smack.

My fingers grip the edge of the desk.

"You don't misbehave because you want to disobey, *Angel*," Lucian says, his tone still maddeningly level. "You do it because you want me to take control, don't you?"

Another hit, again.

"Yes, sir." A choked moan slips from me. I hate him. I hate how much I want this.

His hand glides over my ass again—slow and deliberate, like he's studying the shape of his sin.

"You play the brat so well," he murmurs. "All mouth and no discipline."

Smack.

"Every time you talk back, you're begging for this. Every time you roll your eyes, you're asking me to put you in your place."

I'm trembling now. My breath hitching. My thighs slick and quivering, my core pulsing like I'm seconds from an orgasm I know I won't get.

That's the worst part.

He *won't* give me that.

Lucian's been edging me since the moment I stepped into The Ledger.

Every lingering look.

Every command spoken in that low, lethal voice.

Every brush of his body so close to me that says *mine*—only to pull away before I can have *anything*.

Smack.

"Pathetic," he mutters under his breath. "Dripping all over my desk like a needy little slut, aren't you?"

My breath catches—part humiliation, part helpless arousal that pulses low in my belly. My eyes burn. My skin stings. My thighs try to rub together for friction, but he notices and spreads them wider.

"You think this gets you what you want?" he asks, voice

curling hot against my spine. "You think being desperate makes you deserving?"

He reaches around my hip, to the front of my panties. I suck in a breath and hold it. Begging him to slide his fingers beneath the waistband.

He doesn't. He only allows his fingertips to barely slide between my legs. The faintest touch, stopping just as he feels how truly wet he's made me.

Fuck him.

He bends lower, his palm rubbing over the sting of my ass, soothing and cruel all at once.

"You're soaking," he says, almost to himself, but I hear the satisfaction in it. "So fucking wet for me and I haven't even touched your pretty little cunt."

Smack.

"I know that is what you really want, Angel." His whisper is more growl.

A whimper breaks free before I can stop it.

Not just from shame.

But from fury.

I want to come. I want to scream. I want to claw at him for starting this and leaving me wrecked.

But all I can do is stay there.

Ass high.

Face flushed against the polished desk.

Legs trembling. Clit throbbing.

When the last smack comes—sharp, final—it leaves me breathless.

Then silence.

His hand glides over the tender flesh of my ass again,

slower now. Almost gentle. Like he's proud of his work. Like I'm some lesson taught, punishment delivered.

"Beautiful." He murmurs.

And I hate how much I *liked* it.

How much I wanted *more*.

Lucian leans down, his breath warm at my ear. His cock presses against me—hard, restrained, *untouched*.

"Watch your smart mouth, angel." He takes in a deep breath, inhaling me, his nose pressed into my hair. "I do enjoy shutting it."

That's the end of it. He doesn't kiss me. Doesn't finger me. Doesn't even look at me like I'm worthy of the release I need so badly.

He just steps back, leaving my red ass exposed, my legs spread wide. The cold rush of air stings as he removes his heat from me, and I bolt up.

I'm crying, my nose is running and as I sit up to pull my dress down, he stops me.

"Who gave you permission to get up?"

I want to turn around and slap him, then pull him into me and devour his mouth. Spread my legs and feel him slam his hard cock into me.

Instead, I stay here. My red ass cheeks burning as I stay still, just how he posed me.

He walks around his desk to his chair, unrolling his sleeves and reaching for his first cufflink.

"Go clean yourself up, then you're dismissed."

Without a word or a look back at him, I work my tight dress back down and leave. Slamming his door behind me.

Dismissed. Asshole.

Like it was nothing.

Like *I'm* nothing.

Like I didn't feel his dick throbbing against me, wanting me too.

I know he did. I know he wanted to pull himself out and sink fully into me.

Because I fucking wanted it too.

And when my clit throbs from just imagining it, I think I might actually scream.

Chapter 23
Lucian

I shouldn't have touched her.

Shouldn't have laid my hands on her—spanked that firm little ass and watched her cheeks bounce with each strike. I shouldn't have stared so long at the flush of red I left behind... or felt the sharp bite of pride at the sight of my handprint. *My brand.*

I sure as hell shouldn't have wanted to tear those panties off and *devour* her.

But I did.

I wanted to lick that wet cunt until she sobbed my name, until she forgot why she was mad, until there was no brat left in her—just need.

It's been twenty minutes.

And I haven't moved from my chair.

The Ledger security app glows on my second monitor, and I'm watching it like my fucking life depends on it.

The green dot labeled *S. Knight* is almost home. She's

moving fast, storming her way up that building like she's ready to burn it down.

I know exactly what she's about to do.

So I press a button under my desk. My door locks with a muted *click*, and the monitor to the left blinks to life.

The cameras weren't just installed inside her apartment —though the ones routed only to me? *Those* are hidden. Exclusive. Private.

But there are others. Ones wired through the building.

Visible cameras mounted in the lobby and elevator— obvious, for the sake of deterrence.

Then there are the *others*—discreet angles at the ends of halls, in stairwells, two positioned directly across from Sienna's unit.

I won't take chances.

Not with Lorenzo.

Not with her.

If someone comes for her, I'll see it before they get close.

And when I do?

I'll kill them.

She appears on the monitor now, storming down the hallway from the elevator, heels sharp against tile, fury rippling off her in waves.

Fuck, she's gorgeous when she's pissed.

She fumbles with the lock, her shoulders tense with impatience, and I watch her mouth move as she curses it under her breath.

My cock throbs against the confines of my slacks, straining—*aching*.

The moment the door opens, she throws it shut behind her and marches down the hallway with intent.

She's not even trying to cool off.

She's going straight for relief.

Her hands go to the hem of her dress, yanking it over her head in one smooth pull. I groan, grabbing the base of my cock and squeezing hard to fight the rush that follows.

Black lace bra. Matching panties. Garter belt cinched to those damn stirrups holding up her sheer black stockings.

She kicks off her heels and unclasps her bra.

Her breasts bounce free—perky, flushed, nipples already tight.

I reach for the drawer on the right side of my desk, tugging it open without breaking my gaze. My earbuds are exactly where I left them. I pop them in, syncing them to the audio channel I *never* use.

Until now.

Until her.

Until *this*.

The instant I hear her sigh, a guttural sound leaves me— somewhere between relief and agony. My fist strokes up the length of my cock, slow and tight.

She grabs the vibrator. The purple one I saw on her nightstand the night I dropped her off. The same one I imagined in place of my tongue.

She plops onto her bed, scoots to the center, and spreads her legs wide.

My heart slams against my ribs. I stroke harder.

The vibrator buzzes to life—and her moan?

Her moan breaks me.

Loud. Unashamed. *Wrecked.*

My hips jerk off the chair as my grip tightens. Pre-cum leaks from the tip, and I swipe my thumb over it as her legs tremble on screen.

Her free hand clutches the sheets, her back arches, and she moans again—louder this time.

God, I want her mouth around my cock. Her body writhing under mine. Her nails clawing into my back as she begs for the orgasm I've been denying her for weeks.

This pressure I've been building in her?

It's building in me too.

We're both strung tight, twisted up in this game.

But only one of us is going to win.

And it's not going to be her.

She doesn't even take her panties off.

Just slides the vibrator beneath them, moving in tight, quick circles over her clit. Her thighs twitch as she finds the rhythm she needs, and I can see her hips flexing, chasing that first orgasm like she's been on the edge for hours.

Because she has.

Because I put her there.

I grip my cock tighter, stroking up the shaft as her body jerks—hips bucking—and a sharp moan rips from her lips. Her thighs tremble violently, her cunt pulsing beneath the lace as she cries out her release.

And fuck, it's beautiful.

I throb in my palm, my cock hard as stone, but I *don't* come. Not yet. I know her.

And she's not done.

Her hand slows against her clit, breathing ragged as she

tosses the vibrator—still buzzing—onto the mattress beside her. Her chest heaves as she slides her panties down, finally baring herself.

I growl low in my throat, pumping my cock with a harsh stroke. "Fuck yes, baby."

She kicks the panties to the end of the bed, and I curse again. "Show me that pretty pussy."

Like she heard me, she spreads her legs wide—glistening, pink, swollen, *soaked*. My mouth waters.

God, I need to taste her. To bury my face between her thighs and suck her clit until she cries like she just did.

She grabs the vibrator again and slides the slick bulb down her slit. Teasing herself. Testing how close she is. Her hips twitch when she touches her entrance—fuck, I bet she's so tight—but she doesn't push it in. Just glides it back up and presses it to her clit again.

This time, she turns the dial higher.

Her back bows instantly, her body jolting with a raw, almost pained moan. "Fuuuck."

It's the most beautiful fucking thing I've ever seen.

One hand flies back, bracing on the headboard behind her as she rides the second orgasm with her legs trembling in their stocking-clad sheath. She can't keep them still— friction, need, electricity still running through her.

And me?

I'm right there with her. Grunting. Groaning. My hips flex into every stroke as precum drips from the tip of my cock, my balls drawn up tight.

But she still wants more.

Still isn't satisfied.

My little Angel has *nothing but sin* in her mind.

She shifts—up onto her knees now, thighs spread wide, her body open like a fucking invitation to Hell. One hand stays behind her for balance, while the other works her clit with brutal, desperate determination.

Her breasts sway with every grind of her hips. Her garters bite against her skin. Her head tips back as she cries out to the ceiling, lost to her pleasure.

"That's it, *Angel*," I pant. "Fucking ride it."

I want her on my face. I want her grinding that perfect pussy over my mouth while I taste every goddamn moan she makes.

She starts to shake.

She's close.

And I fall with her.

My cock jerks violently in my grip as the orgasm crashes through me. "Fuck—"

Her voice explodes from the speakers.

"Fuck! *Fuck you. Fuck you, Lucian!*"

The sound pushes me over the edge.

My cum spills hot and thick over my fist as I growl her name, breath ragged.

"Yeah," I mutter darkly, smirking at the screen, still stroking the last of it out of me wiping the tip of my dick with a tissue. "I'm going to fuck you, little rabbit."

My heart is still hammering in my chest when she suddenly... looks up.

Directly into the camera.

Her eyes lock onto mine like she *knows*.

Like she knew the *whole* time.

Her expression is flushed, glowing from orgasm—but that smirk?

That *smirk* tells me everything.

She cocks one brow, smug and dangerous. Then she lifts the vibrator to her mouth and—

Licks it.

Long. Slow. Eyes locked on the lens.

My jaw drops.

My cock twitches.

And I whisper—

"Fuck me."

I was watching her sleep when the call came in.

My little angel curled into her sheets, the fire burned out for the night. Her hair a messy halo around her face, one leg kicked free of the blanket. Lips parted, chest rising slow and even.

She definitely knows where at least two of the cameras are.

How the fuck she found them, I don't know. But Jaxon's getting an earful when I get back.

The alert was *urgent.*

One of my men. Wouldn't say what. Only that it was a client.

And that I needed to come *now.*

So here I am.

The wind sharp with salt and steel.

The full moon casting a ghostly sheen across the industrial wreckage of the shipyard.

"This better be good," I bark, voice echoing off the corrugated metal walls of the warehouse surrounding us.

In the distance, a cargo horn bellows—low and haunting.

The waves slap against the concrete wall in lazy rhythm, but the metallic scent riding the breeze isn't ocean or rust.

It's *blood*.

My men stand silent, solemn. They part when I approach.

I don't need to get close to know he's dead.

Bloated. Pale. Drifted in on the current, tangled in the ropes off the dock. He's been in the water for days. Skin gray, swelling in strange places.

But I know it's a man.

And I know *which* man the moment I see the ring.

His wedding band.

Mateo.

Fuck.

The logo on his shirt confirms it—embroidered right over his heart. The crest of his produce empire. One of the *quiet* clients. The loyal ones. The ones who never asked for more than discretion, and in return, got my protection.

Mateo never wanted to be caught in the middle of this war.

He asked to be released from his contract—quietly, respectfully.

And I told him to stay. Promised he'd be protected. That I had it under control.

I was wrong.

I step closer, my jaw clenched, my men falling silent behind me.

They don't need to follow.

This is my mess.

Mateo didn't go easy. His body tells the story.

The deep bruising. The defensive wounds etched along his arms. A long, vicious gash carved across his stomach—messy, painful, cruel.

He suffered.

But it's his face that stops me cold.

Or what's left of it.

A whiskey bottle—shattered.

The jagged handle driven straight into his eye socket.

And not just any whiskey.

Mine.

The same bottle I brought to Lorenzo's warehouse. A gesture of peace. A final olive branch.

Now it's been returned.

Louder. Bloodier. Impossible to misinterpret.

There will be no truce.

And whatever line I'd been hoping we hadn't crossed—we're miles past it now.

War isn't looming.

It's fucking here.

Chapter 24

Sienna

Something's off at The Ledger.

It's been three days since I've seen Lucian. Three days of silence. No messages. No instructions. No sponsor-led training.

It's like he vanished.

The first day, I was honestly relieved. I didn't know how I was supposed to face him—not after what happened in his office. Not after the spanking. Not after I bent over his desk, dripping wet and panting like a sinner in confession.

Not after I went home, and put on a show just for him... right for *his* camera.

Because once I spotted the first one, it wasn't hard to figure out there were more.

It was like a game.

A very twisted, voyeuristic game and I played it willingly.

I've found six so far.

The first one was in the vent above my bed. That stupid vent has always bothered me—it's been slightly crooked since the day I moved in. I used to ask Ben to fix it. Told him it gave me the ick. That it looked wrong.

He never did.

But after I came home to new locks and a fresh security system, I laid on my bed, furious at Lucian and glaring up at the ceiling, and that's when I noticed it.

The vent wasn't crooked anymore.

Not only was it perfectly straight, but the two tiny screws on either side were lined up... too perfectly. Like someone took the time to tighten them with exact precision. The thin lines on the screw heads pointed directly up and down. Aligned like clock hands.

Lucian.

It had to be.

He didn't install them because I was with him all day at The Ledger, doing all I could to piss in his espresso. But he was responsible for it.

I know it.

He would probably spank me again if he knew how I got up there to check it. I didn't have a ladder, so I dragged my dresser across the room, set a chair on top of it, and climbed up like some short DIY spy.

And there it was.

A camera. Small. Black. Barely visible.

Pointing directly at my bed.

I should be scared. I should report it. Have someone come in and sweep the place. Rip them out and run.

I should quit. Walk away from this whole twisted, gorgeous mess.

I could. I've paid off my credit cards, redecorated my entire apartment and I'm stockpiling a good savings.

I should walk away.

But I'm not going to.

Because there's a part of me that smiled when I saw it.

A part that *liked* knowing Lucian Vale wants to watch me. Wants to know where I am. Wants to make sure I'm safe—and dirty and his.

I won't admit how many times I've fantasized about him watching me masturbate. How often I've imagined him in his office, hand fisting his cock while I come with a vibrator pressed against my clit.

That's exactly what I thought about three days ago.

Right after I stormed out of his office—sore, humiliated, and so fucking turned on I couldn't think straight.

I knew what I wanted.

And I *knew* he would be watching.

So, I gave him something to obsess over.

I spread my legs wide. Teased myself.

Came for him.

Then I licked the vibrator afterward like a lollipop made of desire while I looked right at that fucking camera.

Because if he's going to invade my space, I'm going to make damn sure he regrets it.

Or maybe... maybe he'll beg for more.

The truth?

I *want* him to watch me. I *want* him to taste me.

His brooding, controlling mouth between my thighs. That wicked tongue making me cry out his name.

It's all I can think about.

That—and how it'll feel when Lucian finally stops playing and fucks me into oblivion.

That's the fantasy playing out in my head this morning as I scroll through client profiles, not even seeing them.

Me, straddling Lucian Vale in his office chair—riding him like my life depends on it. His head tipped back, eyes squeezed shut, a low growl rumbling in his throat as my hips slam down again and again. His hands gripping me hard, dragging me closer, guiding every movement.

Fucking me like he owns me.

Like I'm *his*.

My thighs squeeze together under the desk, and I try not to squirm, caught in the spiral, chasing the heat behind my ribcage and the tension between my legs. I don't even realize someone's standing in front of me until I hear the sharp *snap* of fingers.

"Office. Let's go."

I blink up and my fantasy shatters because Lucian is right in front of me.

Startling me with a single word and a flick of his hand. He's already walking away, his broad shoulders cutting through the air with the same deliberate intensity that lingers in every part of him—even when he's not touching me.

I scramble to my feet, nearly knocking my chair over in the process, jogging to catch up to him.

He doesn't look back.

He doesn't *need* to.

My pulse races, my stomach tightens. And when I get close enough to breathe him in—that familiar blend of sharp spice, coffee, and expensive sin—I nearly *groan*.

God, I *missed* this.

Missed *him*.

Even if he drives me insane.

Even if I want to scream every time he pretends like nothing's happening between us.

But the moment we step into his office, the world narrows.

The noise fades.

The Ledger disappears behind the heavy door that clicks shut behind me, sealing us inside.

It's just us.

Only *us*.

I walk forward slowly, but the confidence I usually challenge him with falters under his silence.

Lucian moves around the desk, calm and unreadable. Like the judge of hell deciding whether to tempt or punish.

I have no idea what to say.

No idea what *he's* thinking.

And for the first time in days, I don't feel like the one holding the leash.

Will he say anything?

Will he acknowledge what he did? That he bent me over his desk and made my ass sore for two days? That he *watched* me lick my own pussy off that vibrator like a goddamn dessert and did nothing about it?

Act like none of it happened?

Jesus. Something is wrong with me.

I stand there, pulse thudding in my throat, waiting for something—anything—but all I get is:

"Come over here."

His voice is cool. Commanding. Like we're back to business, like he hasn't seen every inch of me in exquisite, trembling detail.

He slides his office phone closer and presses the speaker button.

One hand braces the desk, the other dials. It rings once. Twice. Then someone answers.

Lucian launches into a pitch—clean, polished, professional. He needs a new supplier for a high-end restaurant uptown. One of those elite places perched at the top of a skyscraper, spinning ever so slowly to give patrons a 360-degree view of the city.

It's the kind of place where you need a tuxedo to blink in the direction of a reservation. Booked a year in advance. Dress code stricter than airport security.

He barely finishes his first sentence before the other end cuts him off with a curt, "No thank you," and hangs up.

His jaw ticks.

Apparently, this isn't the first time.

He slowly removes his hand from the desk, turning to look at me.

"You catch all that?"

His steel-gray eyes pin me to the spot. I feel warm instantly. Like heat is blooming in my chest and rolling downward with dangerous speed.

"Yes, sir."

The words slip out before I can stop them. Reflexive. Instinctual.

His mouth twitches—just barely. Not a smile. Not quite. But something dangerous glints behind his eyes.

He slides a folder across the desk toward me.

"Here's a list. The restaurant info. Find a supplier."

Then he stands—slowly, deliberately—pulling out his leather desk chair and stepping aside. Waiting.

I blink at him. Once. Twice.

I don't move immediately. Not because I don't understand the task. But because I *do*. And I'm not sure if this is just another job or some kind of silent punishment—or worse, a reward.

Eventually, I cross the room.

My hand brushes the back of the chair as I lower into it, his scent clinging to the leather, wrapping around me. That same stormy cologne that makes me want to close my eyes and forget myself.

But I don't.

I keep my face neutral. My spine straight. My fingers grip the folder, and I focus.

At least on the surface.

Because inside?

I'm already unraveling.

The first three vendors are a bust.

Each time I mention the restaurant, the tone changes. The warmth in their voice dies. Some stall. Others go silent for a moment too long before scrambling for an excuse.

And when I mention it's on behalf of *Lucian Vale*?

They practically trip over themselves to get off the phone.

Something is going on.

It's not just about exclusivity or high standards. These people are *nervous*. Like they've been warned.

Like they've been *threatened*.

I sit back, frowning slightly. The rejection stings less than the growing realization that something is wrong. That whatever Lucian's been dealing with for the last three days —whatever kept him away—is bleeding into everything.

I want to ask.

Where he's been.

Who he's been with.

If he was with someone else.

If watching me come undone on his camera made him snap... and he spent the next three nights fucking one of The Ledger's more experienced companions just to burn it off.

The thought makes my stomach turn.

God. What the fuck is *wrong* with me?

This isn't real. He's not mine. I'm not his. This entire arrangement is a game I agreed to play.

And right now, these vendors are playing a game of keep-away.

So, I decide to change the rules a little.

I pull out my phone and do a quick search—details about the restaurant, the executive chef, upcoming press events.

An idea forms.

I dial the fourth number and put on my best composed voice.

"I'm calling about an emergency vendor change for *La Tour du Ciel*," I say smoothly, using the restaurant's full name. "You may already be aware, but renowned Chef Alessandra Lin is in pursuit of her third Michelin star."

Across the room, Lucian perks up from where he's sitting in the leather chair, a file in hand. I don't look at him. Just keep going.

"Several of the world's most prestigious critics are set to dine at the restaurant any moment now, and unfortunately, our current vendor is experiencing a major recall due to contamination at one of their storage facilities. We're looking for someone who can step in immediately with high-quality product."

There's a beat of silence, and then the person on the other end practically *lights up*.

"Oh—we would be honored. I had no idea Chef Lin was pushing for a third star. Absolutely. We can adjust our delivery schedules. Send over your kitchen manager's details and we'll start the onboarding process today."

Bingo.

I smile, letting out a polite, professional laugh. "You're a lifesaver. I'll have my manager get in touch shortly."

Click.

"Done." I say in an overly chipper tone because I am quite pleased with myself.

When I look up, Lucian's watching me.

Not just watching—*studying*. His head tilted slightly, brows raised, mouth curled at the corners in what might be the closest thing to *impressed* I've seen from him.

"Crisis management tactic?" he asks, his voice like silk.

"Something like that," I reply, coy.

He nods once, slow and deliberate, his gaze lingering a little too long before he looks away.

But I see it.

The spark in his eye.

The slow simmer of heat behind that cool exterior.

And just like that, the power shifts again—tilting, dancing between us like a match waiting to be struck.

Chapter 25

Lucian

It starts small.

A few liquor suppliers backing out of pending shipments. Nothing earth-shattering. Just enough to raise an eyebrow.

Then a couple of restaurant clients delay signing their renewal contracts. They ask for more time. Reassurance. Promises. Empty words I've never had to give before.

I don't panic.

I watch. I listen.

Because when things fall apart, they never do it all at once. First, there's a wobble. Then a crack. Then the foundation buckles.

By day three, the ground starts to shift.

Two of my major suppliers pull the plug. No explanation. No apology. Just a call from their legal departments and a sharp, impersonal goodbye.

I make calls—quiet ones. Push through backchannels and old debts. No one wants to say what I already know.

One of my clubs in SoHo goes dark for the night. A shipment was "delayed." The excuse is sloppy, the lie obvious.

And now?

The Masquerade is running low on premium stock.

That gets my attention.

The Masq doesn't *run out* of anything. Especially not the high-end inventory. That floor runs like a machine—flawless, indulgent, and silent.

But the cracks are forming there too.

So I strategize.

I don't flinch. I don't bark. I start moving pieces. Calling in favors. Securing secondary suppliers. Old contacts I haven't spoken to in years suddenly find themselves back in my orbit.

Because my empire won't crumble.

Not while I still draw breath.

But deep down, I know what this is.

This is Lorenzo tightening the noose. Cutting me off at the knees without ever stepping into the ring.

No threats. Mateo was an example to the others.

Lorenzo is sitting back now with nothing but silence surrounding him—and the slow, deliberate collapse of my support.

He's isolating me.

Trying to see how far he can push before I break.

But he should know better.

I wasn't mafia royalty like him—handed an empire, born to rule it with Daddy's blessing and an army of yes-men at his back.

No.

I was an eight year old boy who watched his father swallow a bullet to pay back a debt.

A boy that served in the mafia's ranks, until the little prince got scared the empire would be given to me, instead of him.

But I didn't want that. I left. Left Lorenzo to his inheritance and built my own empire

One built from blood and grit.

I clawed my way up with broken knuckles and broken rules.

And I'll survive *him*.

I just have to make sure the city survives *us*.

Across the room, Sienna's perched at my desk like she's always belonged there—phone in one hand, notes in the other, her brow furrowed in that determined way that makes her look equal parts dangerous and divine.

Whatever magic she's working...it's effective.

She doesn't use my name. Doesn't mention The Ledger. Just plays it smart—saying the right things, pitching new angles, turning vendors who had already said no into eager saviors desperate to be part of the story she's spinning.

It's impressive as hell.

In one hour, she's done what took me three days and a half bottle of whiskey.

By the time she hangs up the last call, my network of clubs and restaurants is back on its feet. Product en route. Deliveries secured. Inventory stocked for at least another week.

I didn't give her The Masquerade.

That bubble still needs to hold.

She hasn't connected me to the Devil who stalks the top floors of that club yet—and I want to keep it that way. I want to see how long she'll look into his eyes and still not realize they're mine.

For now, the other locations will over-order and funnel stock to The Masq quietly.

Let Lorenzo think the cracks are elsewhere.

Let him think I'm bleeding out from a dozen little wounds, not realizing where I'm actually holding the line.

As she works, so do I.

I tap open my phone and send a quick message to Killian.

LUCIAN: How's Sera?

The reply is fast.

KILLIAN: Healing. Pissed. Ready to start killing people.

KILLIAN: Same as the rest of us. When do we hit back?

I stare at the message for a moment. Then type:

LUCIAN: Tonight.

My thumb hovers over the screen for just a moment before I hit send.

Because I know Lorenzo.

I know what makes him tick. What makes him reckless. And what makes him *vulnerable*.

Loyalty.

Not just the kind his men have for him—the kind he demands from everyone else. Absolute. Blind. Unquestioning. It's his pride and his flaw, wrapped in one. The very thing he leans on... and the very thing I can use to break him.

Because loyalty makes a man predictable.

And predictability? That's leverage.

Most of his biggest shipments still run through the waterfront—guns, drugs, cash—moved in silence through rotting docks and dark corners. Guarded by men who are well-paid and well-armed but not half as careful as they should be.

I forward Killian everything.

The location.

The schedule.

The order.

Intercept the shipment, burn the drugs, destroy the weapons.

Leave nothing.

It'll cost him millions. A direct hit to the gut of his operation. But I'm not after his wallet.

Money can be replaced.

Power? Reputation?

Those bleed slowly. Painfully. Publicly.

As the text sends, I glance toward the window, the skyline cutting sharp through the dusk.

LUCIAN: Leave a bottle behind.

Not just any bottle. *Our* bottle.

The same whiskey I brought to his warehouse when I tried to end this before it began. The peace offering he shattered like it meant nothing.

Let's see if he recognizes it now.

If he understands what it means when the message is returned.

This is still his final chance.

Because whether I want this war or not...

One thing is certain.

I'm not going to lose it.

With the messy business handled—orders given, fire set to rise—I shift my focus back to something far more dangerous.

My little rabbit.

Or rather, my Angel.

It's been days since I touched her. Since I corrected her. Since I watched her pant beneath my hand and bite back a moan like she could fight the need clawing at her throat.

I shouldn't be the one training her. I knew that the moment I saw her. I should've passed her file off, let someone else shape her.

But then I saw the way the other men looked at her. That mixer—those hands reaching, those gazes lingering—was all it took.

She's mine to mold.

Mine to command.

Mine to ruin, if I choose.

Tonight, her lesson is different.

Less about rules. More about power. The kind that

doesn't come from spoken commands, but from silence, structure, presence.

She steps out of the bathroom, freshly touched up. I don't speak—just motion her forward from my place in the leather armchair. Sleeves rolled, legs spread, watching her in contemplation.

"Bring me a whiskey," I say simply.

She obeys without hesitation, crossing the office to pour a glass. Two fingers. Two cubes. No more, no less. Her hands are steady, but her breathing isn't.

I take the glass and watch her. "The men who hold these contracts... they crave control. What they're buying is submission."

She swallows hard, her throat bobbing with the motion. I track it like a fucking predator.

My eyes stay on hers as I take a slow sip. I lick the whiskey from my lower lip, and her gaze drops to my mouth. Predictable.

She wants more.

She always does.

I set the glass aside. "Come here."

She steps forward, cautious but curious. The last correction clearly did its job, but I know her—know her bratty little fire only simmers beneath the surface.

"Give me your foot."

She blinks. "Why?"

I don't answer. Just raise an eyebrow and hold out my hand.

She sighs, placing one palm on my shoulder for balance

as she lifts her heel. I slip it off carefully and set it beside my chair.

"The other."

No protest this time. The second shoe joins the first, and I lean back again, the picture of ease.

"On your knees."

She gasps.

I want to see her lips around my thumb, her mouth worshipping anything I give her. But this isn't about what I want.

Not yet.

"Knees," I repeat, voice low. I tap the spot two feet in front of me. "Right there, Angel."

She lowers herself slowly, wary. Uncertain.

"Sit back on your heels. Relax."

That earns me a snort and a roll of her eyes.

My palm twitches. The brat is back.

"Knees apart, Angel." The nickname makes her cheeks flush—still so innocent in ways she doesn't even realize.

She slides her knees out, but not far enough. Testing me.

"More."

Her jaw clenches, but she complies. God, I could play this game for hours.

"Hands on your thighs."

She does it, but her posture's off—slouched, shoulders rounded. She's not using her training.

I rise and move behind her.

My hand smooths down her leg, gently widening her thighs the way I want them.

She tenses and tries to relax with a broken exhale.

I brush her long auburn hair to one side, baring the line of her neck. I don't kiss her. I just lean in, speaking close to her ear, my breath warm on her skin.

"Everything about a Ledger Companion is a piece of art. Always on display."

I correct her posture, one hand at her shoulder, the other at the small of her back.

"I'm paying for these round tits," I murmur, letting my hand skim the side of one breast. My thumb teases beneath the curve.

She exhales sharply. "Lucian..."

That voice.

She's wet for me. Her legs part just slightly more.

I don't reward her. Just continue, letting my hand trail from her hip down her thigh—bare today, no stockings.

While I enjoy those stirrups, I like this even more.

Bare skin, soft and warm under my hands.

The hem of her dress rises as I stroke up her thigh again. "Even if they don't touch you... even if you never fuck them... you're still a masterpiece they're paying to enjoy."

I move back to my chair, seated like a king while she kneels, flushed and needy.

Her eyes are blown wide with lust, her cheeks pink, her chest rising with shallow breaths.

I down the rest of my whiskey. "Let's try again."

She stands, finally getting the game. A temptress. A siren in a short dress and no shoes. Her hips sway as she moves.

"Of course," she purrs near my ear as she bends to take the glass.

She returns with fresh whiskey. This time, she holds my gaze as she lowers herself.

"Knees, Angel."

She starts to look down.

"Eyes on me."

Those blue eyes snap back up instantly.

"Good."

She assumes the position again—but not quite right.

Her knees are too close.

The smirk on her lips tells me she knows it.

She's asking for a correction.

Begging for it.

She hands me the whiskey. "Here you go... sir."

The pause is intentional. Calculated.

I take the glass slowly, leaning in.

"Thank you."

Then I slide my hand between her thighs, just my fingertips.

So slow it almost kills me.

She pants, her mouth parted, her eyes half-lidded.

But she does it. She spreads wider.

I keep going until her legs are parted just how I want them—then I pull back.

Like it was nothing.

Like my cock isn't rock hard beneath these slacks.

I take a slow pull of whiskey, savoring the burn. She's finally still—sitting in the quiet with her knees tucked under her, eyes slightly glazed with submission. No twitching. No fidgeting.

She's learning.

Then, quietly, almost offhandedly, I ask, "Will you fuck them?"

A simple question.

Expected, even.

It's the reality of her role, of the contracts she's here to take. And yet it sends a flash of rage straight through me—hot and violent, sitting just under the surface. I keep it buried, locked tight behind a calm exterior. But it's there.

What catches my attention even more is the flicker of shock that flashes across her face before she masks it again. Her voice is smooth, almost indifferent.

"Probably."

A lie.

I remember her orientation form. The hesitant checkboxes. The hesitations Eve noted.

Inexperienced. Curious. Untouched in ways her bratty confidence tries to hide.

I nod once, slow. "I would like the fire turned on."

The shift in subject is subtle, but she registers it quickly. That's one thing about Sienna—she catches things. Even when she pretends not to.

She moves to stand.

"Let me get that for you," she says, voice soaked in honey and sex. Her knee lands between my thighs on the cushion, one hand bracing behind me on the chair.

She reaches across for the remote, her leg pressing into my cock as she leans.

That's it, baby.

Those full tits are so close, my mouth waters wanting to know how tight her little brown nipples are.

My jaw flexes, but I remain still.

The fire roars to life behind her, blue flame dancing behind glass as she settles back on the floor like a fucking goddess returning to her throne. Still kneeling. Still wrong.

I eye her legs and click my tongue. "This won't do."

I set the whiskey aside and slide to the edge of my chair.

She's quiet—watching me.

Waiting.

One hand strokes along her jaw, tender. The other travels lower. Her breath hitches, eyes shining with anticipation.

But she's still missing the point.

"The art of seduction," I murmur, as if reading from a script only she and I understand.

"You've been a bad girl, Sienna."

She gasps as my hand strokes lower between her legs.

"You've let me seduce you, Angel."

I reach her panties, touch featherlight over the fabric. Her eyes flutter shut when my fingers slide down the length of her pussy.

"Look at you," I whisper. "Soaked for me."

Her lips part. Her eyes open again, heavy with lust, pleading without words. She wants me to slip under the lace. To really feel her.

But I can't.

Because if I touch her bare?

I won't stop.

I lean in closer, my lips barely an inch from hers. Her eyes close, expecting a kiss.

"Eyes on me, Angel."

She opens them instantly.

My fingers slide up again, teasing the same maddening pattern. Down. Up. A promise. A denial.

She's practically trembling. I can feel it in her thighs.

"You'd let me fuck you right now," I murmur.

It's not a question. It's a fact.

"Your contracts will try to take everything from you. Every inch. Every sound. Every drop of cum you have to give."

I press more firmly against her clit through the thin fabric, grinding slow circles with my fingers.

"They'll milk you for it, Angel."

She moans softly, legs spreading wider, the sound of desperation caught in her throat.

"But you..." My voice dips lower. "You must always be the one who seduces. The one who lets them think they're in control."

I lean in, mouth grazing hers without ever touching. "You must always remain in control."

She nods, wild with need. "Yes," she pants.

Two more strokes. Slow. Precise.

Then I pull away.

Just like that.

"Good," I say, reaching for my whiskey. "You're dismissed."

Her breath is uneven. Her hands tremble. Her eyes flicker between rage and need—warring inside her the same way they're tearing through me.

But then, just like that, the heat turns.

All that want ignites into fire.

She gets up with a sharp huff, snatching her heels from beside the chair. She doesn't even bother putting them back on—just clutches them in one hand like a weapon.

Her steps are silent on the carpet, but the fury radiating from her is loud.

She reaches the door. Flings it open. Doesn't look back.

And she doesn't close it, either.

It swings there behind her like a challenge.

I lift my glass and take a slow sip of whiskey, the burn sliding down my throat like victory.

Because I know exactly where she's going.

And exactly who she'll run to.

She can claw and kick and scream all she wants.

But in the end?

She'll always find her way back to me.

Me... or the Devil. But either way, it's me.

Chapter 26

Sienna

et him watch.

Let Lucian sit in his cold, perfect office with his whiskey glass and his walls of control, watching me through every hidden camera he placed in my apartment. Let him trace my path across the city, the chip beneath my nail pulsing with every step. I wanted it there.

Let him track every move I make—because tonight, I'm making one he won't forget.

He's the one who pushed me to this.

And I hope he's watching.

I step into *The Masquerade* without hesitation. The air inside hums with energy—dark, decadent, alive with whispered promises and unsaid things. The lights are low, the music deeper here. Everything pulses like a living, breathing body that thrives on sin.

Tonight, I'm not wandering. I know exactly what I came for.

I only want two men.

Lucian.

Or the Devil.

Lucian won't touch me—won't break his own rules, no matter how desperately I want him to.

But the Devil? The Devil watches me like I'm something he's already claimed. And maybe that's the difference. Lucian trains me. The Devil wants to ruin me.

So if Lucian won't give me what I need, maybe *he* will.

Inside the locker room reserved for Companions, I find what I need: the black rabbit mask that's become second skin at this place.

I pull it over my face, then strip off the simple black mini dress I wore here, revealing what I chose to wear underneath.

A sheer black gown clings to every inch of my skin like water. There's no lining, no bra—just black lace panties. My breasts are fully visible through the fabric, nipples already tight from the cool air and what I know I'm about to do. I step out of my heels and hand them off to the attendant.

I want to be barefoot.

Grounded.

Ready.

And then I ascend.

Floor after floor slips past me like levels of some sinful video game. I don't stop on *Lust*. I don't pause for *Gluttony*. I don't even breathe when I pass *Wrath*.

Because I'm not here for them.

I'm going to the top.

The Devil's Playground.

When the doors open, the world slows.

It's quieter up here. Still. Like the air itself knows to behave.

The lighting is dim but warm, flickering from sconces mounted against black stone walls. There's no music. No moans. No chaos like on the lower levels. This floor isn't about indulgence. It's about power. And every inch of it leads to the man who commands it.

The Devil.

He sits on a throne of black leather and brushed steel at the far end of the room, backlit by shadows and firelight. He wears only black pants, his broad chest bare, every tattoo more sin than ink.

His mask—smooth, angular, cut like horns—is the only thing hiding him. Like the sheer magnitude of his presence could ever be hidden beneath anything.

My pulse stutters.

And then accelerates.

He sees me instantly.

And he doesn't move.

Just raises a hand.

One simple flick of his fingers.

Come.

And I do.

My body moves without hesitation, hips swaying, nerves electric, but my steps sure. When I reach the edge of the throne platform, I don't speak.

I kneel.

Right there at his feet.

Back straight. Knees parted. Hands resting on my thighs.

Exactly the way Lucian trained me.

Exactly the way the Devil seems to like.

I don't dare look away. And he doesn't blink.

The room falls away, leaving only this—the heat of his gaze and the thrum in my core that says I've never been more certain of anything in my life.

I came here to be claimed.

And I know the Devil wants to be the one to do it.

He doesn't speak right away.

He watches me.

That mask—dark, smooth, dangerous—gives nothing away. But I feel his eyes. The weight of them. Curious. Amused. And something else entirely. Something that makes my pulse flutter like wings in my chest.

"The little bunny returns," he says at last, his voice the sound of leather sliding over steel—smooth and slow with an edge that cuts right through me.

I stay perfectly still, spine straight, gaze steady behind my mask. I won't let him see how hard I'm breathing.

"Have you figured out what you're looking for, little one?"

I nod.

A single, precise motion.

He lets the silence stretch, testing me with the absence of sound, with the weight of anticipation. Then:

"And what is that?"

My voice is soft but clear. "Someone to tell a secret to."

His lips twitch in a faint, dark smirk.

But it's gone just as quickly as it came.

He doesn't ask what the secret is. Instead, he reaches out, and with effortless strength, pulls me into his lap.

His hands wrap around my hips, guiding me easily until I'm straddling one of his thick, muscled thighs. The sheer fabric of my dress catches on his pants as I move, riding up until the lace of my panties meets the hard, unforgiving leather of his leg.

I inhale sharply because it's not just leather I'm straddling.

He's got a silicon grinder fixed around his thigh. Deep red covered in black. It's like a cluster of tentacles.

His hands settle beneath the hem of my dress. Warm. Possessive. Palming the bare curve of my ass like he owns it.

"Tell me your secret, little rabbit," he whispers, his mouth close to my ear now, the sound like a dark promise.

I roll my hips slowly, dragging the heat of my pussy along the ribbing of the grinder.

My breath stutters, and I feel his fingers grip tighter. He holds me still, forcing me to feel every groove. Every shift of muscle. Every deliberate flex beneath me.

I turn my head into him. My lips grazing his ear. My voice a whisper.

"No one has ever licked my cunt before."

Everything about him tightens.

His jaw. His thigh. His grip on my skin.

The air around us shifts—heavier now. Hungrier.

He doesn't say a word, but I feel it in the way he breathes. In the dangerous stillness of his body. Like a predator deciding whether to devour his prey here and now, or let the hunger stretch longer.

I roll my hips again, slowly—an invitation, a dare.

The friction is exquisite, the rough grain of the grinder

dragging perfectly against the thin lace between my legs. My clit throbs, and I can't help the way my back arches, my head falling back slightly as I ride the thick muscled thigh beneath me.

The Devil's fingers slide higher. Not rough, not rushed.

Reverent.

Possessive.

"Mmm, little rabbit..." His voice is low, dark silk wrapping around my ears. "That's a dangerous secret to tell."

One of his hands slips away from my hip, trailing down —slow and unhurried. His fingers dip between my thighs, brushing the soaked lace clinging to my heat.

Then, rough knuckles drag across my bare clit as he pushes the fabric aside.

A gasp tears from my lips.

He growls low in his throat, primal and pleased. "You're drenched," he murmurs, voice like smoke and sin. "My little rabbit, sitting all pretty on the Devil's lap... soaking through your panties like this."

I tremble when his fingers glide lower, slipping between the slick folds of my pussy—just once—before retreating. He pulls my panties to the side completely, then guides my hips back down. My bare cunt presses flush against the ribbing of the grinder.

"Fuck," I whisper, breath catching.

Both his hands return to my hips, heavy and demanding. He grips me, guiding my motion. Forward. Back. Slow. Deliberate. Every movement a study in patience and torment.

He's feasting on my reactions.

"Have you come to make a deal with the Devil?" he asks, his voice a decadent purr in my ear.

"Yes," I pant, keeping the rhythm, grinding harder against the thick muscle of his thigh. My clit is throbbing, dragging over the rough texture of the silicon strapped. To him. I'm already climbing fast. Too fast.

"You want my tongue on your needy little pussy, rabbit?"

A whimper escapes me as he leans in, sniffing slowly up the curve of my neck. His breath is hot, his teeth grazing skin, not quite biting.

"Yes." It's a moan. A confession. A prayer.

"What do you have to give the devil in return?"

I hesitate—only a fraction of a second—but he feels it. Sees it in the twitch of my breath, the flutter of my lashes. I try to play it cool, to mask the sharp flicker of panic.

"What do you want?" I ask, grinding harder. Faster. Desperate for the friction. For the release Lucian has denied me again and again.

His answer is a lash wrapped in velvet. "Your trust."

I falter—just slightly—but he doesn't let me slow. His hands return to my hips, urging me forward and back. Thrusting me against him with a rhythm that's turning me inside out.

"Trust is the only thing that matters in my domain," he says, and I can barely hear him through the rush of blood in my ears. "It's more valuable than diamonds. More coveted than power. The ones who give it carelessly?" His hands tighten. "They never survive this place."

My hands clutch his shoulders as my body trembles

with the force of pleasure building inside me. I'm going to come. I can feel it—burning and bright, curling up my spine.

He wraps one strong arm around my waist, the other bracing across my shoulders. His grip is unyielding, his control complete. Every roll of my hips is now at his pace—harder, deeper, rougher.

My eyes lock on his.

I don't look away. Not once.

Even as I unravel.

Even as I lose myself.

And just before I tip over the edge, his voice drips like molten gold into my ear. "Give me your trust, little rabbit... and I'll feast on your greedy cunt until you beg me to stop."

The deal.

The final offer.

"Yes!" I cry out, the word ripped from my throat—desperate and raw—just as my orgasm slams through me.

White-hot and blinding.

My whole body clenches. My legs quake. My voice breaks as I shatter, trembling in his grasp while he holds me together through the storm.

And when the wave finally crashes and I slump against him, chest heaving, I know...

I've just given the Devil more than I meant to.

And he's going to collect.

She shatters in my arms.

Right there on my lap—shaking, panting, her mouth parted in a silent cry. Her entire body trembles as the orgasm collides through her, and I hold her through every second of it.

Every pulse.

Every twitch.

Every greedy little grind of her hips as she rides it out on my thigh like a good girl in heat.

It's beautiful.

And dangerous.

And *mine*.

But just as her breathing starts to slow, just as her lashes flutter and her eyes begin to lift to mine—

Blue lights flood the room.

Security breach.

My head snaps up, and immediately I know—it's not a false alarm. It never is.

A half-dozen of my security personnel pour in through the far side of the Devil's Playground, guns at the ready, eyes scanning.

Sienna stiffens in my lap, startled, her head whipping toward the sudden movement. I don't let her go. My arm locks around her waist, holding her tight as I rise smoothly to my feet, taking her with me.

Her bare thighs slide down the leather of my pants until her feet hit the floor.

She wobbles. I steady her, ripping the grinder from my leg and dropping it to my seat.

"Jacket." The order snaps from my mouth before I even register saying it.

One of my guards peels off his coat without hesitation—a heavy black tactical jacket with SECURITY printed across the back in bold white block letters. I take it and wrap it around her shoulders.

It drowns her.

Swallows her whole.

And it smells like *him*.

That part makes my jaw clench.

But I don't have time to fix it. I don't have time to fix anything.

"Get her out of here," I say, voice flat and deadly.

"Wait—" she starts, turning to me, eyes wide.

I don't wait.

"Take her home. My home. Don't let her leave."

Her lips part in protest. She steps forward.

But I'm already turning my back.

Already gone.

The moment the order is given, she's lifted—hauled effortlessly over one of the guard's shoulders like a defiant, furious little siren. Her legs kick, her fists beat against his back, but he doesn't flinch. He doesn't even slow.

And I don't look back.

I disappear into the shadows of the Devil's Playground.

Because whatever this is—this breach, this threat, this flicker of chaos at the edges of my empire—

It needs to be handled.

And she has no idea what she's just started.

But she will.

Soon.

Very, very soon.

The moment the elevator doors shut behind me, I tear off the Devil's mask.

My skin still hums with the feel of her. The slick heat of her soaked panties pressed against my thigh. Her scent clings to me—sweet, sinful, maddening. I'm still throbbing, my jaw clenched tight as the adrenaline simmers beneath the surface.

One of my floor managers is already waiting, arm extended with a clean black button-down and a quiet, watchful expression. He doesn't meet my eye. Smart.

Because I'm in no fucking mood.

I snatch the shirt from him in silence, handing over the mask without a word.

The shift from predator to polished is a familiar one.

Muscle memory takes over as I pull the shirt on and start buttoning—fast, efficient. No tie. I leave the top two undone and roll the sleeves up my forearms.

My fingers are still twitching with residual tension. The only thing I need now is—

"Gun," I say simply.

The manager places the Glock in my open palm without hesitation. I slide it into the back of my slacks, letting the cool metal ground me as I inhale through my nose and center myself.

"Talk," I order, my voice low.

"Surprise inspection," he says quickly. "Fire Marshal. City Health. Maybe twenty inspectors total. They're downstairs now. Flashing badges, asking for paperwork, threatening to shut us down."

Perfect.

My nostrils flare, but I say nothing else as the elevator dings and the doors slide open.

The main floor is chaos wrapped in forced calm. Lights turned up. Music silenced. Security stationed at all exits. Guests being turned away at the door. A full sweep in motion.

And right at the center of it all stands one of the city commissioners. A man I've done business with. A man who's taken his pick of Ledger contracts over the years and enjoyed every luxury I've afforded him.

Tonight, he's not smiling.

He steps forward slowly, extending a familiar object in his hand—a bottle of whiskey.

Not just any bottle.

My bottle.

The seal is broken. A rag shoved down the neck and into the amber liquid like a makeshift Molotov.

A threat.

A warning.

A declaration of war.

I take it from him, rotating the bottle in my hand as I examine it.

The weight of it is familiar. The message even more so.

This is Lorenzo's way of making sure I know: he's ready to burn everything down. Even *The Masquerade.*

"Looks like you've got some problems, Vale," the commissioner says, too calm.

I don't blink. Don't even let my smile falter.

"I'll handle it."

With deliberate ease, I walk past him to the bar. Then— without ceremony—I throw the bottle into the nearby steel trash can.

Glass shatters. The rag flutters like a white flag scorched in gasoline.

The commissioner flinches.

"Getting a little jumpy, aren't we?" I murmur.

He goes stiff, jaw tightening. Then his hand dips toward the inside of his jacket.

My gun is drawn in a blink.

The barrel is pressed to his forehead before he even realizes I've moved.

Everyone freezes.

He lifts his hands immediately, palms open. "Lucian—"

"You so much as twitch wrong," I growl, "and I'll paint this fucking floor with your brains."

Slowly, his hand retreats, emerging with nothing more than an envelope. Pale yellow. Crumpled edges.

A summons.

"To deliver it personally," he says, trying for composure.

I snatch the paper from him, then lower the gun—but not all the way.

A court order.

A formal investigation into the legality of *The Masquerade's operations*.

Accusations of violating public decency codes.

Obscenity laws.

Operating an unlicensed adult entertainment venue in direct conflict with zoning ordinances.

A hearing date—soon.

They're not coming for *The Ledger*.

Not yet.

They're trying to drag me into the light.

Force my hand.

Pull me out of the shadows where I rule.

Big mistake.

I tuck the Glock back into my waistband, then glance over my shoulder at him.

"You forget which side of neutral you're standing on, and I'll be quick to remind you."

He doesn't reply. He can't.

Because the room's already moved on.

Because I already have.

I've got a war to fight.

A city to defend.

And one stubborn, seductive little rabbit waiting at my home—

A home she has *no* idea she's about to be caged in.

I've been kidnapped by a sadistic sex god in a mask.

Okay, maybe that's dramatic. Technically, I walked into the Masquerade on my own.

Technically, I knelt in front of the Devil on purpose. But the part where I was thrown over the shoulder of a security guard like a duffel bag? That was not voluntary.

The moment the doors closed behind him, the guard carried me down ten flights like I weighed nothing and tossed me into the backseat of a matte-black SUV with windows so dark I couldn't see a damn thing. No explanation. No instructions.

Just slammed the door shut and disappeared.

I didn't bother asking questions. No one answered me the first three times I tried.

At a red light, I reached for the handle, a surge of rebellion in my veins...until I remembered I was barefoot, wearing a sheer nightie with no bra. Not exactly ideal attire for a dramatic escape through Manhattan.

So, I stayed put. Stewed. Simmered.

And thirty minutes later, the car turned into a gated driveway so long I couldn't see the house until it crested into view. A sprawling, single-story estate appeared like something out of Architectural Digest—dark slate exterior, rich wood accents, sharp lines and clean elegance that made my breath hitch.

Modern. Minimalist. Masculine.

The Devil's house.

The driver finally opened the door, barely looking at me. "Go inside. The door's open."

Then he shut it behind me, and a loud beep followed by the click of a lock echoed behind my back.

I spun and yanked on the handle. Nothing.

The door was locked. From the outside.

I'm stuck here. Trapped. In someone's fortress, dressed like a fantasy and completely alone.

My voice carries down the empty entryway. "Hello?"

Silence.

I try another door. Locked.

Another. Locked.

One opens—just a crack—and reveals a pristine garage with three sleek cars inside. Midnight black, blood red, gunmetal gray. They gleam under soft overhead lights like predators resting before the next hunt.

The rest of the house is eerily quiet. No music. No ticking clock. No signs of life.

I find a bathroom. Freshen up. Splash cold water on my face and fix the smudged liner under my eyes.

The kitchen is stocked—everything arranged with

meticulous precision I would expect from him. I grab a bottle of water, cracking the cap as I wander further down the hallway near the garage.

That's when I see the last door.

It's different from the others. Thicker. Heavier.

I hesitate for a second before reaching for the handle.

It's unlocked.

And the second it swings open, I gasp—because I know exactly what I've found.

The Devil's den.

His personal pleasure room.

The air inside is warmer, thicker. Heavy with the scent of leather and something darker beneath it—smoke, spice, and power. It clings to my skin the moment I step inside.

The room is stunning. Every inch of it curated. Designed. Owned.

To the right, a four-poster bed draped in jet-black sheets. The posts are thick and sturdy, with discreet cuffs hanging from the corners.

Directly across from it is a Saint Andrew's cross, polished and menacing. Shelves line one wall, holding coils of rope in every color imaginable—some thick and braided, others thin and delicate like silk thread.

There's a bench. A sling. A swing suspended from the ceiling.

It's not decoration.

It's used. Maintained. Loved.

I feel it in the air. The energy of dominance and submission lingering like a scent. Like a memory.

A mirror covers the ceiling above the bed. Of course, it does.

This isn't just a room. It's a stage.

A place to perform. To be worshipped. To be broken.

My body flushes hot.

I don't know what I was expecting, but it wasn't... this.

I wander toward the bed, fingertips grazing the soft bedding. My skin tingles with every step.

It feels wrong to be in here without him.

And yet, I can't bring myself to leave.

Because this room tells me exactly what he is.

What he wants.

And something deep inside me—something dark and desperate—wants it too.

A voice slides through the room like silk-draped steel, dark and rich and laced with a wicked edge.

"I like seeing my prey wander around my toys."

I spin around, startled, my bare feet hitting the polished wood with a quiet thud. My eyes scan the room, but there's no one there—only the echo of his voice drifting down from the recessed speakers in the ceiling.

It's him.

The Devil.

"Why *am* I here?" I demand, my voice stronger than I expect it to be. "Why bring me here just to leave me alone?"

"Because we made a deal," he replies, smooth and certain, like he's been waiting for me to ask.

"A deal based on trust," I shoot back. "And it's hard to trust someone who locks me in their house."

A low, rich chuckle rolls over me like thunderclouds

gathering above the horizon. It settles in my chest. Between my thighs. Everywhere.

"You're not locked in, little rabbit."

I blink.

"You have a choice," he says, casually amused, like this is the simplest thing in the world. "The SUV is still parked outside. The front door is unlocked. Open it, and you'll be taken home. No consequences. No questions."

There's a beat of silence, heavy with tension. I hear the low, growling hum of a motorcycle engine cutting through the city.

He's coming.

"Or..." His voice dips, hungry and dark. "You can stay. I'll be there in ten minutes."

The air thickens as he continues, his voice lowering to a velvet command.

"When I arrive, I want you naked. Blindfold on. Strapped to the cross in my playroom."

That's it.

No further instructions. No coaxing. No promises of pleasure or safety.

Just an invitation.

And then silence.

My heart kicks into a sprint.

He's racing to me.

I walk to the front door with trembling legs, reaching for the handle. It gives under my palm, not locked like it had been a moment ago. I crack it open, just enough to see the car waiting in the long driveway. Its black matte paint absorbing the faint glow of the house lights.

Freedom is right there.

All I have to do is step through.

But my feet won't move.

Because I asked for this. I chased him down. I begged the Devil to feast on me—and now he's coming. All I have to do is trust him.

Just like the painting from the gallery. The one with the man gripping the woman's throat—possessive, protective, dark.

Trust.

I wave the driver off and close the door slowly, staring at the handle. Then I reach down and slide my panties off, the thin scrap of black lace damp from arousal.

With a smile that's half defiance, half invitation, I hook them around the doorknob like a flag. A message.

I'm still here.

I make my way back through the dark house, down the hallway to the room I was so captivated by only moments ago.

The door closes behind me with a soft snap, and I let the sheer nightgown fall from my shoulders. It flutters to the floor like smoke as I approach the cross.

It looks more imposing now.

Its wide base. The arms stretched just above my head. A monument of submission, carved from wood and metal and dark promise.

"I'll feast on your greedy cunt until you beg me to stop."

His voice still echoes in my mind.

Before I can talk myself out of this—before fear can take

root—I grab a blindfold. One of many hanging from the wall.

Turning around, I put the cross behind me. I bend down and slip my ankles into the thick leather cuffs, securing each one with care.

They lock in with a heavy click.

It's not lost on me that I've been here before. Not physically. But that first night at the Masquerade—when I walked in and saw the woman bound to the cross, body arched in ecstasy—I wanted it.

I wanted this.

And now, I'm here.

I smile, breathless and nervous and buzzing with adrenaline.

I fix the blindfold around my head, not quite on just yet.

Reaching up, I slide one wrist into the cuff. When I pull it, the strap cinches tight. My heart races as I look at the other cuff still hanging loose. I know once I slide my wrist into it, I'm locked in. Exposed. At his mercy.

And yet, I don't hesitate.

Pulling the blind over my eyes, the room is instantly dark. I slide my hand into the cuff and give myself to him.

The click of the clasp making me flinch. So final. Ominous.

I'm spread open and strapped to the Devil's cross.

And all I can do now... is wait.

Chapter 29

Lucian

She's here.

Even before I step inside, I can feel her. That electric pull humming in the air, thick and charged, like the moment before a lightning strike.

I kill the engine at the top of the empty driveway, needing the silence to think—but who the fuck am I kidding?

I've done nothing but think about her since I shoved her out of the Masquerade with security and told them to bring her here. Told them not to let her leave.

She was never going to.

But a kernel of doubt lingers. That small chance she took the offer and ran but what stops me dead in my tracks is what's waiting for me on the doorknob.

Her panties.

Black lace. Damp. Still warm from her body and smelling sweet as sin itself.

I take them in my hand and clench them in my fist.

She chose me.

No excuses. No confusion.

She knew exactly what I asked of her.

And she said yes.

The moment I step inside, I feel her presence like gravity. Every room is quiet, still, steeped in that delicious tension of what's about to happen. I don't call out. I don't need to.

Because I know where she is.

I head down the hallway, past the kitchen, toward the room at the end—the one with soundproof walls, a reinforced door, and every temptation a man like me has no business indulging in.

And when I open that door?

Fuck.

There she is.

My angel.

Naked. Bound. Strapped to the cross like a gift waiting to be unwrapped.

Her wrists are locked above her head, her ankles secured wide on the base. Her back is arched just slightly, enough to make her chest rise and fall with each breath. She's trembling. But not from fear.

No, my girl is shaking with need.

I take my time stepping inside, letting the door close behind me with a heavy, echoing finality.

She gasps.

The sound is soft, barely audible, but it shoots straight to my cock.

Her head turns instinctively toward the noise, blindfolded eyes seeking me out even though she can't see a damn thing. Her breathing stutters, chest rising faster now, like her body knows I'm here.

And fuck, I am.

Every inch of me is wound tight, soaking in the sight of her—strapped down, glistening in the low amber light, ready to be ruined. But not yet. First, I want to watch her squirm.

To let her feel my presence like a storm creeping in.

Because the moment I touch her?

There's no going back.

I hang her panties from a small hook on the wall, a trophy already won. Then I start to strip.

Button by button, my shirt falls open and hits the floor on top of her nighty. Every inch I uncover is deliberate. Controlled.

Because tonight?

There will be no games.

Only promises.

And the devil always keeps his.

I don't speak right away. I let the silence weigh between us, thick and pulsing, until I see the subtle tremble of anticipation roll across her bare skin.

"Easy, now. I'm going to take care of you."

With a slow, deliberate press of a button, the cross begins to tilt back, lowering her body into a horizontal position. Her breath catches at the shift in gravity—her back now flush against the leather padding, arms still extended, legs spread wide, completely at my mercy.

"Just trust me, little rabbit." My voice is dark, husky with want.

I step between her thighs, still in black leather pants, unbuttoned now, my cock straining against the confines. I'm hard—aching—and it only grows worse when I see her glistening cunt on display, exposed, wet, and waiting.

My hands move first to her ankles. A soft touch. Gentle. I massage the tension from her calves, kneading the muscles as I move higher. She shifts under my touch, restless and needy, her breath coming quicker.

"It's time you picked a safeword," I murmur, my voice low and rough with control. "One you won't forget."

She's quiet a moment, then whispers, "Diablo."

A grin curls at my mouth. "Fitting."

I lean down and press a kiss to her thigh—hot and lingering. Then another, and another. I nip gently at her skin, licking the faint sting away, tracing the inside of her leg with my tongue as I move up—closer to the sweet heaven between her legs but not there yet. Not quite.

Straightening, I let both hands explore. My thumbs tease the soft skin near her pussy, a subtle promise of what's coming. But I don't touch her there—not yet.

"If you want me to stop, you only need to say it once."

My fingers drag upward, slow and reverent, over her hips, the dip of her waist, the slight tremble of her stomach.

"Answer me, baby."

"Yes." It's instant and full of breath.

My hands reach her breasts and I pause. Cupping her. Squeezing. Pinching her nipples between my thumbs and forefingers until she gasps again—arches for more.

"Yes, sir." I correct her with a gentle pinch, and she yelps her reply. "Yes, sir."

"Good."

My good girl is so eager to please me.

"You're not getting my cock tonight," I tell her, voice like smoke and sin. "Only my mouth. My fingers."

I lean over her, my body pressing down. She can feel the bulge of my erection pressing against her dripping cunt, the hard line of it grinding against her center with each inhale.

"Do you understand, little rabbit?" I whisper against her cheek. "Do you want them? To be my willing whore?"

"Yes, sir." she breathes. Desperate.

"That's it." I reward her honesty with the drag of my tongue along the edge of her breast. Her nipple stiffens immediately, and I circle it with slow, torturous precision. Then I suck. Hard.

She cries out.

Her skin pebbles. She's so fucking responsive—and I haven't even started yet.

I grab the small leather strap from the wall—a short handle with soft black tassels at the end. It's not for pain. Not tonight. It's for *control*. For *anticipation*.

She's already spread out like a feast, naked, her skin flushed and perfect under the low lights. I trail the tassels over her breasts, watching her nipples pebble instantly. Down her stomach, slow and teasing, and her breath catches.

Mmm. Her body's waking up, every nerve tuned to me.

"Are you a virgin?" I ask, even though I already know from her intake form.

She swallows, but before she can answer, I slide two fingers down her pussy—slick, soft, already dripping for me.

I drag them back up, spreading her open with a gentle but possessive parting. Her clit pulses, swollen and exposed.

God, she's fucking beautiful.

"No," she whispers.

I bring the strap down with a quick flick and smack her clit. She yelps, her back arching.

"No, *what*?" I demand, voice low, quiet, but firm.

"No, sir. I'm not a virgin."

"Hm."

I lean down and blow cool air over her hot, needy cunt. She shivers—nearly vibrates with want.

"Who did you give it to, little rabbit?" I murmur.

"B-Ben."

Ben. That fucking name. My jaw clenches. I repeat the motion with my fingers, sliding down her pussy lips, then up again, spreading her just like before, forcing her to feel it all. Keeping her open. Exposed. Mine.

"And were you Ben's whore?" I ask, dragging the tassels across her slit so gently it borders on reverence. She lets out a long, shaky breath at the sensation.

"No, sir."

"And why not?"

I kiss just above her mound, not quite where she wants me. Her hips twitch, her fingers curl into the leather beneath her.

Before she can respond, I open my mouth and suck hard on the dip of her pelvis, tonguing the spot slowly, deliberately. She groans instead of speaking.

I flick her clit again with the strap. "Answer me, rabbit. Why aren't you Ben's whore?"

I shift to her other thigh, pressing kisses down the inside, marking her. Her legs tremble, her body strung tight with need.

"Because…" she gasps, "I'm *your* whore."

Fuck.

That almost undoes me. Almost makes me forget the promise I made—not to fuck her tonight.

Not with my cock.

But I want to.

I want to bury myself so deep inside her she forgets that fucker ever existed.

Instead, I reward her. "That's very good, little rabbit."

I settle between her legs, centered now. Close. I inhale her. Purposefully let my nose graze her slick pussy as I breathe her in. She whimpers.

"Oh my god," she whispers, voice full of awe, realization, need. She knows I'm about to give her something no one else ever has. What she's been so desperate for.

It hits something dark and possessive inside me. That *Ben* got to her first makes my blood boil. He didn't deserve her. Didn't protect her. Didn't worship her the way I will.

Because she's mine now.

I lift my eyes to her face as I lower my mouth. I want to watch her break for me. Want to see the exact moment she loses herself.

My tongue drags slow and deep over her cunt, parting her, tasting her for the first time. Her flavor hits me like a shot—sharp, salty, divine.

And the way she reacts? Fuck.

Her mouth drops open, and she stops breathing for a second—holding it in like if she lets go, she'll shatter.

She's perfect.

I'm going to make her feel every second of this.

I flatten my tongue and lick her again, slower this time. From bottom to top, savoring every inch, every tremble. She tastes like silk and surrender, and I could drown in it.

She jolts in her bonds, head tilting back even though she can't see me.

"Good girl," I murmur against her, letting my breath tease her before I suck her clit into my mouth.

She jerks, her thighs tensing. I hold them down, my hands spreading her wider, keeping her open for me. There's nowhere to hide. Not from my mouth. Not from my praise.

"So fucking sweet," I growl, licking her again, flicking the tip of my tongue over her clit in quick, purposeful strokes. "You were made for this. For *me*."

She gasps, her hips lifting off the bench, but I press her back down. "Ah ah, rabbit. Let me work."

She moans, high and sweet, her hips twitching, but she can't move far. The straps hold her for me. I circle her clit with my tongue, slow and teasing.

"So sweet. So responsive. Just like I knew you'd be."

She gasps as I suck her clit into my mouth. I hum low, letting the sound roll through her. Her knees tremble, but she's locked in place.

"That's it, Angel," I murmur. "Take it for me. Let me taste what's mine."

Her body shivers. The blindfold makes her focus on every wet stroke of my tongue, every breath I exhale against her sensitive skin. Her hands grip the restraints now, fists clenched.

"You want to come, don't you?" I ask, dragging my tongue down to her entrance, gathering her slick and returning to her clit with another firm lick.

"Y-yes, sir. Please," she pants.

I chuckle against her pussy, and the vibration makes her cry out.

Focusing on her clit again I give it to her—sucking, flicking, devouring. She's right there.

"Okay, baby." I feel it in the way her thighs tighten, in the staccato rhythm of her breathing, the desperation in her moans.

"Please, sir."

This woman.

"Give it to me, rabbit," I command. "Show me how pretty you come."

A few more fast flicks of my tongue. One more strong suck—and she shatters.

Her whole body arches off the bench, her mouth falling open in a silent scream. Her thighs quake around my head.

I don't stop.

I keep licking her through it, prolonging her pleasure, making her ride the high until she's gasping, squirming—too much.

Only then do I slow down. I kiss her pussy, soft now, reverent. Like a thank you. Like a claim.

"Perfect," I murmur. "You're fucking perfect."

She's panting. Legs twitching with every aftershock that rolls through her. Her cunt glistens, pink and trembling, still reacting to my mouth like it doesn't know how to come down.

I blow a cool breath across her hot cunt. Then I lick her once more—slow and deep.

She groans loud and wrecked. Music to my ears.

"Tell me, rabbit," I say, my voice low, rough, but calm. "Why didn't he worship you like this?"

She swallows hard behind the blindfold, voice shaking. "He said—he said he wouldn't like the taste."

I go still.

A slow, cold fury uncoils in my chest.

If that asshole made her feel self-conscious—if he ever made her think that her pussy was anything less than the most delicious fucking meal on this earth—I'll beat his smug little face into the fucking floor.

She keeps going, soft and hesitant. "He didn't like it to be... messy."

"No, baby." My tone darkens. I unzip my pants because I can't fucking take it anymore—my cock is throbbing, swollen, angry, and aching for her.

My fist wraps around it instantly.

I spit on her clit, watching her flinch in surprise. It's not a punishment—it's ownership.

Desire. Need.

My other hand spreads her open again, dragging the slick mix of spit and cum across her swollen bundle of nerves.

"I *like* you messy," I rasp.

My thumb circles her clit. Slow. Steady. Controlled chaos.

She gasps, hips twitching in the straps. I stroke myself in time with the motion, every drag of my hand on my cock matching the rhythm of my thumb over her.

She's not done. Not even close.

I tease her entrance with two fingers, watching her squirm and stretch for me—then slide them inside. She's so fucking wet, the sound alone has me biting back a groan.

We both moan.

Her tight little cunt clenches around my fingers and I lose my rhythm for a second. Fuck. I start pumping faster, searching for that spot inside her that'll make her sing for me.

"Fuck, rabbit," I grit out, jaw clenched. "This tight hole is gonna make me come just thinking about fucking you."

"Holy *shit*," she cries, arching as I curl my fingers deep, hitting her just right.

The slick sounds of me finger-fucking her blend with the wet stroke of my palm dragging over my cock. She clenches tighter. Her head rolls. She's gone.

"That's it," I hiss. "Just think about my big cock splitting you open."

She moans loud, nearly desperate.

"Fucking your sinful mouth," I groan, watching her fall apart.

She's close—so fucking close—but I want us to come *together*.

"Taking your ass," I add, circling her clit faster now, changing the rhythm—driving her up, dropping her down, then dragging her back up again.

"I'm—!" she gasps, but I cut her off with my thumb. Precise. Devastating. Her body jerks in the restraints.

"Is that what you want, rabbit?" I pant, voice fraying. "You want the devil to claim *all* your holes? Make you my slut?"

"Yes!" she cries out, panting, trembling.

I growl deep in my chest. I take my cock and slap it against her clit—wet, swollen, sensitive. She whines.

"Bad rabbit," I say, teasing her with the head of my cock, rubbing it along her slit. She grinds her hips in the straps, chasing it, desperate.

"Yes, sir," she mewls, needy and breathless.

"Come on, baby," I strain. I'm right there with her. So fucking close. "I'm gonna paint you in my cum. Show you just how messy I love this dripping cunt."

"Please," she begs—and that's all it takes.

She starts to come again, breaking with a strangled cry, full body shaking, pulling at the leather restraints like she can't take it, like it's too much—but it's never too much for my rabbit.

I watch her fall—and I fall with her.

I groan, deep and raw, as I stroke my climax out. I come hard, shooting onto her clit, still rubbing her as she pulses around my fingers.

Her orgasm crashes through her like a storm. The second one's worse—stronger. Beautiful.

"That's it," I whisper, still working her slowly through it. "Take it. That's my girl. My good little rabbit."

She's trembling. Sobbing. Her head slumped forward on the restraints, breathing ragged.

And all I can think is:

Mine. So. Fucking. Mine.

My mouth is back on her before she even has time to recover.

Licking. Sucking. *Taking.*

My cum, her slick, my spit—it's all mixed together now, coating her, owning her.

And I want more.

She's wrecked and trembling, but her body responds like it's *mine.* Because it is. She gave it to me the second she walked into my world.

I rip another orgasm from her with my mouth, fingers spreading her wide again. She bucks, crying out—*"fuck, fuck, oh my God—please!"* Her voice breaks on a moan, cursing, praising, begging... for what, she doesn't even know.

But I do.

She wants to *be taken.* To belong to the devil. To be *mine.*

As soon as her third orgasm ebbs away, I lift myself and cover her body with mine, chest to chest, hips flush. My cock presses hard between us, not inside, not yet—but *fuck,* I could bury myself in her right now.

I just came, but my cock doesn't care. I could fuck her all night and still never get enough.

But she's going to wait.

I'm going to make her crave it. *Beg* for it.

Then I do something I really shouldn't fucking do. But I'm going to do it anyway.

My voice is low, guttural when I say, "Taste yourself, baby."

Before she can even respond, I'm kissing her.

She moans into my mouth like she's never been kissed before. I taste *her* on her lips. On her tongue. She tastes like bliss and surrender and something I should never fucking touch.

I don't kiss women. Not at the club. Not here. Not ever.

I fuck them. Eat them. Break them.

But this?

This is different.

She's different.

My tongue claims hers, deep and dirty.

She meets it with her own hunger, grinding her slick cunt against my cock, and fuck—*I move with her.*

I can't help it.

The pressure is torture. My shaft slides against her clit and her whole body tightens.

We're breathless. Desperate. And somehow, even bound and at my mercy, she's the one *taking control.*

Little brat. Through and fucking through.

But I wouldn't stop her for the world.

She grinds harder. Faster. Riding my cock without taking it inside.

When I feel her start to climb again, I pull my mouth from hers and murmur low in her ear, "Rub this dirty pussy on me, baby."

"I'm— I'm going to come again," she breathes, and something inside me—something fierce and *violent*—wants to protect her.

Hold her. Keep her from ever needing anyone else again.

"Take it, rabbit," I growl. "Take what you want from my cock."

She tips her head back and I bite down on the soft skin where her neck meets her shoulder. Marking her again. One more stamp of ownership.

And we *come again.*

Humping like desperate fucking animals.

Not fucking. Not yet.

But it's so close it *hurts.*

When the pleasure finally crests and falls, her body doesn't stop. She slows, but keeps moving, grinding her hips in a slow, lingering rhythm—like she's trying to brand me just as deeply as I've branded her.

I've come twice. Emptied my balls on her stomach. My cum dripping down her sides and soaking the leather behind her.

It's fucking beautiful.

I reach behind her and unclip the shackles at her ankles. The moment she's free, she wraps her legs around me tight, locking me to her like she'll *never* let go.

And fuck... I *don't want her to.*

It would be so easy to slip into her now. Just *push* inside and feel the heat of her cunt swallow me whole.

But not yet.

We breathe together, panting, hips still moving in a lazy, unconscious dance as we come down from the high.

I stroke her face, watching the way she turns into my touch without hesitation. My other hand slides down her side and grips her ass—full, soft, perfect—before I kiss her again.

I shouldn't.

It's *dangerous*—especially now. With the war with

Lorenzo coming to a head. With everything I've built on the line.

But there's nothing—*nothing*—on the face of this fucking planet that could stop me tonight.

"Perfect little rabbit," I whisper, kissing her again as my hand drifts from her ass to the smooth curve of her thigh.

"You did so good for me." Another kiss. Deep. Raw. *Mine.*

"But I'm going to keep fucking you with my mouth until you cry for me to stop." My voice is a promise, low and wicked against her lips.

Another kiss. Harder now.

"Then I'll lick your tears before I make you come again, little rabbit." I smile against her mouth. "So I hope you know the deal you made."

I bite her bottom lip, tugging it between my teeth.

"Because I'm going to make you pay it. *All. Fucking. Night.*"

SIENNA: I think my boss ate my pussy all night.

HARPER: BACK UP.

HARPER: Why are we not sure who the coochie connoisseur is??

I bite my lip as I stare down at my phone. Sitting in the back of the SUV, legs crossed delicately, dress far too short, and thighs still trembling like I ran a marathon. Spoiler: I didn't.

Unless being eaten within an inch of your life counts as cardio.

I start typing again.

SIENNA: Because I didn't see him. I was blindfolded.

SIENNA: But Harper… it was him.

> SIENNA: I kind of went to the Masq and made a deal with the Devil. And he devoured me.

> SIENNA: All night.

Three dots pop up instantly. Then vanish. Then reappear like Harper is going into cardiac arrest and can't decide which question to ask first.

> HARPER: OKAY.

> HARPER: Back it up, Babe.

> HARPER: Why were you at the Masq?

> HARPER: You made a deal with the Devil???

> HARPER: WHAT KIND OF DEAL GETS YOU ORGASMS LIKE THAT??

> HARPER: Be specific. I need to know for science.

I stare out the window as the city rolls by. My reflection in the glass is flushed, my eyes still dazed, my neck marked up like I was mauled by a vampire.

A bite. A literal bite. It rests just above the scoop neckline of my navy-blue dress like it was *meant* to be seen.

I fill Harper in on everything.

It feels like we haven't caught up in weeks. Me being tormented by Lucian and her, being wrapped in Adriano.

But I tell her everything. How he drives me crazy. How he touched me, leaves me wanting.

She was concerned about the hidden cameras but come

on. It's Harper. She completely approved of my revenge arc getting myself off and making him watch.

And last night.

God, last night.

I've never come like that in all my life.

One after another. Again and again.

That mouth. That tongue. Those fingers.

And fuck, the way he talks so nasty.

Blindfolded, I could hear it. I could hear Lucian in every word.

That first round I was so nervous. My heart was pumping so hard, it sounded like the bass music of the club thumping in my ears.

The anticipation of what a tongue would feel like on me.

His tongue.

Then he made me come and come again. He came on me, with me.

His dick, so fucking long and thick sliding against me in such a primal way.

It was the hottest thing I've ever done.

But I heard it. After he kissed me like I was dying, he was so close to my ear.

"You did so good for me." I knew it was him. Lucian.

He's said that to me before in his office, when I did good during my sponsor training.

But fuck, the way he devoured me. Hung my legs over his wide shoulders and feasted.

Moved me to the bed and kept going. He let me take the blindfold off, only because it was pitch-black. He didn't want me to know it was him yet, but I figured it out.

I felt some of the raised lines of his tattoos. The ones that crawl up his forearms, teasing me each time he rolls his sleeves up.

He laid down and I rode his face. My fingers ran through his short hair, finally touching him after weeks of longing.

I couldn't take anymore. And just like he promised, he devoured my tears, taking even my anguish and claiming it for himself. The last time he made me come, it was so gentle. Reverent.

Then he pulled the covers over us, wrapped me in his arms and told me to sleep.

My eyes were closing on their own when he tipped my mouth up to his for one more kiss.

Like he knew it would be the last one.

"I'm breaking every law I've written for you."

Then nothing. Darkness. Sleep. Oblivion.

I woke up hours later. Alone.

The house was silent. No trace of him. Just me, lying in a ridiculously luxurious bed, my body aching in the best way possible.

I'd wandered the sleek halls, slowly coming back to myself. Found a note on the kitchen counter beside a package.

"Shower. Dress. The car will take you wherever you wish."

Inside the package: my phone, my clutch, shoes, a bra and panties. Then a soft, navy-colored dress that skimmed my curves and exposed the *very intentional* marks he'd left on my body.

On my thighs. My breasts. My neck.

Like he'd wanted to make sure I *remembered*.

I had extra time, so I explored more of the house. It looked so different in the daylight.

When I opened a door and saw the big painting, hanging in an office, there was no more doubt.

It was the one from the art gallery. The big one I was looking at when he asked me about it.

Trust.

It can't be a coincidence. Everything tells me Lucian is the Devil and the man breaking all his rules for me.

> HARPER: You're not even pretending to be casual about this, are you?

> HARPER: HE HELD YOU AND KISSED YOU GOODNIGHT?

> HARPER: DID HE TUCK YOU IN AND WHISPER SWEET DEATH THREATS TOO??

> HARPER: I am so proud.

I can't help the grin that pulls at my lips.

> HARPER: So, what are you going to do about it?

I bite my lip, looking out the window again. The Ledger skyrise peek out at me as we turn the corner.

> SIENNA: Make him admit it or make his life hell.

HARPER: That's my girl.

I know he's the Devil.

The one who tied me down. Took me apart with his mouth. Made me forget my own name and moan to the heavens instead.

And now he's pretending like it didn't happen.

Lucian Vale ignores me all damn day.

Doesn't even look at me. He has Eve give me a list of client profiles to review.

Boring. Dry. Useless.

Like I'm a secretary stuck doing homework while my sponsor pretends I don't exist.

The tension between us? Still there. Still *suffocating*. I see it in the way his jaw clenches when I walk past. The way his hands fist on the desk when I get too close.

His gaze lingers just a second too long on my lips, like he's remembering what they tasted like last night. Like he's forcing himself not to look at the bite mark he left on my neck.

So if he wants to play games? Fine.

It's nearly closing time. The office is quiet. Empty. Everyone's gone.

Except me and Lucian.

I slip into his office and close the door behind me. No knock. No hesitation.

Lucian's at his desk, reviewing contracts. He doesn't look up.

"You can be dismissed for the day," he says, tone clipped.

I saunter toward him, keeping my voice sweet. Innocent. *Devious.*

"Okay. I'll just wait here until the driver is ready with the car."

I don't sit in the chair across from him. No. I slide up onto the edge of his desk and cross my legs, the tablet in my hands, pulled up to the client profile section.

I hear the faint grind of his teeth. The flex of his jaw. The tightening grip on his pen.

He leans back slowly in his chair, eyes unreadable. "What are you doing, Sienna?"

I give him a smile like butter wouldn't melt on my tongue.

"You're my sponsor. You should go over some clients with me for my first contract."

His neck tenses so hard I swear I can hear the blood pulsing.

Still pretending? Okay.

I swipe to the first profile. "This one's near your age. Seems well-traveled. Open to light kink. Interested in a Companion who's obedient and curious."

"Sienna." His voice is warning. Low and strained. "No."

I ignore it.

"Oh, or *this one.*" I tap the screen. "He's into foot play. Really into it. Honestly? I think I'm *super* interested in that. My arches are—"

Lucian's chair scrapes back suddenly. He leans forward, forearms on his knees, elbows tense. His head drops for a second like he's trying to summon restraint from the pits of hell.

"Sienna," he says, tightly. "Now is not a good fucking time for this."

I press forward, voice honeyed and dangerous. "Oh, come *on*, this one is *definitely* a dom-daddy if I've ever seen one."

He snaps.

He *surges* from the chair, and I barely flinch as the tablet is yanked from my hands and flung across the room like a damn frisbee. It crashes into the wall and shatters, shards flying across the floor.

My breath catches.

He's between my legs in a second, his hand fisting in my hair, yanking my head back just enough to make me gasp.

"That's fucking enough," he growls, eyes dark and wild. "You're still a trainee until *I* say you're done."

I smile.

Because I know I've got him. And now, it's my turn to burn the lines down.

I soften my body, tilt my hips. Let everything I've learned—and everything that comes *naturally* around him —take over.

"Or," I whisper, "you could keep breaking every law you've written for me."

Something flickers in his eyes. Recognition. Guilt. *Desire.* He doesn't mask it fast enough.

His grip eases in my hair, but he doesn't let go. Doesn't

move. I wrap my legs around his waist, anchoring him to me.

My hand slides down between us, over his slacks. He's hard. *Of course* he is.

He closes his eyes, but doesn't move away. "What are you doing, Sienna?"

I tighten my grip on his cock through the fabric, stroking slowly. "Admit it, Lucian."

"I don't know what you're talking about." His voice is hoarse now. Unsteady.

I lean closer, lips at his ear. "Are you still going to pretend like you didn't devour my pussy all night... *Diablo*?"

His eyes snap open—sharp, furious, *panicked*.

"I don't fuck my employees."

"Bullshit," I hiss, still stroking him, my hips grinding, teasing the pressure between us.

That's when he shuts it down.

Lucian rips himself out of my grip and takes two sharp steps back, leaving me perched on his desk, breathless.

His voice is cold. *Final*.

"Go home, Sienna."

He turns his back to me and walks to his espresso bar like he can just walk away from this. From *me*.

But I follow him. I reach around and press my palm to the front of his pants again.

"Then fire me."

His hand snaps out, grabbing my wrist hard. The warning is in his grip. The storm in his eyes.

And still—I don't flinch.

He releases me a beat later and rises to his full height, towering.

"I'm too old for you," he says.

The words hit me like a slap. I take a single step back, stunned. Not because of his age. But because *that's* the bullshit he's going to pretend will hold any water?

"Is that really what you're going to go with?" I ask, voice low. "After everything?"

We stare at each other.

Neither of us backing down.

Then finally—cold. Controlled. Detached.

"Fine," I say. "If you say so."

I turn and walk toward the door. I refuse to let my hands shake. Refuse to let him see the tears that threaten to sting my eyes.

If he wants to pretend last night never happened—if he wants to hide behind bullshit excuses and pretend like he doesn't want me—I'll make sure he regrets it.

Chapter 31
Lucian

Of all the fucking days for her to figure it out—it had to be today.

She walks out of my office with her head high, her scent still clinging to me, her lips still swollen from the kiss I swore I wouldn't give her. And I just let her go.

The moment the door clicks shut behind her, I turn and drive my fist through the wall.

Plaster cracks. Bone strains. I don't feel it.

All I feel is rage.

At her.

At myself.

At this fucking war that won't wait.

I should've had her this morning. In my bed.

With the morning sun streaking across her skin in a way I've never seen her before. I wanted her to wake up in my arms—blindfold off, body sore and satisfied, my cock sliding into her while she whimpered and begged for more.

From me. Not the Devil. It would be *my* name rolling off her sweet mouth.

But that was taken from me, too.

Killian had shown up near dawn, dragging me out of bed with a warning in his eyes. One look at his face and I knew the news wasn't good.

A high-profile politician. An escort.

A leak splashed all over the front page of every newspaper in the city.

And now media outlets are frothing at the mouth. Running whispers of an exposé on a "secret underground escort agency" that services the elite. They haven't named *The Black Ledger* yet, but it's only a matter of time.

That politician was a client.

And that means the fucking wolves are at the door.

I can handle exposure. I've buried worse. But this? This isn't about scandal.

It's about *survival.*

If The Ledger burns, everything else goes with it. The clubs. The contracts. The women I swore to protect. *Her.*

Clients are pulling out. Inspectors tried to shut down The Masquerade last night—citing false code violations.

And the most infuriating part? Some of those same city officials were clients. Men I've fed, clothed, protected.

Now they're turning on me. Pretending they didn't crawl on their knees for what I gave them.

And Lorenzo... He thinks this is his opportunity. He thinks a little heat will make me sweat. That he can chip away at what I built. That he can break my empire *from the outside in.*

He's wrong.

I don't need bullets to wage war.

I need one thing.

Chaos.

And I am the fucking king of it.

The plan's already in motion. Accounts are shifting. Names are being erased. Favors called in.

Judges, senators, heads of corporations—they'll remember who the fuck *owns* them when their dirty laundry starts leaking in a very curated, very *intentional* sequence.

But Sienna...

Fuck.

I didn't want her to know. Not yet. Not like this.

She cornered me. Played me. Rubbed against my cock and whispered *Diablo* like she already knew she belonged to me.

And I—stupidly, weakly—let her walk away.

Because the timing is wrong. Because I need my head clear. Because if she stays close, Lorenzo will use her as a weapon.

And I will kill for her.

I will fucking burn *everything* for her.

And that would make me vulnerable.

Which means she has to stay away.

For now.

The busted tablet lands in the trash can with a hollow thud just as the door swings open.

Perfect timing.

Jaxon saunters in first, smug as ever in a dark jacket over a faded tee, sunglasses still on despite the setting sun.

Killian's close behind, all sharp lines and lethal silence, his loyalty wrapped in muscle and precision.

"Well," Jaxon drawls, nodding at the broken glass and crumpled tech, "things are going well, I see."

I grunt, already unbuttoning my shirt, striding toward the back of my office where my private closet waits. The black tux hangs ready—custom-made for the kind of evening I hoped I'd never have to face again.

"Is it done?" I ask, shrugging off the ruined dress shirt, letting it drop to the floor.

"Oh ye of little faith," Jaxon says, stepping around the desk and dropping a USB drive beside the espresso machine. "Of course it's done."

He leans casually against the edge, all swagger and brilliance. "It's all on there—every record Lorenzo's ever kept. Family photo albums, emails, financials, account access, even his search history—which, by the way, is *disgusting*."

He gives an exaggerated shudder. "My virus hits the moment you do, and poof." He snaps his fingers. "Generations of business go up in smoke."

Good.

I adjust the cuffs of my tuxedo shirt and glance toward Killian. "Everything set on your side?"

"You know it is." Killian gives a single nod, the kind that ends conversations.

"Who's planting the bombs?"

"I don't trust anyone else with that but me." I lose my dark dress slacks and step into the tuxedo pants.

Killian doesn't hesitate. "Then I'm coming with you."

His loyalty is constant. Fierce. And it's always been appreciated.

But not tonight.

"Sera needs someone close," I say, sliding on my tailored jacket. "Especially on a night when *dozens* of hits are going down at once. She's your priority."

He scowls but doesn't argue.

There's a beat of silence before Killian asks, voice low: "What about—"

Sienna.

He doesn't say her name, but he doesn't have to. He's the only person who knows. He walked in, caught me in bed with her this morning. Saw everything.

He's never judged me before, but I saw it in his eyes—that flicker of surprise. Because *I* broke the rule. The one that's been ironclad for years. Untouchable.

No fucking the girls.

And now it's garbage. Torched by my own obsession.

"She'll be out of the way tonight," I say coldly, even though it tastes like a lie on my tongue.

Her best friend—Harper—is dating one of my men. The guy got a raise and a promotion just for existing near her. I pulled strings without her knowing. Because he's trustworthy. Because he keeps her safe.

Tonight, they're entertaining her at her apartment. Wine. Pizza. Whatever it takes.

Of course, Jaxon and I have alerts set on her building, her phone, her exit points. I'll know the second she walks out the front door.

Because I don't want her *anywhere* near tonight's entertainment.

"Strict orders," I say, tightening the cufflinks on my wrist. "If she leaves, I'm told immediately."

"Lucian," Killian says, quieter now. "You sure?"

No.

But it doesn't matter.

"She's staying in," I say. "She'll be safe."

At least from *everything but me.*

Because tonight, I'll wage a war without a single bullet.

Just the right kind of chaos.

And when it's over... I'll deal with what I've done to her.

What I've let her become to me.

The Governor's Ball is an affair of legend. The elite of New York's power structure gather here each spring, cloaked in velvet and hypocrisy, clonking their champagne flutes above their heads as if the city doesn't rot beneath their feet.

Tonight, Lorenzo hosts it all.

His smile as charming as his lies.

His hands shaking every back he'll later stab.

The ballroom is a temple to wealth—white marble floors, twenty-foot chandeliers glittering with dripping crystals. There are tables lined in gold thread and champagne towers so tall they defy physics.

Cameras flash in bursts as celebrities pose, all teeth and

emptiness. Senators, tycoons, CEOs—the faces of corruption, painted with gloss and pride.

And none of them notice.

Not the shift in the air.

Not the glances between servers.

Not that every chef in the kitchen answers to *me*.

Every tuxedoed waiter.

Every red-lipped cocktail girl.

Every white-jacketed maître d'.

Mine.

The event unfolds exactly as Lorenzo intended—until the part he didn't write.

Dinner is served.

The servers move in perfect unison, synchronized like dancers. Dozens of plates are set before the guests with silver domes polished so perfectly, the chandeliers glint off their surface.

The room hushes, anticipating the dramatic reveal.

Cameras ready. Eyes glinting.

One beat.

Two.

Then the servers *lift* the domes—*all at once*.

A hush falls across the room as confused faces take in what they see on their gilded chargers.

Then beautifully, the room *erupts*.

Dead rats.

Dozens. Hundreds.

Lying lifeless, limp, and grotesque on every plate. Some twisted in rigor, some still wet from whatever gutter they were pulled from. The scent—rotting fur, death, sewer—is instantaneous.

Screams rise like a symphony.

The string section begins with the gasps.

The brass erupts with shrieking violins of horror.

The percussion hits when someone *vomits* onto the floor.

"Oh my God—what is that—"

"Get it away from me—"

"Jesus Christ! Are those—rats?!"

Politicians leap to their feet, knocking over crystal glasses. A woman in a Dior gown scrambles onto her chair. A senator's wife faints. Another slips on spilled champagne, her diamond tiara skidding across the floor.

And then the real show begins.

A soft *hiss* fills the air—barely audible over the chaos.

The ceiling vents slide open with silent precision.

The gas is odorless. Harmless. Just enough to heighten the senses. To make everything feel more raw. More *real*.

And then—they fall.

Hundreds–thousands of live rats, spilling like a biblical plague from the ceiling.

They hit the floor and scatter. A wave of squealing, gnashing teeth. They skitter over heels, climb up satin gowns, crawl beneath tables.

The chaos becomes *carnage*.

None of them knew the tables, the linens, the chairs had been saturated in, what I can only say is a rodent cat-nip.

The tiny beasts are in a frenzy. The guests have become part of the exhibit, the scentless chemical transferred to their ridiculous clothing. And the rats want it all.

Security tries to form lines—fails. Several rats climb the leg of a congressman mid-interview and the cameras catch him shrieking like a child, flailing in a frenzy.

A socialite jumps into the champagne tower, knocking it into a sea of broken glass and foam. Her bare feet bleed as she screams for help.

People run for the exits, trampling over one another, rats hanging from their gowns and tuxes gnawing at the fabrics. An older governor goes down, his security pulling him up by his collar as rats crawl over his shoulders.

But the doors are locked—for now. They'll open in a moment but we need to give the press time to capture *everything*.

Flashbulbs ignite like fireworks—shocking, freezing moments of high-society *humiliation*. Rats climbing Versace. Fear on the face of power. Blood on silk.

It's chaos.

It's *art*.

It's *mine*.

And as I stand on the other side of the ballroom door, watching from a monitor, listening to the symphony of my design, I smile.

Lorenzo's face is frozen in disbelief. Pale. Rage simmering beneath the surface—but powerless.

Exactly how I planned it.

You wanted to embarrass me, old friend?

Now *you're* the scandal.

A man who can't even control his own fundraiser. A man with dead vermin on his china and a rat climbing up his cufflinks.

Lorenzo wanted a war?

I'm giving him one. He just forgot the sewers I came from to get here. And I'm more than happy to remind him.

The chaos is deafening as I step through the ballroom doors—but none of it touches me.

The crowd is in disarray. Guests trip over gowns and scatter across the polished marble in a frantic attempt to escape the rats now swarming the venue.

Silver cutlery clatters to the floor.

Security yells over the noise, powerless to stop the sheer panic erupting in every direction. But through it all, I remain untouched.

The rats give me a wide berth, skittering around my feet without daring to cross my path. The repellent I sprayed earlier—silent, scentless to anyone human—does its job.

I move through the fray like a shadow wrapped in control, chaos peeling away in my wake.

No one sees me, not really. Not yet. But he does.

Lorenzo.

Across the room, he stands frozen amidst the carnage, his once-perfect appearance now marred by the panic unraveling around him. His jacket is wrinkled, collar askew.

One rat climbs onto the corner of his table and he swats at it violently, face twisted with disgust and confusion.

He sees me.

Our eyes lock.

I don't offer him a smile or even the satisfaction of a sneer. There's no need. The destruction speaks for itself.

Instead, I move toward him with calm, measured steps,

each one deliberate, each one signaling the end of something he thought was untouchable.

When I reach his table, I place a single bottle down in front of him.

It's the same whiskey that bottle had once been a symbol of truce.

Tonight, it's a gravestone.

I say nothing. There's no speech. No theatrical monologue. Just silence—he knows what it means.

I turn from him and walk a few paces before slipping the small remote from my jacket pocket. I lift it high enough that only Lorenzo can see, ensuring the message lands with the weight it deserves.

His eyes widen.

I press the button.

The explosion rattles the entire structure—glass trembles in its frames as the first blast echoes through the city.

A second follows almost immediately, closer this time, a deeper boom that makes the chandeliers shiver above our heads.

Gasps turn to shrieks as guests stampede toward the windows, heels skidding, phones raised, mouths agape.

Outside, the parking lot has become a battlefield. Cars and limousines—the prized possessions of the city's wealthiest—are engulfed in flames.

Smoke pours upward in black coils, the orange glow of fire dancing in every reflection. Metal has been torn from its polished form, vehicles reduced to heaps of molten luxury scattered across the lot like a child's overturned toy box.

Lorenzo rushes to the nearest window, pushing past a senator and nearly knocking over a journalist. He presses both hands to the glass, face stricken as he stares at the hell I've created.

Across the harbor is the real explosion.

The new development Lorenzo has been funding with dirty money. It's supposed to be a new jewel added to his crown. Thirty seconds ago, it was still metal framing and scaffolding.

Now, the forty-story condominium goes down as each floor explodes perfectly timed.

But what he can't see is what else crumbled the moment I pressed that button.

Jaxon's virus.

In perfect synchrony with the chaos unfolding outside, his code began devouring Lorenzo's empire from the inside out.

His business accounts, family trusts, offshore holdings, and encrypted files—everything he built with blood, money, and inherited power—has either been redirected to me or reassigned to causes that will never trace back to him.

The St. James' Orphanage will wake to the news of a record-breaking anonymous donation, one that will fund them for the next decade.

Similar institutions across the city will find themselves suddenly, miraculously, whole again.

Everything Lorenzo thought made him untouchable is now burning. Not just in the parking lot, but in the foundation of his legacy.

And me?

I walk through the ballroom's front doors, past security who wouldn't dare stop me, through panicked guests who have no idea what just happened or who orchestrated it.

Untouched.

Unshaken.

Exactly as I planned.

Outside, the night carries a strange stillness, the kind that hums in the air just after something violent has ended —but before the next blow is struck. The chaos of the ballroom fades behind me, muffled by thick walls and the distance I place between us with every step.

No one follows.

No alarms blare.

Just the soft hush of the wind brushing past the marble columns and the subtle click of my shoes against the stone drive.

My car waits where I left it—a midnight-black Aston Martin gleaming beneath the amber lights of the valet circle. Sleek, understated, predatory. Like me, it belongs to the shadows more than the spotlight.

My men are already positioned around the perimeter, unseen by most but ready for anything. If someone inside decides to retaliate tonight, they'll find they're already too late.

I reach for the door handle, already imagining the satisfying quiet of the cabin, the engine's low growl, the open road stretching ahead.

And then—*a sound like a gunshot fractures the calm.*

The crash is sudden, violent. A sharp burst of shattering glass cuts through the night as something slams into the front of the car. I pause, hand still on the handle, eyes narrowing as a web of cracks spreads across the windshield.

I don't need to look closely to know what it was.

The whiskey bottle.

The bottle hurled from above, now nothing more than jagged pieces glinting across the hood. The glass has broken clean through the sheen of the vehicle, amber liquid bleeding across the paint like an accusation.

I glance up, slow and deliberate.

A window above the ballroom remains open, its sheer curtain fluttering like a ghost's breath. I see no face behind it, no silhouette framed in outrage or fear. But presence isn't necessary. The message speaks louder than any scream.

There will be no truce.

No compromise.

No peace.

Whatever civility once existed between us has shattered, right along with that bottle.

I linger there for a breath longer than I should, the crackled windshield gleaming beneath the soft lighting, a mirror of what comes next. Then, without a word or even a sigh, I open the car door and slide into the driver's seat.

The engine roars to life with the press of a button, its power coiled and ready beneath my fingertips. I guide the machine out onto the street, the quiet purr of the tires a stark contrast to the destruction I leave behind.

Lorenzo made his choice tonight.

Now he'll live with the consequences.

Because this isn't just about territory anymore, or busi-ness, or some petty grudge born of ego and betrayal.

This is about *the empire*.

His just crumbled but it looks like my old friend wants to fall a little deeper into Hell.

Tonight, is the Companions Mixer.

It's one of The Ledger's most anticipated events—a curated, high-society evening where new and old clients mix and mingle with the Companions.

A social buffet, dressed up in silk and candlelight, where contracts are whispered over cocktails and glances hold promises. No one signs anything tonight, but deals begin here.

The trainees, all eight of us still under active sponsorship, are invited to attend—not to participate, not officially. We're still considered off-limits. But the exposure matters. It's good practice, they say.

A chance to observe the game before we're allowed to play.

And I fully intend to be there.

Lucian didn't exactly forbid me from going.

When I had completed every ridiculously tedious task

Lucian gave me today, he dismissed me with cold finality. Told me to go home. That I was done for the day.

His tone made it clear he didn't want to see me again. Not tonight.

But he never said I couldn't go to the mixer.

And when I watched the other girls heading downstairs to The Ledger's private salon for hair, makeup, and wardrobe prep—laughing, talking, trailing clouds of perfume and confidence—I knew exactly what he was doing.

Lucian Vale didn't want me there tonight.

So he told me to leave. Because if he'd forbidden me outright, I would've gone just to spite him.

But this? This is a manipulation cloaked in care.

And I'm going anyway.

It's not about spite. Not entirely.

It's about being seen.

About standing in the same room with him and daring him to pretend that I don't matter—that two nights ago didn't happen—that he didn't taste me like I was the only thing on earth worth devouring.

I won't let him rewrite us like that.

I've been building my wardrobe slowly, piece by piece. Learning from the stylists at the Ledger salon. Paying attention to how certain fabrics cling and how others whisper with movement.

I've gotten good at doing my own hair—mastering the art of the perfect blowout with a little bend at the ends, polished but not trying too hard.

And the winged liner, smokey.

Just the right amount of drama to draw attention to my eyes without turning them into weapons.

Tonight, I chose powder blue.

The dress is a sleek mini with a square neckline and sculpted seams that hug me in all the right places. It makes my eyes look richer somehow—deep royal blue instead of soft sky. The color is gentle, romantic. Innocent.

Which is why it's perfect.

Because nothing about tonight is innocent.

I dab perfume at the base of my neck, behind my ears, and down the valley between my breasts. A warm, addictive scent—amber and vanilla and something sinful beneath it all.

I take one last look in the mirror.

My auburn hair catches the light just right. My dress fits like it was made for me. My makeup is a careful whisper of seduction.

My phone pings, a message the ride-share driver is a few minutes away.

I grab my clutch, ready to make Lucian eat his fucking words tonight.

I arrive fashionably late.

Not so late it raises eyebrows—but just enough that the room has settled into its rhythm. The initial introductions are already made, the energy humming at that perfect midpoint between excitement and indulgence.

Exactly how I wanted it.

The event space is stunning, as always—low lighting, gold accents, and the quiet undercurrent of money pulsing through the air like an unspoken language.

Elegant laughter. Clinking crystal.

A room full of people pretending they're not here to buy each other.

And just as I suspected, most of the girls are dressed in black—satin, silk, leather. The unofficial Ledger uniform for mixers and midnight seduction. But me?

Powder blue.

Soft, romantic, memorable.

I stand out in the sea of shadows like a dangerous dream, and I can feel it immediately—the subtle shift in attention as heads turn in my direction.

I smile, poised and polite, offering a graceful wave to a few Companions I recognize from training sessions. One of them arches a brow at me in surprise. The other just smirks knowingly.

But it's the *clients* I'm here for.

And I don't have to wait long.

"Miss Knight," a deep voice greets me near the bar. "I was wondering if we'd see you tonight."

I turn and immediately recognize him—an older gentleman with silver at his temples and a designer watch peeking from beneath his cuff. I met him briefly at the sponsor mixer. His name comes easily.

"Mr. Langston," I reply warmly. "Still wearing Tom Ford. Still refusing to dance?"

He laughs, clearly delighted I remembered. "Guilty on both counts." He takes a flute of champagne from a passing tray and offers it to me with a wink. "Though I might consider breaking that rule, for you."

I accept the glass with a tilt of my head. "Tempting."

He leans in slightly. "I was disappointed, you know. When Lucian pulled you off the sponsor roster."

My smile doesn't waver, but something sharp pierces through me. "Oh?"

"There was nearly a brawl over who would get the bid." He chuckles, sipping from his own glass. "I was certain my bid would win. I heard you were the highest bidding trainee in a long time... possibly ever."

The words land like a slap.

And yet I keep smiling.

Because I remember that day. Sitting in that room, thinking no one had bid for me. That I had somehow failed before I even began. That I was being fired.

Lucian let me believe it.

He watched me squirm. Let me unravel. All while he was the one who outbid everyone else, who *claimed* me without a word.

So, that is why the "top girl" didn't get first pick of sponsors. Because I was the top girl. And someone did the honor of picking for me.

The heat beneath my skin sharpens. My anger curls low and quiet, fueled not just by the betrayal—but by the control.

Fine.

If he wants to play games, I'll show him just how dangerous I can be when I stop pretending not to care.

I thank Mr. Langston with a polite nod and begin scanning the room, hunting.

I'm not here to flirt with the same old names. I'm here to make a point.

Looking across the gathered crowd it doesn't take me long to find my perfect partners in this scheme.

A group of five—clustered near the back of the room, slightly apart from the central buzz of conversation. They look new. Late twenties.. Clean-cut. Fit.

Wealth practically dripping from their expensive shoes and the watches they can't stop adjusting. No visible tattoos. Just money, nerves, and curiosity.

They must be brand new clients.

They're clearly unsure how to approach the Companions, still working out how this world operates.

Perfect.

I run my hand slowly through my hair, fingers sliding through the waves I spent an hour perfecting. Two of them notice immediately, eyes locking on mine.

Bingo.

I tip my head, letting my gaze linger. A smile plays at the edge of my lips.

Time to work.

Time to be unforgettable.

And time to make Lucian fucking *regret* ever thinking he could control me.

They're exactly as I hoped—eager, attractive, just uncertain enough to be grateful for my attention.

My approach is subtle.

Just enough flirtation to stir the air between us, never too much. I laugh lightly at their jokes, tilt my head when one of them says something clever, make a small comment about his cufflinks that has the whole group trying to flash theirs next.

And they eat it up.

For thirty minutes, I work them like pawns on my own personal chessboard, slowly wrapping each one around my finger until they're orbiting me like planets.

And right on cue, just as one leans in to murmur something harmless in my ear—something about how the music makes it hard to hear but *he'd love to get to know me better*—Lucian arrives.

I don't need to look to know.

I *feel* him enter the room.

His presence slices through the atmosphere like a blade, sharp and cold, shifting the energy without a single word. My breath catches before I can stop it, my pulse flickering. Then I glance up—slow, measured.

Our eyes lock.

There he is.

Lucian Vale in a black tux that was clearly made for his body and no one else. Impossibly calm. Thunderously still. His steel-gray gaze is locked on me, eyes narrowing as he takes in the sight: me surrounded by five men, one whispering in my ear, my champagne glass tilted delicately in my hand.

I arch a brow at him—not in challenge, but in acknowledgment. As if to say, *Of course I'm here. Why wouldn't I be?*

I think he'll storm over. I expect it.

But instead, he's intercepted—two clients corner him, hands on his arm, laughter in their voices as they try to draw him into conversation.

He listens. Barely.

But he doesn't break eye contact with me for a full three seconds before finally tearing his gaze away.

I hide my smirk behind the rim of my glass.

Let's see how far I can push you.

"These shoes are killing me," I murmur lightly to the group, casting a look at the wide square planter behind me —an oversized decorative piece doubling as furniture. "If I could get up there without flashing the entire party, I would."

One of them—tall, broad-shouldered, dark-haired— takes the bait like I hoped.

"Need a lift, sweetheart?" he asks, already stepping closer.

"You'd be my hero," I reply with a teasing smile.

He grins, sliding his hands around my ribs—his palms warm through the fabric of my dress—and lifts me easily onto the ledge. I let my legs cross slowly, smoothing my skirt down just enough to remain elegant while still playing the part.

I rest my hand on his shoulder a moment longer than necessary. Letting it linger.

"Oh, so strong," I say with a small, playful squeeze of his bicep. It's ridiculous, transparent, but exactly what they want to hear.

"Fresh champagne, darlin'," another one says, snagging a flute from a passing tray and offering it to me with a wink.

I lower my lashes, feigning bashfulness. "You boys better stop spoiling me. I may want more."

They're practically fawning now, clustered around me like I'm their sun and they're trying to earn the right to be in my path.

Compliments fly, subtle touches land. But my focus never really leaves *him*.

Because I can feel Lucian watching me.

Like daggers dragging down my spine.

His gaze is a weight, burning holes through silk and skin. I don't even need to see him to know—he's getting closer now. Not storming. Not obvious. But with the slow, lethal grace of a tiger stalking prey.

And still, I tip him further.

I run my hand through my hair, flipping it over one shoulder in that offhand way that always seems so innocent.

The man who lifted me takes the bait.

"God, your perfume smells so good."

"Care for a closer sample?" I ask sweetly, turning my head just enough to expose the soft curve of my neck.

He moves in without hesitation. His hand slides around my waist, resting on my hip as he leans forward. His breath is warm against my skin. He inhales deeply, a faint growl slipping from his throat.

If it had been Lucian, I would've flooded my panties right there.

But this?

This is just for show.

And it's working *perfectly*.

Lucian gives up all pretense the moment he breaks through the edge of the crowd.

Gone is the cool composure.

Gone is the carefully practiced detachment.

What walks toward me now is a tightly coiled storm, a man seconds from implosion. Every step is silent and dangerous, heat radiating off him like static before lightning strikes.

He reaches us, eyes locked on mine, and without a word, he plucks the champagne glass from my hand. Turns and gives it right back to the man who gave it to me.

"Lucian," I say, caught between surprise and warning, my tone threaded with a not-so-subtle *don't-be-an-asshole* edge.

"You're needed inside," he replies coldly, his voice low and sharp as steel. His hands find my hips, and with one firm motion, I'm off the ledge and standing in front of him before I can so much as blink.

His hand slides low across my back, guiding me away from the men like I'm nothing more than a prop being rearranged. "Excuse her," he says flatly to the group behind me.

And then he pushes me forward—toward the arched doorway at the far end of the patio, away from the party, the lights, the spectacle I so carefully created.

"You are *not* going to do this," I hiss, my voice low but furious, barely keeping up as he drives us through the crowd.

"I'll do what the fuck I want with my trainee," he growls, his fingers moving from my back to my upper arm, gripping me hard enough that I almost stumble.

"Let go of me," I snarl under my breath.

"Never, Angel."

The name slams into me. Low and reverent and filthy, all at once. It's a curse and a caress, and I hate how it makes me shiver.

We step inside, the elevator ahead of us. The doors open with a soft chime, revealing two Companions laughing as they exit—until they see Lucian's face.

They part like the sea.

He pushes me in without hesitation, following me into the sleek, mirrored interior like a wolf corralling prey. The doors slide closed behind us, sealing us in.

Then he punches the button for the top floor.

Hard.

So hard I swear I hear the plastic flex beneath his knuckle. The number glows red. The elevator hums to life.

But I don't have time to process any of it.

Because Lucian turns on me before the doors even shut completely.

He presses me back against the wall in one fluid movement, his hand on my throat as he tears at the knot of his tie, yanking it loose with a sharp jerk.

His eyes burn into mine—anger, possession, lust—every raw edge of the man he tries so hard not to be.

"Take your fucking panties off," he growls, voice gravel and fire, every word dragged from a place he can no longer suppress.

My heart stutters. Heat floods me instantly.

I back slowly into the corner, my breath shallow, fingers reaching for the hem of my dress. But before I can even draw it up, Lucian drops to his knees in front of me—and the air is stolen from my lungs.

He doesn't say a word.

In one swift, commanding motion, the hem of my dress is shoved up around my waist. The cool elevator air hits my thighs as his hands hook into the sides of my panties and yanks them down.

I barely manage to step one foot free before he punches the emergency stop button behind him. The elevator glides gently to a halt, a soft alarm beginning to pulse above us.

It doesn't matter.

None of it matters.

Because his mouth is on me.

I gasp, hard, my hand flying to his hair to hold on—no, to *anchor* myself.

One of his hands grips my ass tightly, the other anchoring my thigh up and over his shoulder. My back presses deeper into the corner, but there's no escape.

Lucian is eating me like he's furious I ever gave anyone else a taste of me.

His tongue is relentless, every movement sharp and deliberate, circling, pressing, sucking on my clit until I'm gasping his name on every exhale.

He growls into me, the vibration shaking through my core.

He's going to take everything I have and suck it out of me through my cunt.

When he lifts my other leg and drapes it over his opposite shoulder, I cry out, caught off guard as he supports all my weight with infuriating ease. My heels slide against his back as I clutch his head tighter, hips rolling toward him without a thought of control.

I'm completely at his mercy—his face buried between my thighs, devouring me like a starving man who's found the only meal that will save him. His nose presses against me, his mouth utterly ruthless, his grip bruising in the best possible way.

It doesn't take long.

A minute, maybe two.

Then I'm coming undone, my eyes squeezing shut as the orgasm slams through me like a wave I never saw coming. My head drops back with a moan that might border on a sob. My legs shake, my body trembling in his hold as he keeps going until I'm whimpering for breath.

He sets me down roughly, still on his knees, his hands releasing me only when I can stand again.

My panties hang around one ankle. I start to bend to fix them, breathless and dazed, but Lucian's already standing, towering over me.

He reaches over, hits the emergency stop button again.

The soft alarm ceases. The elevator lurches into motion, resuming its swift climb.

I don't even have time to recover before his hand fists in my hair, pulling my head back with a sharp tug.

"You won't need those," he snarls, his mouth crashing into mine, swallowing my breath like it's his to claim.

The kiss is brutal, consuming. His tongue invades, his

teeth graze, and it's all heat and fury and desperation as he presses me back into the wall with his full weight.

I can feel every hard, unrelenting inch of him.

There's nowhere to run.

And God help me—

I don't want to.

The moment the elevator doors slide open, Lucian seizes my hand and storms forward, dragging me behind him.

His grip is tight. Possessive. He moves fast—each stride long and powerful—and I'm practically jogging to keep up, my heels rushing furiously across the tile as I trail behind him, breath catching.

"Lucian," I pant, stumbling a little, still reeling from everything that just happened.

"Shut the fuck up."

The words are a whipcrack—low and laced with fury. He's a storm now, thunder in his shoulders, violence simmering just beneath the surface as we reach his office.

He throws the door open, pulls me inside, and slams it shut behind us, the echo of it rattling the glass.

Lock. Click.

The sound final. Inescapable.

Then he's on me again—turning me roughly, pushing

my chest against the wall. My hands splay to catch myself, palms flat on the cool surface as his body molds to mine from behind. His heat surrounds me. His presence swallows me whole.

His hand tangles in my hair again, yanking my head back with a sharp tug that forces a gasp from my throat.

"You're playing a dangerous fucking game with the wrong man, Sienna."

His voice is gravel and fire, low and lethal as it brushes against the shell of my ear.

I can feel every ounce of his fury pressed into me—especially the rigid length of his cock, straining against his pants and grinding against my ass with punishing force.

"You let those fuckers touch you?" he growls. "Smile at you? Speak to you like they had a fucking right?"

His voice is dark silk over fury, and I open my mouth to answer, but it's too late—he's already moving.

In one furious motion, his hands grab my dress at the neckline and *rips* it. The sound is loud—violent—as the fabric splits clean down the center, and suddenly I'm exposed. Vulnerable. *His.*

He rips again, tearing the dress all the way down before yanking it off me and tossing it aside like it never mattered. My bra is next—his fingers snapping the clasp with terrifying ease, letting it fall to the floor without a second thought.

I'm naked, except for my heels.

He spins me to face him, breath shallow, heart pounding. One of his knees slides between mine, forcing my legs apart as his body cages me in.

He's a wall of fury and heat and restraint on the verge of shattering.

"You think I didn't see what you were doing?" his hands working furiously to unbuckle his belt. "You think I wouldn't fucking punish you?"

His pants fall just low enough to release him, and my breath catches again when I see his cock—thick, long, *hard*. My stomach flips, and for a moment, I forget how to breathe.

Lucian's hand is back in my hair, yanking hard enough to make me squeal. Pain flickers across my scalp, pleasure twisting behind it.

"You want to let those fuckers near my property?" he growls, dragging me closer. "There's a price to pay for that, Angel."

He spits into his palm, stroking his cock with a rough, angry rhythm—and I whimper, knees weakening, knowing exactly what's coming.

Finally.

But he shakes his head, eyes wild and burning as he leans in, gripping my jaw and dragging his mouth over mine.

"Oh no, baby. This isn't for you. This is for *me*."

His kiss is brutal. Possessive.

He bites down on my lip just enough to draw blood, the sharp tang of copper blooming across my tongue. I moan into it, the pain, the intensity, the way he's unraveling everything we've been pretending not to feel.

He breaks away with a snarl and lifts me—*effortless*—his hands under my thighs as he pins me to the wall. My legs wrap around his waist instinctively, my heels digging into the backs of his thighs as he lines himself up.

"I'm going to fuck you hard against this wall," he breathes, voice thick and ragged, "raw, like the slut you are."

And when he slams into me, I see stars.

"I'm going to claim you with my cum from the inside out, Angel."

My back arches off the wall, a broken moan spilling from my lips as he stretches me in one savage thrust.

I dig my nails into his shoulders, holding on like I might fall apart as he fills me—*completely*. The pressure is exquisite, the pain toeing the line of pleasure so perfectly that I don't know whether to cry or beg for more.

He's thick. Hard. Unrelenting.

And he's finally inside me.

Exactly where I've imagined him a thousand times. Exactly where he belongs.

Lucian doesn't give me a moment to adjust.

He pounds into me with savage precision, each thrust a brutal claim. My back is pressed hard against the wall, the cool surface doing nothing to ease the fire burning through my body as he drives into me again and again.

His grip on my thighs is bruising, his hips slamming into mine with a punishing rhythm that makes my vision blur.

"This what you wanted?" he growls into my ear. "To be used like a fucktoy in my office? Dress torn, heels still on, dripping all over my cock?"

All I can do is gasp.

My nails claw into his shoulders, searching for something to hold onto as he fucks me like he's trying to reshape my soul. The sting of his thrusts borders on unbearable, but I don't want it to stop—I want it harder. Deeper. *Worse.*

"Look at you," he grits, voice feral. "Taking me raw like a good little slut. This is what you are now. Mine. You don't need contracts, or clients, or mixers."

He thrusts harder, burying himself so deep I whimper.

"You need *me.*"

My head lolls back as he drives into me again, and again, and again—relentless. My body feels weightless, suspended between the wall and his fury. I can feel my orgasm building, slow and molten, curling low in my stomach like it's waiting for permission to detonate.

Lucian's hand fists my hair again, dragging my mouth back to his as he growls between kisses.

"I'll fuck you however I want. Wherever I want. You belong to *me,* Sienna. This pussy—" he slams into me, and I choke on a moan, "—this tight, greedy fucking pussy is *mine.*"

The words detonate through me, and I almost come on the spot—but before I can fall over the edge, he breaks first.

Lucian's hips stutter, a low groan ripping from his chest as he buries himself deep one last time.

He comes with a brutal thrust and a growl of my name—his cock twitching, thick pulses of heat flooding into me.

It nearly breaks me.

He's still holding me up, panting against my throat, both of us shuddering. My muscles tremble, my orgasm still hanging in the air like a storm that hasn't broken.

He pulls back just slightly, and I feel the mess of us, wet and sticky between my thighs.

Somewhere in the midst of it all, one of my heels fell off —probably from the way he slammed me into the wall over and over like I was weightless. I glance down, dazed, and see the other still hanging on.

I kick it off.

Lucian sets me down roughly, hands still gripping me like he doesn't trust himself to let go. I'm standing on shaky legs, skin flushed, heart racing, dress shredded somewhere in a pile on the floor.

And then he rips his shirt open.

The buttons fly, one of them pinging off the wall, and he yanks it off with a growl, exposing the hard lines of his chest, the tattoos inked across his arms and ribs, the tension pulsing through every muscle.

He looks like something carved from war and sin, standing there half-naked, flushed and furious, cock still heavy and dripping with proof of what we've just done.

I've never seen anything so devastating.

And I've never felt so claimed.

Lucian's hands come up to cradle my face—those big, scarred hands so capable of violence, now holding me like I'm something breakable.

His mouth finds mine again, softer than before but no less possessive. There's a hunger in it still, but now it simmers beneath the surface, slow and consuming.

He kisses me as he walks me backward deeper into the office, our steps uneven, my body still trembling from the way he claimed me against the wall.

Between kisses, his words are like heat curling around my spine.

"You've been such a bad girl tonight, haven't you."

Kiss.

"Flaunting yourself."

Kiss.

"Touching what doesn't fucking belong to them."

Another kiss, harder now, like the memory angers him. His hand moves to the back of my neck.

"I'm going to wreck you, little rabbit. I'm going to show you what it really means to be mine."

The name—*that* name—sends a jolt through me.

Little rabbit.

It makes me whimper.

It's the name the Devil whispered, the one Lucian never used in daylight, never said without the mask. It slips from his lips like a possession all its own, and I realize now—it isn't just a role.

It's *him.*

Lucian and the Devil are the same. Two sides of the same hunger. And I want both.

He reaches the couch and sits down heavily, pulling me forward.

"Face away from me," he murmurs, his voice low and rough, "but straddle me, little rabbit."

My breath hitches. I hesitate for just a second, heart thudding, but then I move—climbing into his lap, my back to his chest, my bare ass pressing into his groin.

He's still hard.

Still ready to ruin me.

One hand snakes around my throat, not choking but holding, a reminder of who's in charge. The other slides between my thighs, his fingers instantly finding my clit, slow circles that make my hips twitch in response.

"My bad girl needs a lesson tonight," he says into my ear. "In pain... and pleasure. Don't you?"

I nod before I can think.

"Yes, sir."

His chuckle rumbles through his chest, deep and knowing.

He shifts, steadying me on his lap as he leans forward, dragging the sleek coffee table in front of us with a single arm.

"Hands on the table, Angel," he commands. "It's time you earn what you've been begging for."

I move as told, placing my palms flat on the table, fingers splayed wide. My knees spread on either side of his thighs, straddling him fully now. I know what I must look like—completely exposed, completely his.

It's mortifying.

It's *exhilarating*.

My clit throbs at the very thought of how he's looking at me now.

He hums behind me, warm lips brushing against the curve of my ass cheek. The kiss is soft. Wet. Almost reverent. Then his hands smooth over me, big palms kneading, spreading, owning.

"Spread your legs wider for me, Angel."

I obey.

His hand moves to the small of my back, pressing me gently downward until I'm arched just right, my pussy nestled against the rough fabric of his pants.

Then his fingers slide between my legs, spreading my wetness, teasing my entrance. He doesn't push in—not yet—but it's enough to make me gasp.

"You're going to remember this every time you sit down tomorrow," he murmurs, voice thick with promise. "You want to act like a brat? Then you get treated like one."

He pauses.

"I'm going to love seeing my handprint on this ass."

The first smack lands across my right cheek—sharp, loud, expected. My whole body tenses in response.

"Relax, baby," he purrs, fingers sliding back up my cunt, slow and deliberate.

The relief is immediate. My breath shudders. The sting fades into heat, into arousal, into *need*.

Then the second smack.

I jolt again—but it's different this time.

His fingers dip lower, circling my entrance before pushing in.

I moan, collapsing slightly forward, my forehead brushing the table.

He keeps the rhythm—punishing spanks followed by soothing fingers, teasing and working me open. One moment pain, the next pleasure, the next both blending into one spiraling sensation that has me humping his lap, my clit grinding against the roughness of his pants.

The sound of my wetness as he fingers me fills the room—filthy, raw, *real*.

My body clenches. My breath comes in gasps. My arms tremble with the effort of holding myself up.

Each time his palm lands on my ass, his fingers sink deeper. Twisting. Curling.

"Such a filthy little thing," he growls. "But you're being good now, aren't you."

"Yes—yes, sir," I choke out, my voice barely audible.

"That's right," he murmurs, thrusting his fingers harder, deeper. "Be my good girl now. Take it. Come for me."

My orgasm obeys him with no warning, no mercy. I cry out, loud and broken, clenching around his fingers, trembling as my body bucks and arches, lost in the overwhelming surge of sensation.

Lucian holds me through it, his free arm wrapped tight around my middle, his mouth at my ear.

"That's it, angel," he whispers. "Just like that. So fucking good for me."

And I believe him.

Because in this moment, I am nothing else.

Only his.

I'm still straddling him, still facing away—my chest heaving, my thighs trembling—when Lucian shifts beneath me.

His hand grips my waist, steadying me. I feel him fisting his cock again, the thick head sliding against my soaked entrance.

My breath catches at the sensation, the tease of it, how *ready* he still is despite already having come once inside me.

He groans low behind me.

"Now that you're my good girl... my *Angel*," he murmurs, voice dragging against my skin like smoke, "I'm going to fuck you good, baby. Just like this. Just like I imagined the first time you sat that sweet ass on my lap."

A moan slips from my lips before I can catch it.

He thought about me then?

That first day, when I'd perched innocently on his thighs during a meeting, trying to play it cool. He'd looked so composed, so unaffected. But all this time, he'd wanted me. He'd *imagined* this.

It undoes me.

I reach between us, guiding him to where I want him most—slick and pulsing and perfect. I lower myself onto him slowly, and he lets out a sound that makes my toes curl.

A dark, guttural chuckle.

"My greedy little slut rabbit is *fucking starving* for my cock, aren't you?"

"Yes," I breathe, palming my breasts as I begin to move.

My body rolls over his, hips circling, rising and falling in an unsteady rhythm as I fuck him like I've never fucked anyone before.

And I haven't.

Not like this.

Not where I feel so *alive*—so wanted, so worshipped and ruined in equal measure.

"You love the way my bare cock slides into your wet cunt, don't you whore?"

I groan as I clinch around him.

He chuckles. "I fucking knew it."

Lucian's hands slide to my hips, his fingers digging into my skin as he matches my rhythm. Then exceeds it. His hips start thrusting up, hard and sure, driving into me from below.

My head falls back onto his shoulder.

He's so deep.

So thick and perfect and *mine.*

But when he senses the control shifting—when my hips start dictating the pace—he doesn't let me keep it.

"No, baby," he growls into my ear. "I'm taking care of you."

One hand clamps firm on my hip, the other moves to my shoulder, anchoring me as he takes over completely.

My hands fall to his thighs, nails biting into muscle as he rocks me the way *he* wants, pulling me back onto his cock over and over until the sound of our bodies meeting is all I can hear.

"You feel that?" he murmurs, voice now laced with something softer—something reverent. "That's how good you feel wrapped around me. Bare. Wet. Fucking heaven."

His praise makes my eyes flutter closed because I love us like this. Nothing between us. No more lies. No condom.

Just us.

I'm not worried. Ledger protocols demand contraceptives and regular tests.

And thank fuck. Because feeling him like this, having him like this–I don't ever want it any other way.

He moves faster now. Deeper. Each thrust pushing me higher, threatening to break me apart. The filthy things he says are softened by the way he says them—possessive and gentle.

"You're the only one I've fucked raw," he says, and every-thing inside me *shatters*. "And I fucking love it."

That one sentence detonates behind my ribs like a bomb.

The only one.

That's all it takes.

My body arches, legs tensing, every nerve alight as I fall —*hard*—my orgasm ripping through me with brutal intensity.

Lucian follows seconds later, groaning behind me, thrusting deep one last time before he stills, his body pressed tight to mine as he spills inside me again.

His breath is hot against my shoulder, his arms wrapped around me like chains. And I don't want to move. Not yet.

Not ever.

Because in this moment... I don't just *belong* to him.

He *belongs* to me too.

Chapter 34

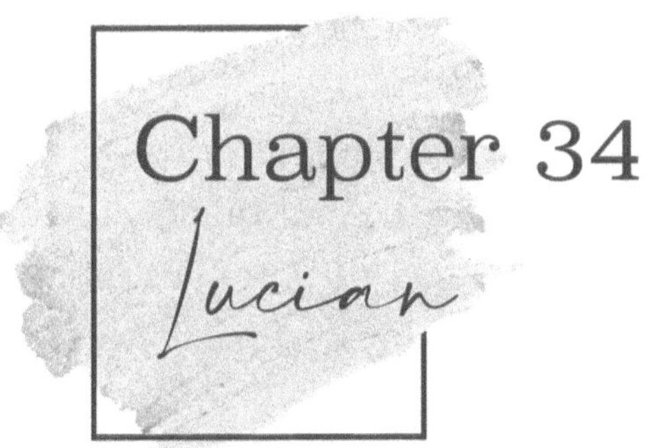

The sun breaks over the city like nothing's wrong.

I stand in front of the floor-to-ceiling windows of my office, espresso in hand, watching the skyline blush with light. The quiet hum of the building stirs around me—elevators starting, voices rising from the lobby, morning security sweeps being logged.

On the surface, it's just another day.

But the smoke still lingers. The ashes of Lorenzo's warehouses still cling to the wind.

That was three nights ago. Simultaneous fires. No alarms. No evidence. Just charred wreckage by morning and millions in unsalvageable inventory turned to dust. I wanted to make him feel exposed. Vulnerable. Unprepared.

But last night?

Last night was *personal.*

While he slept in that fortress of a mansion with his guards posted and his family tucked in safely upstairs... I walked right through his front fucking door.

Jaxon took care of the cameras. My men took care of the locks. And I took care of the art.

Every piece.

The DeLuca family's prized legacy—paintings, portraits, lost artifacts... the gallery of their bloodline—gone. Stolen in silence. Not just the Da Vinci, not just the Monet or the war-era contraband that's passed hands through black market channels for decades.

No.

It's the portraits that matter.

The generations of DeLuca's, hung like royalty along the grand hallway staircase. Lorenzo's wedding portrait—him in black, her in white. Their son, maybe six years old, caught laughing in an oil painting positioned near the piano room. Dozens of frames on side tables, in alcoves, hanging over the fireplace.

All gone.

All mine.

Arranged in a tidy pile in the center of an abandoned warehouse. A single can of gasoline set right beside them. Just enough fuel to make a very clear point.

I take another sip of espresso. The bitterness is welcome.

Right on time, my phone buzzes.

Unknown number.

I don't need caller ID to know who it is.

I answer with silence.

"You arrogant, thieving *son of a bitch!*"

Lorenzo's voice is shaking with rage. Not the cold, calculating kind I respect—but wild, guttural, almost incoherent.

Good. That means he saw the feed.

"I should have fucking killed you when I had the chance," he snaps.

"You tried," I say mildly. "Didn't go well for you."

"You broke into my *home*, Vale."

I take another sip.

"You really should update your security. It's embarrassing."

"You stole from me."

"No," I say, walking to my desk and tapping the tablet with one finger. The live video feed loads instantly, piping straight into Lorenzo's screen on the other end. "I *relocated* some things. Safekeeping. But if you'd like them back…"

I angle the camera.

The artwork. The frames. The family portraits. All of it stacked neatly in the center of the concrete floor.

Then I tilt the angle—just enough for him to see the red gas can at the edge of the frame.

I hear his breathing change.

"You're fucking insane."

"No," I say calmly. "I'm offering a solution. You want to keep what's left of your life? You end this. Right now. Agree to a truce."

He laughs bitterly, but there's panic underneath it. "You think I'd surrender to a man who runs whores in designer heels?"

"Careful," I warn softly. "I don't take well to people disrespecting my employees. You know that."

He scoffs. "If you do this—if you touch that art—you'll regret it. You don't come back from that."

I lean back in my chair.

"No, Lorenzo. *You* don't come back from this."

Silence.

I let it stretch until he speaks again.

But he doesn't.

So, I continue. "You want to come for my empire? Fine. But don't pretend like I started this. Your brother abducted one of my Companions and nearly got her killed. An innocent bystander who stood too close to him when his debt collectors came."

I pause. Let it hang.

"History is bound to repeat itself if you don't give up your pride and admit he got what was coming to him."

More silence because he knows I'm fucking right. His pride just won't let him admit it.

Then I drop the final card.

"Is that the price you're ready to pay?"

A long inhale on his end. No answer.

"I'll give you forty-eight hours," I say. "And then I burn it all."

The line clicks dead.

I stare at the phone for a beat longer, then set it down, draining the rest of my espresso.

He'll call back.

Because he's not just running scared now, he's cornered.

And a man like Lorenzo DeLuca?

Cornered men either surrender.

Or they *keep fighting a war they can't win.*

It's nearly noon, and I'm one shallow breath away from snapping.

Sienna has been driving me insane all fucking morning. A quiet, calculated menace in lipstick and heels—my personal hell dressed in black and white.

She's such a fucking *brat*.

A beautiful, infuriating, untouchable brat. And my palm is *aching* to teach her another lesson.

She walked into the office this morning like she owns it —short, tight dress clinging to her curves like sin. Black and white, classy at first glance... until you actually *look*.

Because it's short. So fucking short I can see the shadow of the garter straps when she walks.

Stirrups.

She's wearing *fucking stirrups*.

Black, sheer stockings attached to garters beneath that tiny little dress—and she's not shy about it either. I know because she's made damn sure I've seen them.

All day.

Meeting after meeting, she's a quiet little shadow just behind the guests, collecting papers, handing out coffee, standing just out of view of the conference camera.

But not *my* view.

Never mine.

She knows exactly where I sit at the head of the table, exactly where my eyes land when someone's speaking.

And she's always in that space—leaning over the sideboard, picking up a file she "dropped," arms straight, legs straighter, ass out, dress sliding high enough that those garter straps peek out and taunt me like little whispers of disobedience.

Smirk locked in place.

Message received.

Please punish me, sir.

Fuck.

But that's not even the worst part.

It's the *panties.*

Red. Dark. Soaked.

I saw them when she crossed her legs during the morning finance briefing. One inch too wide, just long enough for the hem of her dress to pull, just long enough for me to *see* the thin lace stretched over her soaked little cunt.

That wet patch?

It's not innocent.

It's not accidental.

She's *getting off* on this.

Turning herself on by driving me to the edge while I sit through back-to-back boardroom briefings, pretending to give a shit about cost reports while my cock is hard as granite and my blood is boiling.

She's doing it on *purpose.*

Testing me. Poking the bear. Playing with fire.

The conference call ends.

I don't even wait for the final bullshit pleasantries.

I slam my laptop shut with a sharp *crack,* ending the meeting mid-sentence. My jaw is locked, hand clenched around the edge of the desk as I breathe through the storm building in my chest.

I hear her voice before I see her.

Soft. Sweet. Sweet enough to make me fucking dangerous.

"What's the matter?" she says, honey dripping from every syllable. "You seem tense."

I don't answer.

I just slide my chair back, slow and deliberate, rotating it toward her. Letting her see exactly what she's been doing to me.

She saunters forward like she owns the fucking room.

That black-and-white dress hugging her hips like it was made to be torn off. Her heels click with every step—black leather, sharp enough to kill. In her hand, a crystal glass of whiskey—my favorite, neat, precisely two fingers.

She stops in front of me. And then—*fuck me*—she drops.

Right to her knees.

She slips her shoes off one at a time, placing them neatly beside her. Then she settles, slowly, into the pose I taught her. The one I praised her for. Back straight, shoulders soft, chest high and proud. Knees wide. Hands resting perfectly on those silky, creamy thighs.

Her eyes lift to mine, calm and clear—but there's fire underneath.

"Can I help you relax... *sir?*"

My cock throbs behind my zipper.

It's not the whiskey.

It's not the posture.

It's not even the word she dripped like sin between her lips.

It's the *defiance.*

The way she looks up at me like she's innocent—like she

isn't the fucking reason I'm one heartbeat away from bending her over this desk and ruining every inch of her.

And she *knows* it.

This isn't submission.

It's *seduction*.

And she's about to learn that when it comes to me… they're not the same thing.

I take the whiskey from her hand and set it on the desk without a word.

I'm two seconds from grabbing her by the throat and telling her exactly how I plan to use that mouth—when a soft knock hits the doorframe.

Twice.

Fuck.

"Knock, knock," Eve says, already halfway into the room.

Sienna moves *fast*.

She ducks her head and *crawls* under my desk with the elegance of a predator, and suddenly I'm sitting here—raging hard, heart slamming against my ribs—as my training manager walks in like she owns the place.

Oh, nothing to see here, Eve. Just my brat trainee who's been edging me through meetings for three hours now *nesting* under my desk like a well-trained little whore.

Perfect.

"Lucian?" Eve says brightly, dropping into her usual leather chair across from me. "I need a word."

"Not a good time," I grit.

Under the desk, Sienna settles between my legs like she fucking belongs there. She does. And she knows it.

Her hands glide up my thighs, slow and featherlight, like

she's feeling out how far she can push me. My breath catches, but I don't move. Don't *breathe.*

I can feel her smile when she finds my belt buckle.

I grip the arms of my chair, knuckles whitening, and force my gaze to meet Eve's as she crosses one leg over the other and starts talking.

"I've been thinking about shifting how I handle contracts," she says, smoothing down her pencil skirt. "I'm still one of the top-requested Companions, but I'm starting to feel like quantity is wearing me down. I want exclusivity."

Sienna opens my belt. The *click* of the buckle sounds like thunder in my ears.

"Exclusive contracts?" I ask, voice even—too even.

"Mm-hmm," Eve nods. "Same clientele. Fewer engagements. I'd be more like... a girlfriend for hire. A permanent Companion. Intimacy. Familiarity. All the benefits of a relationship without the messy strings."

My zipper slides down.

My cock springs free—and Sienna's fingers wrap around it like she was *born* for this. Warm. Tight. Deliberate.

I force my jaw to stay loose, my breathing steady. "I'm assuming you have a few favorite clients in mind?"

She smirks. "Oh, you know me, Lucian. I *always* have favorites."

Sienna doesn't make a sound. She's a fucking ghost down there. But her mouth is a furnace as it wraps around the head of my cock. Soft lips, wet heat, slow suction. I exhale through my nose like it'll help. It doesn't.

I nod once, pretending to consider Eve's proposal while Sienna bobs lower—tongue teasing just under the crown. I slide my fingers through her hair, holding the side of her head.

A silent approval of my sneaky little minx under the desk.

"I'm just tired of surface-level chemistry," Eve continues. "I want something deeper. Something where the client values... *consistency*."

Sienna slides deeper. Her tongue flattens under my cock as she begins to build a rhythm, stroking me with her mouth, her hand twisting at the base, every movement designed to destroy me.

I grunt—*just* quiet enough to pass for agreement.

Eve quirks a brow. "You okay?"

"Fine." My voice comes out rough. Too rough. "Whiskey's strong."

She shrugs.

"Anyway, I figured I'd take on three... maybe four clients at most. And I'd still be available for Ledger events. Just less public, more refined."

Sienna *hums* around me.

It's over.

The vibration shoots through me like lightning. My balls draw tight, my body taut with restraint, and I *can't* move. Can't fuck up. Can't lose composure—not with Eve sitting ten feet away rambling about client portfolios while her trainee sucks the soul out of me beneath the desk.

I place one hand flat on the surface—trying to ground myself—the other tightens in her hair. I finally find my voice.

"We'll... discuss it more in your review," I manage. "Put your request in writing."

"Of course," Eve says, rising from her seat. "Thanks, Lucian. You really are the best boss."

The fucking irony.

"Anytime," I rasp, watching her disappear through the door.

As soon as it clicks shut, my head falls back against the leather.

Sienna doesn't stop.

She *fucking doubles down.*

I groan—low, filthy, completely *wrecked*—as my hips lift off the chair and I come in her mouth, harder than I have in months.

She swallows every drop.

She looks up at me with those wide, shining eyes like she's done something worth *praise.*

And she has.

But before I reward my good girl...

I have to punish my bad one.

I grab her by the arm and haul her up—not roughly, but with no room for argument. Her breath hitches as I lift her onto the desk and push her back with a firm hand on her chest.

Her legs fall open automatically.

Like she *knows.*

And fuck, does she look obscene like this—panties still damp, her lips, swollen and parted in a soft, breathless dare.

"Such a dirty mouth on such a sweet Angel," I murmur, trailing my fingers over the curve of her inner thigh.

She shudders.

"Keep your legs open for me," I command softly, bending down between them, my breath hot against her soaked lace. "While I suck every drop of cum from your drenched panties..."

My tongue flicks against the seam of red silk, and she whimpers.

"...my *naughty little rabbit.*"

I come with a cry, back arching off the desk, thighs shaking, vision going white at the edges as Lucian's mouth works me through it like he *owns* my pleasure—because he does.

God, he does.

And when I finally collapse against the cool wood, breathless and panting, I manage to gasp out between whimpers, "Honestly? Waiting this long to have my pussy eaten might be the dumbest decision I've ever made."

Lucian chuckles against my thigh, deep and indulgent. His hands are warm on my hips as he pulls back, dark eyes dragging up my body like he's memorizing the wreckage.

"I agree," he says, low and amused.

He helps me down gently, guiding me off the desk and into his lap. I straddle him instinctively, curling into him as he pulls me into a kiss—slower now. Softer. Still possessive, but with something unspoken lingering just beneath it.

I could stay here forever. Wrapped in him. Drenched in sweat and something that feels dangerously close to... more.

But I have to ask.

I hesitate first, trailing a hand down the front of his now half-buttoned shirt, drawing invisible lines over the ink beneath.

"Not to make this weird," I murmur, still breathless, "but when do I get cleared for contracts?"

His fingers still on my thigh.

And just like that, the air shifts.

The warmth in his eyes fades, replaced with that unreadable storm-gray mask he wears so well.

I don't even need him to answer to know I've touched a nerve.

"I mean," I say quickly, trying to make it sound light, "most of the other girls have been cleared by their sponsors. A few already started first contracts. I've been putting up with your shit for *weeks* now."

That earns me the faintest twitch at the corner of his mouth—but it doesn't reach his eyes.

Instead, he leans forward, grabbing the leather folder off his desk and stuffing it full of contracts and paperwork like I'm not still in his lap. Like my question is a line he didn't want me to cross.

"We'll talk about it soon," he says.

My stomach dips.

"Soon?" I echo.

Lucian's jaw ticks as he flips the flap closed on the folder, his focus suddenly laser-pointed on anything *but* me.

"See if you're ready for your first real contract," he adds, standing and setting me aside like I'm light as air. Like I'm *temporary*.

I stay sitting on the edge of his desk, trying to hide how hard that lands. How deep it cuts.

So that's it? A lesson?

Training?

I adjust the strap of my dress, the silence between us louder than anything he could say.

But I see it. The truth he won't speak. The tension in his shoulders. The way his fingers curl too tightly around the leather folder. The flicker in his eyes when he doesn't think I'm looking.

He's lying.

This *isn't* just training.

It hasn't been for a while now.

I'm not expecting some fairytale declaration. I'm not naïve. But this is more than just sex. More than just punishment and control. He touches me like he *needs* me. Kisses me like he'll die if he doesn't.

And yet he won't admit any of it.

Not yet.

But that's fine.

Because I'm not going anywhere.

And if he won't say it?

I'll make him feel it.

One way or another.

He doesn't look at me when he speaks next.

"The conversation's over, Sienna."

Cold. Final.

He grabs his jacket from the chair, slipping it on with

ease. The fix of his buttons, the adjustment of his collar—it's all too precise. Too composed. Like if he lets one detail slip, the entire mask might crack.

"I've got to report to the Capitol. Clear some mess with permits." He says it like it's nothing, but I know better.

Lucian Vale doesn't deal with *permits*. He deals in shadows, in leverage, in threats whispered into the dark. This is a man who controls his empire with brutal efficiency. Whatever this is—it's not paperwork.

"You've been busy with *permits* a lot lately," I say carefully, studying the sharp line of his jaw.

He finally glances at me.

His expression is unreadable. "It's under control."

But it's not.

I can *feel* it.

It's been off for a while now. The tension in the building. The way security has doubled, tripled. The whispered conversations between Jaxon and Killian. The way Lucian disappears more frequently, only to come back looking a little more tired, a little more *dangerous*.

He's keeping something from me.

Something big.

He walks to the door, his hand resting on the knob before he stops and turns halfway back.

"I won't be at the sponsor luncheon tomorrow."

My brows lift, surprised. "Oh?"

"More permit issues." His voice is clipped. Detached. But I hear what he's really saying.

Don't do anything stupid while I'm gone.

Well.

That's adorable.

Because I already know *exactly* what I'm going to do at the sponsor luncheon tomorrow.

And Lucian Vale?

He's going to fucking hate it.

It's the first day of summer, and the weather has the audacity to be perfect.

The kind of warmth that kisses your skin, the kind of breeze that carries secrets. My skirt flutters with it—light blue chiffon, soft and floaty, like innocence stitched into silk.

A lie, of course. But it's a beautiful one.

The glass doors open as I step onto the Ledger's upper patio, and sunlight floods everything—illuminating the marble, the curated florals, the carefully dressed sponsors and companions mingling like this is nothing more than a garden party.

But for me?

It's a chessboard.

Lucian is gone. "Permit issues," he said with that flat, clipped tone that always means *don't ask*. He's off playing king of the shadows while I'm here—*queen by default*.

And queens?

They don't sit on the sidelines.

Trainees aren't allowed full contracts until they're cleared by their sponsors. But a *soft contract*? One made with another sponsor—especially in Lucian's absence?

Technically allowed.

And I plan to exploit *every* inch of that loophole.

Because the last time we had a mixer, Mr. Langston let something very interesting slip. A little comment, a passing remark that I tucked away like a dagger behind my back.

You know, Sienna... you were the top bid, right? We all wanted you. But Lucian pulled you before the decision went public.

He took me for himself. Made me believe no one had wanted me. That I was lucky he gave me a chance at all.

And maybe he thinks I should be grateful for that.

But today?

Today, I rewrite the narrative.

I scan the patio with a practiced eye—polite smiles, half-full champagne glasses, silk dresses and well-tailored suits. Then I see him.

Mr. Langston.

Early forties. Greying at the temples, but sharp in a navy linen blazer. Tall. Broad-shouldered. Handsome in a wealthy, clean-cut sort of way. The kind of man who collects assets for fun. Finance, if I remember correctly. Quiet power.

But for my purpose, he's perfect. An older man, even more so than Lucian. Also handsome. Also rich. Also one that likes to dominate.

He's talking to one of the senior companions. Laughing politely.

I wait until she's called away before I begin moving toward him but he's already spotted me.

Mr. Langston lifts his glass in a quiet acknowledgment, his eyes trailing down my body in that professional, not-so-professional way some men have perfected. I cross the patio toward him with a soft smile, the breeze tugging playfully at my skirt, brushing it against my thighs.

"Miss Knight," he greets, ever the gentleman. "Summer looks good on you."

"And you, Mr. Langston," I reply, letting my tone land somewhere between flirtation and grace. "It's a perfect day, isn't it?"

He smiles, sipping from his glass. "I assume training under Lucian Vale has been... instructive?"

"I only wish it were a little more *hands-on,*" I murmur, reaching for the champagne a server passes behind him. "But he's very busy, as I'm sure you can imagine."

That does the trick.

Langston leans in slightly, voice dropping as if he's the one initiating something forbidden. "Well... some sponsors do make arrangements for a few opportunities with trainees they didn't win. If the interest is mutual, of course."

"That would be wonderful," I say, stepping a little closer. My bare shoulder brushes against his arm resting on the bar, and I make no move to correct it.

As if on cue, the wind lifts the hem of my skirt a bit too high. I reach for it—but so does he.

His hand grazes down the curve of my hip, steadying the fabric, lingering longer than he should before pulling away.

"It is a beautiful dress on you," he says, voice low. "Though I imagine *everything* is."

I glance up at him, lashes low. "Perhaps dinner?"

Langston's smile deepens. "I'd love that. I can log it into the system. Tonight, if you're free."

I tilt my head, eyes gleaming. "Well then... I'm all yours.

Lucian's out of town, after all. I think it's safe to say my sponsor won't be needing me."

And that's when I feel another presence join us.

A man steps into our orbit like he's always belonged there. I haven't seen him before. Not at any event, not in any file.

Which is strange.

Because events like these are *exclusively* for Ledger sponsors. But perhaps he is a new sponsor. I hear they are evaluated as each group of trainees moves on, before a new orientation begins.

"Apologies for interrupting your conversation with the striking Miss...?"

His voice is smooth. Rich. Intentional.

"Knight. Sienna," I say, offering my hand.

He takes it delicately, shaking it like we're on the edge of something that doesn't need words yet.

"Miss Knight," he repeats. "I couldn't help but overhear —you're being sponsored by Lucian Vale?"

"I am," I answer, still holding his gaze. "It's been... very educational."

His smile sharpens. There's something about it that feels too knowing. Like he's seeing beneath my skin. Like he's already decided what part of me he'll bite first.

"You must be a remarkable Companion to catch the attention of Mr. Vale himself," he says, eyes trailing just a little too long.

Langston clears his throat, polite but firm. "If you don't mind, Miss Knight and I have a few things to discuss."

"Of course," the man says smoothly, still holding my

hand with a reverent touch. "Forgive me. My name is *Dominic Salvi*."

The name is unfamiliar.

But the *energy*?

It prickles.

"It's nice to meet you, Mr. Salvi."

His lips brush my knuckles, slow and deliberate before he finally releases me. "I do hope we'll have the chance to speak again. Soon."

"Perhaps."

I turn with Langston, letting him guide me across the patio—but I *feel* Dominic's eyes on me the entire time.

Burning.

Watching.

Something about his feels electric and I catalog it away to look at his file later. If I'm scouting out possible clients to ruffle the feathers of my brooding sponsor, that man would meet the mark.

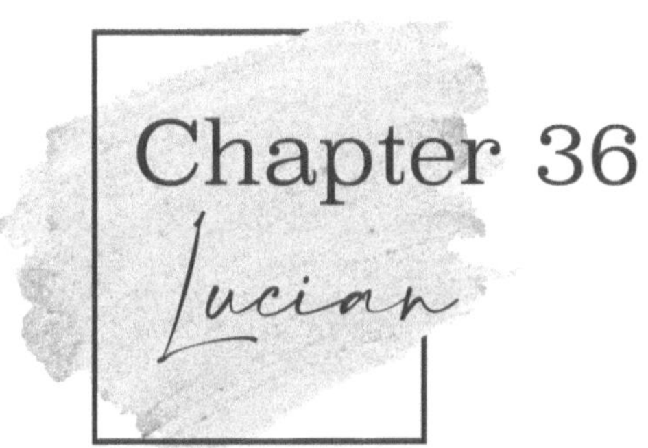

Chapter 36
Lucian

The trip to the Capitol wasn't for fucking permits.

That would've been a waste of time.

The judges were already bought. The summons tossed. The charges, buried. Every signature forged, every roadblock erased.

No—I came for something far more valuable.

A reminder.

Senator William Johnson has forgotten who he belongs to.

He doesn't know about the war brewing between me and Lorenzo—and he doesn't need to. He doesn't need to understand the inner mechanics of organized revenge. Or why the buildings Lorenzo spent decades constructing now lie in ash.

What Bill *does* need is a very sharp, very personal reminder of why he pledged loyalty to me in the first place.

He expected a Companion to meet him tonight.

Someone soft and pretty to indulge his particular... tastes.

Instead, he gets me.

I slide into the booth across from him, ignoring the confusion that crosses his face. It's the panic he tries to swallow that gives him away.

"Lucian." He tries to smooth it over, already reaching for that political charm.

I cut him off before he gets another syllable out. "Let's skip the pleasantries. You betrayed me."

His mouth opens, closing just as quickly. "That's not—"

"You don't get to argue," I interrupt again, calm as ice. "You don't get to explain. You get to listen."

I pull out my phone and press play on a short video. The screen lights up with footage of me—earlier today—seated across from a well-dressed woman at a rooftop café. Elegant. Blonde. Older.

Bill's wife.

He stares at the screen, blinking.

"I had lunch with her this morning," I say casually. "Lovely woman. Kind eyes. A little lonely, maybe."

His jaw tightens. "She told me she had a foundation meeting."

"She did. Just not the kind she thought."

I lift my phone again, switch to the tracking app, and tap the blinking blue dot pulsing on the map.

"She's home now," I say quietly. "Thanks to the tracker I had planted in her purse."

"Jesus," he whispers.

"No, Bill. *Lucian.*"

He flinches.

I lean in slightly, voice dipping. "You sold me out. Took Lorenzo's money. Looked the other way while my businesses were targeted. And now you're wondering if you backed the right man."

"I didn't have a choice," he says, grinding the words through clenched teeth. "He threatened me."

"And what do you think *I'm* doing?"

I move to his side of the booth, sliding in next to him, close enough that he can smell the leather of my gloves, the cold press of my calm.

"If you fuck up around Lorenzo," I say, "he'll put a bullet in your head and be done with it."

Bill swallows hard.

"But *me?*" I chuckle, low and dark. "Bill, when a man breaks his word to *me...* I get creative."

He turns toward me, fear in his eyes.

And I twist the knife.

"Does your wife know," I ask, "that you pay my escorts obscene amounts of money to call you their baby boy while you sit in a diaper twice a month?"

His face goes pale.

"That you shit yourself so they can change you? Feed you a bottle, stroke your wrinkled cock while you cry like a six-month-old?"

"Lucian—"

"That you suck your own cum off their fingers and pretend it's breast milk?"

His throat works. A choke. A stifled sob. His eyes dart toward the empty restaurant, realizing for the first time that it's just the two of us.

No servers. No other guests.

I nod slowly. "It's been cleared out. Just you and me now, Bill. And I'm not done."

"Please…"

"But I don't think *that's* what she'd find most disturbing." I smile. "No. I think it's the *horse* one."

His mouth opens, soundless.

"The one where you wear the mask. Gallop around on all fours. Take cock from my men in every hole while a Companion in cowgirl lingerie spanks your flabby ass with a riding crop."

He's shaking now. Visibly. I can feel the heat of his humiliation rolling off his skin.

"You think she'll understand?" I ask. "That it's just a fetish?"

I lean back slightly, then stand, smoothing my blazer down with one hand.

"I'm not here to kink-shame, Bill. I own a club where every kink imaginable gets indulged. But out *there*?" I nod toward the world beyond the glass walls. "People aren't so understanding. Reporters, especially."

He begins to sob quietly.

I reach around my back, draw my Glock, and slam his head back against the booth before jamming the barrel into his mouth.

He screams around it, muffled and pathetic.

"Betray me again," I whisper, "and I'll fuck your life up so thoroughly, so *unrelentingly*, that you'll beg Lorenzo to end it for you. You'll *swallow* that bullet yourself just to escape the wreckage I leave behind."

His shoulders quake, tears pouring down his cheeks.

"And your poor widow," I murmur, dragging the barrel just slightly. "She'll need comfort. A firm hand. A mouth that doesn't lie."

He sobs harder.

"How long do you think it'll take before she begs me to fuck her out of mourning you, Bill? Before she lets me tie her up and show her what it's like to be fucked by a man who actually finishes what he starts?"

He's saying *please*—I can hear it in the way he gags on the steel.

I shove the barrel in deeper, forcing his head back as he chokes on it.

Then, slowly, I pull it out.

I grab the cloth napkin from his lap and wipe the Glock clean. Fold it neatly. Set it back on the table.

"Your suicide will be the least memorable part of your legacy," I say. "Do you understand?"

He nods frantically, mouthing *yes* again and again.

I grab his jaw, hard, squeezing until his lips pucker.

"Say it, *stallion*. Do you understand?"

"Y-yes," he chokes. "Yes, yes, yes."

He won't betray me again.

Not unless he wants to die choking on more than just his secrets.

I leave him there, still shaking, still sobbing quietly in the booth that now smells like his piss.

The restaurant is silent except for the sound of my steps across the marble floor. My Glock rests cool against my back again, but the heat pulsing through me is *far* from cooled.

Outside, my black SUV idles at the curb. The sky's turned heavy with summer dusk—warm, gold-edged, and lying to everyone about the storm rolling in.

My driver stands beside the open door. He looks at me like he's already apologizing.

Never a good sign.

"What the fuck is it?" I snap, not breaking stride.

He clears his throat. "Sir... it's Miss Knight."

I stop.

Stillness sharpens around me like a blade being drawn.

"What about her?"

He shifts, clearly nervous. "She's accepted a soft contract tonight. With another sponsor."

Everything inside me goes silent.

For a full beat, I say nothing.

"What?"

"She's... currently having dinner. With Mr. Langston. Sir."

My blood turns molten.

Of course she is.

I should have seen this coming. That damn gleam in her eyes when I told her we would talk about ending her sponsorship soon.

She fucking planned this the second I told her I wouldn't be at the luncheon.

Calculating. Fucking. Brat.

Langston should know better. It may not technically

break the rules, but every sponsor at The Ledger knew what I'd made *very clear*—Sienna Knight is off-limits.

I hold out my hand, palm up. "Keys."

My driver doesn't argue. He just tosses them into my hand and wordlessly climbs into the passenger seat, snapping his seatbelt like a man who's been through this before.

I slide into the driver's side, already pulling out my phone.

The app opens with a blink.

Her tracker pulses on the screen—bright and fucking defiant.

With a low growl, I punch the gas, tires squealing against pavement, horns blaring as I shoot into traffic like a fucking missile.

She wants to play games?

She just invited the devil to the table.

And I guarantee she won't like the fucking punishment I'm going to serve her.

I'm half on the curb when the SUV jerks to a stop outside the restaurant.

"Keep it running," I bark, slamming the door before the driver can respond.

The maître d' barely gets a greeting out before I'm brushing past him, scanning the room. It takes no time at all.

Langston's at the corner table, tucked beneath low-hanging glass chandeliers.

Alone.

He stands as I approach, ever the polite gentleman. "Lucian."

"Where is she?" I cut him off before the pleasantries even form.

His brow creases. "Miss Knight only stayed a few minutes. Enough to apologize for canceling."

I don't blink. "Canceling?"

Langston nods, confused but not rattled. "Said you had a last-minute sponsor training session set for her tonight at your club. That you needed her." He sips his wine. "Naturally, I deferred."

What the fuck...

I pull out my phone and glance at the app again. Her tracker still pulses, right here. This restaurant. This *table.*

"She did give me this," Langston says, holding out a small white envelope. "Said I could drop it off at the Ledger tomorrow with my sponsor report, but... if you don't mind."

I snatch it from him, already knowing what it is before I even tear it open.

Inside my palm lands a tiny speck of tech. No bigger than the head of a pin. Lightweight. Nearly invisible.

The tracker.

She removed it. Left it here. With *him.*

Fucking hell.

He would have had this with him all night. No matter when I found out, it would have looked like she was with him.

I clinch my jaw so hard my molars nearly crack.

If I had seen her little dot blinking at this assholes house.

I have to stop that thought before it goes further.

Something in me likes to think I would have kept my calm. Rang the doorbell like a normal fucking human being. But who am I kidding?

I would have blown his goddamn door off the hinges and put a bullet in his face. No questions asked.

She's playing a game. A step ahead. Luring me here on purpose, smiling while she pulled the leash from around her neck and dropped it right in front of my feet.

Smart.

But this is where she loses.

Because now I know exactly where she is.

She told Langston I called her in for training. *At my club.*

Which means she's at *The Masquerade.*

The Devil's Playground.

My domain.

I know every inch of that place. Every corridor. Every secret door. Every two-way mirror, every crawlspace above the suites. I designed it to give the illusion of power to others—while keeping the *real* power in *my* hands.

Let her think she's hiding.

Let her think she's bold.

Because when I find her?

I'm not going to scold her.

I'm going to ruin her.

And the sweet, smug little rabbit who thought she could outmaneuver the devil is about to find out what it means to be *caught.*

I glance back at Langston, who's watching me like he's trying to decide whether to apologize or run.

I give him the answer.

"Off-limits means off-limits, Langston. You're out."

I don't wait for his response.

I'm already moving—out the door, into the heat of the evening, the roar of the city wrapping around me like war drums in the distance.

She thinks she's clever.

She thinks she's unpredictable.

But all she's done is light a match in a room full of gasoline.

Chapter 37

Sienna

This might be the dumbest thing I've ever done.

And that's saying something.

But it's too late to turn back now.

Everything was already set in motion the moment I stood outside the restaurant, waiting for The Ledger's on-call service to answer.

"This is Sienna Knight," I'd said, sweet as sin. "I'm on a soft-contract tonight with another sponsor during my training. I can't get a hold of Lucian to let him know—can someone pass along the message for awareness?"

So polite. So procedural.

So *fucking calculated.*

It was all too easy.

I'd been planning for this.

The moment Mr. Langston invited me to dinner, I knew exactly what I needed to do. I'd peeled off the tiny tracker hidden under my nail polish—filed it down to nothing, wondering if I was screwing with something industrial-grade or fragile as glass. Guess I'll find out later.

But it doesn't matter. Because even if the tracker's toast, Lucian *will* know where Langston planned to meet me.

And that's the point.

He'll think he's caught me.

Until he realizes I'm not there.

Until he realizes *where* I am instead.

I step out of the elevator, making my way through the corridors of The Masquerade, each level a little darker, a little louder, a little more dangerous.

I can feel eyes on me. I can feel the heat of curiosity trailing behind me like fingers across my spine.

And I know exactly why.

Because tonight, I'm wearing the most provocative thing I've ever put on.

A black sheer mesh bodysuit clings to me like smoke, long-sleeved with leather cuffs circling my wrists. No bra. No pasties. Just the bare shape of me, visible beneath the mesh, daring someone to look.

Lucian loves my stirrups. Loves when I wear something that suggests surrender.

There are no stockings—just thin bands around my thighs, elegant gold chains threading up to a delicate leather garter belt. From behind, they form an intricate design, like spider silk meant to trap.

Meant to bind.

Because they *are* bindings.

Each chain can hook the cuffs of my wrists behind my

back, locking me into a helpless position. Exposed. At his mercy.

It's a thong, of course.

A thin one and it makes my ass look fucking *divine*.

I walk level by level, pretending I'm just here for fun, pretending I'm *not* counting the seconds until the door bursts open, and *he* storms through it like a thunderstorm dressed in Armani.

I'm planning on the chase.

I'm *counting* on the punishment.

But I'm not going to give in. Not yet. Not until he admits the truth.

I'm not just a Companion. Not just his trainee.

And that's why he won't let me go.

Because I'm the only one he *won't release*.

The one he *hoards*.

He can't own me in pieces and pretend I don't mean something to him.

Not anymore.

If he wants me—*really* wants me—he'll have to come take me.

And this time, he'll have to say it out loud.

I set the empty glass on the table, letting the last cool traces of water slide down my throat. No alcohol tonight. I need to stay sharp. Nerves like live wire. Mouth dry from anticipation.

The fourth floor—*Greed*—hums around me, plush and indulgent, filled with slow movements, whispered promises, and the sharp glint of power playing at the corners of every smile.

Then the alarm sounds.

Soft. Measured. Controlled. Like everything else at The Masquerade, it doesn't scream—it *suggests*.

I see the shift ripple through the room instantly. Conversations pause. Hands retreat. Eyes lift to the corners where the lights wait. The thirty-second warning gives everyone a chance to reclaim their anonymity, rearrange their masks, or disengage from whatever—or whoever—they might not want to be seen with.

But for me?

It's not a warning.

It's a signal.

The Devil has arrived.

He's here. And he's looking for me.

I'm standing near the stairwell when the sound begins, and my body moves before I've fully made the decision. Fingers on the door. A sharp inhale. And I'm gone.

I push through the stairwell and take the steps two at a time. I barely notice the burn in my thighs or the hitch in my breath.

When I crash through the door onto the fifth floor, I reach the railing just as the lights flicker to life above me.

And the world below me blooms.

Wrath.

The floor unfolds like a fever dream—jagged and sprawling, raw and untamed. It's not a playroom. It's a battlefield. A city swallowed by chaos and rebuilt for predators.

I grip the metal railing and scan the terrain. Faux-ruined buildings stretch wide in fractured symmetry. Steel beams hang like ribs from the ceiling. The floor below twists into a maze of rubble and walkways, hallways of darkness, corners designed to trap and tease.

Even trees—large and gnarled—erupt from the ground, their roots curling like claws across the tile. I blink at them. They look *real.*

And in the middle of it all, glowing like a sacrificial altar, is a raised stage.

It's massive.

So much more than I imagined.

And it's *perfect.* I'll be able to see everything from the platform.

A voice cuts through the quiet, calm and controlled over the loudspeaker:

"Attention guests: due to an unexpected water main break, The Masquerade will be closing for the remainder of the evening. Please retrieve your belongings at the Clerks' Desk. Thank you for your discretion."

I laugh under my breath.

Water main break, my ass.

This is Lucian.

Clearing the floors. Getting rid of the crowd. Locking down his kingdom so he can storm through it without distraction.

And hunt me properly.

Guests begin moving past me—some masked, some leashed, others draped in leather or silk, feathers or chains —filing toward the stairs behind. No one seems particularly concerned. The Masquerade has rules. And when rules are broken, the offender will never step foot back inside.

As they rise, I descend.

Step by step, deeper into *Wrath*.

The further I walk, the more real it becomes—every sound a whisper, every flickering shadow a breath behind me. This floor was built for primal play. For predators. For pursuit.

For the *hunt*.

I reach the center, stepping up onto the raised platform, the cold metal beneath my feet humming with possibility. I turn slowly and take it all in—every corridor, every ruined doorway, every inch of wild design meant to obscure and reveal.

It's not just a room.

It's a *labyrinth*.

And I know exactly who will come looking for me here.

Lucian Vale.

The Devil.

And when he finds me?

He won't just drag me back.

He'll have to admit what he's known all along.

That I'm not just a Companion.

Not just his trainee.

I'm *his*.

And tonight, I want to watch him *lose control* trying to prove it.

The intercom crackles.

A low burst of static, barely more than a hiss—and yet it freezes me in place. The hair on the back of my neck stands up, prickling with instinct. I'm alone, but not *really*. Not anymore.

For a beat, the only think I hear is the deep, labored breath of someone. It sounds like they ran a marathon to get here.

Deep. Controlled. Measured in that way predators breathe when they have their eye fixed on their prey.

My pulse stutters.

A voice follows. Not shouted, not forced—but low and lethal, like smoke curling beneath a locked door.

"Run, little rabbit."

The words are slow, dragged out like a warning... or a curse. But they don't feel like either.

They feel like a *promise.*

A chill slips down my spine, chased by something hotter, heavier, curling low in my belly.

"Run as fast as you can," he continues, every word dipped in hunger. "Because when I catch you..."

There's a pause. Silence thick enough to taste.

Then—

"I'm going to fuck you."

And just like that, the lights go out.

Total darkness swallows the maze.

No flicker. No dimming. Just a full blackout, abrupt and consuming.

I don't scream.

I *smile.*

Because the game has truly begun. And I can already feel him closing in.

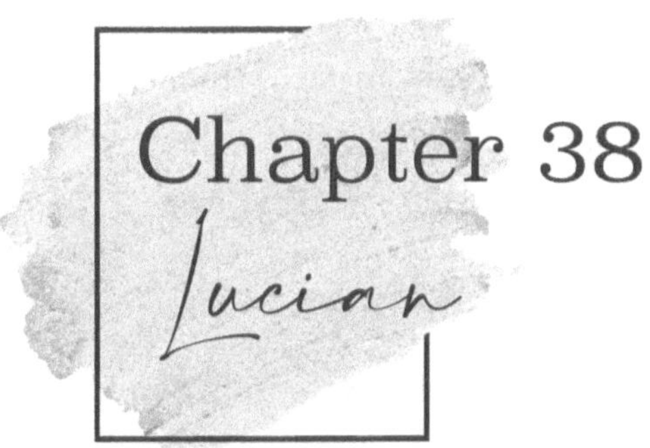

Chapter 38

Lucian

She's on *Wrath.*

I watched her bolt the second the alarm sounded. No hesitation. No second-guessing. Just instinct. The stairwell door was barely swinging closed behind her when I pulled her up on the surveillance feed, following every step.

Up to the fifth floor.

That wild, glorious look in her eyes when she burst through the door and caught sight of the maze stretched out before her. That split-second flicker of panic. The subtle shift to calculation.

I could almost see the map forming behind her eyes as she scanned the terrain—plotting her path, choosing her cover, preparing for the chase.

My little rabbit thinks she's clever.

She is.

Which makes this even more fun.

Outside the control room, my club is emptying. Whispers and murmurs of "water main break" float up the hall-ways as the guests file out, their pleasures postponed. No one questions it. They know better. When I clear the floors, there's always a reason.

And tonight, there's only one thing I want in my kingdom.

Her.

I give her a few minutes—long enough to feel the rush of false confidence, to believe she's making a plan to hide herself well.

Then I lean into the mic and give her my message.

"Run, little rabbit."

Her reaction is instant.

I can't hear it. But I see it. The monitor shows the sharp rise and fall of her chest, the tension in her thighs, the way her head snaps toward the sound like prey catching wind of its predator.

Perfect.

"Run as fast as you can. Because when I catch you..."

I pause. Let it breathe.

"I'm going to fuck you."

And with that, I flip the switch. The entire floor plunges into darkness.

I pull my shirt off in one smooth motion, letting it fall behind me. The belt is next—slipping free of the loops with a snap and wound around my hand.

I grab my mask—the one I only wear when I'm ready to stop playing pretend and start hunting in earnest.

The Devil's mask.

And then I'm on my way to my angel.

No footsteps. No quick breath.

Just a silent descent into *Wrath*.

The floor yawns wide beneath me as I quietly open the door and enter the floor. Shadows curl as the light from the stairwell disappears with the closing door.

My feet are silent on the steps as I descend into the level of madness. The cold of the metal rail biting into my hand. The silence is total—except for the low hum of the lights preparing to come back on.

In a moment, *Wrath* will awaken again—bathed in low, pulsing red light. Just enough to see shapes. Movement. The glint of a bare shoulder or the curve of a thigh disappearing into a corner.

Just enough to *find her.*

At the base of the stairs, I reach the center platform—the raised stage that overlooks the entire floor like a throne over the kingdom. I pause. Let the darkness settle around me.

With a click the lights return, blood-red and pulsing.

A heartbeat for hell.

At the edge of the stage, her heels have been left behind.

Discarded like breadcrumbs.

I grin, slow and dark.

She thinks she can outrun me barefoot?

In my domain?

In *The Devil's Playground?*

No, little rabbit.

You can run all you want.

But you were mine the second you walked through that door.

And now I'm going to prove it.

I step off the stage, silent as shadow, and descend into the labyrinth of *Wrath*.

The moment I enter the first corridor, the temperature shifts. It's warmer here. Claustrophobic. The scent of leather and sweat still clings to the air from earlier scenes of indulgence, but now the space is hollow, stripped of everything but anticipation.

My boots move in silence. Every step calculated. Every breath shallow.

I don't call for her. Don't announce my arrival. I want her to wonder.

Is he close?

Is he watching me?

Because I am.

I listen.

There—a shift of movement to the left. Soft. Like bare feet against the metal grate of a stairwell. She's light on her feet, I'll give her that.

But she's not silent.

She's not *me*.

I change direction, cutting away from the wide path and slipping through one of the ruined doorframes of a collapsed structure. The club spared no expense on the detailing—walls are scorched and cracked, beams splintered, fake dust scattered for realism. I press a hand to the concrete, steadying myself as I listen again.

Nothing.

Clever girl.

She's doubled back.

I turn, slipping between a stack of broken columns, and

climb over a beam to the next chamber. It opens into what looks like an abandoned marketplace—wooden stalls and hanging fabric, designed for primal chases. For capture. For play.

I hear her again. Closer this time.

She's trying to outsmart me.

Her footfalls falter deliberately—pause, shift, pause again. Trying to throw me off her trail.

I smile behind the mask.

"I can hear you, rabbit," I whisper low, just loud enough to carry through the silence.

I don't expect her to respond.

But I hope she trembles.

A door creaks two corridors down.

I move fast now—dodging low under a twisted steel bar, slipping between draped chains that sway as I pass. Another turn, another hallway, then I stop.

Stillness.

I press my hand to the cold metal of the wall and close my eyes.

I *feel* her.

She's close. Her scent clings to the air—warm, sweet, electric with nerves.

I slow my breathing. Let my ears do the rest.

There—behind the old scaffolding, footsteps, barely audible, moving carefully. She's crouched low, trying to stay hidden, heart probably racing like a trapped bird's.

"Are you getting tired yet?" I murmur into the dark. "Because when I catch you, you're not going to be able to walk out of here."

A beat of silence.

Then I hear her gasp.

There you are.

I move fast, surging toward the sound—ducking behind one of the columns, pivoting sharp around the corner.

But she's already gone.

A scrap of black mesh caught on a hook tells me I missed her by seconds.

Clever *fucking* girl.

I chuckle darkly.

"Keep running, rabbit," I growl, low and dangerous. "But you should know… I always catch what's mine."

And she's been mine since the moment I laid eyes on her.

Now it's just a matter of when I take her.

And how hard she begs me to stop.

She's fast. Smarter than I gave her credit for. But that won't save her.

Not here.

Not in *Wrath.*

I double back through a narrow hallway lined with cracked brick, slipping around a steel post that cuts a sharp diagonal through the corridor. She's trying to outthink me, choosing unpredictability over speed—hoping I'll overcommit, that I'll chase in a straight line.

But I've built this floor.

I know its tricks.

Its traps.

And most importantly, I know the way she thinks when she's cornered.

She wants to win.

Which is why I'm about to give her exactly what she *thinks* she wants.

I slow down. Let her hear me.

Boots against tile. Heavy. Measured. Deliberately too loud. I let the sound of my pursuit echo down the main corridor, then dip left—slipping into a side passage hidden behind layers of blackout curtains. She won't see me veer. She'll only hear me moving away.

The bait is set.

I head for the *Echo Chamber.*

It's one of the more sadistic additions to *Wrath*—a circular enclosure filled with fractured mirrors, angled sound walls, and soft floor tiles that absorb footfalls while amplifying others. Disorientation by design.

Sienna doesn't know this floor. Not like I do.

But she will. Soon.

I circle through the outer edge of the maze, taking the longer route around, letting the rhythm of my footsteps continue in the opposite direction.

And right on cue... I hear her.

Her breath. Her steps. Her soft, cautious approach.

She thinks she's flanked me.

Good.

Let her think she's clever. Let her believe she's finally made the right choice.

She slips into the chamber.

I slide in after her through the second entrance.

The space goes silent. So still you could hear her heartbeat if you listened hard enough.

She's careful. Crouched low. Moving slow. Her hand brushes against one of the mirrors, and I see her reflected a dozen times—flickering ghosts of herself stretching into the dark.

She's surrounded.

And has no idea.

I stay behind the wall, circling just outside the main ring, using the mirrors to track her position. Every time she thinks she hears something, she moves toward it. Her own footfalls double back at her. Her own breathing bounces off the glass.

She's *lost.*

I watch her turn in a slow circle, trying to find the source.

Her body is tight with adrenaline. The sheer bodysuit clings to her like a second skin, and those thin chain garters at her thighs are glittering like bait.

She came here to be hunted.

Now, she's exactly where I want her.

I move into the ring—just a few steps behind her. Silent.

She turns again.

Her reflection catches mine, just a glimpse—one flash of the Devil's mask behind her shoulder.

She spins.

But I'm gone.

Another flash in a different mirror. This time to her right.

She backs up, heart in her throat, looking for where I'll appear next.

And then—

I'm behind her.

My hands clamp down on her hips. I pull her flush against me.

"Got you," I breathe against the shell of her ear.

She gasps, one hand flying to the mirror in front of her as if it could anchor her.

Her eyes widen when she sees us—her own reflection, my body towering behind hers, the mask, the bare chest, the belt still coiled in my fist.

"You tricked me," she whispers, breathless.

I smile against her neck. "No, Angel. You tricked *yourself.*"

I walk her backward—right into the wall of mirrors— and trap her there with the weight of my body.

"You wanted to be caught," I murmur, pressing the mask into her shoulder. "You needed to know what happens when you run from me."

I nudge her legs apart with my knee, my belt uncoiling like a serpent between us.

"And now, little rabbit," I growl low and slow, wrapping the belt around her wrists, "I'm going to show you exactly what the Devil does when prey wanders too deep into Hell."

I drop to my knees behind her.

And start collecting my *winnings.*

She's trembling.

Bent forward against the mirror, wrists bound, legs spread, pussy glistening.

My perfect, wicked little rabbit.

I grip her hips, and I don't go gentle. My hands are rough on her ass, pulling her open. My tongue strokes up the length of her slit, slow and possessive, like I'm savoring my favorite dessert. She jolts with every flick, every circle, every press of pressure on her swollen clit.

Her moan is desperate—nearly feral.

"F-fuck—Lucian…"

"Say it," I growl against her pussy, hot breath making her shiver. "Say what you are."

"I'm—" She breaks off, gasping when I suck hard on her clit, rolling it between my lips before letting go. "I'm your slut. I'm yours—God, please—"

"Mmm. There's my girl."

I flatten my tongue and drag it up, then plunge it into

her, fucking her with my mouth until she cries out, thighs shaking. Her body's on a knife's edge, hips grinding, searching for friction, for release.

I give it to her.

For a moment.

I press two fingers inside, curling them deep until I find that spongy spot that makes her *sing* for me. Her breath catches like she's just been knocked out of orbit.

"That's it," I rasp. "Ride it, baby. Let me feel you come all over my fingers like a good little—"

I stop.

Pull out.

Cold.

She lets out a strangled sound, half-whimper, half-wail. Her hips roll back in desperation, chasing the pressure. "No —no, no, don't stop, please—!"

I rise behind her, towering over her small, trembling body as I grip her chin and tilt her face toward the mirror. Her lips are parted, cheeks flushed, eyes wide and *furious*.

"Bad girls don't get to come just because they beg," I say, low and cruel, dragging my soaked fingers across her lips. "You ran from me. Made me hunt. You don't get rewards yet, little rabbit. You get *lessons*."

She licks my fingers anyway. Of *course* she does.

"I'll be good," she breathes. "I swear I'll be good, sir."

I chuckle darkly, already dropping back down. "You're going to say that again in about thirty seconds—right before I take it away *again*."

I dive back in.

This time I'm merciless—tongue and fingers working in

tandem, dragging her toward the edge in rapid, relentless waves. Her thighs quake. Her moans come in broken sobs. She's losing herself—completely unraveling in my grip.

And just as I feel her body lock—

Just as her climax starts to crest—

The club's alarm shrieks.

A brutal, blaring sound that echoes off the walls and slices straight through the haze.

Every hair on my body stands on end.

That's not a club alarm.

That's not a drill.

That's a breach.

I freeze.

Sienna jerks, breathless and still straining against the edge. "Wh-what...?"

"Stay here," I bark, already standing. Rage claws through me like wildfire.

She's blinking, confused and shaking, still on the cusp of her orgasm.

"Lucian—what's happening?"

My jaw tightens. I don't answer. I'm already grabbing my discarded belt, looping it into my hands. Mask still on. My cock still hard and leaking.

My club has been compromised.

And whoever just walked into my house?

They're going to bleed for interrupting me.

All pretense ends in an instant.

The alarm still echoes, but I'm already winding the belt around my hand, tugging it tight until the leather groans. I reach up and rip off my mask, then hers—her face flushed, pupils wide, breath still heavy with arousal and confusion.

Not anymore.

I take her hand, grip firm but steady, and pull her with me. My strides are fast, decisive. No more games. No more play.

We cut through the mirror maze in seconds—my path memorized long before she ever stepped foot on this floor. A wall panel just past the curved glass stage hides the call box. I slam it open, lift the receiver, and press the override code.

Chaos explodes in my ear.

Gunfire. Screaming. One of my men shouting *"They're inside—six—maybe more—fuck—"* before the line goes dead.

But one more word cut through the frey. *"DeLuca."*

My blood turns to ice.

Lorenzo is here.

He wouldn't have come himself. He never does. The bastard doesn't stain his hands. But he sent his dogs. Armed and ready to make a statement.

He picked the wrong fucking place.

I turn to Sienna but she already knows. I see it in her eyes—the shift from playful to terrified. Her body's shaking and her lips part like she wants to speak, but no sound comes out.

I take her face between my hands, holding her steady.

"Sienna. Angel." My voice is calm. Quiet. "I need you to listen to me very carefully."

She nods, chest rising and falling too fast.

"The club is under gunfire. There are men inside, armed, and they're not here to negotiate. We have to get out. I need you to stay behind me, and no matter what happens—*you do not let go of me.* Do you understand?"

"Yes," she whispers, but the word barely comes out. Her whole body is tight, vibrating with fear.

I turn, hit a second panel beside the call box. It clicks open to reveal a hidden stash—handguns lined up like art, each one cleaned and loaded. I grab two, checking them fast, efficient. One goes in my waistband. The other stays in my hand.

I glance back at her. "Have you ever seen anyone get shot before?"

She swallows hard. "No."

"Have you ever seen someone die?"

Her breath catches. "No..."

I nod. "Okay. Baby—listen to me. In order for us to make it out of here, I'm going to kill someone. Probably several someones."

Her eyes widen, breath hitching again. The reality of what I've just said wraps around her like a vice.

"You're going to see blood," I say, gentler now, though my tone is firm. "You're going to see them fall. You're going to see what it looks like when I do what I was made to do. You okay?"

She doesn't answer.

"Sienna—look at me."

I take her chin again, gently but unyielding, tilting her face until her eyes meet mine. Big. Wild. Glassy with unshed tears.

And then I kiss her.

Because there's nothing else I can do.

Because if I die tonight, I need her to know *some part* of this was real.

I rest my forehead to hers, both of us closing our eyes. Her breath shudders out against my lips.

"I won't let anything happen to you. Do you trust me?"

"Yes," she says, voice hoarse but strong this time. "I trust you."

I exhale hard, letting her answer settle into my chest like a weight.

"Good girl," I murmur, backing up.

"Stay close. Stay low. And do not run."

She nods again, trembling fingers brushing the sweat from her brow. Her eyes are wide, but her chin is set. She's scared—but she's ready.

I glance back at the security panel, watching the grainy feed. They're on their way—moving floor by floor, sweeping down from Level Nine. A slow descent with quick intent. They think they're smart. Think they're surgical. Coordinated.

But this is my house.

They were hoping for chaos. For blood. For screams echoing through the corridors while I sat in my goddamn throne in The Devil's Playground, playing host to a hundred masked deviants.

But I cleared the club and they hadn't counted on that. So now it's just them... and me.

And *her.*

Several of my men are down—I can't tell how bad—but I'll grieve for them later. If I make it out. Right now, I only care about the breathing, shaking woman behind me.

And I swear on the fucking flames of Hell itself—I will level this place to dust before I let her bleed here.

I check the hall once more, then turn back to her. "Let's go."

We move in a crouch, slipping between the dark shadows of *Wrath*—structures designed to mimic the ruins of abandoned buildings and crumbling alleyways. Concrete pillars, rusted scaffolding, half-buried rebar twisted like vines. This floor was built for *primal play*—predator and prey.

Tonight? It's real.

We're almost to the rear wall when I hear the crunch of boots on metal.

They're here.

I flatten Sienna against a jagged column, shielding her with my body. "Behind me. Stay small."

She ducks low, her hands balled tight against her stomach.

Voices echo—sharp, alert. I catch them in the reflections —two men clearing the path ahead.

I pull my gun. One breath. Two.

Pop. Pop.

Both drop.

Not fast enough.

I spin, grabbing her hand and tugging her along until a cluster of metal crates blocks our path. I shove her down behind them just as two more shadows close in with fast footsteps.

I hear the click of a weapon being raised—too close. No time to aim.

I surge forward.

The first man rounds the corner. He barely has time to register me before my fist crushes his throat. He gurgles, stumbles, and I grab the barrel of his rifle, turning it into a lever to slam him face-first into the wall. Bone cracks.

The second one lunges—firing blindly.

I'm already inside his guard. My elbow slams into his temple, dazing him. Then my knee rises fast, brutal, shattering his nose. He swings, desperate—I duck, grab the back of his neck, and drive him down onto my knee. He drops like deadweight.

Two more bodies.

I exhale slowly and turn back to find Sienna staring.

Her hands are over her mouth, but I see the shock in her eyes. The tears pushing forward. She just watched me kill two men—one with my hands, one with rage.

I crouch, cup her cheek.

"You okay?"

Her nod is barely there. But it's enough.

"We're almost out."

A gunshot cracks overhead, loud and sudden. I throw her down and cover her body with mine just as the bullet strikes a hanging light above us. Glass shatters, raining down like crystal hail.

She screams—just once—and I feel it vibrate through me.

I twist, shielding her, then rise on instinct—gun raised—and fire.

One shot.

Clean.

The last man stumbles and falls, crashing backward into the broken scaffolding before his body thuds hard against the concrete floor.

Sienna flinches at the sickening sound.

But we have to fucking go.

I grab her, lift her into my arms and run—glass crunching beneath my boots as I move fast and low across the debris field. She buries her face in my shoulder, and I feel her tears against my neck.

The hidden exit is just ahead—disguised by a rusted steel archway and a false ventilation shaft.

I stop long enough to set her down.

Our hands find each other again.

Fingers locked.

I look at her. "We're almost out."

Then we run—side by side—into the shadows of the emergency corridor.

My ears are ringing. Every muscle in my body is on edge, every sense tuned for danger. I reach the stairwell door first and press a hand against it, listening.

Silence.

Stillness.

I wait one more breath, then push it open.

Clear.

I exhale hard, grabbing her hand and pulling her inside with me. The metal door swings closed behind us with a soft thud, and we move—fast.

I take the stairs two at a time, boots pounding against concrete. She's barefoot in nothing but her mesh bodysuit, and I hear the soft slap of her soles with every hurried step, her breathing ragged behind me. Her courage is admirable, but she's unraveling fast—and who the fuck could blame her?

When we hit the bottom, I don't stop. I grip the door handle tight, every instinct screaming this is the final moment. Freedom or a bullet.

I throw it open and burst out—gun raised.

Another barrel meets mine.

"Fuck—" we both start, pulling our weapons back when I realize it's Killian. My head of security. His eyes are wide, gun lowering just as fast.

"Jesus, boss."

"Where are they?" I demand, scanning behind him.

"Still inside. Five of them. Moving slow. We've got eyes."

"How many of ours?"

Killian's face tightens.

"Three injured. But they'll live. No deaths."

I close my eyes for half a second.

Relief hits like a sledgehammer. The ache in my chest loosens enough to let me breathe.

Killian holds up two security jackets. Sees Sienna behind me, still trembling, lips pale, eyes blown wide from adrenaline and fear.

He tosses me the jackets.

"Get her out of here. We've got the rest."

He looks at her, not unkindly.

"Hey," he says gently. "Good thing the club was already cleared. If it hadn't been, this would've been a massacre."

Sienna doesn't speak. Just gives him the faintest nod. She's trying to hold it together. But she's barely tethered.

"Come on," I murmur, taking her hand again.

We round the corner and I lead her straight to the back lot—dark, empty, silent.

My motorcycle sits parked beneath the floodlight. Two helmets wait.

I tug one free and crouch in front of her, gently sliding it on over her head. My fingers graze her cheeks as I adjust the strap.

"Have you ever ridden a motorcycle before?"

She shakes her head. Her breath's shaky. She's holding on by threads.

Fuck.

I lean closer. "Just hold onto me, okay baby?"

She nods again, slower this time. Trusting.

I rise, fix my own helmet, and swing onto the bike. My hands go to the handlebars and I hold one out behind me.

She climbs on, her legs settling behind mine. Then her arms wrap around my waist—tight. So tight.

She's fucking terrified and it breaks my heart.

I cover her locked hands with one of mine and squeeze, just once.

Then I start the engine.

And we fly.

Away from the blood, away from the death.

Toward home.

Chapter 40

The ride home is a blur.

Everything around me feels like echoes, as if I'm flying too fast through a tunnel and the world can't keep up. I hear the wind, but it sounds hollow. I see lights, but they blur into meaningless color.

My arms are locked around Lucian, but even that feels distant—like I'm floating somewhere outside myself.

When the bike finally leans into the turn onto his long, winding driveway, something inside me breaks loose.

I start shaking.

Almost there. Just hold on a little longer.

I repeat it like a prayer.

I need off this bike. I need out of this jacket. I need this suffocating bodysuit peeled off me. I need to be held... or I might come apart entirely.

Lucian must feel it—sense the shift in me—because the moment he cuts the engine and kicks down the stand, he's already turning around and I'm in his arms.

Strong. Steady. Unyielding.

He lifts me like I weigh nothing, one arm under my knees, the other tight behind my back, pulling me against his chest. Our helmets are on the ground in a second.

His lips find the top of my head, pressing soft kisses there, again and again as he murmurs low, calming words against my scalp.

"I've got you, angel. You're okay. I've got you now."

The tremble in me becomes a full-body quake, and I don't realize I'm crying until the tears slide down over my lips. Silent. Hot.

Lucian doesn't let go.

Inside, the house is dim. He moves through it like a man possessed, never once jostling me as he strides back toward his bedroom. Then—his bathroom that surrounds me in soft golden lighting.

He sets me down gently on the cool tile and steadies me, both hands on my waist until I nod. I can stand. I *think* I can stand.

He turns to the tub, checking the water, adjusting the temperature.

And that's when I look down.

That's when I see it.

A dark, wet stain spreads low on the front of the jacket he gave me—just below my ribs. At first, I think it's water. Or oil from the motorcycle.

But when I unclip the front and peel the material open, a sharp, cold shock crashes over me like a tidal wave.

Blood.

A deep red smears across my mesh bodysuit, just above

my hip. I touch it. My fingers come away slick. Shaking, I do it again, pressing against the wet heat blooming through the thin fabric.

Lucian turns just as I sway.

"Sienna—"

I look up at him. My voice doesn't work. I hold up my hand instead, stained red with blood.

His eyes go wide and everything tilts.

I think I'm dying.

I know it sounds dramatic, but there's blood on my hand —a lot of blood—and I can't remember where it came from or when it happened. My stomach feels cold, my fingers even colder, and my vision swims like I'm underwater.

Then he's there.

Lucian's hands are on me in an instant, firm but careful. I think I hear him praying—*please, God. Please, devil. Please, someone.*

His voice is hoarse. Wrecked.

"Let me look, baby. Let me see."

He pulls the jacket off of me, and I see his eyes dart over every inch of me like he's memorizing my body just in case. But then he exhales a breath so deep it shakes his chest.

"It's not yours," he says, his voice ragged. "It was on the jacket. It's not yours."

He says it again, over and over, holding my face in both hands now. His forehead presses against mine, and for the first time since the gunfire started, I can actually focus.

"You're okay, Angel," he murmurs, brushing my hair back. "You're not shot. You're okay."

My knees finally give out, but he's already holding me so

tight it doesn't matter. The sob tears out of me so fast, I don't even feel it until I hear the broken sound echo in the bathroom tiles. Then I crumble.

I cry like a child. Like a woman who saw death up close. I cry for the fear, the confusion, the panic I buried to stay alive. I sob until I can't breathe, and still Lucian holds me—shelters me—like he'll never let go.

At some point, he undresses me. I don't even remember when. All I know is the cold is gone, replaced by warmth and strong arms lifting me again.

He carries me into the bath, the water hot and perfect around us. I curl into his chest, my cheek against his skin, listening to the steady thrum of his heartbeat. One hand strokes up and down my spine. His voice is a quiet hum of praise and reassurance.

"You're safe now, Angel. I've got you. I'm here."

My breathing starts to steady. The panic ebbs. The ache in my bones dulls beneath the water's warmth and the safety of him.

But in its place, something else stirs.

Heat. Desire. A fire that spreads slowly but surely through every part of me as I become acutely aware of his arms, his chest, the feel of his skin under my fingers.

He doesn't stop touching me. Doesn't stop whispering, comforting, claiming me without even trying.

I tilt my head up and find his eyes already on mine. The look in them nearly undoes me.

Desperate. Tormented. Fiercely tender.

I kiss him before I can stop myself.

It's not soft. It's not shy. It's all the emotions I can't say out loud—everything I'm feeling, everything I need. Our mouths crash together like a storm, and he answers me with the same intensity.

I climb into his lap, straddling him without a second thought. When I feel his cock, hard and thick between us, I moan into his mouth.

I need this. I need him. To feel alive. To feel wanted. To remind myself that I made it out.

He doesn't stop me. He just growls deep in his throat as I shift, lining us up.

I slide down on him, slow and steady, and we both groan. He fills me completely. Stretching me, claiming me in the most primal way possible.

Everything else fades.

The world falls silent. The fear is gone. The blood, the screams, the guns—it all disappears.

There's only us.

We move together like we've done it a thousand times, but it still feels brand new. Intimate. Deep. His hands roam my body like it's sacred. My nails dig into his shoulders as I roll my hips, and his lips never stop kissing me.

He holds my face when I come. Whispers my name. Tells me I'm perfect.

And when he follows—his body tense beneath mine, his release thick and hot inside me—I swear I feel it in my soul.

He buries his face in my neck, breathing hard, clutching me tight like letting go would break him.

Maybe it would break me too.

But right now, in this moment, I've never felt more whole.

He washes my hair like it's the most important thing he's ever done.

His strong fingers massage the shampoo into my scalp, slow and soothing. I sigh as he moves with care, rinsing and conditioning, his touch gentle but thorough.

When he wraps my hair in a towel, he makes me bend forward for him to twist and secure it like a makeshift crown. I'm swaddled in warmth and tenderness and a robe so soft it feels like clouds.

It swallows me whole—and I love it.

"I can walk," I mumble, wriggling a little in his arms as he carries me from the bathroom.

"I know." He doesn't stop. Just tightens his hold and keeps moving until I'm seated on the cool marble counter of his kitchen.

"You need to eat something."

His voice is steady again. Controlled. Like he's trying to reestablish some version of calm—for both of us. He moves around the space with confidence, pulling ingredients like it's second nature.

A bottle of red is opened and poured. He hands me a glass, the rim clinking against mine with a soft *cheers* before he takes a sip and starts to cook.

And holy hell—he knows what he's doing.

He minces garlic with exact precision. Blisters cherry tomatoes in olive oil until they pop and burst. Tosses fresh basil in like a flourish. When the pasta is al dente, he drains it and swirls everything together with a handful of grated parmesan.

The entire space smells like heaven.

But nothing compares to the view. The towel slung low on his hips reveals the defined cut of his abs and that sharp V that disappears beneath the cotton. I can't stop looking.

Especially not when the outline of his cock shifts beneath the fabric as he moves.

My thighs clench, heat coiling in my belly like instinct. I'm seconds from dropping to my knees right here in his kitchen when his eyes catch mine.

He grins. Smug. Dangerous. Fucking perfect.

"I didn't peg you as someone who knows how to cook," I say, voice casual, but my insides are a war zone of arousal.

"Contrary to what you may think," he murmurs, lifting a wooden spoon to my lips, "I don't survive off eating your pussy."

The bite is perfect. Garlicky, salty, rich—and my stomach growls in appreciation.

He kisses me quickly. "Though it is my favorite delicacy."

I hum. "I actually thought you lived off espresso."

That earns me a real laugh. Deep and warm.

The whole pot goes to the table—no plates, no pretense. Just two forks. Just a few bites in and I set my utensil down.

He pulls me into his lap without warning, positioning me sideways with one leg on either side of his thighs. The robe falls open between us, exposing the soft heat of my center.

"You need to eat a little more for me, Angel," he murmurs, holding a forkful up to my mouth.

His other hand slides between my legs. No warning. No hesitation.

His fingers graze my folds, parting them as I gasp.

"Can you do that for me?" he whispers, voice like gravel dipped in sin.

I nod, lips parted, eyes already heavy with lust.

"Such a good girl. Open."

I do. I take the bite and moan—not from the pasta but from the way his fingers curl inside me a second later.

He works me slow. Gentle. Unhurried.

Each thrust matches his praise. Each bite is followed by a deeper ache.

Another forkful. Another finger stroke. Another *good girl* whispered against my throat.

It doesn't take long.

I'm moaning. Rocking. Clenching.

And then I'm coming, soft and slow, everything melting around me as he holds me in his arms.

He licks his fingers clean, eyes locked on mine. I kiss him. Desperately. Tasting myself on his lips.

"I want you to fuck me one more time before we go to sleep," I whisper between kisses. "Soft." Another kiss. "Bring me back to life."

His arms are under me in a second.

He carries me to the bedroom, laying me down with care, untying the robe and letting it fall away. His towel hits the floor. His body lowers into mine.

And it's everything.

He doesn't just take me—he worships me. Our bodies move in perfect tandem. His mouth speaks things I never thought I'd hear. Filthy. Reverent. Full of devotion I'm scared to name.

When I come again, it's with his name in my throat and his breath in my mouth. He follows, his arms shaking around me, his release spilling into me like a vow.

I'm drifting. Sleep tugging at the edges of my mind when he moves again.

"Come on, baby. Don't fall asleep with my cum inside you."

I hum, barely awake, but I let him lift me, clean me, and tuck me under the sheets. I feel him curl around me. His warmth. His strength.

And then his lips at my temple.

"I'm so sorry, Angel," he whispers.

A kiss. Another. Then softer still.

"I hope you'll forgive me."

I don't think he's talking about tonight.

And just before sleep takes me completely, it hits me.

Lucian Vale is saying goodbye.

Chapter 41

She's still asleep, curled on her side with one hand tucked beneath her cheek. One of her legs is bared, her skin pale and soft against my black sheets.

She looks like she belongs there—like she's always belonged here—and for one brutal, fleeting second, I let myself imagine what it would be like if this wasn't ending.

If I could keep her.

If I wasn't about to do what I have to do.

I sit on the edge of the bed, elbows on my knees, just watching her breathe. The rise and fall of her chest is steady now, not the shallow panic of last night.

I should be relieved that she's safe, that she's whole. Instead, I feel like I'm being torn in half.

She looks so fucking peaceful, and it guts me.

Because I know I'm about to destroy that look on her face.

Because I know she deserves someone who won't lie to her.

But I will.

Because it's the only way she'll leave me.

Lorenzo's men got into my club. *My* club. Not through brute force, not because we were careless. I can only conclude they got in because someone close to me—someone I trusted—opened a door for them.

And if someone can get inside the Devil's Playground, they can get to her. They already did.

They nearly killed her last night.

When I think about her taking off that blood-soaked jacket... when I thought she had been shot...

My hand curls into a fist. I force myself to breathe.

There's still a leak in my house, and until I find it—until I burn it out at the fucking root—I can't let her stay. Not near me. Not near any of this.

She stirs slightly in her sleep, a soft sigh escaping her lips. My stomach knots. Everything about her is soft when she sleeps. All the fire, the brattiness, the smart mouth—it fades. She looks young. Vulnerable.

And I'm about to break her.

But I have no choice.

Not if I want her to keep this war from touching her.

She doesn't belong in the dark.

She belongs in the light—laughing.

She laughed once in the office—really laughed. I don't even remember what it was about. Probably something Eve said. Something dry and smug that only lands half the time.

But Sienna let out this unfiltered, bright laugh that didn't match the black-on-black pencil skirt she was wearing or the cold marble floors beneath her heels.

It didn't belong in my world.

But I wanted to keep it anyway.

Like a thief with something precious he knows he'll ruin if he holds it too tight.

I remember turning from my desk, pretending to look at the report in my hands, but really just... watching her. Her head tilted back, eyes crinkled at the corners.

That wild auburn hair pulled into one of those lazy knots she thinks passes for professional. Her whole body relaxed for the first time since I brought her into this place.

It only lasted a second. She caught my stare and straightened like she'd done something wrong.

She hadn't.

She was just being happy.

And I wanted to bottle it. Frame it. Lock it the fuck away.

But I don't get to keep that.

I don't get to keep her.

Not when Lorenzo is still out there. Not when someone I trust is leaking blood through the cracks in my empire. Not when the only way to stop this war is to end it on my terms —and I don't know who I'll have to bury to do that.

What I *do* know is this:

If I keep her in my world, it'll chew her up.

And I'm afraid too much damage has already been done.

My phone buzzes on the nightstand.

EVE: I'll be there in ten minutes.

Ten minutes.

Fuck. I wish I had more time.

More time to hold her. To tell her the truth. To kiss her like it means something—because it *does.*

But the clock's ticking on all of this.

This war ends one way—*me or Lorenzo.* And I'm not planning on dying.

Another buzz. This time from Killian. I open the security feed, scan the Masquerade's recovery footage again even though I've already memorized it frame by frame all fucking night long.

> LUCIAN: I want a private meeting within the hour. I'll be at the office soon. We're ending this.

Because I need answers. I need to know how DeLuca's men got through my walls. How they slipped past my protocols. How someone I trust opened the door for them.

If they can get into the Masquerade... they can get into the Ledger.

And if they can get into the Ledger...

They can get to *her.*

My pulse ticks up. I rub the back of my neck and glance back at the woman still sleeping in my bed—still safe. Still soft. Still mine for a few more minutes.

But not for long.

Because this is where the line is drawn.

Between the life she deserves and the war I'm about to wage.

She's still curled into the sheets that smell like me, like us—and I know better than to let myself look too long. But of course I do. Just for a second.

Her features are relaxed, lips parted slightly, her breath steady in the way only sleep can bring. There's a softness there. A safety.

And I'm about to destroy it.

I finish buttoning my shirt, each movement mechanical, deliberate. My fingers find the drawer, searching for the familiar weight of my cufflinks—matte black, the same pair I wore the night we met.

I close the drawer a little too hard. The sound cuts through the stillness like a warning shot.

She stirs, shifting in the sheets. My name follows, quiet and unsure. "Lucian?"

I don't turn. I can't. If I look at her now, I won't do what needs to be done.

I crouch to tie my shoes, slowly. Carefully. Like dressing for war.

With each motion, I retreat further behind the mask she worked so hard to peel away—the man she first met. Cold. Controlled. Untouchable.

Still, I don't turn around. I secure the second cufflink with precision, then finally speak—flat, clipped.

"Take a few days. Report to Eve when you're ready. She'll walk you through your first contract selection."

"What–" There's a pause, and I can hear her sitting up. Sheets shifting. Confusion thick in her tone. "I thought—"

"That was a mistake," I say, cutting her off with surgical precision. My tone leaves no room for questions. Only damage.

The silence that follows is thick, suffocating. I can feel it pressing against my back like her grief is already reaching for me. But I don't flinch. I don't move.

"You don't mean that," she says. Quieter now, but firmer. A soft defiance laced with disbelief.

I grit my teeth. My hand curls around the edge of the dresser until my knuckles burn.

"When have I ever said something I didn't mean?"

The words fall out like a blade, and I know they land the way I need them to. I hear the breath leave her lungs, feel the shift in the air as her world cracks down the middle.

"You bastard," she whispers. "You don't even care, do you?"

Still, I stay silent.

"After everything... after last night... you won't even admit that this meant something?"

Her voice breaks, and for a second, so does something in me. But I can't let her see it.

"Look at me."

It's a command now—low, trembling, laced with a fury that wasn't there before.

I don't move.

"Look at me when you say it, you coward." She yells it, anger cracking through her steady voice.

That word lands. It sinks in and carves a hole right through me. I turn. Slowly. Because if I move too fast, I'll fall apart.

Her hair is a mess. Her eyes are glassy. But she's sitting straight up in my bed like a fucking warrior, holding that sheet to her chest like armor. Her chin trembles but she doesn't back down.

And still, she looks like the strongest person I've ever known.

I look her in the eye and lie through my goddamn teeth.

"You need to learn to separate business from the heart," I tell her, my voice as cold as I can make it.

Her breath hitches, lips parting in disbelief, but I don't stop there.

"Because when it feels real... you have to know it's not."

She stares at me. Waiting. Hoping I'll take it back. But I don't. I can't. Because if I do, she stays—and that's not a risk I'm willing to take. Not with Lorenzo's reach crawling closer to my door.

I grab my watch—black, polished, weightless in my hand—and head toward the door. My voice is flat, final, as I toss the last dagger behind me.

"Eve should be here in five minutes with clothes for you."

She doesn't follow. She doesn't yell.

But I feel her still. I feel the heartbreak trailing behind me like smoke, seeping into my skin, into my lungs.

Outside, the sun is far too bright. The air too still. As if the world dares to continue like nothing inside me has changed.

I step out of the house, jaw clenched, eyes burning. The Rolex presses into my palm. I stare at it for a beat—then with a harsh grunt, I throw it with all the force I can summon.

It hits the stone siding hard, the glass face shattering on impact, sending tiny fragments scattering across the drive like splinters of time I can't get back.

I swing my leg over the motorcycle and start the engine. The roar fills the silence, but it doesn't drown out the echo of her voice, or the echo of my own cowardice.

I don't look back.

I can't.

Because I left her in my bed.

In my world.

A place she never should've belonged.

But God help me...

She did.

Chapter 42
Sienna

It's only been two days.

That's what I keep telling myself.

Two days isn't long. People take longer vacations. Sick days.

Breakups.

But this doesn't feel like a normal breakup.

It feels like someone took a sledgehammer to something fragile inside me and walked away before checking the damage.

I've barely moved from the couch.

The throw blanket is still half-folded from when I tried to sit up and talk myself into going The Ledger this morning.

Didn't happen.

Didn't even get to the part where I put on real clothes.

The air feels heavy. The silence, heavier.

I'm not crying anymore. That stopped sometime around midnight.

Now I'm just... quiet.

Waiting for the ache to dull, even though I know it won't.

Not yet.

The buzzer comes three times in a row. Not the impatient kind, not the angry kind—just the kind that says *I know you're in there, and I'm not leaving.*

I debate ignoring it. But then I hear her voice.

"Sienna, if you don't let me up, I swear I'll call the fire department and tell them you're stuck in the tub with your foot wedged in the drain. Again."

A groan escapes before I can stop it.

I shuffle to the door, buzzing her in and leave the door open a crack before plopping back down on the couch.

The door creaks open a few seconds later, and Harper breezes in like she owns the place—which, emotionally speaking, she kind of does.

"God, it smells like heartbreak and microwave popcorn in here," she says, toeing off her heels and kicking the door shut behind her. "And not the good kind of heartbreak either. The *no one even died and you're still this dramatic* kind."

I don't even lift my head from the couch. "You're welcome for the ambiance."

She walks straight to the window and throws open the curtains, bathing the room in sunlight I didn't ask for and definitely didn't want. "Jesus, Sienna. This isn't mourning. This is light depression with a splash of refusal to shampoo."

"I showered last night," I mumble.

"Not hard to tell. Fuzzy hair, sad eyes, cozy robe. You're

one sad playlist away from becoming a Pinterest cautionary tale."

She walks over, leans down, and squints at me. "Have you eaten anything that wasn't a granola bar or your feelings?"

"I had toast."

Her brow rises. "Dry?"

I hesitate. "...Maybe."

Harper sighs and disappears into my kitchen without another word. A cabinet slams. A fridge opens. Something clinks.

"I'm not in the mood for a pep talk," I mumble, curling deeper into the couch like a feral house cat.

"Oh good," She pops her head back around the corner. "Because I didn't bring one. You *love* grilled cheese and I come bearing brie and reckless opinions. Maybe a sprinkling of rage."

Despite myself, I almost smile.

She reappears with a pan in one hand and cheese in the other, tossing both onto the stovetop like she's about to perform a culinary intervention. "So. Tell me what happened. And don't say 'nothing,' because that look on your face says *everything.*"

I exhale, staring down at my hands like they might offer some kind of answer. "He let me go."

Harper pauses, one hand halfway to the pan. "What do you mean?"

"Lucian. He ended the sponsorship. Said I should report to Eve. Pick a contract."

Her brow furrows slowly, like she's trying to make the pieces fit, and they just... don't.

"Wait," she says, setting the cheese down gently this time. "You're not serious."

I give a hollow laugh. "Dead serious."

"But..." Harper trails off, blinking hard. "What, he just cut you loose like none of it ever happened?"

I nod once, because saying it out loud again might break something I can't put back together.

She walks over, rests a hip against the counter, and crosses her arms. "You guys weren't just playing a game. He felt something."

My chest tightens. "Apparently not enough."

Harper tilts her head, studying me. "What did he say, exactly?"

"That it was a mistake." My voice barely scrapes above a whisper. "That I need to separate business from the heart. And when it feels real... I have to know it's not."

For a long beat, Harper doesn't say anything. She just looks at me like she's trying to see through the cracks in my armor.

Then, softly, she asks, "Do you believe him?"

I swallow, hard. Then lift my eyes to hers.

"No."

And that's the problem.

The apartment falls into silence as Harper absorbs it all. The wheels of mischief are turning and finally, she lifts a brow, her voice quiet but steady.

"So... what are you going to do about it?"

The doors glide open like always, but this time, I walk through them with purpose. Not desperation. Not confusion. Not heartbreak.

Purpose.

It's been three days since Lucian Vale stripped me bare—not just of my clothes, but of the illusion I thought we'd built together. He kissed me like I was everything. Touched me like I was his. And then he shoved me out like I was nothing.

Fine. He wants it to be business?

Let's do business.

I step off the elevator in a tailored dress that hugs every inch of me like armor. My heels echo sharp across the marble. I don't flinch. I don't falter.

I'm here to remind him what he threw away.

Eve looks up from her tablet, her brows lifting in surprise. "Well. Didn't expect to see you this soon."

I offer her a cool smile. "Just needed a couple days to regroup."

She watches me for a beat longer than necessary.

Not prying, but aware. She was there, after all. She saw the aftermath. She helped me piece myself back together without ever asking for the broken details.

"You know, it's okay if you need another week." I see the sympathy in her eyes. Hovering over the words she's not saying. "I mean, damn, take two."

"Thanks, but I'm really okay. I'm ready to review some contracts." I follow, my voice calm. Unshaken. "I want something… high-profile. Exclusive. Something that'll make the room stop when I walk into it."

Eve glances at me over her shoulder. "Making a statement?"

"Making a point," I reply smoothly.

To him. To myself. To anyone who thought I couldn't turn this heartbreak into power.

He wanted to act like I meant nothing?

Then I'll show him what nothing looks like when it walks out of his club on the arm of someone richer, more powerful, and just out of his reach.

I'm going to find the perfect contract.

And when Lucian sees me with someone else—smiling, glowing, desirable—maybe then he'll realize what he lost.

And maybe by then… it'll be too late.

"Alright." She turns and I follow. "Let's get started."

Chapter 43

Sienna

I know exactly what I'm looking for. I just need to find him.

Not *him* him—not Lucian. That ship's been sunk and set ablaze.

No, I'm looking for someone who can help me make a very specific kind of point. Someone powerful. Exclusive. Desired. The kind of man who makes people stop and stare when I walk into a room on his arm.

I sit at the long, sleek conference table inside The Ledger's private suite, a tablet in hand, Eve across from me sipping her matcha like this is just another Tuesday. And for her, maybe it is.

For me, it's the beginning of my revenge arc.

I adjust the filters without hesitation. No short-term contracts. No casual play. I want long-term.

High visibility. Maximum impact.

The list tightens, half the names vanishing from the screen. I swipe through them, one after another. CEOs.

Diplomats. Old money and new tech. None of them give me *that* feeling. Not the one I'm chasing.

Until him.

Dominic Salvi.

The moment his name appears on the screen, my finger pauses mid-swipe. I remember him.

The luncheon. The one where I orchestrated my little performance with Mr. Langston. Salvi was there. Watching.

Even then, something about him made my skin prickle —like I'd stepped into a room with a predator. The kind that doesn't need to growl to be dangerous.

That's what it is.

Power.

It hums beneath his profile like static.

Lucian carries it too—that quiet, devastating sort of authority. The kind that doesn't need to raise its voice. That looks you in the eye and *dares* you to challenge it.

I flick the file onto the big screen. "This one."

Eve glances up, then rises to read. Her brow arches halfway through.

"Check out the bag attached to that one," she says, letting out a low whistle.

I do. And yeah... it's obscene. Like, buy-an-island-and-still-have-change-for-a-helicopter obscene.

She scrolls down with her finger. "Exclusive contract. Long-term, but with a required courting period. Submission preferred. Wants to build trust before committing to full dynamics."

"He's methodical," I murmur.

"More than that," Eve says, still studying. "He's new.

One of the latest additions to the invite-only tier." She taps the note. "Looks like a personal referral... from Lucian."

I don't let my expression shift. Not outwardly.

This can't get any more perfect and I suppress the shit-eating grin that wants to surface.

A personal referral.

That means Lucian will know him on a deeper level. More so than an average client and that is exactly what I need.

"And," Eve continues, tilting her head toward me, "this one's destination-based. Contract specifies a full week at his estate in the Caribbean for the trial phase."

She flops back into her chair and kicks her legs up on the edge of the polished table. "I mean, I wouldn't say no to cocktails on the beach and a payout like that..."

She trails off. "But it's your first contract."

"It's perfect," I say before she can keep going.

Eve studies me for a second. Not in judgment—just curiosity. Then she nods.

"You know what?" She smiles, a spark of respect in her voice. "I think it kinda is."

Eve taps the screen on the console beside her and places the contract on hold. Then, with a smirk that says *watch and learn*, she hits the speaker icon and dials the number listed on Dominic Salvi's private file.

The line rings once. Twice. My heart does a nervous backflip. By the third, my palms are slick, and my breath is shallow like I've just been called to the principal's office—except the principal is a billionaire with a penchant for control.

Then a deep, measured voice answers.

"This is Dom."

Of course it is. No last name. No frills. Just *Dom*. Short, sharp, commanding.

Eve slides into her polished, diplomatic tone like a silk glove. "Good morning, Mr. Salvi. This is Eve with The Black Ledger. I'm reaching out regarding your recent contract listing. We have a compatible Companion available and ready to accept. Her name is Miss Sienna Knight."

There's a pause on the other end. My stomach knots.

Then: "Miss Knight?" His voice warms, just slightly. "Now that's a name I was hoping to hear."

My lips twitch. *Gotcha.*

"She made quite an impression at the luncheon," he continues, thoughtful. "I was hoping she might become available. I'd be honored to have the opportunity to host her."

Honored. The word rolls around in my head like a tiny, private victory. Let Lucian see *that* in the client reports.

"I do have one condition," Dom says, casual but firm. "I'm departing for my island first thing tomorrow. If Miss Knight is available, I'd prefer to host her for the flight."

Eve raises one brow at me. I nod immediately. *Yes.* Hell yes.

Eve covers the receiver with her hand. "It's sudden," she mouths, skeptical.

I nod again, harder this time. *The sooner, the better.*

She sighs, dramatically patient. "Let me see if I can reach Miss Knight and inquire about earlier availability. May I place you on a brief hold?"

"Of course."

She taps the mute button and kicks back in her chair like she has all the time in the world. "What are you doing?" I whisper, trying not to scream. "I said yes."

"Oh, I know." She examines her fingernails with feigned boredom. "I just like to make them wait sometimes. Keeps them grounded. No one else puts men like Dominic Salvi in their place but... *we* can." She throws me a wink.

God, I love her.

After a beat, she unmutes the line. "Mr. Salvi, thank you for your patience. Miss Knight would be pleased to accept your offer."

"Excellent," he replies. "I'll send a car at 8 a.m."

Eve doesn't miss a beat. "Ledger protocol states transportation for all Companion contracts will be arranged through our agency. Miss Knight will arrive at the designated hangar at 9 a.m. sharp."

A small chuckle sounds from the line. "Right. My apologies. Still getting used to your processes."

Eve's voice sweetens with professionalism. "We recommend reviewing the Companion charter once more before tomorrow. Miss Knight will be briefed and ready."

"I look forward to it," he says. "Thank you, both."

The call ends, and silence stretches for a moment.

I finally exhale. "That just happened."

Eve leans forward, drumming her fingers on the edge of the table. "Oh, it's happening, sweetheart. Now the fun part." She wags her dark eyebrows at me. "Let's go raid the Ledger closet and help you pack. You've got a plane to catch."

The car glides through the security gate and into the private tarmac without a delay from security. I suppose they were expecting us, and the rich can bypass such protocols.

Felix has been picking me up every morning since Lucian had the locks changed on my apartment.

The first day, I thought it was to make sure he wasn't inconvenienced by my tardiness. But the second day, and the third. It seemed–nice.

I cross my legs tighter in the back seat, pressing down the flare of irritation that still lingers like phantom heat. I'm not thinking about him today. Not really. Except to picture the exact moment he reads the report of which contract I took.

I hope it burns.

"You nervous?" Felix's voice cuts through my thoughts. It's warm and smooth, like it was aged in oak.

I glance up. His kind brown eyes are wrinkled at the corners, deepened by years of smiling. His hair is still thick, mostly black, but streaked through with enough white coils to say *wise, not old.*

"A little," I admit, smiling faintly.

"Nervous is good," he says, shifting his hands on the wheel. "Means you're still paying attention. Can't teach instinct. But nerves? That'll keep you smart."

I study him for a moment. "You always this philosophical?"

He chuckles. "You remind me of my daughter. She was always nervous going to her contracts."

That makes me pause. "Your daughter?"

"She used to work for The Ledger. A long time ago."

My eyebrows lift. "Seriously? And you drive for them?"

"I know what goes on here but I support my daughter." He shrugs like it's nothing. "Lucian took care of her. Gave her the choice to walk away when she was ready. She's married now." He added. "Eight months pregnant with my first grand-baby."

"Congratulations." I blink, surprised. "Wow. I didn't expect that."

"Most people don't." He glances at me in the rearview mirror, his voice lower now. "But Mr. Vale, he's not the monster people think. He's hard, yeah. But he protects his own. I have a lot of respect for Mr. Vale."

My chest tightens, but I just nod. I don't respond.

Not because I don't agree. But because I *know*.

And still, he let me go.

The car slows as we pull into the hangar lot. The engines of parked planes whine in the distance, but our designated spot is quiet. No jet. No roar of turbines.

One man in a suit and cliché dark sunglasses is already waiting, opening my door when Felix rolls to a stop.

He pops the trunk and gets out, already moving to gather my bags.

"Miss Knight." The man greets me, opening my door. He doesn't offer his hand to help me out and I'm glad I elected to wear a fitting pantsuit and wedge heels. The deep-V in the front is still sensual without giving away too much and it will be a comfortable plane ride to a more tropical environment.

Eve coached me on a few final things and to have an outfit ready to change into on the plane just before landing. *A Ledger girl is nothing if not always looking fresh.*

Felix hands my bags to the suit who promptly turns toward the hangar.

"Miss Knight," Felix says softly, "you sure you're okay?"

I nod again. "I'm good, Felix. Really."

He doesn't look convinced, but he gives me a kind smile.

A moment later, the hangar doors shift open.

And two men step out.

One of them wears a sharp suit and shaded expression like the man who took my bags. Security I presume. The other man... walks like someone who commands a room before he's even in it.

Dominic Salvi.

His dark eyes cut through the distance between us, unapologetically direct. The air around him hums with that same quiet power I recognized the first time we met. A presence that doesn't ask for attention—it simply claims it.

He walks straight toward me like I've already agreed to belong to him.

And maybe, for now, I have.

Chapter 44

Lucian

TWO DAYS LATER

It's been five days since I ripped my heart out of my chest and left it tangled in the sheets of my bed.

Five days since I looked Sienna in the eye and told her a lie so brutal it still tastes like blood in my mouth.

I haven't been back to the house outside the city. I can't. Not yet. The memory of her is too loud there.

In the curve of the bathtub she melted into after the attack.

In the pillow that still holds the indent of her sleep. In the goddamn kitchen—where her laugh lingered in the air while I cooked her pasta and pretended I didn't want to devour her instead.

So I've been living at the club.

Avoiding the house. Avoiding the quiet. Avoiding the truth.

Crack.

A sharp right hook connects with my jaw, snapping my head to the side.

"Jesus, are we sparring or reminiscing, Master Yoda?" Jaxon bounces back on the balls of his feet, grinning like a devil with a death wish. His black tank is soaked through with sweat, and his knuckles are already taped from an earlier bout with Killian.

I swipe at the blood in my mouth with the back of my hand and spit onto the mat.

"You either grew a pair overnight," I growl, circling him, "or you're the dumbest bastard alive getting in the ring with me while I'm in this kind of mood."

"Why not both?" he shrugs, keeping light on his feet. "Call it a character flaw. I like punching you when you're brooding."

I lunge forward and land a vicious jab to his ribs. He grunts but rolls with it, dodging my next strike and throwing a low kick toward my thigh. I block it and counter with a quick elbow, grazing his shoulder.

"You fight like someone who hasn't slept," Jaxon taunts, dancing back.

"I fight like someone who's about to make you eat the mat."

"Then stop pulling your punches, old man."

That earns him a brutal left hook. My fist connects with his side hard enough to knock the wind out of him. He stumbles, catching himself against the ropes, but doesn't drop.

He grins instead. "There he is. I was starting to miss the Devil."

"You're not funny."

"I'm hilarious. You're just in denial." He straightens, cracking his neck. "You want to talk about it?"

"No."

"Then hit me harder." He steps forward again, fists up. "Might help."

I grit my teeth and take a step forward.

Jaxon lunges with a jab, which I dodge without effort, but my follow-up swing comes half a second too late.

"Sloppy," he says, panting, "but I'll take it."

"Shut up."

"Just saying. Whatever's got you brooding like Batman in a thunderstorm—it's getting in your way."

I aim a high kick. He blocks, grinning like a man who's not taking this nearly as seriously as I am.

"Maybe I should send Sienna a thank-you basket," he adds. "Clearly got you all twisted up."

I slam him with a punch to the stomach. It lands with a satisfying *thud*.

"Right," he wheezes, doubling slightly. "Touched a nerve. Got it."

"You're supposed to be running diagnostics on the Ledger's firewall and making sure the backdoor route you built into the Masquerade server can't be used against us," I snap, grabbing his arm and flipping him onto the mat with a satisfying crash. "Not giving me relationship advice."

"Multitasking," he grunts from the floor. "It's a skill."

The gym door opens and Killian walks in, phone pressed to his ear. His face is grim, voice clipped and low. Jaxon sees him and rolls to his feet, brushing sweat from his arms with a towel.

Killian finally ends the call, pocketing his phone with a sharp look.

"Still nothing," he says.

That lands harder than any punch.

"Lorenzo's gone dark?" Jaxon asks, already unwrapping his fists.

I nod. "His properties are cold. Phones dead. Staff turned over. No confirmed sightings in two days.

"We can't even get eyes on his wife and kid." Kill adds.

"Coward." My voice is low, dangerous.

"He knows he's running out of options," Killian replies. "He's hiding because he's afraid of what you'll do next."

I know Lorenzo. He's not afraid.

After he invaded my club, shot up my guys, he knows I'll be looking for him. He's laying low to stay alive long enough to make his next move.

I step out of the ring and grab my water bottle, chugging half of it before tossing it back onto the bench.

"This is going to end," I say. "I'm done letting his mess bleed into mine."

Killian's jaw tics. "What do you want to do?"

"I'll handle things the old fashion way." I dry my face with a towel and toss it aside. "Just me and him. We settle it in blood."

"Old school." Jaxon lets out a low whistle. "You're serious."

"Dead serious."

Jax and Kill fall into a conversation about The Godfather

movies and I find myself looking toward the windows. It's late morning. Sunlight slants through the glass in gold ribbons across the floor.

And all I can think about is her.

I wonder if she's still taking time off. If she's lounging in that small apartment of hers, pretending not to miss me.

Pretending she's not checking the door every time footsteps echo in the hall. Waiting for me to barge in, throw her over my shoulder, and tell her I was wrong.

Because that's what I want to do.

Every second since I left her, I've wanted to go back. Wrap her in my arms. Apologize for every lie I told to protect her. Tell her the truth—that she's not just a Companion. Not just a trainee.

She's mine.

But I can't go to her yet.

Not until Lorenzo is handled.

When I walk away from this, when Lorenzo's body is cold in the dirt, and this blood war is finally over...

Then I'm going to her.

And I'm not leaving without her.

Killian suddenly jolts upright. "Yes!"

I freeze mid-wrap on my wrist tape. "What did you find?"

"Uh..." He blinks, sheepish. "Nothing. Eve's on her way over. Said she's bringing breakfast. Coffee. And cheesecake."

Jaxon's head snaps up like a dog hearing the word *treat*. "I love free food."

I narrow my eyes. "You have more money than God. Why do you get excited about free food?"

He shrugs, grinning. "Because I wasn't always rich. Used to live for the free samples at the grocery store. Didn't realize till later that was how my mom was feeding me dinner some nights."

That sobers the air for a beat. But Jaxon just throws his towel over his shoulder and heads for the bench like nothing happened. He's always been good at tossing out pieces of his past and pretending they don't sting.

His phone chimes as he grabs it from his duffel. "Scan's done," he mutters, unlocking it and squinting at the code.

Right then, the gym door swings open and Eve barrels in, her arms loaded with branded takeout bags and one dangerously overfilled coffee tray.

"Delivery service with better heels and more attitude," she calls, kicking the door closed with one stilettoed foot. "Somebody better clear space before I drop this on the floor and cry."

"Is that from Elena's?" Killian perks up like a golden retriever.

"With extra sugar and shame," Eve confirms, already setting the bags on the bench. "Lucian, I brought you black with a splash of spite. Just how you like it."

I arch a brow as I take the cup. "Cheesecake?"

She grins. "Lemon. I figured you could use something sweet since your mood's been sour as hell."

Jaxon whistles low. "And here I thought *I* was the emotional one."

I ignore them all, sipping the coffee and watching Jaxon's face tighten as he scrolls through the final scan.

"Something?" I ask.

He nods once, serious now. "Maybe. I need ten minutes to verify the path, but there's a fingerprint on the server. And it doesn't belong to any of your registered users."

That's all I need to hear.

The playfulness drains from the room as I set my coffee down and crack my knuckles.

About fucking time, I catch a break with this asshole.

For more than ten minutes, Eve won't leave me the hell alone until I try the damn cheesecake.

"It's from my bestie," she insists, nudging the box closer like it's a peace offering. "At least pretend you're human for five seconds and take a bite."

I sigh, take the smallest forkful I can manage, and give in. The moment it hits my tongue, I know I've been manipulated.

It's perfect.

Tart lemon, buttery graham crust, and some kind of whipped cream topping that practically evaporates.

Of course it's delicious. Elena made it.

But I can't enjoy it.

Not when Jaxon hasn't looked up from his phone in fifteen minutes and that scowl on his face is digging deeper by the second. I can tell he's close to finding something. His thumbs move fast. His brow furrows. His jaw ticks.

"How the fuck did he get in?" I mutter.

No one answers. But we all know I mean Lorenzo.

The bastard slithered into my club like a snake through a crack in the foundation. I need to know how. I need to know who helped him. Because if there's a rat in my empire, they're already dead—they just don't know it yet.

Killian lounges back, sipping his coffee like he's got all the time in the world. Eve is daintily picking at another slice of cheesecake, making soft noises of appreciation as if we aren't quietly orchestrating the end of a war.

Her words land like a fucking bomb in my mind.

Casual. Light. Like she's talking about the weather.

"So," she muses, "how do you think Sienna's doing on her first contract?"

The fork freezes midair. Killian glances at me from the corner of his eye but says nothing.

She took a contract.

I don't move.

I don't blink.

I definitely don't let any of them see the way the words stab straight into my ribs and twist.

Eve's pretending she's just making conversation. But she knows exactly what the fuck she's doing. Goading me. Teasing the Devil.

"She's got fire, that one," Eve continues, her tone breezy but her eyes sharp. "I admire that. I think it'll serve her well. Especially with the contract she took."

That gets my attention.

My gaze snaps to her, but I school my face into stone.

Jaxon snorts. "Damn, Eve. You playing chess today or just poking the bear for fun?"

Eve only smiles, licking cheesecake from her fork like the fucking cat who caught the canary. "Oh, I'm just proud of her. She didn't waste any time. Jumped right in, head held high."

My grip tightens around my coffee mug. I swallow hard. Force the lump in my throat down like it's poison.

I won't ask.

I won't give her the satisfaction.

But the truth is—I'm already bleeding from the inside out.

Because I need to know where she is.

And who the fuck she's with.

"Whelp." Eve claps her hands together, rising with the grace of a queen and the mischief of a gremlin. She starts boxing up the rest of her cheesecake, tucking it carefully into a sleek black container like its treasure. "Looks like my work here is done. I'm off to The Ledger."

Her oversized purse swings into the crook of her elbow, her coffee cup is in hand, and she turns toward the exit. "Have fun murdering people," she calls over her shoulder, stilettos clicking across the polished gym floor like gunfire. Killian chuckles under his breath.

I don't. Not even close.

Jaxon hasn't looked up once. The bastard's practically fused to his laptop now, shoulders hunched as he taps through firewalls and encrypted tunnels like he's orchestrating a symphony of digital destruction. It's been ten minutes, and my patience is paper-thin.

My leg bounces restlessly. My phone sits in my hand, screen black, thumb hovering over the button like it might bite me.

I don't want to look.

Because if I do—if I open her file and see the contract she picked—I'll see him.

I'll see every goddamn line of service he requested. I'll see how much he paid. What dates. What limits. What liberties. I'll see if he's fucking touched her.

And I'll kill him for it.

I stare at the phone for another minute. Maybe more.

Then I open it.

My fingers aren't steady, not even a little, and that pisses me off too. I swipe through The Ledger's internal network, punch in my credentials, and pull up Sienna Knight's Companion file.

Her photo hits me first.

It's from the week after she joined—hair in soft waves, eyes uncertain, lips just barely turned up like she wasn't sure she deserved to smile.

She had no fucking idea how dangerous she was back then. How fucking *mine* she was.

I click deeper.

The screen loads slowly—my punishment, maybe—and then the profile appears.

Client Name: Dominic Salvi

My breath catches.

And then the world goes fucking still.

Because *I know that name.*

That name is a ghost from the past.

My past.

I made it up.

We were sixteen—me and Lorenzo. Drunk off our asses, pulled over in my old black Challenger with beer bottles rolling around the backseat. If his father had found out we'd been drinking and driving?

He wouldn't have beat us. He would've buried us.

So when the cop leaned in and asked for our names, I didn't hesitate.

"Matthew Cole," I'd said. Calm. Stone-cold.

Then I added, "He's Dominic Salvi." I pointed to Lorenzo.

The officer gave us a look, went back to run the names through his cruiser computer, and I took the fuck off.

We were never caught.

Not then. Not for that.

But ever since... Lorenzo held onto that name.

Used it. *Adopted* it. Turned it into his mask.

Dominic Salvi became his cloak of invisibility—an alias tied to a ghost of a night that should've ended in handcuffs.

And now he's using it here. In *my fucking system.*

My entire body goes cold.

Because I didn't see it. I didn't fucking *see it.*

And now he's not just in my system.

He's got Sienna.

Chapter 45
Sienna

The moment I step into the airplane hangar, something feels off.

It's subtle at first—a faint chill in the air despite the warmth of the sun, the hush of an empty hangar that should be alive with the quiet bustle of pre-flight activity.

There's no jet waiting, no crew in uniform, not even the soft murmur of idle conversation. Just silence and steel and the unmistakable sense that I've walked into something I can't quite see.

My gaze shifts back to Felix's SUV just as he eases away, calm and deliberate, like it's any other day. Because it should be.

I'm sure he's dropped many companions off for their contract. Why should this one be any different?

But something *is* wrong.

And I realize that far too late.

A rush of movement hits me from the side. Before I can react, a powerful hand slams into me and shoves me backward, hard enough to knock the breath from my lungs.

My back collides with the wall of the hangar, the cold metal rattling behind me as a body pins mine with brutal force. Fingers grip my jaw. My throat.

Dominic is in my face.

But the polished, composed man I met at the luncheon is nowhere to be found.

The man holding me now is unhinged—eyes bloodshot and wild, face twisted with a fury so volatile it takes me a second to even recognize him.

His breath comes fast and sharp through clenched teeth, and I feel the tremble in his fingers as they clamp around my throat.

"Where the fuck is my son?" he snarls, tightening his grip until my breath comes in short, desperate gasps. "You think I don't know Lucian has him?"

I try to shake my head no. That he's wrong. That I don't know anything he's talking about. I claw at his wrists, but he doesn't budge. His voice rises, a manic edge creeping into every word.

"You're not just one of Lucian's girls. You're *his*. His fucking *whore*."

The word lands like a slap, but it's the next that makes my blood run cold.

"He has my son," Dominic growls, spittle dotting my

cheek as he leans in, the madness in his eyes nearly vibrating. "Lucian Vale took him from me—so I'm taking something from him in return?"

The grip around my throat tightens. My lungs scream. Panic surges. I flail against him, desperate now.

I slam my first into his throat—sharp and vicious. He chokes, breath gasping, just long enough for me to claw my nails down the side of his face with everything I have. Four angry red lines bloom instantly, blood beading along his cheekbone.

He stumbles back, howling, and I run.

I don't look back. I just run.

"Help!" I shout, lungs burning as I sprint across the open stretch of tarmac. "Felix—somebody help!"

My arms wave wildly, my voice breaking on his name, but the SUV keeps moving. Smooth. Steady. Unaware.

Please Felix. Just look in the fucking mirror.

If he would just glance... just once...

But he doesn't.

Behind me, I hear footsteps—fast, heavy, too close. The sound spurs me faster, though my shoes weren't made for this. The moment my wedge catches on the edge of the pavement, my ankle twist painfully beneath me.

My body pitches forward.

And just as I scream, a heavy force collides with me from behind.

The impact knocks me off my feet, slamming me into the concrete. My knees hit first. Then my shoulder.

Then—my head.

A sickening crack echoes through my skull, and a white-hot bolt of pain bursts behind my eyes. The world spins wildly, then fades at the edges, the color bleeding from everything until it's gone entirely.

The world turns dark.

Chapter 46
Lucian

I can't breathe.

The air thins around me as the truth settles in like a fucking vice around my chest. My hands curl into fists. My breath comes ragged.

Lorenzo has Sienna.

Jaxon stands slowly, eyes still fixed on the glowing monitor. His mouth is moving, but I don't hear a word. My pulse is too loud—thundering in my ears, drowning everything else out.

I need to know when the fuck she left. How long he's had her.

That she's still alive.

I snatch my phone off the bench–I don't even remember dropping it–and call Eve. She picks up immediately.

"Lucian—this one thing was bothering me," she starts. "Her contract... Dominic. He's listed as a new client, but he said he met her at the luncheon. I thought that was only for sponsors—"

"Eve," I cut her off, my voice gravel and fire.

She goes quiet. I hear her footsteps stop, the bustle of the street around her fading out.

"That's not a client," I say through clenched teeth. "It's not a fucking client."

Killian straightens, his full attention locking on me.

"It's Lorenzo," I grind out. "He has her, Eve. He has Sienna. How long?"

A beat of silence. I can hear her breath catch. I can see her in my head, frozen in place on some city sidewalk, realization flooding her face.

"How long has she been gone, Eve?" My roar shakes the rafters as I slam my fist into the table hard enough that the windows rattle.

"Two... two days." Her voice breaks into a whisper. She's crying now. "Lucian, I didn't know. I swear to God—"

"Lucian," Jaxon cuts in, voice tight. "I found the bug."

I end the phone call and whip around. He turns the laptop toward me, and it's the same fucking profile I just found.

The smug fucking picture of my old childhood friend smiling at me in an open challenge.

Behind him is a wall of whiskey bottles.

Our whiskey bottles. The ones I've been leaving after every battle in this cold war we've been fighting. *I'm going to fucking kill him.*

"He submitted a client application," Jaxon says quickly. "It wasn't a profile—it was a fucking virus. When your staff opened it, the breach was complete. He had access to the system."

My vision goes red at the edges.

"But there's one more thing," Jaxon adds, hesitating and I know it's fucking bad. "There's a file in her contract folder. A video."

The blood drains from my head. My legs nearly buckle, but I catch myself on the edge of the table. I nod once.

"It was uploaded last night."

"Open it."

The screen flickers, then the footage loads.

I nearly drop to my knees.

Sienna.

She's slumped in a chair—metal, rusted, cold. Her wrists are bound to the arms, her ankles strapped to the legs. Her head hangs limp to the side, auburn hair dull and tangled, a curtain of dirt hiding her face.

She looks... lifeless.

"Please," I whisper to no one. "Please be alive."

A shadow passes across the frame, and a bucket of water is thrown over her. She jerks awake with a cry, sputtering, blinking against the light. My lungs finally expand.

Until Lorenzo fucking DeLuca steps into view.

He grips the top of her head and yanks it back. Her face tilts up—split lip, swollen eye, a knot the size of a fist on her forehead.

My heart beats so hard I swear it's going to tear through my ribcage.

He looks straight into the camera. Into me.

"You took my son," Lorenzo says, voice smooth, venomous. "So, I took your girl."

I blink. What?

"I don't have his fucking son."

I might be a monster, but I wouldn't go after a kid. That's a line I've never crossed.

Lorenzo pulls a switchblade from his pocket. Clicks it open. Presses it to Sienna's throat.

She whimpers, swallows—but stays still. Brave little rabbit.

A thin line of red appears on her skin where the blade kisses too hard. My world narrows to that drop of blood.

"I want him back," Lorenzo growls. "You have twenty-four hours. Or I start sending you pieces of your whore-for-hire in bloody boxes."

The screen goes black.

But I'm already moving.

Killian and Jaxon are right behind me as I storm out of the office, adrenaline crackling beneath my skin like wildfire.

I turn to Jax first. "Wipe everything. I want full diagnostics. Clean every fucking server, every terminal, every file he could've touched. If he downloaded anything, I want to know how much and how fast—and I want it ten minutes ago."

Jaxon nods, already flipping through security clearances on his tablet.

Now Killian. "Call Wolfe. I need his helicopter."

Killian's eyebrows lift. "You planning on asking nice?"

"He owes me." I growl.

We're out of the gym in seconds, the cool blast of outside air doing nothing to temper the fury roaring through me. We pile into my Aston Martin, tires screeching as we peel into traffic, Killian's phone already to his ear.

"Who else are we calling?" he asks as Wolfe picks up on the first ring.

"Everyone."

This isn't a rescue mission.

It's a goddamn war.

In thirty minutes, I've mobilized a fucking army and I'm on the helipad at the top of Wolfe Industries arguing with my head of security about who is going to fly.

The chopper is sleek—top of the line, customized, and grotesquely expensive. Wolfe's personal toy. He's not here to fly it himself, of course, but I'm not planning on waiting for a goddamn pilot to arrive.

"I can fly it," I mutter, inspecting the instrument panel with sharp, practiced eyes.

Killian gives me a look like I'm full of shit. "You can fly a *plane*, Lucian. Helicopters are a whole different beast."

I slide into the pilot's seat anyway but he pushes me over.

Killian climbs in after me with a sigh. "Fine. I'll fly. But you're explaining the bloodstains to Wolfe."

I smirk, just barely. "He'll be lucky if there's a helicopter left *to* give back."

The cabin is silent except for the roar of blades overhead and the occasional flick of Killian adjusting flight controls. I don't speak. I can't. Every second we're in the air is another second she's in Lorenzo's hands.

Every breath I take is a fight not to punch through the glass and start jumping early.

My knee bounces uncontrollably. My fingers twitch over the handle of my Glock, my mind painting a hundred ways this ends.

Every one of them involves me walking out of there with Sienna in my arms and that bastard's head in a fucking bag.

As soon as I watched that video, I knew exactly where he was keeping her.

It's a warehouse from our past. Not one he owns anymore so ironically it survived my destruction of his other properties.

It's where Lorenzo and I made our first kills. Seventeen years old. Still boys with blood on our hands and his father watching with cold pride in his eyes. That was our initiation into the DeLuca crime family. That's where we proved we were monsters.

And now Lorenzo's brought it full circle.

That sentimental fuck chose that place for a reason.

He wants me to see it. Feel it. Bleed in it.

Well, good.

Because I want him to hear me coming.

And he fucking does.

The helicopter touches down with a bone-rattling thrum, the gravel lot kicking up in swirling clouds as Killian keeps it steady. I'm already out, my boots hitting the ground hard a second before Killian pulls away.

The wind slaps me, the late-morning sky dim with

smoke-stained clouds, and the warehouse looms ahead like the grave it's always been.

Lorenzo is waiting.

He's standing dead center at the far end of the lot, hands in his coat pockets, like we're here to negotiate a fucking real estate deal instead of trade blood and bones. A long series of scratches down his face that look fresh.

I walk toward him slow, steady. Every step an exercise in restraint.

We stop with a stretch of open ground between us— neutral territory that won't stay neutral for long.

He studies me, his expression unreadable. "Where is he?"

I don't answer.

"Don't fuck with me, Lucian."

I nod once at him. "My girl do that?" My eyes linger on the harsh scratches that had to have come from Sienna. My little warrior angel fought back.

He glares at me and I smile smugly.

"Knew you wouldn't be able to handle her."

His face nearly turns purple. "I know you have him!" Spit flies from his mouth as he screams.

"I don't," I say flatly, voice like broken glass. "You're fucking paranoid."

"You think I'm stupid?"

"No," I snap. "I think you're a desperate, arrogant piece of shit who's grasping at shadows because your empire is crumbling, and you need someone to blame."

His mouth curls into a bitter sneer. "You stole my brother's life and now you need my fucking son?"

"You know damn good and well this is not about your fucking brother anymore."

"You're so full of righteous bullshit," Lorenzo spits. "But it's always been like that, hasn't it? You pretending to be more superior than the rest of us while hiding your sins under tailored suits and expensive clubs."

"I'm not pretending anything. I just clean up better than you."

"Give me my son," he growls, stepping forward.

I don't flinch. "Let me see Sienna."

His eyes narrow.

"I'm not playing games, Lorenzo," I bite out. "You show me she's alive or I start carving your fucking eyes out, so you'll really never see your son again."

Too far? Not even fucking close.

"She's fine."

"Prove it."

"I'm not here to prove anything."

"Then I'm not here to negotiate."

We stand there—two kings with proverbial knives pressed to each other's throats. The air between us is sharp with rage, the kind that's been simmering for years.

Decades.

This has been coming since the moment I walked away from the family. That meant walking away from Lorenzo too.

And now here we are.

At the bottom of the mountain, deciding who's going to die on it.

The gravel stirs behind me as I hear engines. A lot more than one.

The high whine of performance tires followed by the roar of multiple vehicles charging in fast.

I whirl around, hand on my gun. "Call your fucking men off Lorenzo."

Lorenzo is already turning. "This isn't yours?"

We lock eyes.

Shit.

The convoy speeds into the lot like a storm—three matte-black SUVs, one bulletproof van, and a pair of souped-up bikes. They don't stop gently. They grind into the gravel, dust and exhaust choking the air as doors slam and feet hit the ground.

Men pour out—a dozen of them. Armed. Smug fucking pricks like they're walking into a party.

And at the front, stepping out with a fucking *swagger*, is Shawn O'Mally.

"I'll be damned," I mutter.

Lorenzo's face drains of color.

Because he knows exactly what this means.

His brother's debt is catching up to him. The Irish have arrived—and they didn't come to negotiate. They came to collect what's owed to them.

Lorenzo's little brother was in bad. Too much debt and he couldn't settle it.

That's why he bailed with *my* Companion. Took her hostage and ended up with my bullet between his eyes.

Seems like his debt transferred to Lorenzo. Maybe

instead of fighting me, he should have been cleaning up his brothers' mess.

Shawn adjusts the collar of his leather jacket, takes a long, dramatic breath like the afternoon air is made just for him, and smiles wide.

"Ahh," he drawls. "Isn't this a family reunion to remember?"

Behind him, a car door opens and I go on high alert.

One of Shawn's men is dragging a terrified, struggling boy out by the roots of his hair.

You'd be able to spot Lorenzo's son from a mile away. He looks just like his father.

He's kicking, screaming, crying out in broken Italian.

Lorenzo moves like he's going to bolt.

I raise a hand. "Don't."

He doesn't listen.

"Give me my fucking son!" Lorenzo shouts, voice cracking.

Shawn laughs, stepping forward, calm as the devil at Sunday mass. "Funny how you answer me now, eh, Lorenzo? Where was this—enthusiasm when your brother fucked me out of three hundred grand and six kilos of product?"

"*His* problem is not *my* problem!" Lorenzo yells, fists shaking.

"Oh, it is now," Shawn smirks, reaching back to ruffle the boy's hair mockingly. "But I'm a man of opportunity. Seeing this *friendly* gathering—I want more than just my money back."

He gestures to me now, eyes bright. "I want leverage."

Satan himself would be jealous of the grin on his face.

"Now," Shawn says, stepping into the space between us like a maestro about to conduct his bloody orchestra, "who's ready to make a fucking deal?"

I sure as hell didn't come here to negotiate.

I came for her.

But as much as I want to put a bullet through every bastard here—including the two standing front and center like they're hosting a reunion—I can't ignore the terrified little boy being dragged by his hair into the center of this chaos.

I was no older than he was when I watched a man put a bullet between my father's eyes. No kid should have to see that.

His wide, tear-streaked face locks on mine for a single beat, and something primal rises in my chest. He's innocent in all this. And now he's part of it—used like a pawn in a game he doesn't understand.

I give Killian a single nod from where he's perched on the rooftop. It's all he needs.

The sniper rifle cracks through the air with surgical precision, and a split-second later, Shawn O'Mally stumbles, blood blooming from his shoulder. Chaos erupts as the tension detonates—men drawing weapons, shouting, diving for cover.

But I'm already moving.

My gun is up and steady, sights locked. A clean shot drops the man holding the kid—center of his fucking head. He drops like a sack of bricks, and I'm sprinting forward before his body even hits the gravel.

The boy flinches as I scoop him up under my arm and bolt for the warehouse.

Gunfire rips through the air like thunder cracking open the sky. Chaos erupts around me—shouts, bullets, the acrid scent of smoke curling into my lungs.

But I don't stop. I don't hesitate. I move through the fray like a man possessed, the boy tucked under my arm, his terrified weight reminding me why I can't fucking fail.

The warehouse looms ahead, the same one from the video. If she's not inside... no. I won't finish that thought. She's here. She has to be.

My boots skid on the dirt-slick floor as I shove open the rusted door, gun drawn and sweeping the room. And there—Jesus—there she is.

Sienna.

She's bound to the chair, gagged, her eyes wide and wild with panic, skin bruised, blood dried beneath her temple. Her entire body stiffens when she looks just past me, and for a breath, neither of us moves.

I realize just in time what's about to happen and I can't fucking let it.

I spin putting the boy behind me and blocking Sienna with my body. My arm raises as just a shot cracks through the air.

A bolt of searing pain explodes through my shoulder, the force jolting me and sending the boy tumbling from my grip.

But my bullet races through the air and hits the gunman between the eyes. He hits the ground just after the boy does who scrambles upright like a frightened animal. He bolts toward the exit before I can grab him.

Right into the fucking gunfight.

"Fuck!"

Gun still in hand, I put pressure on the wound. Warm blood coats my palm, but I don't stop moving. I rush toward her, adrenaline overriding everything else. I crouch beside her, untucking the switchblade from my boot and slice it through the rope binding one hand. I slip it into her now-freed hand as I push the gag from her mouth.

My lips are on hers in a chaste kiss, needing to feel her to know she's really here.

"Cut yourself loose, Angel. I have to get him."

She nods, lips trembling, and starts sawing through the rope as I turn and push back into the chaos.

Outside, the firefight is peaking. My men have closed in —silent, lethal, efficient. The O'Malleys are going down one by one, caught in the crossfire they didn't prepare for.

Killian's on the roof, sniping with surgical precision.

The boy's darting through the crossfire, a blur of panicked motion too small to stay safe.

His father is screaming at him across the yard to stop and hide but I don't think he can hear it.

I duck low and sprint, weaving between crates and scattered bodies until I spot him—cornered, trembling, and inches from one of O'Malley's men readying to grab him.

That fucking asshole. I hate a goddamn coward.

I surge forward, my shoulder screaming in protest, and tackle the bastard to the ground.

"Get back inside the fucking warehouse boy."

Thank fuck he listens—and I let this asshole go, planting

my knee on the man's chest and driving my fist into his jaw. Two bullets later and he stops moving.

It's nearly over now. The dust is settling. Gunfire dies down, replaced by groans and silence. The air hangs thick with smoke and vengeance.

I rise slowly, my shoulder throbbing but my grip steady as I step through the haze.

O'Malley has a gun pointed at Lorenzo's head. My old friend, now enemy, has nothing but an empty gun. He raises his hands in surrender but I'm fucking over this.

I want to get my girl out of here. But first, Lorenzo owes me my pound of flesh.

Blood coats the gravel around us. All their men are gone. My gun lifts on instinct, aimed straight at O'Malleys head and he meets the same end as the rest of his men.

Lorenzo gets my gun next, knowing we're not fucking done yet.

Behind me, I hear Sienna's ragged breaths as she shields the boy with her arms, pulling him back against the warehouse wall. Her eyes are locked on me, and I can feel her fear —and her fury—radiating like heat.

"Don't let him see." I tell her, my voice deadly low.

Lorenzo stares at me, chest heaving, the glint of something manic in his eyes.

"You wanted a war," I say, my voice low, dangerous. "This is how it ends."

Chapter 47
Sienna

My legs barely work.

I'm leaning against the cold metal of the warehouse, one arm wrapped tight around the boy's small, trembling body, the other gripping the wall behind me like it might hold me upright through sheer will.

My wrists are raw.

Torn skin, dried blood. Ankles the same. My whole body feels bruised and battered, like I've been through a war.

Because I have.

My heart punches hard against my ribs as Lucian stands over Lorenzo, gun steady, eyes unreadable. The devil in human form. A man I love—I fucking love—even like this.

Maybe especially like this.

Because he didn't just come for me. He brought a goddamn army ready to level this place, just to get me out. He created a river of my captor's blood just to cross it and free me.

"On your fucking knees, Lorenzo."

Lucian's voice cracks like lightning through the smoke-filled air. The man drops. Just collapses. A far cry from the wild-eyed monster who slammed me against a hangar wall and screamed about bloodlines and betrayal. Now he's just a broken man, begging.

He pleads for his life. For his son. For mercy.

Lucian gives none.

"You know what's owed to me," he says coldly. "And you damn sure know I'm here to collect it. Because I'm the Devil you helped create."

I don't move. I barely breathe.

The boy in my arms starts to tremble harder. I shift, pulling him closer, shielding his face with my hand. Covering his ear. He shouldn't have to see this. Hear this. No child should.

But I do. I watch everything. I wouldn't be able to look away from it if I tried.

Lucian orders Lorenzo to throw down his knife. When it lands at his feet, Lucian picks it up and flips it open with a snap that makes Lorenzo flinch. I feel it in my spine. A jolt that steals my breath.

"Please," Lorenzo begs. "Not in front of my son—please, Lucian."

Lucian crouches beside him. His hand grips the mans wrist, forcing it to the gravel ground. Fingers spread wide and flat.

His voice a lethal whisper. "You took my girl."

I can't see the cut. But I see Lucian pressing. The weight of him going into the blade, taking what he wants from Lorenzo's body.

His pound of flesh.

Lorenzo's scream that tears through the air and vibrates all the way down to my bones. I squeeze the boy tighter as he jerks, trying not to cry out myself.

Lucian keeps going, listing Lorenzo's offenses.

"You called her a *whore*," he growls, grabbing Lorenzo's other hand. "Put your *fucking* hands on her."

Another slice. Another finger.

The scream this time is quieter. Choked off by pain, or shock, or maybe the reality of what Lucian Vale has become in this moment—a man with nothing left to lose.

My stomach churns at the guttural noises coming from Lorenzo. His blood staining the grey rocks he's kneeling upon.

Then the blade hovers over Lorenzo's right ring finger, a thick black and gold band glinting in the firelight.

"You were so afraid your empire would be handed over to me." Lucian's rage is controlled. Alarmingly appearing calm but the fire in his eyes tells otherwise. "That it would be me that climbed to the top of the DeLuca empire. So, I fucking walked away."

He readies the blade.

"No—please," Lorenzo sobs. "Not that one. Please, I—"

Lucian doesn't wait for the plea to finish.

"I've earned this one, you motherfucker."

The blade comes down. Another finger gone, ring and all. Then Lucian stabs the blade through his hand, pinning him to the ground.

Lorenzo's mouth opens but no sound comes out. His eyes are wide and wet, his entire body trembling.

Lucian picks up the ring like it's a crown. Looks at it.

"I left you to be the king of your empire but it wasn't good enough. And you want to know why?"

The man has been reduced to a huddled mass, wanting to hold his wounds but he can't. He wants to pull the knife from his hand but his other is shaking too badly.

The wound where his pinky used to be looking like a dark hole, oozing blood.

"You're done, Lorenzo," he says, his voice like ice and thunder. "Just like you feared. I've taken your empire from you."

The man sobs now. A sound so broken it barely resembles a man at all.

"You should've just let me walk away," Lucian adds, standing tall, towering over him. "Taken the fucking truce I offered. But you had to drag it into the light because of your fucking ego and your goddamn insecurities."

He hurls the ring—Lorenzo's pride, his name, his legacy—into the water behind us, and I hear it splash into nothing.

I feel like this act is sacred. Like it means something.

It feels like the power Lorenzo had, disappears with the gold band.

Then Lucian retrieves the blade, unpinning Lorenzo from the ground.

Without care, he tosses the three severed digits into a pile of burning debris like kindling for the fire and turns to me.

His eyes find mine through the smoke and haze. And for

a moment, the violence slips from his features, leaving only the man beneath it. My man.

"Let the boy go," he says.

I do. Gently.

He sprints toward his father, screaming through the wreckage.

Lucian slides the blade closed and shoves it into his back pocket as he comes to me, his arm curling around me—his wounded arm slides easily under my legs and he carries me.

"Let's get you out of here," he says softly, pulling me closer.

My arms fix themselves around his neck and I breathe him in. My face buried into him as the tears start to fall.

But he's here.

He came for me.

Because I am his but he's also finally admitting, showing, that he is just as much mine.

The sound of helicopter blades thunders in the distance, growing closer by the second. Wind kicks up around us, lifting my tangled hair, brushing against my bruised skin.

And for the first time in days—I let myself fall apart.

The rotor still spins overhead, a dull roar muffling everything but the sound of my heartbeat.

Lucian hasn't said a word.

Not during takeoff. Not during the flight. Not even when the man stitching up his shoulder winced at the depth of the wound.

He just sits there beside me, rigid, unreadable.

His good arm is caged across my body like a human seat-belt—keeping me tucked firmly against his side. But not for comfort. Not for warmth. Not even for me, I think.

It's instinct.

Control.

Possession.

Maybe all of it.

His jaw is locked, teeth clenched so tightly I can see the tension twitching in his cheek. His chest rises in short, measured breaths. The kind you take when you're trying not to come completely undone.

No one else speaks either.

Not the medic. Not Killian. Not the pilot.

Just the humming silence of fear and fury and the weight of everything that wasn't said.

I can feel the hollow pit already forming in my stomach, carving me out from the inside.

He's going to send me away.

I can feel it coming.

And I can't even blame him.

I took a contract to get back at him. Stepped blindly into a war I didn't even know existed. Got myself captured, held hostage, turned into bait in some sick fucking revenge plot —and now here I am, waiting for him to do the inevitable.

To cut ties.

To protect The Ledger.

He's going to end it all for good.

The aircraft touches down with the softest jolt, the wheels kissing the ground like the quiet before a final goodbye. The doors open and his men file out in practiced forma-tion. Killian moves first, already barking orders into his comm.

Lucian doesn't move.

Not until everyone else is gone.

Then he stands on the rooftop just outside the helicopter.

And I prepare myself for it—that last flicker of connec-tion severed like a thread snapped under too much tension.

I shift to the seat near the door, ready to follow, but his arm shoots out, bracing against the frame of the craft.

Blocking me in.

"Wait."

His voice is low. Strained. But not cold.

He's still not looking at me, and I can feel my breath catch in my throat.

Don't do this. Please don't do this.

I can't make myself say it. I can't even look at him when he finally speaks again.

"I sent you away."

There it is. The words I've been bracing for.

"It should have kept you safe."

His arm drops, but he still doesn't step away. He just stands there, head bowed, like he's not sure what to do with the weight of his own thoughts.

"I should've told you everything. About the war. About Lorenzo. About how close it was getting."

He breathes in sharply through his nose.

"I kept you too close to it. To me."

I glance at him then, just enough to see the side of his face—and the way his expression cracks at the edges.

His voice dips, guttural now.

"When that video came through... when I saw you—tied to that fucking chair, your head hanging like—" He chokes on the words and grips the back of the seat in front of him like he's anchoring himself to the earth.

"I thought I was going to lose you."

His head finally turns. Slowly. Eyes meeting mine.

"I didn't care about the empire. About the business. About anything. I just needed to get to you."

He swallows hard, voice barely a whisper.

"I've been in shootouts. I've killed men with my bare hands. I've seen things that don't leave you—things that turn your soul black."

He takes in a shaky breath.

"But nothing... nothing ever scared me like the thought of losing you."

My mouth parts but no sound comes out.

I'm drowning in the wreckage of him. The weight of his confession crushes every defense I have left.

"I don't know how to do this, Sienna," he whispers. "How to care about someone. How to let someone care about me."

His eyes drop to my hands, still raw and red from the ropes. He holds his hand out to me and I take it, stepping out of the aircraft with him.

He lifts my wrist to his mouth, placing a tender kiss just above the sore wounds. Closing his eyes, he squeezes them tight, fighting to keep everything pushed down.

But it refuses to stay buried any longer.

"I only know how to destroy."

His words hover between us, heavy as stone, delicate as glass.

Lucian's jaw ticks once, then again—like he's fighting something inside him that doesn't want to be named.

That doesn't want to be *felt*. His eyes drop to the floor, to the space between our shoes like it holds the answer to how he's supposed to survive this.

Survive *me*.

"You should've had someone soft," he says quietly. "Someone safe. A man who works nine to five and comes home on time and remembers your coffee order. Someone who hasn't put bullets through dozens of men and lied to you every time he tried to protect you."

He looks up. The storm in his eyes is still there, but the walls are breaking.

"I'm not that man, Sienna."

I already know that.

He swallows hard and his voice drops, barely above a whisper.

"But I wanted to be."

His hand flexes at his side like it's aching to reach for me, but still—he doesn't move.

"I didn't lie to protect the business. I didn't push you away because of some fucking protocol. I did it because I didn't know what to do with the way you made me feel."

His voice breaks then—just a little, but enough for me to hear the man underneath the legend.

"I thought I could let you go. Thought I could live with

it. I told myself if I kept you safe, that was enough. That I'd done my part."

He shakes his head.

"But when I saw you there, tied up and bleeding and too still... I unraveled. I *snapped*."

He exhales slowly, brokenly.

"Because if I lost you, Sienna—if something happened to you because of me—I wouldn't come back from it. I *wouldn't want to*."

He takes a step closer now. Hesitant. Like he's approaching something holy.

"And I'm sorry. For all of it. For hurting you. For lying. For making you think, even for a second, that I didn't want you."

Finally, finally, he lifts a hand and touches the side of my face—so gently it undoes me.

"I fucking love you," he breathes. "And it terrifies me. But I do. I love you more than I've ever let myself want anything before."

He's shaking now, just barely—but it's there.

"You got under my skin so fast I didn't know how to breathe without you. I still don't."

His forehead drops to mine, the touch of his skin like an anchor against the storm inside me.

"Come back to me, Sienna," he whispers. "Even if I don't know how to do this the right way. Even if all I know how to do is burn."

For a moment, I can't breathe.

I can't think.

Because the man in front of me isn't the Devil of the

Masquerade. He's not the cold king of The Black Ledger or the ruthless shadow that haunts the underworld.

He's *Lucian.*

And he's mine.

I lift my hand to his jaw, running my thumb across the stubble there. He leans into it like it hurts not to.

"You didn't destroy me," I whisper. "You saved me."

His eyes close, like the weight of those words is almost too much.

"You're afraid of the fire," I continue. "But I was already burning when I met you."

My lips brush his, feather-light. A promise. A homecoming.

"I love you too."

And when I say it, his mouth finds mine like we've both been holding our breath for years.

There's nothing soft about this kiss—not at first. It's all teeth and desperation and unsaid things poured into the space between us.

But then he gentles.

His hands come to my waist, to my hips, pulling me close like he needs to feel every inch of me to believe I'm still here. He kisses me like a man starving.

And I kiss him like he's the only thing I've ever needed to survive.

I don't know how long we stay like this—his arms around me, the world falling away.

The wind curls around us like it knows what we are. Something broken. Something rebuilt.

Lucian's breath moves against my cheek, steady and warm. He doesn't let go. Not even a little.

His hand lifts to cradle the back of my head, his lips brushing mine again—slower this time. Reverent. A kiss that doesn't ask, or take, or claim.

It just... is.

I sigh into it, my fingers tangling in the collar of his shirt. "You don't have to do it alone anymore." I whisper.

His answer is immediate, murmured into my mouth like a secret. "I've never been whole, Sienna. But when I'm with you... I forget what it feels like to be broken."

We stay like that—just breathing, holding, existing.

Beneath us, the city pulses. Around us, the night moves.

But up here, in this moment, there is only him. Only me.

And the quiet promise that whatever comes next... we'll face it together.

The Devil and his Angel.

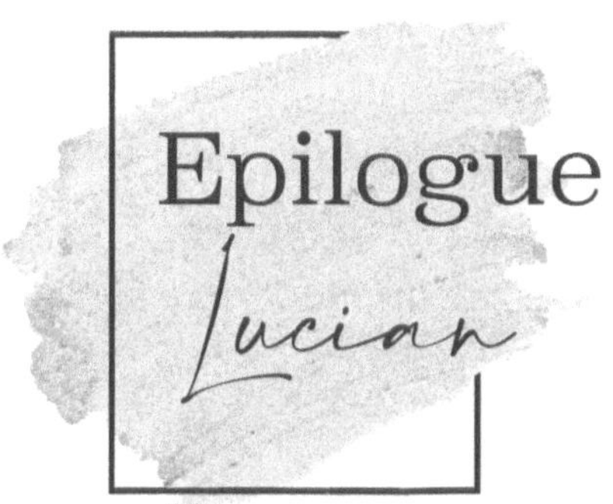

SIX WEEKS LATER

The bullet wound doesn't ache much anymore. Not unless I stretch too far or lift something the wrong way.

But the truth?

The only thing that's been healing me is her.

Sienna.

She's the most dangerous thing that's ever walked into my world—and the only thing that's ever made it feel worth surviving.

She's not just *mine* anymore. She's running shit.

Head of Crisis Management at The Black Ledger.

A role only she could fill—grace with a backbone, charm with bite. When my world catches fire, she doesn't just put it out. She makes sure it never happened in the first place.

Blackmail. High-profile disasters.

She handles it all without flinching. And somehow, even

when she's elbow-deep in chaos, she still answers when I call.

Her line rings once.

"Lucian Vale," she answers, voice low and lethal, pure seduction. "What can I do for you, sir?"

A growl curls in my throat. "Come to my office and make out with me."

She huffs a laugh. "You are a walking HR violation."

"Is that a yes?"

"Maybe..." A pause. "My meeting ends in five minutes."

"I'll be waiting."

And I am.

Five minutes and twenty-eight seconds later, she walks in—black pencil skirt, cream blouse, heels I want to see pointed at the fucking ceiling. She's got her tablet under one arm and that unreadable expression she uses when she's about to serve me my own balls in a negotiation.

She stops in front of my desk. Cocks her head.

"You're stretching again."

I don't deny it. My fingers had been massaging the scar tissue under my shirt just before she walked in.

She eyes me perching her sweet ass on my desk, then hikes her heel onto my chest—slowly pressing it there with just enough pressure to make me lean back.

"Let's go home," I trail my hand up her leg, slow and hungry.

"Yours or mine?"

"Mine," I answer, my smirk curling. "I have a surprise for you."

She hums. "Does it involve me wearing just these heels and the new collar you left on my nightstand—"

"I love the way your dirty mind works." I try to part her legs but she pulls her knees back together.

"One condition," she cuts in, leaning closer, her foot still pressed to me. Her skirt hikes higher with each move.

I narrow my eyes. "You always have to argue, don't you, little rabbit?"

She swings her leg over and settles in my lap, arm curling around my neck, her lips a breath from mine.

"Let me take care of your shoulder first."

"You drive a hard bargain."

I slide my hand under her skirt, fingers spreading over bare thighs. She moans softly when I grind up into her, my cock hard beneath her and getting harder by the second.

"If you sit here much longer, I'm going to fuck you right on this desk."

She slides off my lap slow, deliberate—her fingers grazing my chest, my cock. Teasing like she doesn't know I'm already two seconds from losing control. But she does. She knows *exactly* what she's doing.

She moves toward the door with that little smirk on her lips and murmurs, "Hm. I have a much better idea."

My growl follows her down the hall, rough and low. A promise. A threat. I don't know which yet. I just know I'm already rock hard and following her like a fucking puppy.

We make it home in record time, walking down the hall together in step. Because I can't stop from touching her. Kissing her.

I press her against me as she leads us forward. My arms

wrap around her, my mouth is on her neck, sweeping her hair out of the way.

She opens the door to our bedroom—*mine*, but she's made it hers in a hundred quiet ways—and gestures for me to step inside.

I do.

She closes the door behind us.

When I turn, she's already moving. Her hand grasps my throat, pushing me against the door. Her other hand around my cock, squeezing the fucking life out of me and I swear, I could come right now.

Fuck.

"Sienna," I say, voice low and tight.

She raises a brow. "No, you're going to listen." She grips me. Her fingers around my shaft, stroking me over my pants. "I want you to take your clothes off."

She rips my shirt open; her hot mouth immediately moves to my nipple. Her hand back on my cock. God I love this side of her.

"You're going to get on the bed."

Sienna licks my nipple, keeping her eyes on me before she bites me. Marking me as hers. And I'll wear it with fucking pride. In fact, she's coming with me for a new tattoo tomorrow and she's going to bite me again. Then I'll wear it forever like a badge of honor.

"You're going to be my whore tonight, Devil." Oh, hell yes. "My fucktoy."

She takes my bottom lip between her teeth and pulls. "And I'm going to take everything I want from you. And you," She slaps me. Just hard enough for the sting to send a pulse right to my cock. "you're going to let me use you, aren't you?"

She raises one sharp eyebrow waiting for my answer.

I hesitate. Just a breath. Just long enough for her to see that I don't do this for anyone.

Except her.

"As you wish, mistress." I take her hand and raise it to my mouth, giving her knuckles a gentle peck before I kick off my shoes and shove my pants down.

I climb onto the bed without a word. Watch her with piercing, unblinking eyes as she approaches like a predator in heels.

I'm not sure if I'm turned on or terrified. Probably both. Abso-fucking-lutely both.

So slowly, she unbuttons her blouse and I bite back a groan looking at what she's wearing. When she loses her skirt, my cock twitches, pre-cum leaking at the sight of her.

She fucking planned this all day.

The complex network of straps and rings hide just enough while still revealing everything. Black latex, shiny, smooth and begging for my touch.

"You sneaky little rabbit."

"Arms up," she says softly with a grin that would seduce the devil. *Because she already has.*

I obey.

The silk winds around my wrists with slow, practiced grace. Tight. Intentional. She checks every knot, makes sure I can't break free. Yet.

When she's done, I'm spread wide. Helpless. Bound. My

heart's pounding, not from fear—but from the ache to touch her. To take her. To *ruin* her.

She kisses me once. Soft. Slow.

"Color?" she whispers.

"Green," I rasp. "So fucking green."

She smiles. And climbs on top of me.

"Lick, slut."

God, what did I do so right in this life to deserve her?

Her thighs straddle my shoulders, and the moment she lowers herself onto my mouth, I stop breathing. *Finally.* My tongue flicks out, slow and reverent. She grinds against my face, moaning like she's trying to kill me sweetly.

I groan into her—lost in the taste, in the power she has right now. Every part of me is coiled, my cock straining, but she's in no rush.

"Are you ready for my toy, baby?"

I don't know what she has in mind but there's no chance in hell I'm saying no.

With a nod and a muffled "yes", spoken against her sweet cunt, she takes my meal away all too soon. When I see what she has in her hands, my devilish smirk matches her.

"Green."

She hears the challenge in my tone as she coats the plug generously in lube.

She twists around, and sits on my face, pussy back to riding my mouth and I'm in heaven.

Sienna leans forward, taking my cock in her lubed hand, stroking before her lips slide down my length. I groan so loud it vibrates against her.

Then her hand moves between my thighs and I part them more for her.

Click.

She teases my ass with the vibrating plug, sinking her hot mouth further down my shaft as she slowly works it in.

I jerk against the restraints, a broken sound tearing out of my throat because she goes feral on my dick. Sucking, squeezing, scraping with her teeth as she works me. The plug against my prostate and her ungodly fucking mouth is going to make me come fast and hard.

"Fuck—"

But she sinks down harder on my face, silencing me with her cunt as I choke on a groan.

"Stay still," she pants. "No coming."

I'm shaking now. Panting. Every nerve in my body is on fire. My cock is throbbing. My fists are clinched, muscles are tight.

And still, I hold on.

For her.

She rides my face like I was made for it. Her mouth sucks me like she owns me—and right now, she does. My hips twitch, the plug's vibrations driving me closer and closer to the edge.

She comes first. Her thighs clench around me. Her moans fill the air. She grinds hard against my mouth as her release rips through her.

And me?

I get nothing.

Her mouth is off me in an instant and she switches off the plug.

She slides off, slow and smug, dragging the wetness from her thighs and crawling down my body until she's hovering over my cock. She's facing away from me, and I get a perfect view of her tight ass.

"You're going to be good for me," she whispers, brushing her hair back. "And don't come until I say."

My eyes lock with hers—wild. Desperate. Drenched in something that's not just lust anymore. It's deeper than that. Darker. More dangerous.

It's love.

And she owns it.

Every part of me.

She's mine.

And I'm hers.

She's watching me over her shoulder when I hear her little purple vibrator turn on. I see her moving and can tell she's pressing it against her clit when her head hangs back. She closes her eyes and parts her mouth like a fucking goddess but turns away from me.

This is pure fucking torture.

"Oh, baby, turn around and let me see."

She starts rolling her hips, moaning. Her vibrator, her pussy rubs along my shaft. Teasing. Tormenting as I watch her ass flex.

"Please let me see you, Angel." I'm not too proud to beg. "You're so beautiful when you come."

"Oh," She turns up the intensity, calling out the pleasures she's giving herself.

"God, Sienna."

She leans forward, spreading her ass open and letting

me see exactly what I don't get to have. I can see between her legs as she works the vibrator against her pussy until she's arching her back while she comes again.

She's relentless.

Every inch of me is strung tight, my muscles twitching, my thighs straining. I can feel the silk at my wrist fray with every jerk of resistance, every ounce of control I lose by the second. I'm holding on by threads, literally and figuratively, and she knows it.

Fuck, she *loves* it.

"You're being such a good boy." Her voice is smoother than the ties binding me. "You want a little taste?"

I nod but it's not what she wants. She reaches between my legs and squeezes my balls at the same time she turns on the butt plug.

"I didn't hear you."

My eyes slam shut and I tilt my head back. My cock throbs wanting to be stroked but she denies me.

"Yes mistress. Can I please have a taste?"

"Of course baby."

She turns off the plug and slides up my body, working the straps of her harnessed bodysuit off and letting her breasts out. She pushes them together, holding the vibrator, wet with her juices in her cleavage.

"Suck it for me." It's nearly a whispered command and I follow on instinct.

My tongue comes out, lavishing the taste of her off the toy before I take one of her nipples in my mouth, between my teeth.

God I could live off the noise she makes for all of eternity. She starts working her pussy on me. Dragging her wet cunt along my chest as I suck her. "Just like that, baby." Her nails drag across my scalp, and I groan in appreciation.

I move to the other one, loving the slick feel of her as she takes her pleasure from every part of my body.

"You're such a good fucktoy." She sits up and moves down. Pausing to run her tongue up my chest, and my dick has a pulse that refuses to stop beating for her.

"Please Angel, fuck me."

"Do you need to feel this wet pussy around your dick?"

"Fuck, yes I do." And I nearly fall apart when she lowers herself down, fully suffocating me as she clinches around me. "Yes, thank you, mistress."

She rides me with slow, torturous rhythm—grinding down like she's trying to break me without ever giving me the satisfaction of falling apart.

And I'm *so close.*

The heat's pouring off me in waves. My cock is pulsing, straining for release. Every nerve ending is on fire, and all I can do is *feel* her—wrapped around me, teasing me, denying me.

And God, she fucking works me.

Her pussy, the vibrations of the plug against me as she turns it on, rides me, turns it off and pulls my orgasm back.

She comes but doesn't let me.

I growl. I fucking beg. "Sienna, fuck—please."

She has the nerve to *pretend* to think about it. "Hmm. No."

That word hits harder than any gunshot I've ever taken.

"You don't know what you're doing, little rabbit," I grit out, my voice wrecked.

But she just purrs back, hips circling, deliberately slow. "Oh, I know exactly what I'm doing. And you love it."

"I'm going to fucking ruin you."

"Big promises," she murmurs, nails dragging down my abs like a fucking weapon, "for someone who can't move."

My jaw clenches. I buck once, hard, and she gasps—but the sound isn't fear. It's arousal. She loves that she's provoking me. Tempting me to snap.

She changes position, straddling my thighs, dragging my cock through her slick cunt again and again without letting me inside. I'm soaked in sweat, flushed and burning, holding myself back with the last shreds of self-control I have left.

"You think you're in charge," I grind out through clenched teeth.

She leans in, kisses me like she's sealing a deal with Lucifer. "No. I know I am."

Her mouth is hot, greedy, devouring mine as she grinds harder, rubbing her soaked pussy against me until she shudders again—coming hard, crying out against my neck.

And just when I think she's finally going to give in and let me finish—

She pulls away.

Leaves me trembling, on the edge of release, and snatches it from me like a sadistic fucking queen.

"No," she whispers at my ear. "Not yet." As she sinks down onto me again. Both feet flat on the bed, ready to bounce that hot fucking cunt on my dick until I die from need.

My eyes snap open.

And something inside me *breaks*.

"You little fucking tease—" I buck again, and again. Even from the bottom, tied up in her web, I take my girl for a fucking ride, and she loves it. Her hands brace on my chest like she was hoping for this.

Well, it's not in me to deny my little rabbit of what she wants.

I fuck her from the bottom, gritting out her name between my clinched teeth as I pull on the straps with everything I have.

The left restraint rips with a sharp crack. Silk tears. My arm shoots free and the other follows, splintering the wood of the headboard as I tear myself loose.

I rip the straps binding my ankles with ease.

She gasps—but she doesn't move fast enough.

I grab her by the waist and her throat and flip her onto her back, covering her body with mine in one breathless second.

My weight. My heat. My fury.

It's all bearing down on her now.

"You had your fun," I growl, my cock pressing between her thighs, already poised to take. "Now it's my turn."

I hook my elbow under one knee, pulling her leg up and opening her sweet cunt to me.

I drive into her, deep and hard, burying myself to the hilt in one brutal thrust that makes her arch and cry out.

And then I *fuck her*.

Like I'm branding her from the inside. Like every inch of her is mine and I'm never letting her forget it. My hips pound into her, savage and hungry. My mouth devours hers. My hand fists in her hair.

"You're mine," I rasp, voice pure possession. "You fucking hear me?"

"Yes," she gasps. "Yes, Lucian—God, yes."

I groan like a wild animal when she turns on the vibrator in my ass again. I take her harder. Faster. Until the world dissolves and it's just her and me, colliding in one final, desperate crescendo.

We come together, trembling, shaking, pulsing with it—and even then, I don't let go.

I stay inside her. Stay on top of her because I'm already about to come again.

I grab the purple vibrator and turn it the fuck up. Pressing it hard against her clit, she scratches down my back and I arch into her hard against the pain.

"Fuck, Sienna." I call out, unable to stop the flood of pleasure barreling through me, through her as I make her come again with me.

"Fucking take this." I pick up the pace as her orgasm crests. "Take every drop of my fucking cum, my beautiful whore."

"Lucian!" More scratches as I work my dick into her, the vibrator against her.

"I want you so full of my cum, it's dripping out of your slut pussy for weeks."

"Yes. Fuck yes." She repeats as I bring her down with me. The last pulses of my climax shooting into her as I slow my hips. We both turn off the toys we used to torment each other, and I toss the vibrator on the mattress.

My forehead presses against hers, my arms lock around her, like if I hold tight enough, the whole world might stop spinning.

"Fuck," I whisper. "I love you."

She kisses me again, soft and sweet, like she knows what that costs me to say. "I know, baby. I love you too."

And there it is.

The Devil—finally brought to his knees.

Only for her.

I kiss her everywhere—lips, throat, collarbone—like I'm trying to memorize her with my mouth. I don't want to part from a single inch of her. I never do. Every part of her is mine, and I want her to feel it long after the ache from our fucking subsides.

"Stay with me," I whisper against her lips, my voice raw from the storm we just walked through—outside and in.

"I am," she says.

I shake my head, my mouth brushing her jaw, breathing her in. "You know what I mean. Forever. Put me out of my misery and finally say you'll live with me. Every day."

My arms lock around her back, and hers settle around my neck.

"I don't know..." she teases, soft and quiet, but there's something trembling beneath it. "What if you get tired of me? Break up with me and keep the espresso machine in the divorce?"

My eyes narrow, the devil in me flashing. "Don't say things that'll make me angry, little rabbit." I pin her wrists to the mattress in one quick motion, rolling her perfect nipple between my thumb and finger. "I'll have to tie you up and spank that pretty little ass until your cheeks are red and throbbing for me."

She sucks in a breath, and I grin. Wicked. Wild. In love.

"Just the thought of it's got me hard again already," I murmur, thrusting my hips against hers.

She feels me. I know she does. Already hard again. Already aching for her.

"There is no one else for me, baby," I breathe against her skin. "And I want to build this life with you. Run my empire with you. You didn't just clean up Lorenzo's fucking mess— you've made The Ledger untouchable."

She blinks up at me, surprised. "You want me to... what?"

"I want you at the table," I say, clear and unwavering. "Not as staff. Not as support. A seat, Sienna. A real one. Right next to me."

She stares at me like I've lost my mind. "You want a partnership?"

"Exactly."

She starts to laugh, nervous and sweet. "I don't know what to say..."

I don't push. Just smile. Lean in like I'm about to kiss her again when my phone chimes. I glance over and smirk.

"But if you need more convincing..." I slide off her and whisper, "Stay right here. Don't move a muscle."

I grab my lounge pants and slide them on quickly before half-jogging from the room.

She watches me go, confused and grinning. Flustered and naked in my bed. Right where I fucking love her.

When I return, it's with a wriggling, brown-and-black shepherd pup in my arms. Big paws. Floppy ears. Tail wagging like it's powered by joy alone.

Her eyes light up. "Oh my God. What—"

I watch happiness swell within her as she takes him in, and I can't stop smiling knowing she loves him. I knew she would.

"If you're not ready to move in yet, that's fine," I tell her, placing the little beast on the bed. "But I still want you protected when you're not here. He'll be trained. Fully. He'll guard you with his life."

The pup whimpers, scrambles toward her like he already knows she's his favorite person. She scoops him up, scratches behind his ears, and he immediately starts drooling on the sheets.

"I love him."

"What are you going to name him?"

She smirks. "Maple."

I blink. "Maple?"

"It's perfect," she insists, beaming.

You've got to be fucking kidding me.

I groan. "This dog is going to be a killer, and you're naming him *Maple*?"

"Yes. And my baby is *not* going to be a killer."

Oh my god, this fucking woman.

The pup makes a move to jump off the bed. She gently sets him down and watches him wobble like his legs are still learning how to work.

She pulls me down, her legs wrapping around my waist in an instant. "Thank you. He's perfect." Her tongue sweeps across my mouth and I gladly part for her. Groaning as I taste the two of us on her lips. *God I fucking need more of her.*

"Name him whatever you want," I murmur into her hair. "Just say yes."

She rubs her soft hands down my hard chest, tracing the lines of my tattoos with her gentle touch. "To what?"

"To all of it... but first..." I know I'm begging but I don't give a shit. I want my woman. "The Ledger. Partner."

She nods, smiling. "Partner."

She kisses me like she means it—like she finally believes this is real.

And I break the kiss just enough to whisper, "Live with me."

Her hand snakes beneath the waistband of my pants. I'm hard. *Still* hard. Of course, I am.

I can't not be when she's got me like this. Her sinful grip wraps around my cock and I groan, rolling my hips into her touch.

"Not in front of our child." I grunt into her neck when she squeezes me.

"Our child?" She grins, moving to the head of my cock and driving me wild.

"We're co-parenting now. Visitation rights. Shared custody. Weekend trips to the park."

I groan louder when she sneaks her other hand into my pants, both her talented hands stroking me in tandem. I can't fucking think like this so I pin her wrists against the mattress just because I *can*. She lets out a laugh, throwing her head back.

"Live with me, little rabbit," I growl into her neck with a bite. "Don't let our boy come from a broken home."

She laughs again, and I release her hands.

Sienna trails her fingers over the scar on my chest and presses a soft kiss there.

No words.

Just that knowing look between us.

She's not leaving.

Because she's mine.

And me?

The Devil—the man, the monster—that has never belonged to anyone.

But now I belong to her.

She drags her lips over my throat and whispers, "You think you can handle being a full-time brat tamer?"

"I'm the only one that can." I groan, my cock twitching in answer. "I was made for you, Angel."

Then I kiss the corner of her mouth, my voice low and sure. "And I want to wake up looking at your beautiful face and go to sleep with you in my arms. Every day."

She smiles.

And this time, she doesn't hesitate. "Yes."

I breathe it in like it's oxygen. Like the answer *saved* me.

Because maybe it did.

She's the only thing I've ever believed in. And she said yes to forever.

I spent my whole life building an empire... and somehow, she became the only thing in it that matters.

She said yes—and for the rest of my life, I'll spend every breath proving she made the right choice.

Good girl.

I knew you'd read every last filthy word.
Now I want you dripping, ruined, shaking.
So get that toy, angel—
and let me hear you scream for the Devil
one. more. time.

Welcome to
The Black Ledger

Where every desire has a price...
and every contract is final.

*Love The Owner's Temptation? Don't stop now.
The next Black Ledger book awaits...*

The Black Ledger
Billionaires

Check Out www.RebekahSinclairWrites.com for more!

www.ingramcontent.com/pod-product-compliance
Lightning Source LLC
Chambersburg PA
CBHW061033310726
48969CB00004B/939